PRAISE FOR MARIA V. SNYDER

"Smart, witty, and full of heart, *Navigating the Stars* had me hooked from the very first page!" Lynette Noni, bestselling author of *Whisper*

"This is one of those rare books that will keep readers dreaming long after they've read it." *Publishers Weekly*, starred review on *Poison Study*

"Snyder deftly weaves information about glassblowing into her tale of magic and murder." *Library Journal* on *Storm Glass*

"Filled with Snyder's trademark sarcastic humor, fast-paced action, and creepy villainy, *Touch of Power* is a spellbinding fantasy adventure." *USA TODAY*

"This deftly plotted story will engage readers of both genders with its fresh story line." *Kirkus Reviews* on *Storm Watcher*

"A wonderful, thoughtful book full of vivid characters and a place—Inside—that is by turns alien, and breathtakingly familiar." Rachael Caine, etc.... on *Inside Out*

D1593641

ALSO BY MARIA V. SNYDER

Study Series

POISON STUDY
MAGIC STUDY
FIRE STUDY
SHADOW STUDY
NIGHT STUDY
DAWN STUDY
ICE STUDY
(Available as an ebook)

Glass Series

STORM GLASS
SEA GLASS
SPY GLASS

Healer Series

TOUCH OF POWER
SCENT OF MAGIC
TASTE OF DARKNESS

Discover other titles by
Maria V. Snyder at
MariaVSnyder.com

Invisible Sword Series

THE EYES OF
TAMBURAH

THE CITY OF ZIRDAI
(coming June 2020)

THE KING OF KORAHA
(coming June 2021)

Sentinels Series

NAVIGATING THE
STARS

CHASING THE
SHADOWS

DEFENDING THE
GALAXY
(coming November 2020)

Inside Series

INSIDE OUT
OUTSIDE IN
(collected as INSIDE)

CHASING

THE

SHADOWS

MARIA V. SNYDER

Chasing the Shadows / Maria V. Snyder—1st edition
Cover design by Design by Committee
Published by Maria V. Snyder

Print ISBN 978-1-946381-04-0
Digital ISBN 978-1-946381-05-7

For Michelle Mioff-Haring and Cupboard Maker Books.

Keep living the dream!

2522:190

"You're dead," Elese says as she presses her forearm against my neck, cutting off my air.

With no breath to speak, I slap my hand down on the mat. Hard. Probably harder than needed to concede the match, but, give me a break, at least this time I didn't panic.

Elese rolls off me and I remain prone on my back, gasping. The odor of hot sweat mixed with the funk of feet is a fine perfume to my starved lungs. I'm already well acquainted with the view of the bland cream-colored ceiling above the training room and it's only been eight days since my funeral.

Yes, you read that right. I officially died—killed by my ex-friend Jarren, the murdering looter—for about a minute before the good Dr. Edwards revived me. The funeral was to say goodbye to Lyra Tian Daniels and hello to Ara Yinhexi Lawrence—my snazzy new name. But I've gone almost eighteen Actual years being called Lyra so it's gonna take me quite a while to get used to it.

With a groan, I push up to a sitting position. Muscles unused to such activity ache in protest. Elese stands next to me. Her chestnut-colored skin contrasts nicely with her white—still very clean and dry—training uniform. Not a single short brown curl is out of place on her head. Unlike me. Most of my long hair has sprung from its braid. Black strands stick to the side of my face, which, despite my olive-colored skin, is probably dark red from exertion. And let's just say I'm damp in places better left unmentioned. Ugh.

Around us, a couple other off-duty security officers spar. Their grunts echo off the walls, two of which are covered in floor-to-ceiling mirrors. Yep, my face is red. Along the opposite side is a row of workout equipment. Bendix lifts weights. Figures. The muscular guy is about as wide as he's tall. Elese says she can toss his "fat ass" across the room despite the fact she's a hundred and seventy-seven centimeters tall—about ten more than me—and is lean. After seven days of working with her, I now believe she can do anything.

"What went wrong?" she asks me.

I consider the fight. "I blocked too wide, leaving my solar plexus unguarded." Rubbing my stomach, I remember her jab—not too hard as this is training after all. "Distracted with the need to breathe, I allowed you to get too close and you took me down."

"Yup. Classic rookie mistake. All right, on your feet, Recruit. Let's try again."

Rookie. Recruit. Newbie. Take your pick, I've been called

all of them by various officers of Planet Yulin's security team. As the newest member, I take it in stride and hope it's a phase. It's a thin hope as all the rest of the team have nicknames.

"Once more." Elese sets her feet into what I now know is a fighting stance.

I face her, copying her posture. She attacks, I block. Or I try. In my defense, she has years of experience. This time I last a bit longer before she takes me down…again. I wonder if I could decorate the ceiling—maybe have Niall paint a mural.

"You need to keep your guard up," she says.

Talk about stating the obvious. I bite down on my sarcasm—she is trying to teach me—and climb to my feet.

"Let's work on your blocks." Elese faces me.

Overheated, I roll up the sleeves on my tunic, exposing arms covered with an assortment of colored bruises from dark red to muddy green and a few mat burns just to make it interesting. My legs and torso sport the same coloration. Sexy, I'm not. But, at least my stomach no longer twists with apprehension when I put on the loose cotton training pants and shirt. Progress.

I block her punches and kicks for hours. Okay that's an exaggeration, but at the end of a long day, I'm entitled. Training, I've learned, is repetition. Lots and lots of doing the exact same thing over and over and over again. Words like "muscle memory" and "instinctual reactions" are drilled into my mind and body. I understand why. After spending eight hours a day in the training room, I've seen the other officers also come in each day and work out for a couple hours to keep their skills sharp. Plus this will probably save my life someday.

And that's the kicker right there. Jarren, the murdering looter, is still somewhere out there. He could be anywhere in the Milky Way Galaxy or he could be hiding right on Yulin. Yeah, we've no idea. Scary, right? He might figure out that I didn't stay dead and come back for me. Which will endanger all the scientists on the base as well as my new family—the security team.

He already killed Officer Menz, but I'm determined that he's not getting anyone else so I'm gonna train hard, lay low, and not attract attention. Don't laugh. I am capable of…oh, all right. I admit, it's killing me not to entangle with the Q-net and hunt him and his looter thugs down. Happy now?

"That's enough for today, Recruit. Read chapters eight through ten in the security handbook tonight. See you tomorrow at oh-eight-hundred." Elese gives me a jaunty wave.

The security handbook is actually rather interesting. It has lessons on how to deal with criminals, how to read body language, how to decipher a crime scene, etc... Elese and I discuss these lessons the next day between practice bouts.

I chug water as I navigate the hallways. The biggest downside of being "dead" is not being able to leave this section of the base since only my parents and a few others know I'm still alive. The perks are that I don't have to attend socialization time, no more required school work and I can walk around without an escort. I fought for that last one.

The Chief of Security and my new boss, Tace Radcliff, is rather overprotective and paranoid. Good qualities for a security chief, but I argued, since the other officers don't have a partner—his word for bodyguard—with them constantly, I don't need one either. Plus the camera feeds in the security area have been put on a special closed loop, meaning they're not connected to the Q-net so no one can worm into them. Only the security officer on watch can see what's going on.

If my partner could be Niall, his son, then I'd reconsider. However, Officer Radcliff seems determined to keep us too busy to do more than cuddle on the couch after dinner, which usually ends up with one or both of us sound asleep.

Entering housing unit three-oh-one, I pause and breathe in the heavenly scent of garlic and tomatoes. Radcliff might be a pain in the butt, but the man sure can cook especially when you consider the poor and artificial quality of the ingredients—we are on an exoplanet quadrillions of kilometers from Earth—or fifty thousand light years if that helps you picture it better. Space is big. Really big.

And the fact he spends the time feeding me and my parents despite being crazy busy also goes in his favor. After all, there are sixteen looters confined in detention and armed shadow-blobs in the Warrior pits. Oh, excuse me…Hostile Life Forms (HoLFs). Lots going on. You can read a detailed report in Q-cluster 978-1946-3810-19 if you're so inclined.

I hurry through the living area, bypass the kitchen and duck into the washroom before Radcliff orders me to set the table. Showering is the priority. Once clean and dressed in jeans and one of Elese's hand-me-down T-shirts, I emerge from my room. Yes, I'm still living with Radcliff. My parents insisted I stay here until I turn eighteen A-years old. Plus there's no Q-net terminal in the room so I won't be tempted. Although I think my mom's more worried I'd be more tempted by Niall than the Q-net if I had my own unit. And she would be right. Not that I'll ever tell her.

Radcliff glances at me as I grab the stack of plates. After spending forty days living with him, I'm somewhat immune to his glowers. He's close to my parents' ages—mid-forties—with bristle-short black hair that's streaked with gray. Broad shoulders and a solid muscular build, Radcliff looms over me by a good twenty centimeters.

My parents arrive and I'm squished between them. They've been rather clingy since I died. Guess I can't blame them. They watched Jarren, the murdering looter, shoot me, and if it wasn't for Menz's quick action, I'd be ashes. The parent sandwich doesn't last long. The smell of food entices my dad over to the oven, but my mom remains.

Examining my expression with her mom X-ray vision, she says, "You don't look as tired today. How did training go?"

"My bruises have bruises." I joke...sort of. Looking at my mother is like staring into my future. I inherited her straight hair, coloring and eye shape, except mine are hazel while hers are brown. She appears younger than her forty-four A-years, which I'm hoping is also in my DNA. "Elese pinned me a hundred times at least." I huff.

Mom presses a hand to her chest. "You mean you're not going to become a super woman overnight?" She tsks. "Such a disappointment."

"Ha ha." Normally, I have to endure my dad's lame humor.

I'm not sure I can handle it from both of them.

"Do I need to remind you how many years it took you to become proficient at reconstructing the Warriors?"

"No lectures, please."

"All right, but because of your experience, you're the only one I trust to finish putting the General back together. That is when we can get back into the pits." She presses her lips together. Her stiff posture radiates frustration.

I understand all too well. We time jumped fifty-years into the future to travel to Planet Yulin so my parents, the archeological Experts (the capital is not a typo) could study the ancient Chinese Terracotta Warriors buried in sixty-four pits underneath Yulin's desert. Only four pits had been uncovered before looters arrived. They stole hundreds and destroyed the rest. Then the shadow-blobs appeared—and attacked us— they're not called hostile life forms for nothing. The pits were sealed for everyone's safety.

When the unit's door opens to admit the last of the guests, my mom takes over setting the table so I can greet him in semi-private.

Niall waits for me in the living room. He's not in his security uniform, nor am I, which means I'm allowed to wrap my arms around his neck, go up on my tiptoes and pull him close for a hello kiss. He responds, deepening it as his hands press on my back. Warmth spreads through me and tingles dance along my skin. With parents in the next room, our kiss is unfortunately short.

Still holding me tight, he rests his forehead on mine. "Hi,

7

Mouse."

"Toad." That earns me a tired laugh.

Poor guy's been working long hours since Jarren's attack. All of the security officers have been. There are dark smudges under his blue-green eyes.

"Dinner," his dad calls from the kitchen.

Niall sighs. "How long until you're eighteen?"

"One hundred and twenty-four days."

"That's one hundred and twenty-three days too many." Releasing me, he grabs my hand and tows me into the kitchen.

The conversation limps along with stilted small talk. It's odd and I wonder if this is normal or if it's because this is the first meal where I actually have enough energy to pay attention. By half way through, I suspect there's a topic that the adults are dancing around. And my instincts tell me that I'm not going to like what they really wish to discuss.

I meet Niall's gaze and raise my eyebrows. Does he know? A small shake of his head. But at least he confirms I'm not crazy.

Interrupting the fascinating discussion about the research base's air filters, I say, "All right, spit it out."

Mom exchanges a glance with my dad. They do that silent communication thing as Radcliff's expression remains neutral. Too neutral, which worries me more.

Finally my dad says, "Officer Morgan has been working with the astrophysicists to create a light weapon that might affect the HoLFs."

So far so good. "And?" I prompt.

"And they need more information that only you can

provide," Radcliff says.

Ah. Makes sense since I'm the sole person in the base who can actually see the shadow-blobs…er…HoLFs. So why the hesitation? Unease gnaws on my stomach. "You need me to go into the pits?"

"No," my parents and Radcliff say in unison. Impressive.

"Nothing so drastic," Mom says.

"Not yet," Dad mutters, but clamps his mouth shut when my mom glares at him.

"Not at all." Mom's grip on her fork is so tight, I expect it to bend in half.

Radcliff interrupts. "We discussed this and the best way is for you to talk to the scientists directly."

Which means more people knowing I'm alive. "How many?"

"Two and I'll ensure they keep your status secret."

Not an idle promise. Radcliff threatened to tear Jarren, the murdering looter, apart with his bare hands if he harmed me. I would have been flattered if I wasn't terrified out of my mind at the time.

"All right, I'll talk to them."

"Are you sure?" Mom asks because that's what moms do.

"Of course. If those shadow-blobs find a way out of the pits, then we're going to have more to worry about than Jarren returning."

A tense silence follows as everyone is no doubt remembering Planet Xinji. Looters raided the pits, stealing and destroying

Warriors. Soon after the attack, the planet went silent. No communications and no signs of life. The entire population of the research base dead—killed by HoLFs.

When the shadow-blobs appeared in our pits after a similar raid, I speculated that the Warriors were protecting us from the HoLFs and, when they were broken or stolen by the looters, the Warriors could no longer do their job. Let's just say the others are skeptical about my theory.

At least they believed me about the invisible-to-them blobs…eventually. It took an attack where Beau almost died and a bunch of us were injured for them to trust me. As to why I'm the only one who can see them, I think it's because I touched a Warrior Heart. We found these lifelike human hearts crafted from a strange black material in a factory below the pits. Despite a lifetime of knowing better—sorry again, Mom—I picked one up. Or I tried. The heart disintegrated into nothing as an icy cold stabbed my hand and traveled up my arm. My explanation about my super power hasn't been met with much enthusiasm either.

"When do you want me to talk to the astrophysicists?" I ask. Then a more important question pops to mind. "Does this mean I can leave security? Oooh, I can dye my hair blonde and wear a disguise!"

"You can't risk being recognized, Ara," Radcliff says.

Killjoy.

"They're coming to my office at oh-seven-hundred tomorrow." He gives me an evil little grin. "Don't worry, you won't miss training."

Uncomplimentary thoughts whirl, but I wisely keep them to myself.

"Do you want us to be there as well?" Mom asks me.

Nice of her not to add "in case you freak out" in front of the Radcliffs. "I'll be fine, Mom." Besides, I prefer to have my freak outs in private.

The rest of dinner is more…normal—for lack of a better word. My mom pulls me aside before she leaves with a let-me-know-if-you-change-your-mind talk. I refrain from rolling my eyes.

After dinner's cleaned up, Niall and I collapse onto the couch. Radcliff goes into his bedroom to work. He shuts the door, giving us the illusion of privacy.

Niall drapes his arm around my shoulders and tucks me close. I rest my head on his chest, breathing in his unique scent of sage grass and soaking in his body heat. The tension flows from my sore muscles. For a while, we're content to just sit.

"I'll be watching the cameras tomorrow morning until oh-eight-hundred if you need me," Niall says.

I groan. "Not you, too."

"Can you blame us?"

"No."

He chuckles. It's a deep masculine sound that vibrates against my cheek. "Can you say that without sounding grumpy?"

"No."

He waits.

"I just need everyone to stop being so...careful with me. If Elese invites me over for a sleepover one more time, I'll..." The proper description fails me.

"Why is that bad?"

"It's her cure for PTSD."

He pulls back to look down at me. "Do you—"

"No. I've no symptoms."

He studies me. "Maybe she's just being friendly."

"Well after eight hours of her torturing me, I'm not inclined to spend my free time with her. I'd rather spend it with you."

"I can't argue with that." He closes the distance between us.

I tilt my head back as his lips touch mine. Fire ignites in my core, burning away all my peevishness. Instead, my world fills with Niall. The minty taste of him on my tongue, the smell of his shampoo and his hands under my shirt, caressing my skin. I straddle him. He reaches higher and sucks in a breath.

Breaking away, he stares at me. "You're...not wearing..."

"My ribs are sore."

Niall closes his eyes. "You're making it very difficult for me to be the sensible one. My father..."

We both glance at Radcliff's bedroom door. I sigh and sit next to him.

He takes my hand. "On my next day off, we'll have another proper date."

I squeeze his fingers. "That would be lovely." I wait a beat. "What are the chances of you getting a day off?"

"Ah...well, what's that expression...? It's the thought that counts."

It does. But it's too bad that the eleven people comprising the security force are not enough. Then again, no one expected shadow-blobs and murdering looters at a scientific research base on the edge of Explored Space. A Protector Class ship is enroute, but it's going to take another year and a half for it to arrive.

"How are the techs doing?" I ask. Since the pits are closed, Mom lent Radcliff her idle techs to help with security.

"About what you'd expect from a group of people who have no interest in anything other than archeology."

"That good, eh?"

"We set up another monitoring station on the other side of the base. All the guys have to do is watch the camera feeds. I found them both asleep. It was the middle of the day. And none of them want to guard the entrance to the pits."

"You can't blame them. That's ground zero if the shadow-blobs escape. Plus in the pits they were…er…"

"Useless when we were attacked?"

"I wouldn't say that. They did help carry Beau. It saved his life."

"I guess," he grudgingly admits.

"Then let's hope the astrophysicists can develop a weapon to counter the blobs and everyone can go back to normal." Except me. I'll have to find a new normal.

Niall yawns.

"You better go. You have to be up at oh-so-early."

He groans, but stands. I walk with him to the door.

Facing me, he says, "And you have an early day as well."

That's right. I do. "I'm actually looking forward to it."

"Really?"

"Yeah." The truth. "New faces. Something to think about other than keeping up my guard. A change."

His gaze grows distant. "I never thought about it that way."

"About what?"

"You had more freedom when you were on probation."

True. I shrug. "I'm not going to complain. I like having a heartbeat."

A slow smile softens the angles of Niall's face. "And I enjoy affecting the pace of that heartbeat."

"Oh?"

He draws me in for a kiss. A deep passionate kiss that sends bolts of heat all the way to my feet. Pushing me against the wall, he rakes his fingers through my hair as his other hand strokes the side of my breast through the T-shirt. All sensations increase by an order of magnitude.

Way too soon Niall slows then stops. Good thing he's supporting me or I'd topple over.

He presses his fingertips to my neck for ten seconds. "Pulse rate one-twenty." Then he whispers in my ear, "I'll do better next time."

Oh my stars.

"Good night, Mouse."

"Night." My voice is rough, which earns me a smug grin. I lean on the wall for a long while after he leaves.

I enter Radcliff's office at oh-seven-hundred. Two familiar women wearing science chic—lab coats over nerdy jumpsuits— sit in front of his desk. But Officer Morgan and not Radcliff is behind it. Morgan's the same age as my mother, about my height and has super short blond hair. I noticed that all four female security officers have short hair, although none as…buzzed as Morgan's. Good for them. I remember Niall's fingers entwined in my hair and there's no way I'm cutting mine no matter how unruly it gets during training.

Instead of wearing my training uniform, I dressed in the everyday security uniform—a light gray long-sleeved polo shirt with black tactical pants and black boots. I've a belt and holster. Except for a flashlight, I don't have a weapon. Not yet. However, I have Lawrence embroidered over my left breast right under the word security. 'Cause the uniform might not be obvious enough. Sheesh.

Morgan introduces me to the lady with her hair pulled into a messy bun. "This is Dr. Roberta Carson."

She extends her hand. "Call me Bertie." There's a spark of amusement in her brown eyes.

I shake it as if I've just met her.

"And this is Dr. Zhang Yenay." Morgan nods to the woman whose shoulder length black hair is thick and glossy. I'm so gonna ask her what shampoo she uses.

"Yenay," she says, pumping my hand once before letting go.

"And this is Junior Officer Ara Lawrence," Morgan says.

"Uh…call me Ara," I say. This is weird. I've nodded hello to both these women dozens of times in the hallways of the base. They're in their early thirties—I think.

"All right, let's get started," Bertie says. She sits at the visitor terminal—my name for it since Radcliff has another terminal at his desk, which Morgan accesses. Yenay stands behind Bertie.

The terminal is a plain plate made of a rare metal and built into a desk. Rather underwhelming considering it's the gateway to the Quantum net or Q-net for short.

I press my hands to my sides. The desire to insert my entanglers pulses through me. It's been twenty days since I accessed the vast scientific wonder that is the Q-net. Invented back in 2066, it changed our world. New technology developed, including the Bucherer-Plank Crinkler engine that allows us to travel across immense distances in space in seconds, giving all the countries on Earth a reason to unite and they formed the Department of Explored Space (DES) which uses the Q-net for…everything.

Bertie brings up a file on the screen above the desk. It's labeled HoLFs and there's not much data. "Please describe the alien creatures," she says to me.

This ought to be interesting. "They resemble shadows. But they move as if they're made of liquid and they're…translucent. They float and seem to have no mass. I call them blobs because they remind me of those amoebas. They can grow as big as two meters and will form…appendages—lots of them that solidify into sharp blades." I rub my left hip, thinking of the one that stabbed me. But it wasn't as bad as when they attacked Beau.

My description appears in the file. Alarmed, I ask, "How safe is it? Wormers can get to the file and might be able to connect it to me."

"Officer Dorey assured us it's well protected," Bertie said.

Beau is good, but I'm better.

"And Jarren already knows we'll be trying to figure out a way to stop the HoLFs," Morgan says.

Still. "Mind if I take a look?"

Yenay glances at Morgan. "Is Ara authorized?"

I almost laugh. "I can go in without the Q-net recording my identity."

"Really? That's possible?" Yenay seems impressed.

"It's possible for *Ara*," Morgan says, giving the woman a pointed look. "But there's no need, Officer Dorey has established your new identity, Ara."

Swell. "I'd feel better skipping that part."

"All right."

Excited, I insert my tangs. The little round plugs fit right into my ears. They, along with the sensors implanted in my brain, allow me to access the Q-net. You have to be next to a terminal, though. To entangle with the Q-net for more than twelve-hours can lead to insanity. Nice, huh? So everyone must be able to completely disentangle.

My consciousness flows into the Q-net. To me, it's like a universe-sized ball of yarn with zillions of layers. And I've learned how to squeeze and wiggle between those layers, entering data clusters and other secure areas. It's called worming and it's illegal unless you're doing it for a good reason—like hunting down murdering looters.

But this time, it feels like home. I ease into deeper layers as if sinking into a tub of hot water. Ahhh.

"Well?" Morgan asks.

Ignoring the temptation to descend to the star roads, I check Beau's protective measures. They'll do.

"Let's continue," Bertie says. "How does the light affect these beings?"

"They shied away from the beam or vanished."

"How close were they at that point?"

"About a meter to a meter and a half. When they closed in, I could make them disappear with the light."

"Disappear? Is that different than vanishing?" Bertie asks.

"Yes. Vanishing is like they moved out of the way too fast for me to see where they went. Disappearing is when I shone the light right into their core and they…poofed. It seemed more…drastic. And I don't know if it's permanent either. They could have reformed in the darkness."

"I see."

Too bad Bertie still sounds confused.

"What type of light?" Yenay asks.

I pull the flashlight from my belt and hand it to her.

She clicks it on. "It's not very powerful."

"Which is probably why they were able to get through our defenses. That and the fact we only had three."

"Do you know how they were able to turn off all the lights?"

"No, but I can guess they used their sharp blades to cut the wires."

"Including the emergency lights," Morgan adds.

Quiet descends as the fact that the HoLFs showed signs of intention sinks in. It shouldn't be a surprise to me as I was there, but at the time it seemed as though I fought mindless shadow-zombies.

"We have the video of when you first saw them," Bertie says, breaking the tension. "Can I show it to you?"

There's that caution again. Morgan must have said something to them. I ignore it. "Sure."

The video plays. It's only a minute long, but Bertie stops it when I take a step toward the back wall of the pit. "Can you point out where the HoLF is?"

"Which one?"

She glances at me. "There's more than one?"

"There's five."

Stunned silence. Clearing her throat, she says, "Okay. Can you point them out?"

Yes, but what good would it do? They can't see them. I consider the problem. Maybe I could outline them, but I'd need to go deeper. Various possibilities pop into my head.

"I've seen that look before," Morgan says. "I'm not going to like this, am I?"

I explain. "I'll keep everything...quiet. It's low risk."

"On one condition."

I wait.

"That Officer Dorey trails you."

"Fine."

Beau is summoned and Bertie relinquishes her seat to me when he arrives.

"Keep everything on the screen," Morgan orders. "And if Dorey tells you to back off, you listen."

"Yes, sir."

I meet Beau's gaze.

His brown hair is spiked and the ends are dyed yellow, which is the reason everyone calls him Hedgehog. Mischief sparks in his amber eyes, but he inserts his tangs and says, "Let's go."

I worm through a few layers, easing into the gaps without causing ripples that would alert others. It's easier than I remember. And the intricacies of the Q-net are sharper, brighter, and bigger. Odd. Perhaps it's because I haven't entangled with the Q-net in twenty days. I've accessed it at least once every day since my sensors were implanted when I was ten A-years old.

Beau stays close to me as I navigate. A pang vibrates in my chest. It's just like old times, when we worked together plugging DES's security holes. I missed it. Who knew?

Taking the video file, I drag it down to my Q-cluster. It's hard to explain—nothing is anyone's in the Q-net. As long as you have the proper clearance, you can go as deep as the star roads. But this particular cluster responds to me. I know, sounds crazy and I did have a concussion when I discovered it. Time to see if it still recognizes me.

I've woven a tight security net around it and it appears intact.

Once inside, I stretch the video like taffy around me, pulling it until each second is visible. The effect is similar to a panorama photo. The entire sequence of events can now be seen.

"Damn, girl," Beau whispers.

Pride swells. It's hard to impress him. Focusing on the task at hand, I concentrate on one shadow-blob at the beginning of the clip and think about outlining it. The Q-net follows my instructions and a shape forms. Still a blob. Then I move to the next second and repeat. It's tedious. And perhaps stretching the time into sixty seconds wasn't my best idea. I finally finish and start on blob two.

Except after I outline the second one, the Q-net takes over and does the remaining fifty-nine seconds.

"Stars, girl," Beau says. "What the fu—"

"This cluster likes me," I say.

I pick out number three and whoosh. Same with four and five. Both finished in a blink of an eye. Astonished, I'm speechless.

Beau gapes at me. "Was that real? Did I just see that?"

"Yeah." My voice is rough.

"See what?" Morgan demands.

I turn toward her. "The Q-net..." Still overwhelmed, words fail me.

"The Q-net," she prompts.

"Recognized the shadow-blobs."

2522:191

Morgan grabs my shoulder and turns my swivel chair toward her. "Recognized as in…?"

I draw in a deep breath and clasp my hands together to stop the tremors. "As in, the Q-net can see the shadow-blobs."

"See how?"

"I don't know. Maybe there's a visual element on the video that only the Q-net can sense. Does it matter? Think about the implications."

Beau straightens in his chair. "We can use the Q-net to pinpoint their locations."

"Exactly." We grin at each other.

He flashes his teeth, which seem bright compared to his bronze skin. Handsome and he knows it, he enjoys goading Niall, making him jealous.

Bertie taps the screen. "Can you have the Q-net scan for other wavelengths besides visible light?"

"You think they're emitting X-rays or microwaves or something?" I ask.

"Nice to know your education included physics," Bertie says. "Yes. And if they do, then we can learn more about them. Since there are no terminals in the pits, it would also make it easier for us to develop a way to see them without having to rely on the Q-net."

"And invent a weapon to kill them?" Morgan asks.

"One thing at a time, Officer," Yenay says. "Ara, can you do the scan?"

I consider the problem, but then realize why it won't work.

"Wait," Bertie says, figuring it out at the same time. "It's a video feed. The camera only records visible light."

"Then we need to get a sensor in the pits to record the full electromagnetic spectrum," Yenay says.

Both astrophysicists turn to Morgan.

"Too dangerous," she says.

"We can provide hand-held lasers to the security team," Bertie says. "If the HoLFs...poof...when the flashlight's beam hits them straight on, then the amplified light of a laser should work as well. And with a laser, the beam goes much further than a flashlight's and that should keep them away from us long enough to install a sensor."

"We can use floodlights as well," Beau says. "Plus we don't have to go in far. Pit 1 is right across from the archeology lab. I'll volunteer for the mission."

And I'd have to go as well to spot the shadow-blobs or I wouldn't be able to live with myself if something happened to

Beau or the scientists. "Me, too."

Morgan shakes her head, muttering something about idiots. "Officer Radcliff would have to approve it. How many people do you need to set up a sensor, Bertie?"

Color drains from poor Bertie's face. "Uh…we'd need…" She glances at Yenay, who crosses her arms over her lab coat as if that would protect her.

But then Yenay's spine stiffens and her hesitation transforms into determination. At the moment she resembles my mom. She gestures, indicating Bertie and herself. "Us," she says. "We're supposed to keep all this under wraps, right? So it's the two of us."

"How long to install it?" Morgan asks Yenay.

"Five minutes."

"Make sure the sensors have a battery and a way to connect to the Q-net without wires," I say, remembering the lights.

"How far into the pits do you need to go?" Morgan asks.

Now Bertie and Yenay do a silent communication thing. And I guess they've worked together before. Maybe as partners like me and Beau.

"Ara, did you see HoLFs in all the Warrior pits?" Yenay asks.

"Yes. I saw the most in Pit 4, but that's where I spent all my time." Reconstructing the General, which I also miss doing, which I'll never admit to my parents.

"Then we only need to install the sensor in Pit 1. A couple of meters from the entrance should work."

"I'll discuss this with the boss," Morgan says.

A shudder rips through me. The looters referred to Jarren as The Boss. And I'd be happy never to see him again. No. That's not entirely accurate. I'd love to see him locked in a cell. Plus he has answers that I desperately want to know—like what do those alien symbols on the Warriors mean? And why are they so important? Why kill over them? My curiosity is going to get me into trouble—actually, more trouble since it was my involvement that brought Jarren back to Planet Yulin. He said I was too clever and would figure it out. I think he overestimated my abilities.

Beau touches my right arm. I'm hugging it to my body as if I'm about to lose it. Relaxing, I smile thanks.

"Disentangle from the Q-net, Lawrence. I believe you need to report to training with Officer Keir soon," Morgan says.

Ah, rub it in. I slip from my Q-cluster and check that my web of security remains undisturbed before I exit.

"I'll contact you if the project is a go," Morgan says to the two scientists. "Do you have any more questions for Junior Officer Lawrence?"

"Not right now, but can we contact her?" Bertie asks.

"Only through me. For now," Morgan says.

The ladies leave.

"Come on, I'll walk back with you." Beau hooks his arm through mine.

I glance at the door on the left wall. It leads to the monitoring room where Niall's been watching the camera feeds of the base's public areas and labs. There's no audio and no cameras are allowed in the housing units—that would be creepy.

"You don't have time to say hello," Beau says.

Annoyed that he read me so well, I drop his arm and head for the exit.

Chuckling, Beau catches up in a few strides. "Too easy. You need to learn how to hide your emotions or Keir will keep slamming you down on the mat."

Easier said than done. "How long?"

"For what?"

"Until I stop training all day and get to do something else."

Beau slows. "What else do you want to do?"

I huff. Is he being dense on purpose? "Jarren's out there. We need to find him and stop him."

"It's only been twenty days since you…" He clears his throat. "Actively searching for him may tip him off about you."

We stop outside my unit. "Then we'll just have to be subtle about it."

"It's not that simple. I can't even determine where he's gone in the Q-net or even a hint about his physical location."

"Even more reason I should be helping you." When he doesn't say anything, my fingers itch with the desire to strangle the man. "You saw what I did. It was easy, Beau. You can't say you weren't impressed."

He fights a smile. "I see your ego hasn't been affected by your recent adventures."

"Come on, face it, you need your partner."

"I do."

Ha! Progress finally. "And Radcliff did say that Junior

Officer Lawrence would be helping you track down Jarren."

"He did."

Yes! "So what's the problem?"

"Your parents."

My excitement deflates. Everyone in my life is overprotective—boyfriend, boss, and my parents. Okay, yes my parents have the biological right to be, but…sheesh. They can't see anything beyond my lifeless body on the floor. I'm not helpless. After all, I did manage to rescue the security team when Jarren locked them in detention. I sigh. Guess I need to have a private discussion with them.

Beau taps his chest with a finger. "And you didn't hear it from me. Agreed?"

"Chicken."

"Damn right. Your mother scares me."

I can't help it. I laugh.

Rushing into my room, I change into the comfortable training uniform. Not bothering with shoes, I hurry out into the hallway and stop in surprise. Niall is standing in front of his unit. His hand hovers over the lock mechanism. Oh-eight-hundred already?

"You're late," he says with a smile.

"Aren't you supposed to be guarding the entrance to the pits?" I counter.

"I get thirty minutes to eat breakfast."

Ah. He opens his door and I follow him inside.

"What do you think you're doing? Keir's gonna—"

"I'm already late. The damage is done. Besides, I need a hug."

He raises an eyebrow. "The meeting didn't go well?"

"It was fine. Just…" I rub my arms. "Memories."

Niall pulls me in close. I'm pressed against his chest. Feeling safe and warm, I listen to his heartbeat. Strong and steady. He rests his cheek on the top of my head. We stay like that for…a while.

I draw back and meet his gaze.

"Better?" he asks.

"Yes, thanks."

He dips his head down for a quick kiss. "Then you should skedaddle."

"Is that a real word or did Beau make that up?" I ask.

"Knowing Beau, he found it in some obscure file. And you're procrastinating."

"I know, but I wanted to talk to you about tonight. After dinner, I need to have a conversation with my parents alone. Can I meet you in the rec room later instead of us hanging out on the couch?"

"Sure." His forehead creases in concern. "Is something wrong?"

"No. I'll tell you about it later."

"All right. Now—"

"I'm going, I'm going."

I race through the hallways until I reach the training room.

Officer Elese Keir is doing a kata with a knife. A kata is a predetermined set of moves, like a waltz, to help you when fighting. So you don't just punch once and hope for the best, but follow that move up with a kick and a jab and a roundhouse because that combination has been drilled into you so it's automatic. It's a part of martial arts, which I've also been learning.

Elese is wearing a tank top instead of the standard long-sleeved tunic. Her arms and shoulders are wrapped with muscles. The fluorescent lights shine off a sheen of sweat on her dark skin. As I watch her, I learn two things. One, she's been going easy on me, and, two, there's a grace and deadly beauty to the kata. Her fluid movements make me question if she is who I should aspire to be. If I'm going to choose to stay in security when I reach my eighteenth birthday, this physical conditioning would be an integral part of my life. And she's a perfect role model…well, no one's perfect, but she's close.

However, the star roads call to me. I learned how to dive deep into the Q-net and navigate the star roads during my internship with Chief Hoshi on the Interstellar Class space ship. And the view of the universe from the bridge…there isn't a word to describe the overwhelming amazement it stirs deep inside me. But to join DES as a navigator means leaving my family and perhaps Niall—if he decided to stay on the planet—far in the past.

"You're late, Recruit," Elese barks at me. The knife is still in her hand and she waves it at me. "What happened? Couldn't get your pampered ass out of bed? Did you need more beauty sleep?"

"I'm sorry I'm late."

"What? No excuses?"

"No. It's on me. Late is late." I just quoted my mother. Kill. Me. Now.

"Refreshing. Too bad it won't help you. You're ten minutes late so times that by ten and…give me a hundred laps around the room, a hundred push-ups, and a hundred sit-ups. Go!"

Yikes. I jog around the training room. It's not huge like the base's port, but it's a decent size. Running thirty laps has been a part of my training so I'm not winded right away. One thing about this type of physical exercise, it allows my mind to go in a different direction. I mull over the problem of Jarren. He's managed to get deep within the Q-net. Before we identified him, we called him the super worm because of his mad skills entering secured DES areas and covering his tracks. And he must have access to the star roads. How else can he travel this far out?

Except there's no indication that he used a star road or that he did a time jump. To get to Yulin, my family traveled on the ship for ninety days, but we jumped fifty Earth years into the future due to the time dilation. I'm actually a hundred and eighty-four Earth years old, but since I've done three time jumps, I've only lived seventeen Actual years. Confusing, right?

If Jarren did a time jump, he should be younger. Instead he appeared to be around thirty-eight A-years old, which lines up with his last trip being from Xinji to Suzhou. But what about the looter that said the time dilation sucked for us, implying not for them? He also mentioned an obscenely rich patron. Maybe they discovered a way to travel without causing a time dilation. Argh. Too many unknowns!

By my forty-fourth lap, I'm sucking air. Sweat drips from my forehead and my tunic sticks to my back. When I hit fifty, I count down instead of up. A mental trick that gives me some energy. The laps start to blur together. My tongue turns into a dried-out piece of jerky. The material of my uniform rubs painfully against my inner thighs. As a headache thumps in my temples and bile churns in my stomach, I'm glad I didn't have time to eat breakfast this morning. My world shrinks to the blue mat right in front of my feet. I lose track of...everything.

Then I almost run into Elese. She's standing in my way. I stop and stare at her.

"That's one hundred," she says.

"That's...nice," I pant. Then the mat rushes up to meet me.

Cold water splashes on my face, filling my nose. I gasp and sit up. Well, I try. Hands press on my shoulders, pushing me back down. Elese leans over me.

"Easy there."

I stare at her. "What happened?"

"You fainted."

Great. "I'm okay. Let me up."

She moves off and I sit up, but the room tilts and I close my eyes until the floor steadies. A cold container is placed in my hand. I chug the water without opening my eyes.

"And eat this," Elese says, shoving an energy bar in my other hand. "Let me guess, you didn't eat this morning."

I grunt between bites. The food and drink revive me and I peek out. The room remains still, but Elese is frowning. Glancing around, I spot a couple of the other officers watching me. Great, just great. They haven't really accepted me yet and now I've gone and given them another reason to doubt me.

"Don't tell my parents or Radcliff about this. Please," I add because her frown deepens. "They've been so…"

"I know." Her face smooths. She plops down next to me. "Why do you think I've been so hard on you?"

"'Cause you're sadistic?" I joke.

She huffs. "Not my thing. Training gives you poise."

"Poise?"

"Confidence, competence, remaining calm under pressure. Poise." Elese taps my chest with a finger. "What it isn't is being cocky. Rather, being careful and controlled at all times. Being aware of the dangers around you."

Her comment reminds me of when I joined the mission to check the base for looters when we first arrived at Yulin. The body language of the security team was a calm confidence, while I fumbled with my harness and almost threw up in zero gee.

"That incident with Jarren has shaken you," Elese says. "You need to get your poise back. Once you've reclaimed it, then everyone will stop being so careful with you."

That surprises me. "You mean I actually had it at one point?"

"Girl, if you didn't, you would have curled up into a ball in the pits when the enemy attacked and we'd all be dead."

I mull it over. Now Beau's comments make more sense. I've been waiting for someone to say, okay you're good to go, while they've been waiting for me to say, I'm ready to go. If it wasn't for the meeting with the astrophysicists, I wonder how much longer it would have taken me to figure it out.

Feeling better, I ask, "What is your thing?"

She smirks. "Dump Niall and I'll show you."

I laugh. "Not my thing."

"Pity. But no worries, I've been getting to know one of the chemistry techs. She says my eyes are beautiful." She flutters her long dark eyelashes at me.

"They are. It's a shame your feet stink."

"Uh-huh. I see you're recovered. All right, Recruit. Time to finish your punishment."

Groaning, I hand my water jug to Elese, and do a sit-up. Only ninety-nine more to go.

After a grueling day, I drag my sore and tired body back to my unit. I've learned two lessons. One, don't be late. Ever. Two, don't tease my instructor. It's a bad combination. The fabric of my uniform is plastered to my body. Ugh. Staggering to my room, I'm focused on grabbing clean clothes and showering.

The light switches on and—

I freeze, gaping at the marvel. Bright colors fill my walls. I blink and the colors form shapes...paintings. There must be twenty of them. Landscapes and cityscapes and nebula clusters and animals stalking through jungles all arranged in a pleasing manner. All inviting me to step closer and drink them in. Amazing.

When I'm able to think again, I realize these are Niall's mother's paintings. She died over two, maybe three A-years ago, leaving behind hundreds of them. Niall hasn't said much about how or when she died and I've been reluctant to ask. His pain is obviously still raw.

Footsteps sound behind me. I turn. Radcliff stands there, staring into my room. His posture is stiff, expression flat.

"Did Niall do this?" I ask.

"Yes. He said you needed a change of scenery."

My heart melts. So sweet. But Radcliff hasn't relaxed. "Is it okay with you?" After all, this is Radcliff's unit and these are his wife's.

"Do you like it?" he asks.

"Very much!" My enthusiasm earns me a slight smile.

"Then I approve." The tension in his shoulders disappears, but his nose crinkles. "Better shower before dinner. You stink."

And just when I thought we were having a nice moment... I resist the urge to stick my tongue out at him. Instead, I clean up. The hot water loosens the knots in my muscles. By the time I'm finished, Radcliff is setting a steaming casserole on the kitchen table. Ravenous is too mild a word to describe my stomach's sudden need for food.

My mother is the only person at the table.

"Where's Dad?" I ask.

"Equipment troubles. I'm starting to miss the forests of Xinji. I'd rather roots in my pits than sand in the gears."

I glance at the living room.

"Niall's on duty until twenty-two hundred hours," Radcliff says, sitting down. "Seems he switched shifts with Officer Tora so he'd have the afternoon off."

Warmth flows through me. I'd have to return the favor...somehow. Plus Radcliff allowed it. Progress.

"He mentioned seeing you later?" Radcliff asks.

"We're meeting in the rec room."

He grunts. "He'll only have a few hours to sleep before his next shift."

And the Chief of Security is back. Funny I didn't miss him.

My mom changes the subject and asks me about the meeting with the astrophysicists. As expected, she isn't happy about my worming in the Q-net. And let's just say her reaction to the possibility of me going into the pits makes an exploding star seem like a benign experience in comparison. Radcliff keeps quiet. Like Beau said, it's up to me.

Not wanting to argue in front of Radcliff, I invite my mom to see my room after we finish eating.

"Oh my, these are wonderful! Did Niall paint them?" she asks, while moving slowly from one to another.

"No, his mother did."

She sighs. "Such a shame about her. Oooh...look at the

detail on this one."

I join her in front of a leopard sitting on a branch. Its fur is so realistic, I'm tempted to reach out and stroke its back. Another part of me wishes to ask about Niall's mother, but that's not what I need to do now.

Straightening my spine, I think about what Elese said. I draw on my training and breathe in deep, exhaling stress and tension. Poise.

"Mom."

She turns to me, probably sensing this is important. "No."

So much for poise. "Please give me the courtesy of listening to me first."

"All right." Mom perches on the edge of my bed with her arms crossed.

"In one hundred and twenty-three days I will be eighteen and won't need your permission."

"I'm still in charge of the base," she counters.

Poise. "But not security." A mulish tightening of my mother's jaw is a warning sign even though she knows I'm right. I continue, "In the time it takes to reach my birthday, anything can happen. The shadow-blobs could invade the base or looters could attack us again. You can't put my safety above all the others who live here."

I let that sink in for a moment. "You need to trust me. I know my life is at stake, but I refuse to let Jarren win. That's unacceptable."

Mom's arms relax into her lap as she studies me. "Is that

what I look like when I'm being stubborn?"

I glance in the mirror. "No. It's what you look like when you're being confident and logical."

"Nice." Then she sighs. "It hasn't been that long since the attack. Jarren could be monitoring all our activity on the Q-net."

"He has been monitoring our activity since we arrived on Yulin, Mom. But now we know what he can do."

"And he knows what you can do."

Fair point. Except. "But Lyra is dead. He has no idea what Ara can do. She has a new perspective on navigating the Q-net."

"Because of your internship with Chief Hoshi?"

"That certainly helped."

She pins me with one of her I-know-you're-not-telling-me-everything stares. If she pushes it, I might have to lie. I'm not ready to explain to anyone that my consciousness flew through the Q-net when I was officially dead—no terminal or tangs needed. Yes, I know all about hallucinations, but, deep inside my mind, past the area that normally denies things like this, I know it was real. Everyone thought those shadow-blobs were a figment of my concussed imagination and look how that turned out. However, I don't have the energy to argue another this-really-happened-and-I'm-not-crazy situation.

When she doesn't respond, I say, "You need to allow me to be an active member of the security team."

"I'll talk this over with your father," Mom says.

"All right." I keep my tone neutral even though excitement pumps through my heart. My father defers to Mom when it's a family decision.

I get another look from her, but thankfully she doesn't go into interrogation mode.

"I suggest you get to bed early tonight, Ara," Radcliff says as I head toward the door. He's sitting on the couch, reading from a portable.

There's a hint of smugness in his tone so I stop and meet his gaze. He knows about earlier. "Who ratted me out?"

"The officer monitoring the security cameras."

Ah. I forgot. "I'm surprised you didn't tell my mother."

"Training is hard. You're not the first nor the last recruit to pass out. I've seen big men topple just at the sight of blood. As long as you don't make a habit of it."

So why bother with this entire conversation? To imply I can't get away with anything? What does he expect me to do? Perhaps I need to practice some of my poise on him.

"Officer Radcliff, thanks for the…advice." Warning is more like it. "I appreciate your concern. However, I'm under the impression that your security officers are able to use their free time as they wish. I assume that as long as I stay in security that applies to me as well?"

A reluctant nod along with a pained expression as if he wanted to say more.

I don't give him a chance. "I won't be long."

As I walk to the rec room, I pass a few other officers and nod a hello. Most have dark circles under their eyes. They move as if a heavy wet blanket is wrapped around their shoulders and dragging behind them.

The double doors to the training room are closed. Odd. I assumed that since the officers worked around the clock, the room would be available as well. Clanks of metal and muffled voices seep from the gap under the door. Perhaps there's a special training session going on. That makes more sense.

But I slow. The hallway is bright. Too bright. Every colony planet and Warrior planet keeps Earth time. We have twenty-four hour days and three hundred and sixty-five days in a year with that lucky leap day every fourth one. It's archaic and can be quite comical when you're living on a planet with over twenty-four hours of daylight and one season lasting an entire Earth year, but it unifies us Earthlings who are spread across the Milky Way Galaxy. Plus the light/dark cycle matches our natural circadian rhythm.

Normally, at this time of night, the hall lights would be dim. All public areas of the base have muted "night time" lights for about twelve hours a day. The overly bright hallway ends and, by the time I reach the recreation room, the illumination is normal.

No one is in the rec room. Not a surprise as everyone's been so busy. I'm lucky to actually have free time. Although I suspect that will soon change. I tug a small couch over to the spot the cameras can't see—not because I plan to jump Niall as soon as he arrives…hmmm…no, it's way too public of an area. But because I'm tired of being under the microscope all the time.

Niall enters, lugging that same exhaustion. Although his eyes spark with humor when he notices that I've rearranged the furniture.

Plopping down next to me, he says, "Nice."

"Not near as nice as what you did for me."

"You liked it?"

"Of course. The paintings are fantastic. Thank you."

Niall tucks me close. "They certainly brightened your room. Except now that pencil drawing I drew for you looks—"

"Just as fabulous. Don't diss King Toad and Queen Mouse or I'll have to hurt you." I framed Niall's gift and it's the last thing I see before I turn off the light. Its very presence helps reduce my nightmares.

He lifts his hands as if surrendering. "I wouldn't dream of it."

"Good." I snuggle closer.

"So what's with meeting here?" His tone is casual. Too casual.

This is gonna be fun. "I'm thinking of doing some worming and—"

"Are you insane?" His grip tightens.

I laugh. "Do you really have to ask that question?"

A sigh. "No."

"Don't worry, *Officer* Radcliff. I needed some one-on-one time with my mom. I think I've convinced her to lift the restrictions."

"Restrictions?"

Pulling away, I study his face. "Wow you must be really tired. You're usually a better actor."

He runs a hand through his black hair, leaving spikes. "I'm the lowest ranked officer, I'm not privy to everything."

"You had to guess my parents must have given your father conditions about me."

"Yeah. And before you get mad, I knew you'd figure it out."

"Took me long enough," I grump.

Drawing me against him, he says, "I wish it took you longer. You'd have been safer."

"It's a temporary illusion. No one's safe until Jarren's stopped."

A shrug. "It helps me sleep at night."

That's actually very sweet. I squeeze him. But he mentioned the S-word. Sleep, people!

"Come on." I break away and stand, hauling him to his feet. "It's twenty-two thirty. You're only going to get three hours of sleep. Time for bed."

"You're being sensible." He squints at me in suspicion.

"I can be sensible."

"No. You're up to something and trying to hide it by being sensible."

"So being sensible is a bad thing?"

"No. Yes. No."

"Which one is it?" I wait, suppressing a grin.

"In your case, it's a bad thing."

"All right. Then I won't be sensible anymore."

"That's not…" He sighs.

We hold hands on the way back to the officers' housing. When we reach the corridor that runs along the training room, I ask Niall about the brightness. "Is there a reason?"

His gaze grows wary and the silence lengthens. Confused, I'm about to prod when the doors of the training room open. The entrance is about a few meters ahead of us. Niall stops, releasing my hand, as Elese and Officer Zaim back out into the hallway. They point pulse guns at a group of people wearing neon green jumpsuits—and I thought the light was intense. The group are paired up in a line and each pair is shackled together at their wrist and ankle, causing them to walk in step. Their expressions range from defeated, bored, hostile and neutral. Officers Ho and Bendix follow the slow parade. They're also aiming pulse guns at the vivid group.

It clicks. They're the looters. Security captured sixteen of them during the attack—four women and twelve men. I peer at them. It's easy to see their faces in the brightness—oh, that's the reason for the daytime conditions. Do I recognize any of them? No. They wore jumpsuits and masks to hide their identities.

Niall puts his arm out, stopping me from getting closer.

"Wait," he says. Niall rests his hand on my shoulder. Is he worried I'm going to do something? Jarren killed Menz, not these thugs.

"What were they doing in the training room?" I ask.

"Exercising, stretching, moving around. Those detention cells are small for one person, but six of the units have two people." He frowns. Probably remembering the few hours he spent in one with Officer Morgan. "It would be inhumane to keep them in there all day."

Oh. I didn't think of that. In fact, I've been avoiding the topic altogether. Denial in all its glory.

At the sound of our voices, a few of the prisoners glance at us.

"Hey. It's her," one of the women cries. "That little worm The Boss was so keen to capture."

Uh oh. I step back as the prisoners all stop and stare at me. Maybe I should have cut my hair short. Grins and delight now shine on their faces even though Bendix is yelling at them to get moving. Niall blocks me from their view, but the damage is done.

"She's alive," a man says. "Which means—"

"The Boss is coming back!"

Cheers erupt.

Not good. Not good at all. Remembering the purple fire that danced on my skin and stopped my heart, I wrap my arms around my chest.

"We should tell The Boss she's here," one burly looter says.

"Back to your cells, now," Zaim orders, aiming his pulse gun at the big man.

Instead of obeying, the man surges toward Zaim, dragging his partner with him. Ho shoots, but the pulse goes wide and Burly slams Zaim into the wall hard enough to knock him unconscious.

The rest of the prisoners cheer and rush toward the three remaining security officers. Shocked by the speed and intensity of the attack, I'm rooted to the floor. Niall curses and grabs for his gun. But he's not in uniform.

All my training dissolves into a jumble in my mind, but I

step forward anyway. I have to help.

Niall grabs my arm, holding me back. "Reinforcements are coming."

"How do—"

He tilts his head at the cameras. "Rance is on duty and he'll sound the alarm, alerting the rest of the team."

"But—"

"Stay here." Niall rushes in to help the officers.

Sizzles from the pulse guns add to the cries and bellows. A few looters go down, taking their partners with them, but four of the pairs are now fighting hand to hand with the officers—two to one. Or in Bendix's case, four to one. The weapons have fallen to the floor. At least the guns can't be used by the looters. But they can't be used by us either as they're each set to only one person's electromagnetic signature.

The sizzles of multiple pulse guns crack through the air. Stunned, looters drop to the floor until no one is left standing except the officers and Niall. Lined up on the other side of the fallen prisoners are Radcliff, Morgan, Beau, and Rance. All are pointing their weapons at the prisoners. When no one moves, they lower them. Morgan and Rance are in uniform, but Beau is wearing a tight T-shirt and a pair of pajama pants. He must have been on call.

The other officers recover from the fight. Ho presses a hand to his nose, trying to staunch the flow of blood. Examining her torn and bloody shirt, Elese curses. Bendix leans against the wall. And poor Zaim is still out cold.

Radcliff quickly takes charge, ordering Morgan to call a

medic, sending Rance back to monitor the cameras, having Beau check on Zaim, asking us to explain what happened. Niall tells him what sparked the fight. Radcliff focuses on me and the desire to melt into the floor flushes through me. I brace for his anger.

Instead, Radcliff says to us, "Return to your units, I'll talk to you both later."

"Yes, sir," we say in unison and bolt.

But once we're out of sight, Niall takes my hand. I slow as the realization that it was all my fault catches up to me. The prisoners thought I'd be a way to gain their freedom. They cheered at the prospect of Jarren returning to kill me.

Niall stops and turns to me. "You're shaking."

"I am?" Sure enough my muscles are trembling.

"Don't listen to them," he says, pulling me into a hug. "There's no way they can contact Jarren. He won't find out you're alive." Niall leans back and meets my gaze. "The Protector Class ship will be here in six hundred and forty days. And you're surrounded by security."

Who were almost overwhelmed. And who Jarren got the drop on. Twice. But I wisely keep those thoughts to myself. Plus I've already figured out that Jarren will at some future point figure out I'm alive. It's inevitable. The key will be to find him first. That thought steadies me. Weird, right?

Cupping his cheek, I run my thumb over his stubble. "I'm better, thanks."

We continue to Niall's unit. I follow him in for a private good-night kiss, but something about what he said bugs me.

"How do you know the exact number of days until the Protector ship arrives?" I ask him. Has he changed his mind and plans to enlist? A pulse of unease ripples through me.

His shoulders droop as he reveals the depth of his exhaustion. "It's what gets us through the days of double shifts, little to no free time, the constant vigilance. To know there's an end point helps."

The knot in my throat loosens. And now I understand. The officers need more help and the techs haven't been that keen to fill in. Granted, they didn't sign up to— "I know a way you can motivate my mom's archeology techs."

"Don't keep me in suspense."

"Ha ha. Seriously, all they want to do is return to normal, like you do. If they know what they're doing is actually helping security, that we're figuring out a way to open the pits and there's an end point, they'll be more inclined to assist us."

"My dad—"

"Probably keeping a tight lid on everything. Doesn't want the details about the looters and HoLFs scaring the scientists. Right?" The answer is in Niall's stiff posture. "Well, if you want them to be part of the team, they need to feel like part of the team, working on a common goal. You have to trust them with the truth."

Niall shakes his head, giving me a tired smile. "And here I thought the prisoners' revolt would spook you. Instead, you're giving advice."

"Good advice," I clarify.

"And you're modest too, no wonder I like you so much," he

teases. Then he sobers. "What changed, Mouse?"

"I'm motivated."

I'm still awake when Radcliff returns. He glances at me sitting on the couch then at the clock. It's oh-two-hundred hours.

"I couldn't sleep." The truth. Every time I closed my eyes, the riot replayed in my mind.

He relaxes. "I'm sorry about tonight."

Surprised, I blurt, "That's what I'm supposed to say. It's because of me. I'm—"

"Not your fault. I assigned four officers to watch sixteen prisoners." Radcliff straightens. "It won't happen again. Only eight prisoners will be allowed to exercise at one time."

A good idea, except that means more work for the officers.

"Get some sleep, Ara," he says, heading toward his room.

Not so fast. I surge off the couch and block his way.

He raises an eyebrow. "Do you need something?"

"Yes. I want a shift."

"A shift?"

"A security shift. Everyone's exhausted. I can take a turn monitoring cameras or guarding the entrance to the pits. In fact, I should be there since I can actually see the shadow…er…HoLFs."

"You're still in training."

"Does everyone train eight hours a day every day when they

start?" I already know the answer is no.

"Your case is different," he says, but it's weak.

I wait.

"Your parents—"

"Are not in charge of security."

Radcliff studies me. He's pissed I interrupted him, yet there's approval there as well. I'm getting better at reading him.

"Am I part of this team or not?"

"You are."

"Then please put me on the schedule."

The next day I'm a few minutes early for training. A nasty bruise is purpling on Elese's swollen right cheek. It's hard for me to believe that last night was not my fault.

"I'm sor—"

"None of that," she says, holding up her hand. "They've been spoiling for a fight." Elese shrugs. "It's all part of the job. You gotta be ready for anything." To prove her point she jabs a punch at my ribs.

Without thinking, I block it.

"Ah, progress." She launches into a series of attacks.

And I spend most of the morning practicing blocks, punches and kicks with Elese before we move on to self-defense—a typical day. Frustration builds—did no one listen to me? But after lunch something is finally different.

Elese hands me a pulse gun. "This one is yours."

Interesting that Radcliff kept the gun set to my electromagnetic signature. The weapon is nonlethal and built so I can't accidentally shoot myself because it recognizes me. Plus no one can use the gun on me or the other officers. But, as I witnessed last night, it will send an electromagnetic pulse at the enemy, rendering them unconscious.

She leads me to the shooting range. It adjoins the training area and is long and narrow. There's a wide red stripe crossing the short width of the floor.

"Ever shoot one of these?" Elese brandishes her own weapon.

"No."

"There's no kickback and you're not going to see anything. But you'll hear—"

"A sizzle. I've plenty of experience with that."

We share a rueful grin.

She tilts the gun to the side. "See this yellow bar? It means the gun is fully charged. As you use it, the bar will shrink. Once it's gone, you need to recharge your weapon."

"How?"

"Ask Radcliff for a pulse kit—it has a charger."

"What if the gun runs out of power when you're in the middle of a fight?"

"There are power packs." Opening the bottom of the gun's handle, she pulls out a round cylinder and replaces it with another one from her pocket. "Tactical pants are the best. You wouldn't believe what I have stored in all these pockets." Her brown eyes gleam. "Wanna see?"

"Er…no thanks. A little mystery between friends is a good thing," I say.

Her laugh is spicy and rich like hot chocolate mixed with coffee. Elese then shows me how to properly hold the gun, set my stance, square my shoulders to a target and press the trigger with my thumb.

Then she steps on the red strip and says, "Beginner target."

About ten meters down the room a circle drops from the ceiling. The center of it glows orange. Elese aims and fires. A burst of sizzle, then the orange light flashes and winks out.

"Your turn." She moves out of my way.

I step onto the strip. The orange light returns. Concentrating on my body's position, I lift the gun, aim, and press the trigger. Warmth fills my palm as a sizzle flies and keeps right on going, missing the target.

"Freeze," Elese orders. She adjusts my stance, turns my shoulders slightly, and lifts my arm. "Try again."

Another miss. Another adjustment. And…repeat…about ten…twelve times before the stubborn orange light finally dies. Yes! I killed a light, my parents will be so proud.

"Again," she says.

A sizzle and a miss. Sigh.

"Again."

Miss.

"Again."

Hit!

"Again."

Miss.

When my hits outnumber my misses, Elese is satisfied. She slaps me on the back and says, "The shooting range is yours until seventeen hundred. When you can hit the target twenty times in a row, you can move on. Just say 'intermediate target' while standing on the sensor."

"What if I don't reach twenty in a row?"

"Then tomorrow you try again and again and again."

"I'm beginning to hate that word."

"So worming is easy? You figured it out right away?"

"Shut up."

She flashes me a smile and leaves.

I squint at the target. Okay, Mr. Orange Light, you're mine.

After a couple hours, I hate the color orange. I can't hit the target more than six times in a row. Now, if I had one of those energy wave guns...Mr. Orange Light would be Mr. Shattered Into A Million Pieces Light.

When I finish, Elese is doing bicep curls on one of the weight machines. Her arms flex and her muscles pop to an impressive bulge with each pull, lifting a stack of ten heavy metal plates. I can lift two. Who knew all those hours worming in the Q-net doesn't build upper body strength, or lower body strength, or core strength? However, my butt muscles are like steel.

When she finishes, I hold out the gun. "Where should I put this?"

"In your holster, Junior Officer Lawrence."

I stare. Did she just—

"It's not going to do you any good in a locked armory."

Just like that, my sour mood vanishes. Yup, I'm that easy.

The divine smell of chicken greets me when I enter my unit. If Radcliff notices the gun as I go to my room, he doesn't say anything. After a moment to recover from the blast of colors—it's gonna take me a while to get use it to all the paintings—I tuck the gun—no, my gun—into my leather holster on my belt. All the security officers are armed when dressed in their uniforms. The weapon is also required when wearing the combat jumpsuit—a form fitting material that resists pulse hits and reduces the impact of other lethal weapons. My jumpsuit helped save my life when Jarren shot me. And if I'm not being modest, I look good in it. Even though the black color is slimming, it still shows off my curves.

After a quick shower and change of clothes, I join my parents, Niall and Radcliff. Dinner is a rather normal affair. Well, normal for me. My mom sneaks probing glances at me and I wonder if Radcliff told her about the looters rioting last night.

It's not until my parents leave that I learn why Mom was being extra mom-ish. Niall and I are on the couch just hanging out when Radcliff approaches.

"You're on the schedule," he says to me. "You have the twenty-two-hundred to oh-two-hundred shift watching the camera monitors."

I'm uncertain whether to be excited or suspicious. "And training?"

"Ongoing. Officer Keir still expects you at oh-eight-hundred hours. You'll have three and a half hours of training, two hours of weapon drills and you'll report to Officer Dorey from fourteen hundred until sixteen-thirty. Understand?"

Excitement wins despite the fact I'll only get six hours of sleep a day. "Yes, sir."

"Good."

Before he retreats, I ask him about the pulse kit.

He points to a small leather bag sitting on the end table. "Inside is a charger and a couple power packs. Always have at least one extra power pack with you when you're armed." Radcliff goes into his bedroom.

Niall doesn't say anything, but his arm around my shoulder tenses.

"Okay, spit it out," I say.

"Is this because of last night?"

"No, it's—"

"It's because I complained about the long hours," he says.

I lean close to him and whisper, "Can I tell you a secret?"

Instantly wary—he knows me too well—he nods.

"You are not the center of the universe." I pat his hand. "I know it's a blow to your ego, but, despite being coddled by your father all your life—"

"Yeah, he's such a cuddle bunny," Niall says dryly.

"Exactly." I hold onto my fake condescension until I imagine Radcliff as a cuddle bunny. Laughter ruins my act.

Except Niall is not amused. "Mouse."

"All right, all right. First, you really didn't complain. Just stating a fact. Second, what I said about the archeology techs and them feeling like a part of the team is a concept I've been thinking over these last couple days. I'm a security officer, but I don't feel like part of the team. It's time for me to do my share of the work."

He exhales and the tightness drains from him. "You're right, but I'm going to miss our evenings together."

"Wait, why do you think that will stop?"

Tucking a strand of my hair behind my ear, he says, "You're going to need to sleep before your shift."

"I don't need that much time. We can still hang out a few hours, then I'll nap until my shift. Plus this way you'll get more sleep."

"I'd rather fall asleep here with you on the couch than in my bed."

"Okay, then we'll nap on the couch together. It's only six hundred and thirty-nine more days."

He groans. "I'd rather think about the one hundred and twenty-two days until you're eighteen."

"How about during our couple hours together, we don't think about work at all?"

He straightens. "Do you have something else in mind?"

Once again, I whisper in his ear, "Yes. Come to my room so you can…" I run my fingers through his hair.

Sucking in a breath, he closes his eyes.

"…tell me about your mother's paintings and why you choose those for my walls."

Now he's glaring at me. "You're evil, Mouse. And you can't do that without paying a price."

"What price?"

"A kiss."

I oblige. A chaste kiss turns into…more. When we break for air, I tug him into my room. My hormones spike, sending heat to a number of unexpected places, but I leave the door wide open and avoid skin contact to allow my pulse return to normal.

Niall explains the various paintings. The Cat's Eye Nebula, the jungle on Planet Jieshou, the capital city on Planet Omega, an Earth leopard, Planet Anqing—

"I didn't know Anqing has so many rings," I say, marveling over the red spirals.

"It's beautiful."

But I don't think he's referring to the painting. "You've seen it?" I ask. It's over a hundred E-years from Yulin.

"Yes."

That surprises me. "When?"

"I think it was around twenty-one ninety. When they closed Anqing, we transported the scientists to another Warrior planet…Heshan, I think."

Once the assessment of a Warrior planet is finished and the statues have all been cataloged, there's nothing more to do. Not until DES decides if they want to colonize the planet or leave it as a historical site. In the meantime, there's no reason to stay. Except...

"What about the looters?" I ask. "Those closed planets are just ripe for the picking."

"The Protectorate deployed a bunch of military satellites in orbit around the planet. If a ship doesn't have the right clearance codes, they won't allow it to get close."

Oh. "Why don't they do that to the active Warrior planets?"

"They are, it just takes time."

Of course. Stupid time dilation.

Now I'm curious about how many Warrior planets are empty. Anqing was the second exoplanet discovered with the Warriors. Xi'an was the first, then DES named the rest after cities in China in alphabetical order. Heshan was the eighth and Yulin is the twenty-second, unless you consider Earth as a Warrior planet, then it's the twenty-third—my parents are still debating over that even though DES didn't give another Warrior planet a name starting with the letter E.

I study the paintings and am struck by how many different places are represented. Plus these are just a fraction of what Niall's mother created. And then the significance of the date he mentioned—twenty-one ninety—finally hits me.

"How old are you in E-years?" I ask.

He avoids my gaze. Instead he moves to the next painting. That's concerning. I do the math...he has to be at least over three hundred and thirty some E-years. The first Explorer Class ships went out in twenty-eighty-two and he said he was born on a ship... It's quite possible that he's four hundred and forty E-years old. Oh my stars.

Niall glances at me. "You have that look."

"What look?"

"The pained one that says you're trying to do math."

"I can do math, you know. And I already figured you have to be older than three hundred and thirty." When he doesn't say anything, I add, "Why don't you want to tell me? I'm a hundred and eighty-four and don't look a day over a hundred." My joke falls flat.

"It's just…some people act…weird about it." He fidgets with his sleeve.

I'm a little hurt—well, more than a little—to be classed with "some people," but I don't want to make him uncomfortable. "Don't worry about it." I point to a picture of a dark green Chinese male guardian lion. Its massive right paw rests on an orb. "Was this carved from jade?"

"I think so. One of the archeologists we met had two of them on her desk. They were only about eight centimeters tall, but my mom was fascinated. She painted both. I have the female guardian lion in my unit." He stands behind me. "They represent yin and yang, male and female. I thought it's appropriate for us to each have one." A pause. "I think of us— the security officers—as guardian lions. Silly, I know."

I turn around. "Not really. After all, you and your father were quite growly when I first met you, roaring out orders." I tease.

"Which you didn't listen to."

"Of course not. I didn't speak lion."

"And now that you do?"

"Ara, shouldn't you be resting before your shift?" Radcliff asks. He's standing at the threshold of my room, the familiar crease of annoyance on his forehead.

I wonder if he panicked when Niall and I weren't on the couch. "I will soon."

He stabs Niall with a stare then walks away.

"Speaking of guardian lions…" I mutter.

Niall laughs. "I better get going." But he pauses. "I'm sorry about…earlier. I know I haven't told you much about my life before. It's just all my good memories include my mom and it's…still hard to talk about her."

"That's understandable. When you're ready, I'll be here to listen. In the meantime, you'll just have to suffer through some of my stories."

"Some?"

"I'm not going to tell you all of them."

"Why not?"

"'Cause you'd arrest me."

He stills. "It's probably best I don't know."

"No probably about it." I wink.

Ugh. Waking up at twenty-one-thirty hours after only sleeping for ninety minutes sucks. I change into my uniform, French braid my hair, and strap on my weapon belt.

Flashlight, check.

Pulse gun, check.

A bit of pride swells when I rest my hand on the weapon. I'm armed and dangerous…well, more like a mild threat, but some day, baby, watch out.

I make a cup of coffee. Normally, I don't indulge, but I suspect it might be the difference between me being awake when Niall shows up at oh-two-hundred hours and me drooling on the counter.

The halls are empty and quiet, the light dimmed for night time. No one is in Radcliff's office as I cross to the door into the monitor room.

When I enter, Officer Tora turns to me. "At least you're early and not out causing more trouble." Her disgusted tone suggests we're not about to have a bonding moment.

A brief thought—too bad I can't shoot her—flashes through my mind. I do the mature thing and keep my mouth shut.

The woman is about thirty A-years old and always smells like roses. Her bobbed brown hair bounces when she moves her head. After the first looter attack, Radcliff assigned two officers to monitor the camera feeds, but with the shadow-blobs and prisoners, there aren't enough people so the shift is down to one person. Tora sits in the narrow walkway between Radcliff's office and Beau's office. "Just don't stand there, come closer so I can show you what to do and be out of here on time for once." She sweeps her hands out, indicating to the two long side walls filled with screens on either side of her. Views of empty hallways, labs, the canteen, the port, and about ten meters of the ground outside the base fill them.

"It's easy. Watch the feeds. If you see anyone who doesn't belong or anyone doing something illegal or harming another or rioting, then press this button. That will alert Officers Radcliff, Morgan, and the officer on call." She glances at the mug in my hand. "If you need to use the washroom, there's a small one in Radcliff's office. Be quick and make sure you rewind the feed and watch what you've missed. You can speed it up. Since you are here, I doubt you'll see anything at this time of night. Questions?"

Yeah, like why are you being such a bitch? "How do you know if anyone tries to tamper with the feeds?" I ask instead.

"Unless they flash black or ripple you can't know for sure, but Dorey has secured them."

Her answer fails to reassure me. "Can you stay another couple of minutes so I can make sure they're showing live feed?" And that no one has altered the special security loop.

She glares. "Dorey—"

"Is very good, but worming into camera feeds is super easy and I'd feel better knowing they were secure."

Tora folds her arms and huffs. "I'm sure if I refuse, you'll run to Radcliff and whine about it. Make it quick."

I'm torn between calling her out for her nasty comment and not upsetting her further—she might just be exhausted. With no time for drama, I hurry. Beau's office is unlocked. No surprise since the camera room is the only way into his domain, and it's always monitored. I insert my tangs, sit at his desk and access the Q-net. Worming through all the security Beau heaped around the cameras, I check to ensure they are indeed showing our base at the current time and date. They are. And just to be on the safe side, I ensure the closed loop is still inaccessible to everyone except me, Radcliff, and Beau. It is. Then I hurry to set up an alarm in case a worm tries to alter any of our cameras.

"Happy now?" Tora leaves before I can answer another snide question.

I am happier, thanks for asking. Scanning the screens, I watch a few dedicated scientists—probably techs—still working. A couple people are in the halls. Most are heading back to their units. Nothing moves outside the base. Not even a breeze stirs the sand. All is quiet in the security area.

After an hour of nothing, I'm bored. I wonder why there's no terminal in here. Keeping an eye out for intruders would be easier through the Q-net. In fact, the Q-net could do this job.

To keep awake as I scan the feeds, I consider how to make it work. My parents have pictures of everyone who has been assigned to the planet. The Q-net could sound an alarm if an unfamiliar face appeared. But what about fights or crimes? That's extremely rare in a research base, but sometimes when the chemists mix up a batch of hooch they can get rowdy. I puzzle out how to set up a protocol for the Q-net for those cases. Maybe I could convince Radcliff to let the Q-net monitor the feeds so the officers would get a break. But what about the closed loop? Hmmm. I could write a standard plug and chug program to check the loop.

The best part of my shift is when Niall arrives. Freshly showered, his wet hair is combed back and he smells like shampoo and sage grass. The desire to hug him pushes on my body, but even though no one can see us, we're in uniform and we made a promise.

"How did your first shift go?" he asks.

"Uneventful." I gesture at the monitors. "Not even an inappropriate liaison that I could gossip about."

"Pity. But that's how it goes for most of security. Long periods of boredom, followed by intense action, then back to boredom."

"Similar to archeology. Lots of grunt work with discoveries few and far between."

"Then you should be used to this."

I yawn.

"Go to bed, Mouse. I've got this."

I tell him about the Q-net alarm I set up.

"You don't think Beau's measures are enough?"

"I bypassed them in a few minutes without using my security clearance. Jarren could do it faster."

"Wow. I'm wide awake now. Could Jarren slip by your alarm?"

"It's subtle. I wove it through a few layers, but we didn't call him the super worm for nothing."

"Not helping."

"Jarren won't be looking for it. Not with all of Beau's safeguards. And not if he believes I'm dead."

"Better."

I say good night and head back to my unit. My conversation

with Niall replays in my mind and I wonder just how…integrated Jarren is in our communications to DES. I assume he's been monitoring them, deleting the ones that report on his attack and activities. Perhaps there's a way to bypass him or to hide the information so he doesn't stop that file. I'm sure he has a list of words that will trigger his attention. Then those files will be rerouted to a cluster where he could review them. If it was me I'd— Oh my stars!

I almost trip over my feet at the thought. But I stay upright by sheer will because I don't want Niall to abandon his post to rush to my side. After a few steps, I steady my nerves. I'm probably overreacting. And if not, there isn't anything I could do about it at this time. Tomorrow when I'm working with Beau, I'll ask him.

When I reach the door to my unit, I press my hand on the pad to unlock it. Before going inside, I turn to the closest camera and wave good night to Niall.

Due to my overactive imagination, it takes me longer to fall asleep than I planned so it's an effort to leave my warm comfortable bed in the morning. At least I'm waking up surrounded by beauty and calm. Is it weird to feel that a part of Niall's mother's soul is watching over me? In a good way—not a creepy way. The paintings remind me of the Terracotta Warriors. When I stand near an intact Warrior, I sense a part of the craftsman's soul was worked into the clay thousands of years ago. I guess that is weird. Must be the start of sleep deprivation.

Elese is way too chipper for this time of the morning. We drill and spar and work out and drill and spar and work out. Then a break for lunch before I stand in a shooter's stance and attempt to make Mr. Orange Light go away twenty times in a row. My arms are sore from yesterday's fruitless efforts. Finally, the part of the day I'm most looking forward to arrives and I dash back to get a shower before going to Beau's office as an official security officer.

"You're late," he says.

"Did you want me to stink up your office?"

"No. Next time leave training earlier."

"Fine with me." I plop next to him.

Beau has dual Q-net terminals—I'm so jealous—along with a regular terminal at his desk. He spends the most time securing the Q-net. Although the other officers are trained, he has a natural talent. Radcliff is rather good at tracing worms as well. That's how I met him. He caught me illegally worming on the ship. Back before I interned with Chief Hoshi. I doubt he'd catch me now, but I learned early on never to underestimate Officer Tace Radcliff.

"Tora told me you checked my security around the camera feeds," Beau says in a flat tone.

Tora, eh? And she accused me of running to Radcliff to whine. I gauge his mood. Normally, he's a terrible flirt, cocky and easy going. I wonder if I've offended him or broken some protocol. We're supposed to be partners on this.

"I wanted to make sure they hadn't been compromised," I say.

"You don't trust my protections?"

Ah. I hurt his feelings. "I trust you to do the best you can. Jarren is better than both of us and, I'm sorry, but I'm super paranoid."

He grunts, slightly mollified. "Setting up an alarm was a good idea. Now we need to figure out where Jarren's hiding." He picks up his tangs.

Time to tell Beau about my worries. "I think we should test to see if DES is getting messages from us."

His hands freeze halfway to his ears. "Where did this come from?"

"Last night, I was trying to think of a way to determine which files Jarren was monitoring or stopping from reaching DES, when I thought, if it were me, I'd stop them all so there's no risk one will get by me. We should confirm that we have reestablished contact with DES. Remember that at one point during the attack Jarren had cut us off from them." Not that DES could do anything to help us. But they should know what's going on so they can at least warn the other Warrior planets about Jarren.

"We're in contact with DES," Beau says. "That's the first thing I checked when I was cleared for duty."

Beau was sliced by the shadow-blobs and then pulsed by the looters. "How are you doing?"

"I've a cool crisscross shaped scar, you wanna see?" He pulls his shirt, untucking it.

I grab his wrist. "No. Niall and I can't even hold hands in uniform; I don't think Radcliff would approve of you flashing your abs at me."

"You ain't seen abs like these." He winks.

Nice to know he doesn't hold a grudge. "Don't worry, I have."

He pishes. "Oh please, Niall's got nothin' on me."

"Who said anything about Niall? I'm talking about Elese."

Beau opens his mouth, but nothing comes out. He snaps it closed.

Score one for Elese. I switch my focus back to work. "Can we test the connection to DES again? Jarren might have blocked us since you checked." Before he could pout, I add, "Indulge my paranoia please."

"All right. How do you want to do it?"

I mull over the problem. Worming is good at getting into places that are supposed to be protected. I wish I could trail a file as it travels to DES's data clusters. I'd see right where it's intercepted. But that's not possible. Not while I'm alive. When I died, I flew through the Q-net and it would have been easy. It was probably just my own version of the afterlife, but...my interactions with the Q-net have been different since then.

My idea might be unconventional and impossible, but worth a try. "Can you send a report to DES's security marked urgent?"

"What should I write?"

"Just nonsense. It's not the contents that are important. It's more the destination. I'm going to try to follow it."

Beau turns and stares at me. "You can't do that. No one

can."

I don't say anything.

"Those routes are for text files. Which you're not. You can worm into DES's cluster for urgent information and see if my file shows up. That's what I did."

"Can I at least try?"

"But…" He glances away. Drumming his fingers on the desk, he remains quiet for a long while. Finally he says, "After you had the Q-net outline the HoLFs, Radcliff asked me to take the video footage of the pits from after you first saw them and have the Q-net mark the HoLFs."

Huh. I cross my arms. Why didn't he ask me? "And?"

"It wouldn't work. I even took it to your cluster. Nothing."

"You wormed into my cluster?"

"Took me hours, and the only reason I got in without setting off any alarms was because I was there when you layered in the security measures."

In that case, my ego isn't as bruised. However, more important than my ego are the results. "Nothing at all?"

"Nope."

Am I surprised? I do call it my cluster for a reason. But still…

"That's why I'm going to let you waste both our time to try to follow that file. I reserve the right to say, 'I told you so' when it fails."

"Duly noted."

Beau writes up a short report that says, 'This is an exercise in futility.' Then he marks it urgent. Ready? he asks through the

Q-net.

I close my eyes for a more immersive experience and concentrate on the file. Towing it into my cluster, I imagine in detail what I wish to do. The file transforms into a snake of data strung together like beads. It wraps around me. It's hard to describe because, in the Q-net, you don't have a form, but you have a presence. And now there's a weight to my presence. A strange unease flicks through me. What if I get trapped or lost? Would I forever be entangled in the Q-net? Or would I go insane?

It's too late for doubts. Go, I say.

Beau hits send. And I fly. Pulled along on the invisible paths through the Q-net. Similar to the star roads, but not as…complex and beautiful. It's linear, making sharp, nausea-inducing turns.

Until it smacks into a wall. A painful wave ricochets in my head—talk about solid security measures. Then the file is sucked into a huge sorting cluster. Lots of information from Yulin. So far so good. A plug and chug program sorts them and puts all the biology reports together, matches the administrative files, sends messages on to their final destination, etc...

My urgent file is tugged from the big cluster and put into a database with others marked urgent. Lots of others. All sitting there. I scan dates, the oldest is 2522:139. That's too old. These shouldn't be stored, but sent to the proper personnel in DES. The older ones might have gone on and then been stored here after they've been read, but the new one shouldn't have stopped.

Beau worms through a tight gap. *See, I told you it's getting to DES.*

Is this the same place you checked for your other test file? I ask.

Yes. What's wrong?

Can't you see all these files?

I see the urgent file and a few other reports.

There's hundreds here.

You must have damaged your brain with this stunt, Beau says.

I'm fine. Can you go out and come back the official way, using your clearance?

This is a waste of time.

Please.

All right. Beau disappears.

While I wait, I check the rest of the database, looking at the dates. Nothing marked before day 139. What happened on that date?

Beau enters as if he's strolling through a door. Having clearance makes navigating the Q-net vastly easier.

What do you see now? I ask.

Same thing as before except now that urgent file is gone. I'm probably going to get into trouble.

I've a moment of doubt. Did that wave of pain make me see things that aren't here? Why can't he see them? There must be another layer of protection. I examine the security programs. And...there! Woven into one of the basic codes is another delicate set of instructions, hiding all the files from both wormers and those with permission to be in this cluster. But not from me because I arrived in an unconventional way. I unwind it, turning it off temporarily.

Beau yelps. *Stars, girl! Give a guy some warning. A pause. What the fu—*

Loads more files, right? I ask.

Yeah.

I let him figure it out.

Nothing's gone through to DES since day 139. It's all been collected here. Something big must have happened on that day.

It clicks. *It was the day of the first looter attack!*

You mean nothing has reached DES since they stole those Warriors? Beau asks.

Yes.

So that means DES believes—

Planet Yulin went silent. Just like Xinji.

2522:193

Stunned, Beau and I take a moment to just…absorb. If DES hasn't received any messages or reports from us since 2522:139, then they're not aware of the second attack or the shadow-blobs. And they probably believe everyone on Yulin is dead just like when Planet Xinji went silent.

Then who has been responding to our—Jarren, the murdering looter.

Let's go, Beau says. *You worm out of here and I'll leave via official channels.*

Okay. I rewind the program and cover my tracks without causing ripples, which takes much longer. Ripples would alert Jarren and could be traced back to me. While the Q-net is similar to a gigantic ball of yarn with a gazillion layers, the…strands act like they're made of liquid. Confusing, I know. Wormers find gaps in layers and squirm/worm through. However, those layers will flex and undulate, especially if the wormer is inexperienced. The more experience a wormer has, the less the disturbance. Jarren has been worming all over the Q-net with nary a ripple. Scary, right?

By the time I disentangle, Beau is already on his feet. He's crossing his office with short agitated strides.

"This is bad, really bad," he says. "How long have they been blocking us?"

At least the math is easy. "Fifty-four days. But we should assume Jarren's been monitoring us since we arrived on Yulin."

"And he probably decided on what files to let through to DES once we were planetside."

"I'd bet those odd responses from DES were really from Jarren," I say.

"We're completely cut off!" He fists his hands in his hair.

I've never seen Beau so freaked before. "Not *completely*."

He whips around. "What do you mean?"

"I found a way *out* during that second attack. I reached Chief Ritsa. That was real because she gave me the override codes for the base." It'd been a worming feat driven by pure terror and desperation. In other words, I've no idea how I managed it and am not sure I could do it again. But I keep that little nugget to myself.

Beau takes a breath. "All right, we need to report this to Radcliff."

"And my parents."

It didn't take long to assemble everyone in security's conference room. My parents were already enroute to Radcliff's for dinner. Officer Morgan sits on Radcliff's right and Drs. Milo Jeffries and Kara Gage complete the group. The two scientists are second in command after my mom and dad. Plus they know all about my situation. I claim a chair next to my mother.

Beau stands and explains what we learned during our foray into the Q-net. A moment of silence follows.

"Are you sure?" Dr. Gage asks.

"They just confirmed what we've suspected," Radcliff says to her.

We? That doesn't include me or Beau. I glance around. Or Gage. Or Jeffries, if I'm reading their pinched expressions correctly.

"Why wasn't I informed?" Beau asks with an even tone, but his hands are balled into fists and pressed against his legs.

"It was a guess, Officer Dorey. We didn't want to tip Jarren off by actively probing the blockade," Radcliff says. "If he discovers we suspect, then he'll search for our attempts to bypass his measures."

"Have you been trying to reach DES?" I ask.

"No. On the off chance we were right, we've been feeding him misinformation about our security. The other science reports are being filed as usual," Morgan says.

"Permission to speak freely, sir?" Beau asks Radcliff.

Oh boy. This ought to be interesting.

"Granted."

"Do you really think *I* would have tipped Jarren off, sir? If that's the case, then I wish to tender my resignation."

"This isn't about your ego, Dorey," Morgan snaps. "It's about survival."

Her words hit me hard. I didn't think of it that way before. And it's way scarier than just being blocked. It also deflates the puff from Beau's chest.

"You were doing your job," Radcliff says. "Securing the camera feeds, checking for a block using conventional methods. That's what we needed you to do. That's what Jarren expects us to do." He turns to me. "Why didn't you trust Officer Dorey's security measures?"

Now I'm on the hot seat—is that really a thing? How do I explain without sounding like I'm boasting? "I don't want to die again. So I'm being extra careful and super paranoid."

My mom clasps my hand under the table in silent support. But everyone else is waiting for me to continue.

"I trust Beau to do his very best, but I've a unique way to navigate the Q-net and it's...more accurate, so I wanted to ensure that our messages were reaching DES."

"Diplomatic," Jefferies mutters.

"Did you tip off the looters?" Gage asks.

"No," Beau answers. "I didn't trigger anything and Ara was a ghost."

Technically, Lyra is a ghost.

"What does all this mean for us?" Jefferies asks. "Is that Protectorate ship still enroute?"

Mom tips her head at Radcliff.

"Yes," Radcliff answers. "It was dispatched prior to the block. Even if DES suspects we're all dead, they are still required to confirm it beyond a doubt and make an effort to search for survivors."

"However, if Jarren wishes to keep his activities secret, he has to…" Dad glances at me.

Mom squeezes my hand. Uh oh.

"Has to what?" Gage prompts.

"Eliminate the rest of us before that ship arrives," my father finishes in a rush.

I suspected as much. Yet hearing it said aloud lends it more weight. The news sinks to the bottom of my stomach with a sickening thud.

Gage is clasping her hands so tight her fingertips turn red. "That means we have…"

"Less than six hundred and thirty-eight days," I say. No one remarks on the speed of my math. Tough room.

Jefferies pales. "To live?"

"No. To find Jarren and stop him," Radcliff says with confidence.

"What about the HoLFs?" Gage asks in a shaky voice. "He let them do his dirty work for him on Xinji. That's why he destroyed so many Warriors."

"That's still a theory," Dad says. "We haven't proven that the arrival of the HoLFs is due to the destruction of the Warriors."

Unable to keep quiet, I say, "That's not quite right. Jarren didn't destroy the Warriors to release the shadow…HoLFs. He wasn't expecting them when he attacked Xinji. Now when he attacked us, he knew what would happen. But Jarren didn't particularly care if we survived or not." A shudder zips up my spine as the memory of his words, *they might survive until the Protector ship arrives* repeats in my mind. "He also didn't indicate that he was counting on it. In fact, he was going to send you all the information he had about the shadow-blobs."

"However, at that time, he thought he had you in his custody," Radcliff says. "It was probably a lie to keep you calm and cooperative."

True. Yet it *felt* genuine. It was only when I was rescued that our deal was broken, which was why he returned to kill me. I clutch my mom's hand with both of mine at a sudden realization. "I've killed us all!"

Mom leans toward me until our shoulders are touching. "Nonsense. None of this is your fault."

"It is. As part of the deal, Jarren made me promise not to tell anyone, including his thugs, his real name. I had enough time to tell you before he came back to kill me."

"Let's not jump to conclusions," Radcliff says in his Security Chief voice or his I-must-be-obeyed voice, depending on who you're talking to. "We stick to the routine, keep sending out reports. The only thing that changes is we search for a way to contact DES without alerting Jarren's organization. Is that possible, Ara?"

Everyone stares at me, including Beau. Although his expression is flat, he can't hide the sparks of anger in his amber eyes. Thanks, Radcliff.

I relax my death grip on my poor mother's hand. "What do you think, Officer Dorey?"

There's a slight softening in his posture. "Anything is possible. In my experience, nothing is entirely secure."

"Then you and Junior Officer Lawrence will make that a priority," Radcliff says to Beau. "Do you need a higher clearance terminal?"

"That would help," Beau says.

"There's the one in the Control Center, but it's staffed around the clock," my dad says.

"We could clear the room for a few hours," Mom says.

"No," I say. "Nothing can change or that will alert Jarren."

"I thought he couldn't access the camera feeds in the base," Gage says alarmed.

"Right now the feeds are secure and are showing live footage. However, like Dorey said, nothing is entirely secure. There's no reason to take a chance. The terminals in Dorey's office will be fine."

Once again I'm the center of attention. Go me. Suppressing a sigh, I explain about reaching the interstellar navigator through Beau's terminal in his unit, which has less access than the ones in his office. And that was before I died. But I keep that tidbit to myself to avoid upsetting my parents.

"What we need is more time in the Q-net," I say.

"We can shift your schedule to report to Dorey at twelve-thirty and you can go until seventeen hundred. Is that enough?"

Radcliff asks.

"Yes."

"Good." Radcliff meets my gaze.

"Hold on just a minute," Jefferies says, slapping the table with his fingers. "If Ara's actions in the Q-net alert Jarren that we're aware of his blockade, then he'll come to Yulin sooner and kill us all." He glances at everyone. Two red splotches bloom on his cheeks. "It's *insane* to have the fate of the *entire* base in the hands of a *teenager.*"

"Officer Dorey—" Morgan starts.

"No offense to Officer Dorey," Jefferies says. "But you call Jarren a super wormer because he's been manipulating us from the very beginning with *none* of us the wiser."

He has a point. Radcliff gives the man a long cold look. Unaffected, Jefferies glares back.

"I agree with Milo. It's suicide," Gage chimes in. "We can wait for—"

"Waiting is suicide," Dad says. "We need to contact DES."

"Junior Officer Lawrence is especially cognizant of the danger," Radcliff says to Jefferies. His tone turns the blood in my veins to ice and I'm not even the one he's aiming it at! Then he looks to me. "Tread with the ultimate care."

"Of course she will," Mom snaps.

Way to go, Mom.

Jefferies stands up. "I want it noted in the record that I do not approve this endeavor."

"The record that Jarren will read?" Mom counters.

"You know what I mean."

"When we contact DES, I'll ensure your disapproval is noted, Dr. Jefferies."

When? No pressure there. Thanks, Mom.

"Mine, too." Gage stands.

"All right. You're both dismissed," Mom orders, reminding them she is in charge.

With stiff shoulders and stern expressions, they leave. There's a moment when we all just take a breath. Radcliff glances at the time—it's eighteen hundred. My stomach growls. Sensing the meeting is over, I let go of my mom's hand.

She places both arms on the table, leans forward and says, "Since we're all together, I want to discuss opening another Warrior pit. Wait." Mom holds up a hand. "Not one adjacent to the infected pits, but one further away. One that hasn't collapsed."

Infected. That fits.

"For what purpose?" Radcliff asks Mom in a tight, almost annoyed tone.

"So we can keep doing our job. And to further our knowledge about the significance of those alien symbols on the Warriors."

"And to test Ara's theory," Dad says. "The field team has been analyzing the data and identified Pit 21 as one that has all fourteen hundred and forty-eight Warriors intact. It's twenty kilometers east of the base. We can dig from the surface, letting in sunlight just in case there are HoLFs. Also we have big floodlights that run on batteries for night time."

"My security force is already spread thin," Radcliff says.

"The techs have been training. Surely they can fill in for a couple days," Mom says. "If we don't encounter HoLFs, then the security can return to base."

Mom's reasonable tones fail to placate Radcliff's inner guardian lion. The danger signs are there—posture ramrod straight, neck muscles straining, hand clutching the handle of his pulse gun. Wow, I really need to find a hobby.

"We haven't confirmed Jarren's physical location. He could still be on the planet."

"The satellite—"

"Can be compromised and isn't infallible. There are plenty of places to hide from a life scan. You'd be risking your team and my officers' lives."

A good point.

Mom turns to me. Oh no. "Are you able to check the satellite to make sure its feeds are clean?"

"Yes."

Her focus returns to Radcliff. "The satellite can scan the desert's surface, searching for any holes or tunnels in the sand that could be potential hiding places. It's only twenty klicks."

"What if opening this pit brings Jarren out of hiding?" Radcliff asks.

"He has digging machines and heavy equipment," Dad says. "Right now, he could park in the middle of the desert and open all the pits if he wanted. We can't stop him. Not with our limited resources. He obviously has a hidden agenda. All we know is that when he attacked the first time, he selected specific Warriors to steal and destroyed the rest. There must be a reason."

"If the activity draws Jarren out, that will answer the question of where he is," Morgan—ever practical—says.

Radcliff grips the armrests of his seat. Hard. "The last time Jarren showed up, your daughter died."

Wow. Them's fighting words.

Mom stands up.

"Ming," my dad warns.

"Thank you for the reminder, Officer Radcliff."

If words were tangible, my mom's would be coated in ice and have sharp edges.

"Once we confirm there's no one hiding nearby, Dorey and I can fix the satellite cameras to show an empty desert," I say.

Radcliff tenses, which I didn't think was possible considering before this a small child could bounce on his abs.

"That reduces the risk," Dad says into the silence.

"And we need more answers," Mom says. "Yes, it's a risk. I'm not going to force anyone to go. We'll ask for volunteers. If we don't get enough, then we won't do it."

Time to state the obvious. "Mom, *I* would have to go. You can't send techs into a pit without me ensuring there are no shadow-blobs."

"We'll bring a camera that's not routed through the Q-net; you can watch the feed."

"No. It's not the same thing. And I wouldn't be able to live with myself if I missed one and someone died."

My skin tingles with Radcliff's approval. Too bad I'm going

to ruin it. "I'll volunteer. You're right. We need more answers. And time is running out."

Mom, Dad and Radcliff are all about to protest.

"Without me, there's no mission. No one else will volunteer."

My mother's icy gaze turns on me even though she knows I'm right. I suppress a shiver.

"If Ara goes, I'll volunteer," Beau says.

"You're a bunch of idiots." Morgan shakes her head in disgust.

"You're going to need another two security officers to volunteer before I allow my team to be a part of this mission." Radcliff just about growls.

"I'll check with them," Morgan offers.

My father stands. "And we'll see about the techs."

Although it appears as if my parents will get their team, they fail to look happy about it. They depart to go recruit more team members. Radcliff leaves, but Beau touches my arm, stopping me from following Radcliff.

"Thanks," Beau says.

"You're risking your life again. No need to thank me," I say.

"No, for backing me up. Asking my opinion about the Q-net."

"Isn't that what partners do?"

He flashes me a grin. "You got that right." Then he sobers. "Your worming skills took a gigantic leap forward. What happened?"

I don't hesitate for long. We're partners. He deserves to

know. "When I died, I flew through the Q-net. I've no idea how, but It must have done something to my brain."

"Other people have been revived and no one else reported being better at navigating the Q-net."

"That you know," I add. "Becoming a better wormer is not something one would advertise.'

Beau crosses his arms. Stubborn man.

"It's my best guess, all right? It could be the combination of dying, having a concussion, and touching a Warrior heart."

"Or you could be suffering from significant brain damage."

"Do I act like I'm suffering?"

He tenses so much his biceps practically rip through his sleeves.

I sigh. "I'm sorry. But I've had a number of brain scans and they all show I'm fine."

He glares at me. Apology *not* accepted. "What if doing the exacting work needed to worm through Jarren's blockage triggers a medical problem?"

"That's a fair question. Right now, I don't have any symptoms. No migraines, no extreme dizziness, no blurry vision, no fainting spells. And, if I do, I'll let you—and my parents—know right away."

Beau drops his arms, but still appears unhappy.

"Can't we just celebrate our good fortune and use my super power to stop Jarren, the murdering bastard?"

After a few moments, he says, "Super power? No ego there."

"I'm learning how to be modest from my partner."

A huff, but there's a slight smile. "And you're learning from the best."

My Beau is back.

"See you tomorrow." I wave and head out.

"Hey, I bet you ten credits the other two officers who are going to volunteer are Niall and Elese," he calls as I reach the door.

"Sorry, but Ara Lawrence has no credits." I checked.

"Payday is every thirty days. It won't be long until you have credits."

"I get paid?"

"Why are you surprised? Didn't your mom pay you when you helped reconstruct broken Warriors?"

"Yeah, but— Wait." I turn back. "Did you get paid? If Jarren's been blocking us for the last…" I do a quick calculation. "Fifty-four days, then wouldn't DES stop paying you? Especially since they think we're all dead."

"They won't stop payments until our deaths are confirmed. I'm sure everyone who worked on Xinji is still earning credits. Once DES proves their deaths beyond a doubt, the payments will stop and all their income will be distributed to their next of kin." Beau's gaze grows distant and little crinkles spread on his forehead—his thinking face. "I didn't notice a missed payment."

Interesting. "If Jarren is allowing the payment notices through his blockade, then maybe we can use that point of entry to get a message to DES when the next deposit is made."

"The timing would have to be exact. It'd be difficult to do."

"For us, but not for the Q-net. When is the next payment?"

"Day two hundred and ten. That gives us seventeen days to find another way through, but, if we're desperate, getting one message out will be better than none." He grins. "Until then, I can spot you ten credits for that bet about who's going to volunteer for the Pit 21 mission."

"No deal."

"Aww. You're no fun."

"We might be fighting shadow-blobs in 21. That's fun."

"No," Beau says, rubbing his stomach. "That's revenge."

It's nineteen hundred by the time I arrive back at Radcliff's unit. Niall's sound asleep on the couch. I pause next to him, drinking in his peaceful expression—a rare sight. The desire to stroke his cheek and smooth his hair propels me to reach out. But I stop. Poor guy's exhausted. I tiptoe past and join Radcliff in the kitchen.

He's rummaging in the fridge, removing containers. "Leftovers tonight."

I sort through them, pick out chicken pot pie and heat it up. Radcliff does the same and soon we're sitting at the table in companionable silence.

When we finish, Radcliff leans back and asks, "Can you really alter the satellite feeds so Jarren doesn't see the team in the desert?"

"Yes, and I have an idea about how you can save time."

"I'm listening."

I tell him about using the Q-net instead of his officers to monitor the base. "I can set it up. It won't take long."

He taps his fingers on the table as he considers my idea. "It's a big risk. Jarren's people could modify the camera feeds at any time. I'm not sure we'd survive another surprise attack."

"We're already taking the risk. Jarren's people are good enough that even with an officer watching the feeds, he or she won't even see the change. Think about it, that's what happened before."

Radcliff stills. Not a good sign.

I continue. "It's a dilemma, I know. We can't rely on the Q-net because of Jarren, but we have to rely on it because you don't have enough people to secure the base. Now we know he's blocking us, but he thinks we're still clueless. The advantage is ours. We can be super subtle and set up a series of alarms that he won't be searching for. If he tampers with the feeds, we'll know."

"And you and Dorey can do this on his terminals?"

"Yes."

"How? That's deep level programming."

I start to explain about weaving the programming into the existing protocols.

"That's not what I meant. When I asked you to search for the missing Xinji files, you needed to use the terminal in the Control Center."

"I'm…" Terrible at lying. So for the second time, I explain about my new worming abilities. His stony expression and rigid posture mean one thing.

"I already got a lecture from Beau." Then I add about my promise to alert my parents about any troubling symptoms. Still no response. "At least let me tweak the cameras before you tell my parents. You know they'll freak and forbid me to use the Q-net until I have my brain scanned." Again. Which will find nothing wrong. Again. I sigh. It's *my* brain, it should be *my* decision.

"You'll lose a valuable resource," Niall says from the doorway.

I jump in surprise, but Radcliff doesn't react except to ask, "How long have you been standing there?"

"Long enough to know Jarren's put up a blockade. When were you going to tell the rest of us?" Niall demands.

"When you needed to know," Radcliff says.

"We just figured it out today," I say. "That's why we were late for dinner."

Radcliff huffs at me as if I ruined his fun. Then he turns to Niall. "I'm calling a staff meeting tomorrow morning."

"Good."

"Glad I have your permission," Radcliff says with plenty of sarcasm. "As for you…"

"Me?" I squeak and curse under my breath as amusement glitters in Niall's eyes.

"Do your tweak. I'm trusting you to know your limits and to not get us all killed."

"Yes, sir."

I decide to wait until I'm with Beau before doing the tweaks to the cameras. Radcliff schedules the meeting at oh-eight-hundred and I volunteer to man the cameras since I already know what it's about. Morgan guards detention. Watching the feeds during the base's busy morning activities is more interesting than the middle of the night. And it's harder, as people clad in lab coats tend to look alike when they're hurrying through the corridors.

My mom and dad are in the archeology lab. Both are armed with large flashlights and pulse guns. Nice of them to cover for security. I check on them quite often, looking for shadow-blobs.

There's a camera in the conference room. I keep an eye on the meeting, scanning expressions as Radcliff updates the team about Jarren's blockade. There's a variety of glum, determined, and angry faces. At least no one is freaked. Although at one point, Niall and Beau exchange words—heated words by their body language. Boys.

The meeting ends and everyone leaves except Radcliff. A few officers talk in the hallway as the others disperse. Two go to relieve Morgan. Beau and Rance head my way while Niall and Zaim turn toward the archeology lab. Niall flashes me a tired smile before leaving security. I concentrate on the rest of the base.

Rance's gravelly voice sounds on the other side of the door. "…not volunteering to go to Pit 21. It's a suicide mission."

"You'd rather sit here and wait for an ambush? Not me,"

Beau says as he enters the monitor room. "Anything to report?" he asks me.

"No. All's quiet. How did the meeting go?"

Beau scowls and Rance huffs. That good, eh?

"Your schedule's been altered for today. You're working with me," Beau says. "We have quite the To-Do list."

Interesting. Rance takes my seat. The chair appears small underneath his muscular frame. He's tall and burly and one of the few officers with a family. He, his wife, and two sons all live in a housing unit in the main base for safety reasons. A good thing, too, or they'd have been in trouble when Jarren attacked.

Beau and I go into his office and shut the door behind us.

"What's on our list?" I ask, sitting at the dual terminals.

"All the crazy stuff you told Radcliff you can do with the feeds and monitoring the base. Getting through Jarren's blockage not enough for you?" Beau's tone is gruff.

Oh boy. "Look—"

"It doesn't matter what *I* think. It's Radcliff's call, but I hope you're not putting the entire base at risk."

I clamp down on my response. He's right, it's Radcliff's decision. I'd hoped my partner would be supportive. Guess there's only one way to prove to him that having the Q-net monitor the camera feeds is safer overall.

"Are you going to help or are you just going to stand there?" I don't wait for an answer. Inserting my tangs, I access the Q-net.

After a minute, Beau joins me. Then we worm.

I explain what we need to do. He's sullen, but agrees. While I worm into the base's personnel files for the photos, Beau remains in my Q-cluster, building the programs for the cameras. Once completed, I weave them into the security clusters in such a way they're almost invisible. Then we link with the satellite to ensure no one has tampered with it. Except someone already has.

Before panic sets in, I check the camera feeds. They're clean, showing an accurate picture of Yulin's surface. But there's a sneaky little program wrapped around the main Q-cluster. It's unusual. In order to determine its function, I have to pull it apart. The process is like separating the individual strands from a rope without breaking them. With the utmost care, I ease the threads away from each other far enough to see what it's programmed to do. It takes…a while for me to fully understand its purpose.

Fear claws at my heart. I curse.

What's wrong? Beau asks.

Its purpose is to report no life signs on the planet to DES, and DES has already sent two requests for scans.

There's a pause. *We already suspected DES believes we went silent.*

But this is proof! It makes it more…real.

Beau touches my shoulder and gives me a reassuring squeeze. *It's more information, which is good for us.*

True.

Can you disable it? he asks.

A number of the strands are alarms. If I cut the program, it will signal Jarren—I think. It's a work of genius, but it doesn't match Jarren's style. Which is more evidence that my guess that Jarren is working with other super wormers is correct. This is just getting better and better. Yes, I'm being sarcastic. It beats hyperventilating.

Ara?

No, I can't. Not without alerting the person who planted it. I rewind the strands, putting it back to its original construction.

The person? Beau pauses. *Yeah, I thought it didn't look like our boy's work. Is there anything hidden in the video feeds?*

No.

Good. I'll add a few hidden alarms in case anyone tries to alter them. Beau works fast and when he's finished, I help him tuck them deep.

Then we move on to our next task with the satellite. Detailed scans of the surface show no one hiding between the base and Pit 21. I access the satellite's recordings of the surface, going back until I find a boring day and night that shows nothing but empty sands. Copying it, I store it in my Q-cluster until we need it to cover our activities when we're outside the base.

It's delicate, exacting work that takes us hours. By the time we finish, pain thumps in my temples and I'm as exhausted as if I spent the day doing drills with Elese. Pulling out my tangs, I rest my head on my arms.

Beau's chair squeaks. I tilt my head and peek at him with one eye. He's leaning back with his eyes closed, rubbing his forehead. My stomach growls. Loudly.

"That's what happens when you work through lunch," he

says, meeting my one-eyed gaze.

I lift my head. It's sixteen hundred. We wormed for seven hours straight. No wonder my head hurts. "I don't know about you, but after putting those measures in place, I've gotten my appetite back."

"They're masterpieces, Ly...Ara."

Not bad for an apology. "I couldn't have done it without you." The truth.

After we recover, we leave his office. Tora has replaced Rance. Beau tells her she's off duty. The Q-net is monitoring the feeds.

Instead of leaving, she crosses her arms. "I'll stay until Radcliff returns."

Beau gives her a sour look. "Suit yourself."

I glance at the screens. "Will Radcliff turn them off?"

"No. We'll still check them from time to time. Plus Radcliff likes to ensure his team is where they're supposed to be," Beau says.

Speaking of Radcliff, he's in the conference room with my parents and...I peer closer...all the archeology techs.

"Do you know what he's doing?" I ask Tora.

"I believe he's *motivating* them," she says. Her tone is far from friendly.

Okay that's it. "What's wrong this time?" I ask her.

"You've been just full of advice about important security measures lately."

"And that's a *bad* thing?"

She tilts her pointed chin up, meeting my gaze. "For someone in your position, yes."

"My position?" I glance at Beau, but he's being very careful to stay out of it.

"You're living with Radcliff and dating his son," she says. "They're listening to your advice, but you have no experience with security. It's making the rest of the officers nervous."

That explains the increased tension. "Oh yeah, because Radcliff is so *easy* to sway."

"You know what I mean."

"No. Not really. Radcliff puts the safety of his team and the base above everything else. You, with all your vast experience, should know that." I can't believe I just *defended* the man. Kill me now.

She stabs a finger at the screen. "I know that you don't go telling techs things they don't need—"

"Stop right there. I know *exactly* what they need. I've worked with them since I was big enough to hold a brush. If you want them to cooperate, then they should be fully aware of the situation. And I was under the impression that suggestions were welcome in this team. Are you telling me I shouldn't voice my opinion?"

"You're going to get us all killed."

Ah. There it is. Nothing like brutal honesty. How do I respond? She might be right. Just by surviving Jarren's murder attempt, I might be the reason the entire base will be killed. Beau and Tora are both waiting for my response.

Funny, I thought Beau would come to my defense. Does that mean he believes it too? Is that why he and Niall argued at the staff meeting? Pain pulses in my head. I look past Beau's shoulder to the dual Q-net terminals.

Masterpieces, Beau said. Damn right they are.

I gather my poise and stare at Beau then Tora. "*Jarren's* the enemy. Not me. Try not to forget that." I turn my back on them and leave.

2522:194

My anger at Tora and Beau fuels my steps. I go straight back to my…er…Radcliff's unit. Grrr. Now I'm gonna worry about everything I say. Yes, where I live is out of my hands. But still…I don't want the team to think I'm getting special treatment.

Taking a painkiller, I change into comfy clothes, turn off the light in my room, and crawl under the covers. In the cool darkness, I wonder if we're going to survive this. If Jarren returns, he won't be concerned about altering camera feeds. No reason to. He has a small army, heavy earth moving equipment, and weapons. These thoughts don't help my headache.

Eventually I fall asleep. Only to be woken two seconds later by an insistent tapping on my door. I groan, which is translated by the tapper as "come in" because light stabs the darkness. I pull the blanket over my head.

The mattress dips as someone sits on the edge and touches

my shoulder. Mom. I'd know that touch anywhere.

"Did you over-do it today?" she asks.

Did I? "A little."

"We were worried when we couldn't find you."

Huh? I sit up. "What time is it?"

"Eighteen hundred."

Oh. I slept for two hours. The aroma of Radcliff's casserole wakes the sleeping lion in my stomach. Its claws dig in and it roars, reminding me I haven't eaten all day.

Mom laughs. "You can't be feeling too bad. Come on."

I follow her to the kitchen as I unwind my messy braid and comb my fingers through my hair. My dad and Niall are already sitting at the table. Radcliff scowls at me. What did I do wrong now?

"If my team isn't visible on the screens when I look, and since no one is watching the feeds to tell me where they might be, how do I locate them?" Radcliff asks.

Oh. Mom's earlier comment makes more sense now. "You can ask the Q-net."

He stares at me as if I had just spoken another language.

"Come on, I'll show you. You, too. Mom and Dad." They follow me into Radcliff's bedroom along with Niall who stands near the door. I gesture to his desk. "Access the Q-net and ask where Officer Dorey is."

Radcliff inserts his tangs. The screen shows Beau having dinner in the cafeteria. "What about someone who's in a private location?"

"Ask about Niall."

The screen switches to the view of the corridor time stamped seventeen-fifty. Niall exits his unit and then enters Radcliff's.

"The Q-net is tracking *everyone*?" Dad asks. "It knows where everyone is right now?"

"Yes. And only you, Mom, and Officer Radcliff can access the information."

"What about you?" Radcliff asks me.

"Me and Beau can as well. Why, is that a bad thing?"

"It could be a violation of privacy," Mom says.

"What's the difference between a person watching the feeds and being able to tell my dad where someone is versus the Q-net?" Niall asks.

"The Q-net doesn't forget and this feels like surveillance," Mom says.

"As long as you don't ask it for…patterns," I say. "It's meant to look for intruders. I think using it to find someone is okay. We all know there are cameras in public areas."

"This is only due to unforeseen circumstances," Radcliff says. "It's temporary and as soon as we're no longer in danger, we'll return to the normal monitoring."

We troop back to the kitchen. Conversation is light and I just about inhale a large portion of casserole. When I finish, I slump back in my seat, thinking of going into a food coma. I don't have to monitor the camera feeds tonight. But I still want to help.

"What else can I do?" I ask Radcliff.

"You already freed up so much time," he says.

"I want a shift. How about guarding detention?"

"No," my mom answers. "We don't need another riot. It's too dangerous. Besides, Ara needs to rest after today's marathon Q-net session."

"I'll be fine by tomorrow," I say.

"Then you can resume training," Radcliff says with an evil little half-grin.

"I can also resume working with Beau." We still need to find a way to reach DES. "And I can do a security shift. How about guarding the entrance to the pits?"

The chorus of reactions is instant. Great, I've three parents and one over-protective boyfriend all yelling at me.

"I'll think about it," Radcliff says, ending the discussion.

After dinner, Niall and I go to the rec room since we actually have some free time.

"I'm looking forward to my first full night of sleep," Niall says as we enter. There's no one else there. "Of course I'm not naïve enough to think I'll get more than one." He turns to me. "What do you want to do, Mouse?"

There's a pool table, ping-pong table, game/video system, various couches, chairs, and a table for old-fashioned cards and puzzles. Not sure my brain can handle anything more complicated, I pick pool. How hard can it be to knock the white ball into a colored ball?

Turns out I suck at pool and ping-pong. Niall crushes me at

both. We end up playing Sevens where luck of drawing certain cards beats out strategy.

"Do you really want to guard the pits?" Niall asks.

"Yes. I'm the only one who can—" An idea pops into my mind. I almost smack my forehead.

"You can what?"

"I can have the Q-net monitor the lab for escaping shadow-blobs. I should have thought of it sooner!"

"Wait, the Q-net can see the HoLFs?"

Guess that news didn't travel to the entire team. I explain. "…only my Q-cluster can do it, though, so I'm going to need to link it into the camera feed."

"Wow." He leans back in his chair. His gaze turns inward. "But I'm not sure my dad will approve that."

"Why not? Right now the guards are basically bait. They can't see the shadow-blobs so it'll only be when they're attacked and maybe killed that they will know something's not right. Plus it'll give the officers more free time."

"They'd rather be there than trust everyone's lives to the Q-net." Niall's grip on his cards tighten. "You've taught us just how much it can be manipulated."

True. I remember Tora's reluctance to leave the screens earlier. She certainly didn't trust the Q-net, or me for that matter. And Beau didn't back me up. Niall seems…uncomfortable. I wonder if he thinks I'm using my *position* to influence his father. He should know better than anyone else just how inflexible Radcliff can be. Or is it because of what he's heard from the others? Do I want to find out? Not really. Denial has its perks.

I suppress a sigh. "Speaking of being manipulated, does everyone think I'm...overstepping my role as a junior officer?"

Niall hesitates. And there's my answer. Great, just great. I stand.

"Wait." He jumps to his feet. "*I* don't believe that."

"That's because you're dating me."

"No, it's because I know you and what you can do with the Q-net. I tried to tell them, but..."

"You're biased. So why hasn't Beau defended me?"

"I don't know, but I can guess."

I think back over the last few days. "He's jealous of my worming skills."

"That's my take," Niall says.

Not much I can do about that. Unless I back off and stop making suggestions, stop doing "impossible" things with the Q-net. Except...it's so not my style. I refuse to let Jarren win and if that's going to make the rest of the team uneasy, that's on them.

"What are you thinking about?" Niall asks. There's a crease of worry in his brow.

"That I have to go talk to your father."

He's not happy, but Niall accompanies me back to my—yes, *mine* damn it—unit. Radcliff's sitting on the couch, working on his portable. Before he can say anything, I tell him about my idea.

This time I add, "At least allow me to rig up an alarm to alert the officers on duty if a shadow-blob escapes."

"Will any of the activity tip off Jarren?" Radcliff asks.

"No."

"How can you be so sure?" Niall asks.

A legitimate question, but why does it…hurt, coming from him? "Because Jarren doesn't know about my Q-cluster. Also he won't be searching for such a minor routine laced into the camera feeds."

Radcliff considers my request. Finally he says, "Set up the alarm, but we'll keep personnel in the lab for now." Then he turns to Niall. "Don't tell anyone about the Q-net's ability to spot the HoLFs. It only worked for Ara so far."

"Yes, sir," Niall says a bit stiffly.

But I need clarification. "So you don't tell the team everything you learn?" I ask Radcliff.

He gives me a wry smile. "No. Only what they need to know, which is about eighty percent. For the future, please check with me before you share information."

"Even with Niall? Talking to him is what sparked the idea for this and for how to motivate the techs."

"Yes, even with Niall." He holds up a hand. "However, I trust him to be discreet."

Nice save. "Can I set up the alarm now? I'll use the guest terminal in your office."

"I thought you said your brain was fried," Niall says.

"It won't take long and I'll sleep better once it's done."

"Officer Dorey isn't available," Radcliff says.

"He can't help in this case." Which Radcliff should know.

The tight set of his shoulders say he's not happy, but he doesn't have a legitimate excuse to force the issue. "All right. Please keep Officer Morgan in the loop. She's on duty."

"Yes, sir."

Niall follows me out to the hallway. Once the door closes, I say, "You don't have to come along. That full night of sleep is waiting for you."

"It can wait some more. I'm curious how the Q-net can see invisible creatures."

We go to Radcliff's office. Morgan is working on the terminal at the desk. She disentangles as soon as we approach. Her expression is guarded. "Something wrong?"

I explain about setting the alarm.

She grunts, but inclines her head to the other terminal. "Knock yourself out. But keep the screen on."

Ah. Seems trust is a hard thing to get lately. Funny, they trusted me when I rescued them from detention—actually, at the time, Morgan wanted to lock me in detention—guess I should redact that snide comment.

I sit at the terminal and insert my tangs. Niall pulls over an extra chair and follows me into the Q-net. Worming into the cameras in the archeology lab, I create a link to my Q-cluster. Then I access the cluster and immediately spot the tunnel where Beau wormed through. A couple hours to break in, eh? I plan to fix it right after this job. Pulling up the video of me in the pits the first time I saw the shadow-blobs, I check that it's the one marked with the outlines.

Huh, Niall says, sounding surprised.

I play the video for him. Why not show him how the blobs move and hide? The rest of the team should view this as well. Yet another unwelcome idea. Too bad. I'm Ara Lawrence, Refuses to be Ignored. I'll make all the suggestions I think are necessary.

For now, I ask the Q-net to watch for shadow-blobs through the camera feed and sound an alarm in the lab if one escapes the pits. Then I fix the hole in my security, setting a trap. No way Beau can worm into my cluster now. Who are you calling petty?

Nice, Niall thinks. *Of course, it won't help with his jealousy.*

I'm not going to stop so he'll just have to get over it.

Good luck with that.

We disentangle. Pain throbs in my head, but it's not as bad as earlier.

Morgan is standing behind us. "Are you willing to outline the HoLFs on the rest of the video from the pits?" she asks me.

"Yes, but I'm sure you'll have to get Officer Radcliff's permission."

"How much time will you need?" she asks. "It's seven days' worth for four pits."

I consider. Do I be honest? Will that make them uneasy? Once everything's set up, my Q-cluster can do it in ten to twenty minutes. "An hour."

Silence.

Finally Morgan says, "I'll talk to Radcliff."

On the way back to my unit, Niall doesn't say a word until we're at the door. "I've been meaning to ask you. Why didn't you tell me about what happened when you…died?" His voice catches on the d-word.

"First I thought it was just a delusion due to dying. I'm not a big believer in the afterlife, but if there's a heaven, flying through the Q-net would be my own personal version."

Niall huffs. "By yourself?"

Ah the fragile male ego. "You were still alive."

He crosses his arms. "Delusions don't have to be logical, you know."

"I do, but then when I finally was able to access the Q-net after I died, it felt different. Which made me suspect it might not be a delusion."

"Except you weren't entangled at that time."

"I know, but it's the only explanation for my improved worming abilities."

Niall relaxes. "Maybe the energy from the weapon affected the sensors in your brain."

That's not a lovely thought. As if in response, the pain in my head intensifies. I rub my temples. "Does it really matter why? Do you think having a reason will make everyone more comfortable?" Including you, but I'm not dumb enough to say that aloud.

"It might. Or it might not. Everyone's on edge waiting for another attack."

I drop my hands. "That's why we need to locate Jarren and make sure that doesn't happen."

He agrees. We enter the unit. Radcliff's on the couch and demands a report right away.

"The alarm is installed," I say.

"It's well hidden," Niall adds.

My chest warms. Perhaps Niall isn't as freaked over my abilities as I thought. "Tell the officers on duty that if a siren sounds they should leave the lab right away."

"I will. Good job, Lawrence."

"Thank you, sir."

"I'm going to bed." Radcliff gives us one of his forceful stares, meaning we should follow his example. Now.

Except Niall and I are somewhat immune. We say good night, but remain in the living area. Once his bedroom door closes, we plop onto the couch. A spike of pain jabs into my forehead.

Niall notices my wince. "You did too much today."

"Probably."

He waits.

"Yes."

Standing, Niall grabs my hand and pulls me to my feet. "Come on." He tows me to my bedroom. "Take a painkiller. Change into your pajamas."

I'm pushed inside. The door closes behind me. Annoyed, I open it only to be confronted with Stubborn Niall. Nothing I can do or say will influence this man. I try anyway. "No good night kiss?"

"Not until you're in bed." He shoos me.

I hurry and change into a soft T-shirt and shorts, downing a pill. Ah, better living through chemistry. The legal kind, people! I already had a concussion, no need to kill off any more of my brain cells. Hopping into bed, I call Niall.

He enters. "Bunnies?"

Most of my clothes are hand-me-downs from…others. I've no idea where my mother found them. But after Jarren took off with my bag of clothes in his shuttle, I've had to lower my standards—not that they were very high, but a girl likes to look nice on occasion.

"Not just any bunnies, Toad. But dust bunny *assassins*."

He smiles at the memory. "I stand corrected." Moving closer, he points to my pillow.

"I'm technically in bed."

Doesn't matter. Niall's not to be deterred. Only when I'm lying down with the covers pulled up to my chest is he satisfied. He sits on the edge and leans in for a kiss. A frizzle of heat shoots through me when our lips connect. I yank my hands free from the covers and pull him closer, deepening the kiss. Then it's the taste of Niall, his familiar scent, his hands in my hair causing goosebumps to spread over my skin.

He stops and rests his forehead on mine. "My father…" he says.

"Yeah."

"Night, Mouse." He turns off the light and leaves.

I groan into my pillow. This lack of privacy sucks. Not that I'm planning on going wild, but Niall and I need some serious make out time.

Over the course of the next few days, I train with Elese in the mornings and work with Beau to probe Jarren's blockade in the afternoons. We worm deep, searching for a hole in his defenses while moving with the ultimate care. Which means, so slow a snail could lap us. It's also delicate work, as if we were navigating through a tunnel of playing cards. One wrong move and… Poof! Everything collapses, revealing Beau and I trying to sneak into Jarren's fort.

Radcliff has yet to give me a security shift. And I have to admit I'm glad, as the long hours spent crawling through the Q-net are mentally exhausting.

Five days after Morgan asked me about working on the video feeds from the pits, Radcliff gives us permission. So after dinner, I return to Beau's office. Except tonight Morgan, not Beau is partnering with me. She has access to the videos that I'll need. I also suspect she wants to experience my worming for herself rather than watch on the screen.

I'd planned to slow things down, but with her in my cluster it would be pointless. Hoping not to freak her out, I insert my tangs and get to work.

Unlike Beau, Morgan is quiet. No grunts or huffs or whoops or sound effects. She's silent and able to keep up with me. I approve her efficient style.

When we reach my cluster, I check my security measures for tampering. There's scratches on a few protective channels as if someone tried to find a way through and failed. I suspect Beau, but it could be Jarren. No, he wouldn't leave a trace. Maybe one of his minions. Which is not much of a relief.

Morgan brings in the video feeds. I pick one and pull it out like taffy, revealing ten-minute sections. It's of Pit 2 from day one-sixty-three. I expect the Q-net to find all the shadow-blobs and outline them, but it doesn't. It waits until I have outlined each one, then the Q-cluster takes over and finishes the job. Then it's only a matter of opening all the video files, outlining the blobs, and letting the Q-net do the rest. I send the altered files to Morgan so she can do…well, whatever analysis she plans.

Easy, right? Except a dawning realization hits me. Hard. That alarm in the lab won't work. Not without me to point out the shadow-blobs. It seems the Q-net doesn't recognize them until after I've outlined them. At least Radcliff was smart enough to keep security in the lab. I tell Morgan about the flaw in my shadow-blob alarm.

Make sure to inform Radcliff, is all she says, and then remains quiet until we disentangle.

"How did you find that cluster?" she asks me.

Oh boy. "I didn't. It found me."

"Can you clarify?"

I wish. "I was using various empty clusters to help with organizing data." There's a million of them. "I used one for my friend Lan's research. She was working on translating the alien symbols on the Warriors before Xinji went silent. Lan sent me her files, I didn't steal them," I add, just in case. "I didn't have time to do much with them before Jarren looted the pits and I was shot. But the Q-net kept sorting the symbols and making connections. After I tried and failed to find out how Jarren traveled to Yulin without anyone knowing, I was detoured to this Q-cluster where all the results were arranged." I shrug. "Ever since then, it's been rather...perceptive about what I want to accomplish."

Morgan absorbs the information with a stillness that reminds me of a predator waiting for prey.

"Do you have any more of these perceptive clusters?" she asks.

"No. I—" A memory sparks to life. I've hidden files in a couple of clusters. I wonder if the Q-net has done anything with them. Then I remember— Oh boy.

"You?" she prompts.

"There may be other clusters." One with files I accessed illegally.

"May? Either there are or aren't."

I debate what I should divulge. "There are, but *Lyra* might have been worming at the time she used one of those clusters."

Her focus sharpens and I squelch the desire to duck. "Just tell me. We'll worry about the consequences later."

"Uh...okay. There's a couple of files from Xinji that I copied to a cluster. This was after they were marked classified by DES." I wait for the admonishment.

Instead, she asks, "What are the files about?"

"I did a search for Warrior hearts and any mention of an underground factory and had two hits, but I didn't get a chance to read through them." Because Niall caught me worming and threatened to arrest me. Obviously before we got together, but I called in a favor and then I promised not to rat him out. "The looters invaded the pits soon after."

Morgan's gaze turns inward. "You were tasked to recover those files before Jarren attacked the base."

Nice loophole.

"What about the other clusters?" Morgan asks.

"Those are legit. Niall and I were sorting the alien symbols in Lan's research notes, matching them to one of the eight rows of glyphs on that octagon we found on Xinji." And we only completed five rows because, soon after, DES confirmed that everyone on Xinji died.

"Is there any way you can reach the Xinji files now?"

"Not with Jarren's blockade, but as soon as we find a way through, I might be able to."

That earns me a small smile. "You're confident you'll get through?"

I consider. Nothing is ever completely secure. There are gaps in the Q-net, but many are so tiny that not even the best wormers can find them. "Confidence isn't a factor, Officer Morgan. Our lives depend on it and I'm staying optimistic about our chances."

"Fair enough." She leans forward and rests her elbows on her knees. "Since you marked those video files so fast, we still have another hour. Let's go take a look at those files you recovered from Xinji."

"Yes, sir." I insert my tangs.

It doesn't take long to find the hidden cluster and bypass my own security. In fact, it's ridiculously easy and I make a mental note to fix all of Lyra's protective measures.

The files aren't big. Morgan opens the first one. It's about hearts and it's a bit disjointed with references to romaine lettuce hearts as well as the blood pumping organs of a couple of the native animal species on Xinji. Not a big surprise as the Q-net had ripped apart hundreds of files and reorganized them into smaller groupings.

I scan the text until my gaze snags on a reference to the alien symbols. My friend Lan sent her mother, Dr. Mindy Maddrey, who had retired to Planet Rho, a couple personal messages about her research.

2520:072: It's so frustrating! I've deciphered enough of the alien symbols to translate their language, but full understanding of what it all means just slips through my fingers. <sigh> Here's an example, I discovered there are eight symbols that are needed for the "heart" of the Warriors. Does that mean a literal heart or a symbolic one? And then once these hearts are woken—whatever that means—the Warrior then serves as a sentinel. This implies the aliens also believed the Warriors will guard them in the afterlife. But it made me think, do the Warriors have hearts? We've X-rayed the Warriors and examined broken ones, but what if the hearts are very fragile or dissolve when exposed to air—like the paint that had all flaked away as soon as the air hit the original Warriors on Earth. I know Havier will refuse—how dare I suggest we drill a hole into one of his precious Warriors!—but I'm still going to try to convince him to let me look inside—in a vacuum chamber of course. In other news, Kate is doing well at university and I think she's fallen in love. Of course she won't admit it to her mom—I've gotten the text version of an eye roll—but the way she goes on and on about Maddie has me convinced.

Seems Lan was on the right track.

Acts as a sentinel, Morgan says. *Do you think that could be a reference to your Warrior ghosts, Ara?*

The desire to correct her—they're not mine—pulses. But because I saw ghostly versions of the Warriors near the hearts when the lights went out, they will be mine until someone else confirms they exist. Along with being able to see the shadow-blobs, seeing the ghosts, I believe, is another side effect of picking up one of those hearts—sorry again, Mom. *It's possible,* I reply to Morgan.

I keep reading and after a few irrelevant passages and a recipe using chicken hearts—yuck—there's another message from Lan to Dr. Maddrey.

2520:104: Good news, Mom! I pestered Havier until he agreed to let me peek inside a Warrior with a camera. We found a black heart with silver symbols etched on it! The heart appeared to match a human heart in size and shape and was attached to the Warrior in the proper position. It proved to everyone I've correctly translated some of the symbols. And, all the archeologists are beyond excited. Havier picked me up and twirled me around. Then his team did open heart surgery on the Warrior to remove it, but as soon as Havier touched it, the heart disintegrated so fast no one was able to get a sample! Still, it's a great discovery and I have more clout with Havier. Now to figure out why the Warriors have hearts! Also I'm glad to hear you're enjoying retirement. Did Daddy really catch a fish that's a hundred and twenty-five centimeters long?

I wonder if Xinji's reports about the hearts reached DES or if Jarren intercepted them. Are they important to what he's planning? I remember the care his thugs took when they stole certain Warriors, yet they destroyed all the remaining ones. Was it to break the hearts? Hard to tell.

There's one last message from Lan to her mom.

2520:147: I still can't believe it! Yes, I know you verified my results and Havier is convinced (his archeologists practically carried me around on their shoulders as they opened the champagne), but it's mind-blowing to finally understand why. The aliens believed there were demons that threatened our Galaxy—not ones that haunted an afterlife, but real ones. Believed it enough to build over two million Warriors with special hearts to act as sentinels and keep the demons from crossing into our dimension. And that's mind-blowing as well. None of our astrophysicists have been able to prove there are other dimensions even with the help of the Q-net. Did the aliens discover an alternate dimension? Or did these demons arrive, surprising the aliens and they had to figure out a way to protect themselves? Yet more questions! Like are these demons real or part of the aliens' belief system? Of course no one wants to test the theory. Can you imagine destroying all those Warrior hearts just to discover the aliens are right about the demons? How would we protect ourselves? <shudder> Good thing we're smarter than that.

I re-read Lan's message. Twice. Another dimension? Demons? Mind-blowing is putting it mildly. Did Jarren read this and decide to test the alien's theory? That would be...horrific. No, he said he didn't know about the shadow-blobs. But he is a murdering looter and has no trouble lying. Argh.

Sucking in a breath, I calm my chaotic thoughts. No, Jarren isn't trying to kill everyone in the Galaxy. He lives here, too. If murder-suicide is his goal, he wouldn't have taken so many Warriors and he would have destroyed all of them on the planet. He has the heavy equipment to dig into the rest of the pits, he could just have—

Oh my stars!

Officer Morgan, I think—

I see it. I'll let the astrophysicists know about Lan's speculation about a possible alternate dimension.

It's not—

Her translation, whatever you call it.

Not that. What if Jarren is planning to destroy all the Warriors except enough to keep him and his goons safe? He could have already targeted more pits on Yulin. Another idea stabs me in the guts. *Or he plans to sell those Warriors to very rich people to keep them safe as well. Jarren's goon mentioned an obscenely rich patron. Perhaps they are the first of many future rich clients.* Then my imagination kicked it up another notch. *Or he could ransom the Galaxy! Think about it! He could threaten to destroy all the Warriors unless DES pays him.*

2522:199

*Y*ou have quite the imagination, Morgan says, seemingly unperturbed.

Niall once suggested that I could be a criminal mastermind. He'd been joking. Okay, half-joking, but still.

We need to check the other pits. There was a gap in time between his two attacks. Jarren could have been raiding them. And it would either confirm my crazy theory or set my mind at ease.

I'll discuss it with Radcliff. In the meantime, let's look at the other file. Unless you're not done plotting how to overthrow the Galaxy?

Nice. *You're just mad you didn't think of it first.*

Oh don't worry. I'll give you all the credit.

Smart ass. I pull up the second file. It's much larger than the other. This one has references to factories. There's a report from Lan about Havier opening a few more Warriors so they could examine the hearts. She speculated that they were made from a material not found on Earth and constructed in an alien factory. And her excitement when she matched the symbols on the hearts to those in her research is clear.

Sadness wells inside me. Poor Lan would never learn the outcome of all her hard work. If I survive all this, I will ensure she receives full credit.

There's nothing relevant in the rest of the file. Morgan and I finish and disentangle.

She stands and stretches. "Let's go talk to Radcliff."

Radcliff is equally unperturbed. The three of us are sitting at the kitchen table in our unit.

"Considering there is no proof of an alternate dimension, nor has one ever been discovered, that's a huge leap in logic," Radcliff says.

"Those HoLFs came from somewhere," I say.

"And we will figure it out."

"Since your son and Officer Keir have volunteered, the expedition to Pit 21 is a go," Morgan says.

No surprise those two volunteered.

"Don't remind me." Radcliff shoots her a glare, but it's at half wattage—he must be tired.

Unaffected—does anything upset the woman?—Morgan says, "At least the trip opening another pit will address some of Junior Officer Lawrence's concerns. The initial planetary scans show Pit 21 is intact, but that was done before the looter attack. In the meantime, I'll schedule a meeting with the astrophysicists."

"Good," Radcliff says. "Anything else?"

"I believe Ara has something to tell you."

Oh yeah. I inform Radcliff about my failure with the shadow-blob alarm.

"It did seem too good to be true." Radcliff rubs his face.

I'm just as disappointed. I hate that the security officers in the lab will have no warning of an attack. If only I could— Why not? I mull it over.

"Uh oh, she's got that look," Morgan says. "Spit it out, Lawrence. Yet another insight into Jarren's machinations?"

Ignoring her sarcasm, I say, "I could monitor the camera feeds in the lab with a portable. Well, at least when I'm awake."

Radcliff leans back and drums his fingers on the arm of his chair. "I'm tempted, but I need your full attention on discovering a way to contact DES."

"Then how about a shift in the lab? In fact, I could do it alone because I can see the danger."

"And what happens if a HoLF breaches the lab?" Morgan asks.

"I sound the alarm and get the hell out of there."

"What if it surprises you? You won't have backup."

"It won't." I shudder, remembering the heavy pressure on my shoulders whenever they were around. Truthfully, I'd rather have a shift guarding detention. Looters, even rioting looters, are less scary than shadow-blobs. But my conscience refuses to allow me to be a chicken.

"You're supposed to be dead. You can't be seen." Morgan points out.

"I can take one of the overnight shifts. You know no one dares enter the lab except for security."

"I'll think about it," Radcliff says, ending the discussion.

A familiar response. At least he didn't say no. When Morgan leaves, I glance at the time. Maybe Niall is still awake.

As if he can read my mind, Radcliff says, "Go to sleep, Ara. Take advantage of a full night's rest while you can."

Does that mean he's decided? As usual, his expression gives nothing away. I wonder when Elese will teach me the how-to-look-intimidating-without-even-trying lesson or the how-to-suppress-your-emotions lesson. Too tired to argue, I get ready for bed.

"An alternative dimension is the stuff of science fiction, Ara," Yenay says. "While there's always speculation, there's been no evidence that such a thing exists."

At that moment, she reminds me of my mother. Although younger and with shorter hair, she has that you-are-wasting-my-time-with-this-nonsense demeanor.

"Plus the Q-net failed to produce a mathematical theorem that would prove its existence," Bertie adds, in a gentler voice. "The fact that the aliens believed in demons is a very important discovery. It explains why all these Warriors are spread throughout the Galaxy. Your parents must be thrilled."

They are. Lan's translations of the alien symbols are the first big breakthrough since the discovery of the Warriors on other planets. Except their excitement is tempered by large doses of frustration because they can't get into the Warrior pits. I hope this meeting will help get us closer to that goal.

We're in Radcliff's office. It's oh-seven-hundred so I can still report to training on time. Lucky me. Lan's messages to her mother are on the screen above his guest terminal. It's been three days since Morgan and I opened the files. The astrophysicists delayed the meeting until they finished the laser weapons and the sensor that will record the full electromagnetic spectrum in the pits.

"So where did the HoLFs come from?" I ask.

"We have a few theories," Bertie says.

"Like what?" I'm not letting her get away with a vague answer.

"They could be native to Yulin and were disturbed by the destruction of the Warriors."

"And native to Planet Xinji as well? The HoLFs killed—"

"We can't know that for sure," Morgan says. "Jarren said the HoLFs appeared after they raided the Warrior pits, but we can't trust him. And there wasn't enough information in the files from Xinji aside from mention of the first deaths."

Which included multiple lacerations, evisceration, and exsanguination, but I guess that could be attributed to your average murdering psychopath. Too bad those files were stolen.

Even though they're mere pieces of the vast amount of data that is sent to DES from a research base, we really need to recover them—that's next on my worming To-Do list after we contact DES.

"Or the looters could have brought the HoLFs," Yenay says.

"The looters didn't bring them," I say. "They arrived because the Warriors were removed and destroyed." But I might as well have been talking to one of the Warriors.

"You were in Pit 4 during the attack," Morgan says. "They could have released them in the other pits."

Huh. Well that would certainly be…I can't think of a horrible enough word to describe it. Did Jarren lie to me about what happened on Xinji? He seemed sincere at the time, but, then again, he planned to leave everyone on Yulin at the mercy of the shadow-blobs. So he's more than capable of deliberately killing an entire base.

"The important thing is to learn more about the HoLFs," Yenay says.

I agree, but I'm not buying their theories, no matter how logical. I'll stick with my gut intuition thank you very much.

"Officer Radcliff is waiting for us in the conference room," Morgan says.

Ah, part two. The four of us join him. He's sitting at the head of the large rectangular table. Niall, Beau, Elese, and Rance are also seated. The screen behind Radcliff shows a diagram of the archeology lab, the entrance to the pits, and the corridor that runs parallel to Pits 1 to 4.

We settle into the empty chairs. I choose the one next to

Beau. He grins at me.

Radcliff's gaze scans the room, ensuring we're all paying attention. "Drs. Carson and Zhang have built a sensor that we need to install in Pit 1." He pauses as if expecting resistance. When no one speaks, he continues. "Here's how it's going down. Officers Keir, Dorey, Rance, and Radcliff will move in step and set floodlights in an arc, creating a perimeter of light around the work area."

A curved line appears on the diagram. It balloons out from the entrance to the lab and stops just inside Pit 1. It's egg-shaped. Fancy.

"The floodlights in the lab will be aimed at the corridor between the pit and the lab," Radcliff says. "Drs. Carson and Zhang will install the sensor and activate it. Once they return to the lab, the officers will back out of the pit in step." The balloon deflates. "When all personnel are in the lab, the doors will be secured. Officer Morgan and I will be on stand-by in the lab. Junior Officer Lawrence will be our spotter. If she sees a HoLF, those in the pits will retreat A-sap. Any questions?"

"When is the operation, sir?" Bendix asks.

"2522:204 at oh-one-hundred."

Rance frowns at me because I'm the reason we're going in an hour after midnight—so no one will see me. I ignore him. The fluttering in my stomach has me quite distracted. Not tonight, but tomorrow night, we're really going to open the doors to the pits, putting the nine of us in danger. Or more if the shadow-blobs escape into the rest of the base.

"How will we know if the sensor is working?" Beau asks.

"Bertie and I will have a portable with us. As soon as the signal is acquired, we can leave," Yenay says.

"How long will it take to get the signal?" Rance asks.

"Seconds after it's turned on."

"This op should be quick," Morgan says. "We get in and we get out in less than five minutes."

"What about the laser weapons? How can we aim at the hostiles if we can't see them?" Rance asks.

"Lawrence," Radcliff says.

"If the HoLFs attack, I will mark their locations for you," I say.

Another frown. Rance is clearly not happy to be part of this mission. Unlike the excursion to Pit 21, Radcliff didn't ask for volunteers.

"Any more questions?" Radcliff asks.

Nothing but a tense silence, which Beau breaks by asking, "Can we call ourselves the shadow team?"

Groans and sighs.

"Any more *legitimate* questions?" A beat. "All right, you're dismissed. Back to work."

Everyone gets up and we file out. When Beau passes me, I grab his arm, stopping him. "I think the shadow team is a cool name."

"Thanks, partner." He gives me a quick one arm sideways hug.

It's just to annoy Niall, who's right behind us. My back warms with the glower I'm sure is on Niall's face.

The last time I wiggled into my form-fitting security jumpsuit, I'd been Jarren's prisoner. Then I'd tossed my clothes over the garment to conceal it, which ended up saving my life. This time, I'm not as stressed or sweaty. The stretchy black fabric is like a second skin and leaves nothing to the imagination. It resists punctures and cuts, but isn't impenetrable.

I rub the scar over my left hip and wonder if the material is strong enough to block the shadow-blobs' sharp appendages. No. It won't come to that. I finish dressing and secure the belt, sliding my pulse gun into its holster. Its weight on my right hip balances out the more important weapon for this mission—the laser. I also have a flashlight just in case and an extra power pack.

Dimming down the lights in my room, I click the laser on. The thin red beam slices through the darkness. Nice. After lacing on my black boots, I'm ready.

Both Radcliffs are waiting for me in the living area. Also clad in the combat jumpsuits and sporting that confident ready-for-anything demeanor. When Niall turns to follow his father from the unit, I take a moment to appreciate the view. Oh come on, you'd do it too. He has a fine muscular…er…back.

We meet up with Beau and Elese in Radcliff's office.

"Where are Officers Morgan and Rance?" Elese asks.

"Already in the lab on guard duty," Radcliff says. "When we leave security, the four of us will surround Junior Officer Lawrence, to keep her hidden in case we encounter anyone in the base."

I've put my hair up into a tight bun so it won't get in the way. Not exactly the best disguise.

Once we exit the area that's dedicated to security, Radcliff takes point, while Beau and Niall walk on each side of me, Elese following right behind. It's hard to see within the ring of officers. Although I doubt anything has changed. I grew up in research bases and they're all the same design. Still, I've been cooped up in security for the last thirty-one days, so it's a nice change of scenery, even if we're walking toward danger and the creatures that have been haunting my dreams since the first looter attack. Minor details.

We reach the lab without encountering anyone. No surprise as it's almost oh-one-hundred and even the most dedicated scientists are tucked into their beds. Probably dreaming of making a monumental discovery in their field. I wonder if they know we're cut off from DES and have hostile alien blobs trapped in the pits.

My parents, Rance, Morgan, and the two astrophysicists are waiting for us inside. Mom and Dad clutch heavy-duty flashlights. Uh oh. Radcliff frowns and orders—well, asks them with a forceful politeness —to leave.

"No," Mom says. "This is our lab and the base is our responsibility. We won't get in the way. We'll be backups to your backups."

Radcliff stills. In this situation, where their personal safety is at risk, he does have the power to kick them out. Will he exercise it? Everyone is waiting.

"Stay right by the door. If I tell you to go, you leave. No. Matter. What. Understand?" There's a growly rumble in his voice. Radcliff's inner guardian lion is showing.

Niall and I exchange an amused look.

"Yes," my parents say together. They stand right in front of the exit.

At least they'll be the first to safety if this mission goes sideways. That thought doesn't help my nerves. Lots of people I care about are in this room. What if I don't spot the shadow-blobs in time?

Radcliff issues orders. Four giant floodlights on tripods are turned on. Beau, Rance, Niall, and Elese pick them up and aim them at the entrance to the pits. The extra brightness sears my eyes. Bertie and Yenay hold a metallic box between them as they wait behind the four light bearers. With laser weapon in hand, I join them.

"It's a go," Radcliff says.

Morgan unlocks the double doors and pushes them wide. They swing into the corridor as she circles back around to stand with Radcliff. Cool damp air flows into the lab. Nothing but dust motes stir in the harsh stream of white light.

"One," Beau calls and steps from the smooth lab floor onto the sandstone.

The other three match his stride. Their boots crunch in unison.

"Two. Three. Four..."

The wall of light moves further in until it reaches just inside Pit 1. A couple rows of Warriors are illuminated. The techs reconstructed a number of them after the attack. Cracks zigzag through their uniforms. The statues stand almost two meters tall. Each face is unique, but they're all Chinese and crafted from terracotta. The red color faded to gray after thousands of years buried underground. They were never painted, unlike the ones on Earth.

My father thinks the aliens learned how to make the Warriors from the ancient Chinese craftsmen and then constructed the ones that they buried on sixty-four exoplanets. But my mom believes they were made on Earth and then transported to those other planets. Why am I *even* thinking about this? Better than the possibility of encountering shadow-blobs.

I focus on the task at hand as I walk behind Bertie and Yenay. The light pushes back the darkness. The only shadows are those created by the floodlights from the lab. And they're all human or box-shaped.

"Lights set," Beau calls, putting down his tripod at the same time that the others set theirs. All four then pull their lasers and rest their fingers on the triggers.

The astrophysicists install the sensor, securing it to the ground, and fiddling with…whatever it is they need to adjust. I spin in a slow circle, scanning the shadows, especially the ones that connect to the perimeter.

"Two minutes," Radcliff calls from the lab.

"Not enough," Yenay says. "We need five more, the link is being difficult." She curses under her breath in Chinese.

My mother tried to teach me Chinese. She was often

frustrated, which is how I learned the more colorful phrases of the language.

"You have three," Radcliff says.

Without warning, needles of cold stab my skin. The air thickens around me, pressing in, suffocating. It's a familiar and very unwelcome sensation. Fear sloshes in my stomach as I check all the shadows. An image of an army of shadow-blobs massing in the darkness forms in my mind.

Hurry, hurry, hurry, I silently urge the scientists. Movement catches my attention. Why is Beau— Not him, but his shadow is rising!

I aim my laser at my partner. "Beau, duck."

He dives for the ground. The laser goes right through the HoLF. Nothing happens. It keeps advancing. I toss the laser to the ground, yank my flashlight, click it on, and…poof.

"Lasers are useless," I yell. More shadow-blobs loom behind the others. "Everyone down," I order.

They comply and I sweep my light over them. Poof, poof, and poof.

"Retreat." Radcliff's command echoes.

The four officers hop to their feet, but Bertie continues to tap on her portable. Her fingers dance over the surface. "Just a sec."

"Now!" Radcliff is standing in the threshold. "Leave the floodlights."

Rance grabs Bertie's arm and yanks her toward the lab. Yenay kneels next to the sensor and fiddles with something before Elese hauls her to her feet.

A sizzle and pop sounds and one of the floodlights dies in a shower of sparks and shattered glass. We sprint for the lab. Another crack rends the air. Two more follow. All that's left are the lights from the lab. Behind us is nothing but darkness.

"Turn around! Use your flashlights," I just about scream. Okay, yes, I screamed.

Elese and Rance shove the women toward the lab before spinning around. The five of us back up while sweeping our beams of light. I poof a few more.

"The doors are closing," Bertie shrieks.

I glance over my shoulder. Radcliff and Morgan are fighting to hold the doors open. Stars!

"Double time," Radcliff orders through gritted teeth.

The shadow-blobs thread through the gaps in our defenses. Their sharp appendages slice the fabric of our jumpsuits. The column of light from the lab narrows. Now my parents have joined Radcliff and Morgan, helping to keep the doors open. If they closed— No. Not going there.

We finally reach the lab and dive through the gap. The doors bang shut and Morgan rushes to lock them. No one says a word for a long while. We're all huffing either from the effort or from almost being killed.

"Lawrence, did any of the HoLFs escape?" Morgan asks.

Good question. I inspect all the shadows in the lab. Nothing. Plus the heavy pressure is gone along with the cold. "No."

"Did you activate the sensor?" Dad asks Bertie. "Is it

CHASING THE SHADOWS

working?"

She jerks as if startled, then consults the portable. The rest of us hold our collective breaths. Did we just risk our lives for nothing?

"It's...collecting data," Bertie says.

The relief is palpable. We share grins and Beau slaps Niall on the back.

"You're bleeding," Mom says to me.

I glance down. An assortment of cuts mark my arms, torso, and legs. Lovely. But I'm not the only one. Beau, Niall, Rance, and Elese also have multiple lacerations. Niall has one on his forehead. Blood streaks the side of his face. I squelch the desire to fuss over him. At least the astrophysicists are unharmed.

"Morgan, ask Dr. Edwards to meet us in security," Radcliff says.

"Yes, sir."

"The rest of you report to the conference room to be stitched up."

"What about the lab?" Rance asks. "Who's going to guard it?"

"I'll stay until the next shift arrives," Radcliff says.

"I should stay as well." Before they can protest, I gesture at the entrance. "They blew out the floodlights and tried to close the doors. I think I should ensure they don't find a way into the lab."

Radcliff gives me his hard stare. I meet it.

"Morgan, change of plans. Have Dr. Edwards come here

first," Radcliff says.

I don't alter my expression, but inside I'm celebrating my small victory. Morgan and the others leave. Niall catches my eye on the way out. His amused smile is all I need to know that he's applauding my efforts on the inside as well. My parents remain in the lab.

"We'll wait until Dr. Edwards is finished," Mom says to me when I tell them to go to bed.

I can't believe it's only oh-one-fifteen. Time must have slowed while we fought off the shadow-blobs. Or it could have been the adrenaline, which is wearing off.

"Did you expect them to try to close the doors?" Dad asks Radcliff.

"Obviously not. Truthfully, we didn't know what to expect. We only have limited information about them." He turns to me. "Do you know why the laser didn't work?"

"No. It went right through them. Perhaps it's too concentrated. Maybe Drs. Zhang and Carson will know better."

"Did they show any signs of this level of intelligence before?" Radcliff asks.

The word *intelligence* hits me like a pulse wave. It's one thing to think they're mindless killing machines, another to believe they know what they're doing and are purposely doing it. My heart rate spikes to unhealthy levels.

"Ara?"

Uh. I sort through my memories. "It seems like they waited until they had enough of them before they attacked us, so I guess that's a sign. And they cut the lights in the pits." Hard to forget the instant blackness and Beau's cry of pain.

"And the emergency back-up lights," my dad adds.

Even scarier.

"I'd hoped that was instinctual," Radcliff says. "But the doors…" He rubs his right bicep. "Either they're very strong or there were a lot of them. Did you see how many, Ara?"

"No. I poofed at least a dozen, but I didn't see the ones pushing the doors." Too busy fighting for my life.

My mom's dark eyebrows crinkle together. "You said they waited for more HoLFs. That implies they didn't all arrive at once."

I mull over her comment. "I wasn't in the pits that much, but each time I was, I spotted more." Or was I more aware of their presence? No, the pressure increased. "If they're coming from an alternate dimension, and the gateway is guarded by the Warriors, then, when Warriors are destroyed, maybe it gives the shadow-blobs an opportunity to cross over."

"There's no proof—"

"Of another dimension. I know, Mom. But there was no indication that these HoLFs existed, yet here they are." Except that's not quite right. Lan's translation of the alien symbols did say the Warriors were built to protect against demons. What if the HoLFs aren't the demons they're referring to? What if— I gasp.

"What's wrong?" Mom asks. "You're pale. You should sit down. Spencer, get the first aid kit."

"I'm fine." I bat away her efforts to guide me to a chair. "What if these HoLFs are the ones who built and installed the

Warriors? And the reason they're trying to kill us is they're pissed because their Warriors were destroyed!"

All three adults stare at me as if I've just grown antennas. I review my logic and I don't think it warrants such a reaction.

My dad is first to break the awkward silence. "That's...an interesting way to look at it."

"If that were the case..." Mom stares into the distance. "Being averse to light would be problematic. They'd have to travel through space in order to place the Warriors."

Good point. Unless... "Space ships don't need windows. Our Interstellar Class ships can navigate without them. And all the Warriors have been found underground, sealed off from natural light. Or, if they are from another dimension, maybe that one doesn't have visible light."

"Yet you hypothesized that the Warrior ghosts in the factory kept the HoLFs from attacking," Radcliff says. "Wouldn't that mean they are at odds?"

Another good point.

"Regardless, it's all pure speculation," Radcliff says. "Let's hope that sensor comes up with some real answers."

We all stare at the doors that lead to the pits. I imagine words mysteriously appearing on them one letter at a time with ominous music playing in the background. It spells out: *Here there be demons.*

2522:047

A throat clears behind us. Dr. Edwards stands at the threshold with his medical kit. His short gray hair is sticking up on one side. "Why wasn't I informed ahead of time that you planned a dangerous mission, Officer Radcliff? I would have been happy to assign you a medic to be onsite."

I look at Radcliff. The Chief of Security actually appears abashed. He probably didn't want more people in harm's way and I wonder if he's going to offer an excuse.

"Sorry, Doc. It won't happen again," Radcliff says.

Huh. So he *does* know how to apologize. He still owes me one.

"Good. I don't appreciate being woken in the middle of the night. Now, Ara, sit down before you fall over."

Yes, the doctor knows about my new name. He saved my life. I'm indebted to this man so I sit and hold out my arms and then my legs for inspection. Five of the cuts require a couple small stitches that will dissolve in a few days. The rest of the lacerations aren't deep, but they sting like crazy when he cleans them with a sharp antiseptic. Which makes me ponder the possibility of cross contamination. The shadow-blobs drew blood so they have to have our blood on their appendages. And what if they left behind some alien bacteria or a strange incurable disease in my wound. Could I turn into one of them?

My imagination must be set on overactive. I'd been stabbed by them before and I haven't had any ill effects. Not that I noticed. As for them…would one of our viruses kill them? I don't think the good doctor has a vial of Pavartian pox in his bag. And I doubt the adults would appreciate yet another wild speculation from me.

When Dr. Edwards leaves to tend to the others, my parents don't follow him. Now what?

My mother sweeps her hand out, indicating me and the entrance to the pits. "How does this factor into our expedition to Pit 21?" she asks Radcliff.

"You saw the HoLFs in action. I'm hoping it has changed your mind about opening another pit."

"None of the Warriors in Pit 21 have been damaged. The HoLFs appeared after the looters destroyed the ones in Pits 1 to 4."

Not one to be out-stubborned—is that a word?—Radcliff says, "All the security volunteers for your team are covered with lacerations. They might not be willing to risk their lives again."

Uncertain, Mom glances at me.

"I'm still going."

"Why?" Radcliff asks me in a flat tone.

"We need information. The HoLFs aren't our only problem."

"You're right. We still have Jarren's blockade to breech. Once we can contact DES, then you'll have time to search for the stolen files from Xinji. If you recover all of Lan's research notes, you will have plenty of information," Radcliff says.

"The key word being *if.* We can't risk everyone's lives for an if. We need to explore as many options as possible."

My parents appear queasy. As if they're torn between being proud of me and worried for me. Radcliff just shakes his head.

Dad goes over to one of the terminals in the lab. He inserts his tangs, but he keeps the screen dark. I check the shadows. Frequently.

"If everything stays on schedule, we'll leave for Pit 21 on day two-fourteen," my dad says. He disentangles and stands. "Li-Li, can you ask the other officers if they're still willing to go?"

"I can, but I'm pretty sure they will be." And will probably be offended to be asked.

"Good. Do you need us to stay? Just in case?" He picks up his flashlight.

"No, go to bed." I shoo them, but they each hug me before leaving.

Now it's just me and Radcliff. He faces the entrance with his flashlight in hand. And do you know what? Guard duty is super boring. After an hour, I almost wish a shadow-blob would peek out just to give me something to do besides yawning. The desire to sleep grows with every passing second.

Soon not even my throbbing cuts are enough to keep me alert. I lean against one of the lab tables and fight the pull of gravity. Which, in spite of the law of physics, grows stronger each eternal minute.

I jerk awake when a head bob almost sends me crashing to the floor. Despite the late hour, Radcliff's still vigilant.

"How do you do it?" I ask him.

"Do what?"

"Stay awake when nothing's happening."

"I've had years of practice." He peers at me in amusement. "You don't think I started out as the Chief of Security?"

Actually I couldn't imagine him doing anything else. And that's saying something considering my imagination lately. "You mean you weren't born with a pulse gun in your hand?"

He laughs. And I just about faint. That's only the second time I've made Radcliff laugh since I've known him.

"I'm sure my mother would have mentioned that," he says, still smiling. "No, I began like you and Niall. A junior officer."

Wow. "Did you grow up on a space ship like Niall?"

"No. I grew up on Earth and joined DES when they sent out a recruiting call in twenty-eighty." His smile fades as he glances at his hands, then me. "I didn't have any skills except with my fists—I lived in a rough neighborhood—so they assigned me to security."

Ah. "Was it hard to leave your family and Earth behind?" I think of my brother who I still miss. Phoenix is in a time jump and due to arrive at Earth in forty-two years. At that time, he'll still be eighteen and I'll be fifty-nine A-years old if I stay on

Yulin. Ugh.

"No. Best thing I ever did." His gaze turns—if I didn't know any better I'd say wistful. "I met Janela—Niall's mother—on that first assignment. She worked in the galley until her paintings became famous."

Famous? I learned about a bunch of painters from old Earth up to the new space-faring pioneers. I run through the names but no Janela Lawrence. Maybe Janela Radcliff? Recalling the paintings in my room, I try to envision the signature. And then it hits me. "She's Jay El!"

"She was."

Was. That heavy word just slices right through me. Way to go. "I'm sorry." An inadequate, weak, stupid response.

He nods.

At least I'm smart enough not to ask how she died. Instead, I think of her paintings. My room is filled with them. "Niall didn't tell me."

"To him, she was just Mom." A touch of amusement returns to Radcliff's eyes. "Your mother is well known and highly respected in the scientific community. Do you tell your friends that?"

"No way. I complain to my friends about how annoying and overprotective she is."

"Funny," he says, deadpan. "I believe you think the same thing of me."

"At least I'm not playing favorites."

He huffs.

"Come on, you gotta admit I'm surrounded by guardian

lions."

"Guardian lions?"

Oops. "The ones in China. They guard—"

"I've heard of them." Radcliff stares at the door to the pits. "It's an apt description."

And I can't take any credit. "It's Niall's."

No comment. I mull over all the stuff I've learned about Radcliff. If he joined DES in twenty-eighty, he had to be at least eighteen, which means…Radcliff is at least four hundred and sixty E-years old. Oh my stars. A million questions about Earth and the places he's been bubble up my throat, but I swallow them all down. Bad enough I reminded him of his dead wife. Instead, I switch to a safer topic.

"With all those years of practice guarding…er…things, have you learned a trick to keep awake?" I ask.

"Coffee helps, and talking to your colleagues like we're doing now. Except there are some situations where having a conversation is distracting and all your attention must be focused on the *thing* you're keeping safe."

I ignore the jab. "And then what do you do?"

"I imagine what would happen if I failed at my duty. Who would get hurt? What would happen?" He gestures to the entrance. "In this case, if the HoLFs escaped the pits, they would kill everyone on the base. That's enough to keep me alert."

And it should do the same for me. Yet after twenty minutes of quiet, I'm struggling to stay awake. I rub my arms, inflaming the healing cuts. Pain pushes the fatigue away. Eventually, though, that stops working. Maybe it's because I know there's no threat. No pressure or spikes of cold to indicate lurking shadow-blobs. I try pacing and bouncing on the balls of my feet. Maybe if I do a kata—

"There's a reason I haven't assigned you a shift to guard the lab or detention," Radcliff says.

This ought to be good. "And that is?"

"It's not in your skill set."

Huh. "I've been training and I think I've shown I can handle the shadow—"

"That's not what I meant. This is mindless work. You don't do mindless. You never have. I need your sharp mind in the Q-net. Not sleep-deprived."

"But I want to help the team."

"And that's how you can help the best. Think about it. What happens if we don't contact DES? What happens if we don't figure out how to counter the HoLFs?"

Fair point. Except, doing that isn't being a part of the team. "Beau does both."

"He does. However, he doesn't have as many shifts on guard duty as some of the others."

Oh. I'd hoped doing my share of guard duty would ease the tension between me and the majority of the officers.

"From what I've heard, you're making an impression on the team," Radcliff says.

Did the man just read my mind? Scary thought. "Yeah, the wrong one." The words just slipped out of my mouth. I blame my exhaustion.

"Oh?" He focuses on me.

How to explain without sounding like a whiny four-year-old? "I think my...propensity for making suggestions and speaking my mind hasn't been welcome." And that Beau is scared of my new worming skills. Huh. Where did that come from? But when I examine our encounters, it makes more sense than jealousy.

"What are you going to do about it?" Radcliff asks.

Me? I tried easing their workload, but that didn't work. I asked for a shift. I...sense this is a trick question. "Nothing."

"Good. Keep making those suggestions. It's *my* job to decide if they're worthwhile or not. The safety of this team is on me, not *you*."

I knew that. Yet I obviously needed to hear it because it helps. A lot.

Bendix and Ho arrive at oh-five-hundred for their shift in the lab. I'm struck by how Ho Liu is the complete opposite of Gordy Bendix. He's thin and wiry with black hair and olive colored skin like mine. I'm glad the swelling around his nose has gone.

"All's quiet," Radcliff says.

The men look at me as if waiting for confirmation.

"The lab is clean," I say. "No signs of HoLFs."

"Any chance they'll get through?" Bendix gestures to the entrance to the pits.

I cover my surprise over the fact he asked *me*. "They

couldn't get past the floodlights in the lab when we had the doors open. But there's always a chance they might find a way in." An idea occurs to me. "Did you feel cold when you were at the door?" I ask Radcliff.

"It did seem cooler, but I thought it was from the pits."

I'll have to check with the others to see if they noticed. In the meantime, I say, "If the temperature quickly drops in here, skedaddle and sound the alarm."

Bendix's wide shoulders relax a bit. Ho shoots me a grateful smile. Progress.

Radcliff raises an eyebrow. "Skedaddle?"

"Move with the utmost haste, sir," Bendix supplies.

"I see Officer Dorey has been in the dictionary cluster again. Let's go before everyone wakes up, Lawrence."

Radcliff and I head back to security. The hallways are mostly deserted. Radcliff takes point and checks each corridor first. We only have to change routes twice to avoid a couple early risers. We arrive back at our unit at oh-five-thirty. I aim for my bedroom.

"Training at oh-eight-hundred," he calls, sounding gleeful.

I bite my lip to keep a groan from escaping. It's all part of the lesson. Plus I can handle one day without a good night's sleep. Right?

Oh-seven-thirty arrives two seconds after my head settled on the pillow. I swear time is plotting against me. Dragging my body out of bed is a colossal effort, but I manage to change into my workout clothes, eat, and arrive in the training room one minute early. I squint in the bright lights as Elese scans me.

"You look like hell, Lawrence," she says.

"Good morning to you, too."

She grunts in amusement. "How deep are your injuries?"

Pushing up the tunic's sleeves, I examine the rows of healing cuts. The ointment Dr. Edward used accelerates the process, but it still takes time. "Eleven stitches. You?"

She reveals her arms. "Fifteen stitches."

"So I guess we won't be sparring today."

"You got that right. We'll focus on cardio and strength. Give me forty laps around the room, Recruit."

We really means *me* doing all the work while Elese supervises. The morning turns into a blur of endless exercises, but I remember to ask her about the temperature change in the pits before I start target practice.

She rubs her leg. "Nah. My adrenaline was jacked. Too busy dodging invisible weapons to notice."

I pause. The shadow-blobs scare me and I can *see* them. Not being able to see the threat must be terrifying. And that reminds me.

"My father wants to know if you are still willing to go on the expedition."

Elese snorts in derision. "Of course. Who else is gonna protect that pampered ass of yours?"

Thought so.

Despite my fatigue, target practice goes well. Mr. Orange

Light winks out more times than ever—my best session so far. It's either due to being motivated by the attack or because my muscles don't have the energy to be tense. I'm hoping for the former. There's no way I'll be relaxed around shadow-blobs or looters.

When I meet up with Beau after lunch, he's sporting a similar collection of cuts. His are harder to spot among the spiderweb tattoos around both his elbows.

"Seventeen stitches," he says, almost proud of the fact.

"You beat me and Elese."

"But not Niall. He has twenty-five."

Ouch. Poor guy.

"Don't look like that," Beau admonishes. "Doc gave him the day off, the lucky bugger. He gets to lie in bed all day."

The desire to join him pulses in my chest. Right now heaven would be curling up in bed with Niall. To sleep, people! I doubt I'd have energy to do more. Besides, we're both injured.

Wait. Concern flares around my heart. "Why did Niall get the day off?"

"It's nothing to worry about. A couple of his wounds were deep and the Doc was concerned about blood loss. A day in bed should fix him right up. Now, let's get to work."

Beau and I entangle with the Q-net and gently probe Jarren's blockade for a weakness or hole we could slip through. It takes a light touch and super focused concentration. After a couple of hours, I'm straining to stay on task. A headache thumps in my temples. I hate to admit this, and I'll never say it to Radcliff, but the man is right. Lack of sleep and worming are a bad combination.

Careful, Beau warns.

I back away before my clumsiness sets off the alarm. That was close. Beau and I go to a neutral Q-cluster to regroup.

The door behind us opens. The intrusion of the physical world while deep in the Q-net is an odd sensation. Normally no one bothers us while we're worming.

"Dorey, I need you for a few minutes," Morgan says. "It's important."

A vibration flutters through the cluster, probably due to Beau's annoyance over being interrupted.

Stay here, I'll be back. Beau disentangles.

While I wait, I consider possible routes to DES. I wish I understood exactly how the Q-net transmits messages and reports over vast distances without being affected by the time dilation. If I could comprehend the equations used by the Q-net, perhaps I could discover a way to send a message to DES without alerting Jarren. However, I'd need another four years of advanced mathematics just to learn the basics.

The pain in my head intensifies. I cross my arms on the desk and rest my forehead on them. There's nothing of interest in this cluster. To me, a cluster is like a cavern in a cave system that has a bunch of narrow tunnels leading to and away from it.

This cluster only has one tunnel coming in and one going out. Rather boring until the "walls" turn transparent. That's never happened before. Beyond the cluster is—star roads!

And then I'm flying. I swirl and dip and swim through the Q-net. It's exhilarating. It's amazing. I'm...welcomed.

Embraced. Twirled and flung to the very edges of space. Time is fluid and spread across the universe like peanut butter on bread. All the answers are right here. I could find a way to DES. But DES is such a tiny part of the Q-net. It's irritating. A parasite. Better to soar along the star roads. To become—

"Ara!" Beau shakes my shoulder. "Wake up."

The Q-net shrinks. Once again the "walls" are opaque and I'm confined to the dull Q-cluster. I mourn the loss.

"Disentangle. Now," he orders.

"I'm okay." I sit up. The motion ignites the pain in my head and I press my fingertips on my temples to keep my skull from exploding. Imagining Beau's office walls covered with bits of splattered brain doesn't help.

"Disentangle." Beau's tone is firm.

The effort sends spikes of fire from my hair to my toes. Ouch. I pull out my tangs then cradle my head in my hands, closing my eyes.

"Should I call the doctor?" he asks.

"No. I just need a painkiller."

Beau rustles around, opening drawers. The door creaks open. It's quiet for a few seconds before his footsteps sound.

"Here."

I open one eye. He hands me a glass of water and two pills. Ah. I down them in one gulp—relief can't come soon enough.

"That was really dangerous and stupid," Beau says.

"I…" At a loss for words, I consider what happened. The sensations and feelings I experienced were similar to when I'd died, which should alarm me, but it doesn't.

"You, what?"

"I didn't know I fell asleep. I just thought…" This time he waited for me to find the right description. "I thought I'd found the…heart of the Q-net." And it was just about to reveal itself to me. Crazy, I know.

"Which is why you never ever fall asleep while entangled. Stars, girl. You could have gone catatonic."

Now he's being dramatic. "There's only a very tiny chance." Almost everyone who dozes off wakes up disentangled.

"With your track record, I wouldn't be surprised if you fall into that tiny percentage." His tone is hard and angry. "And don't forget, I woke you. Who knows what would have happened if you'd slept longer or deeper."

I may have found a way to communicate with DES. However, I keep that to myself or risk having my head examined.

"Well, you're no good to me now," he says, still grumpy. "Go get some rest."

I'm about to protest when I recall how I almost triggered an alarm before I fell asleep. "Okay."

He squints at me in suspicion. I turn to go before he can question me, then pause, remembering to ask him about the encounter with the HoLFs. "Did you feel anything before they attacked?"

Beau rubs his arm. "Yeah, cold. The pits are always damp, but there was a wave of cold air that hit me from behind right before you told me to duck. Why?"

I explained how that could alert the officers guarding the

pits. "Also, are you still willing to go on the expedition to Pit 21?"

"I'm insulted that you thought you needed to ask."

"Not me, my father."

Beau grunts. "You know my answer."

I did.

"On your way out tell Morgan I'll be finished with the analysis sooner than expected. Seems I have some free time this afternoon." He gives me a pointed look.

"Is that what Morgan interrupted us for?" I ask.

"No. There was a situation in detention. Morgan rearranged roommates and needed a couple extra guards to keep everyone civil."

"Another riot?"

"No. Nothing on that scale. It was a fight between two prisoners. Tempers have been flaring. Morgan's mixing it up so two people don't get on each other's nerves as often, give some a cell to themselves for a while, things like that, hoping to settle everyone down. You know those cells are too small for even one person let alone two."

"Actually, I don't. I've never been in one." I smirk.

"Brat." He gives me a grudging smile, though. "If you're feeling better, I have—"

"Ow, my head." I press my hand to my forehead and skedaddle before he can assign me to some mundane task.

I relay his message to Morgan and then head back to my unit. Except I stop outside Niall's instead. Standing there, I debate. The desire to check on him and ensure he's okay wars with being unwilling to disturb his rest.

The door opens before I can make up my mind. Niall's wearing pajama pants and nothing else. Oh my stars.

His bare torso is sculpted with muscles. The desire to run my hands over his chest presses on me. Then I spot the lacerations along his arms and shoulders. And the gash on his forehead sports a row of stitches. His hair is damp and slicked back from a recent shower. The intoxicating scent of sage grass reaches me, confirming my guess. An image of Niall in the shower sends a bolt of heat through me.

"Something wrong, Mouse?" he asks when I continue to stand there like an idiot and stare.

"I came to check on you. Beau said..." I draw in a breath—get a grip, girl. "Why aren't you resting?"

"Because I heard footsteps pause outside my unit. Why didn't you knock?"

"I didn't want to bother you."

He huffs in amusement.

"How are you feeling?" I ask.

Instead of answering, he grabs my hand and tugs me inside, closing the door behind me. I follow him into the small living area. On the floor next to the couch is a sketchpad and pencil. On the open page is a half-finished drawing of...me wearing my security jumpsuit. My posture is tense and I'm wielding my flashlight like a weapon. Wisps of hair frame my face. My expression is...fierce.

I meet Niall's gaze.

"I'm going to call it 'Chasing the Shadows' when it's done," he says.

"Technically shadow-blobs."

"That doesn't sound as good."

"You never answered my question."

He pulls me down to sit next to him on the couch. "I'm much better now that you're here."

"Have you rested at all?"

"I slept until a decadent hour. Besides, drawing is relaxing and you were on my mind." He drapes his arm over my shoulder, tucking me close.

The scent of his shampoo is now mixed with a decidedly male musk. I inhale, filling my lungs.

"Beau said you needed twenty-five stitches."

He snorts in derision. "Everything's a competition with him."

Still. "Your dad's worried about the expedition to Pit 21. My dad—"

"I'm still going."

No surprise. I snuggle in, resting my head on his shoulder.

"Aren't you supposed to be worming with Dorey?" he asks.

I explain what happened and endure the admonishments. Good thing I didn't mention flying along the star roads. It's one of those things that I know I should fess up to, but am reluctant for reasons unknown…Okay, I wish to avoid the unpleasantness that will no doubt occur. Brain scans aren't fun, people. When I reassure him that my headache has gone—it has—I say, "It got me a few hours off to rest." I trace the cut on his forehead with a gentle fingertip. "We can rest together."

Heat flares in his blue-green eyes. Then his lips press on mine and I deepen the kiss. We shift so I'm sitting in his lap and we're facing each other. I finally get to do what I've wanted since he opened the door. I run my hands over his bare skin. He shivers under my touch. Emboldened, I explore the planes of his chest and tangle my fingers in his damp hair. Groaning, he leans forward. I rake my nails lightly down his spine, dipping toward his waistband.

He breaks the kiss off. His eyes shine and he's a bit breathless. "I fear you have me at a disadvantage."

I'm well more than a bit breathless. "I do?"

"Yes, and I need to rectify the situation." He tugs at the bottom of my shirt until it pulls free. Then he pauses, seeking my permission.

My heart rate jacks up as I nod. In one smooth move, he takes off my shirt and tosses it to the floor. He studies me and I'm super glad I'm wearing a decent bra. It's not sexy, 'cause I wasn't expecting *this* when I dressed. His hands snake around me and grab the clasp of my bra. Again he waits for my nod before unhooking the garment. I'm impressed with his skill and gasp when he cups my breasts. Fire races over my skin and gathers deep down.

Niall reclaims my lips and then it's all raw sensations and pulsating desire. Being skin to skin heightens each touch. After a good long time, we stop to catch our breaths. Somehow we ended up lying down on the couch side by side.

"You're beautiful, Mouse," Niall whispers in my ear.

His words warm my insides. I stroke his cheek, rubbing my

thumb over the stubble on his jaw.

He grabs my wrist. "You're bleeding."

One of my stitches ripped open. I didn't even feel it. Of course now that I'm aware of it, pain needles into my arm. I'd ignore it, but Niall insists on bandaging it. And when he gets up to fetch the first aid kit, I see that he's torn a few of his as well.

By the time we're done, I'm cold and hug my arms to my chest. Niall grabs a blanket and we return to the couch. He covers us and nestles in next to me. It's warm and comfortable and I can't keep my eyes open. We've fallen asleep together before, but this time, with skin on skin, it is so much nicer.

What's not so nice is the pounding on the door that startles us awake. Niall surges to his feet and goes over to see who's making all the noise. He turns on the screen.

"It's my dad," he says.

2522:204

"Shit," I say, scrambling to put on my bra and shirt, tucking it in.

The banging grows louder. Radcliff must be pissed.

Niall glances at me. I'm pulling my hair into a ponytail. He waits a beat before opening the door.

"What's the emergency?" he asks his father.

"Is Ara with you?" Radcliff demands.

My emotions swing from embarrassed to confused. Shouldn't Radcliff know exactly where I am?

Niall steps back. "Yes."

Radcliff storms into the living room. Uh oh. He glares at me. Okay, that's not the reaction I expected. Not that Niall and I were doing anything wrong, but why is his father angry at just me?

"What did you do to the Q-net?" Radcliff asks.

Wait... "What do you mean?"

"Don't act innocent. What did you do to prevent me from finding you?"

"Nothing."

"Don't lie."

Oh no, he doesn't get away with that. I stand up and glare right on back at him. "I'm not. All you need to do is ask the Q-net where I am."

"I did and it wouldn't tell me."

It wouldn't? Those two words just didn't go together. The cameras in security are on a closed loop so no one can worm into them and see me. But Radcliff should be able to access that loop. "That doesn't make sense."

"Not helping," Radcliff almost growls.

I pull my tangs from my pocket and head toward Niall's terminal.

Radcliff grabs my arm. "Where do you think you're going?"

"To figure out the problem."

He releases me. "Leave the screen on."

Seriously? "Put your tangs in and trail me then."

His surprise lasts a millisecond before he follows me to the terminal. I sit down, insert my entanglers, and suck in a breath.

"What's wrong?" Niall asks.

The Q-net is different. It's like someone came in and changed all the colors. The layers shine and appear more...translucent.

"Mouse?"

"Nothing's wrong." I access the security camera feeds. They appear to be functioning normally and correctly pinpoint the other officers. But when I inquire about my whereabouts, it shows nothing. Odd. I look at the feeds from the training room earlier today. Elese is there, but I'm…not. And I fail to show up in any of the feeds from the last couple days. In fact, the places where I should have been are changed so it doesn't look like people are talking to an invisible person. As if I've been erased from existence.

"Care to explain that?" Radcliff asks aloud probably for Niall's benefit. "I can't. Not yet." I check the programming and nothing triggered the alarms. All is as it should be. So what happened? I need to go deeper. Problem is I shouldn't be able to do it on this terminal and with Radcliff tagging along… Oh well, he's bound to find out sometime.

I go deeper and examine the protective measures around the security cameras in detail. It's a slow process and takes a while to tease out the problem. Oh my stars.

"Is that—"

"Yes," I interrupt Radcliff. "Jarren tried to access the cameras in security."

"Can he do that?" Niall asks in alarm.

That's the thing. "Sort of."

"What the hell does that mean?"

"It means that when I programmed the Q-net to watch our cameras, I had to create a very small link to that closed loop in security—otherwise the Q-net wouldn't be able to locate the officers or check for intruders. When Jarren wormed into the camera feeds for the base, he found that tiny link. So the Q-net allowed him to view the security feeds, but it removed all images of me."

"Can it do that?" Niall asks.

Radcliff is quiet. Too quiet. And that worries me.

"Obviously, but, more importantly, *why* did it do it?" I dig into the cluster. "Huh."

"Huh, what? Talk to me, Mouse."

"When I was setting up the programs for monitoring the base's cameras, I must have inadvertently included an extra protection around my image." I don't remember doing it, but I was worried about Jarren finding me at the time. "So when Jarren wormed into the feeds, the Q-net translated that into erasing my image. It's odd, but it saved me."

"But if Jarren was worming into the feeds, why didn't it alert us?" Niall asks.

"He didn't trigger any of the alarms." Disgust that our measures weren't enough mixes with admiration for his mad worming skills. He's still a murdering looter, though.

"Except the Q-net seemed to know he wasn't supposed to be there."

True. "Yeah, but without a breach in the security protocols, it couldn't stop him."

"The bigger problem is why didn't it let us know it *altered* the feeds?" Radcliff asks, but I don't think he expects me to answer.

It's a good question. If the Q-net had let Radcliff know, then he wouldn't have come barging in here accusing me of lying. I shoot him another glare, but he's not paying attention. Instead, I try to figure out an answer. "The Q-net isn't programmed to message us if that happens. I can put in a program for any future occurrences."

"All right."

It doesn't take me long to weave in another protocol that will alert Radcliff of any alterations to our security made by the Q-net. "Done."

"Is Jarren still monitoring the camera feeds in security?" Radcliff asks.

"It appears that he, or someone who works with him, checks in from time to time. Do you want me to fix the hole he's worming through?"

"Not now," Radcliff says. "You can do it tomorrow when you're rested. Besides, it seems the Q-net is doing a good job protecting you."

We disentangle. And I wait for an apology. Of course I don't get it. Radcliff squints at his son. While we were in the Q-net, Niall put on a shirt. Smart man.

Radcliff turns to me. "Officer Dorey sent you back to rest. Why didn't you?"

"I came to check on Niall and fell asleep on his couch." The truth.

A grunt. "We better get back. Your parents are worried."

Oh no. Seems when my mother came to wake me up for dinner, she found my room empty. Radcliff asked the Q-net for my location and you know the rest.

My parents' reaction to the Q-net's odd response and the fact Jarren wormed into the feeds is the same as mine—a combination of gratitude and fear.

"It would probably be a good idea to keep Ara out of the Q-net since Jarren's snooping around, except we need to reestablish contact with DES," Radcliff says while we're eating.

I keep quiet despite the fact that he practically blamed me for the Q-net's strange behavior. Am I to blame? The Q-net did appear to be different. Falling asleep while entangled shouldn't have had any effect. Well, there's that chance of going catatonic. Maybe I am catatonic! And all this is just happening in my mind.

Trying not to panic, I press my fingers on one of my deeper cuts. Pain spreads. It's a relief until I think— No. I need to stop thinking or I'm going to go crazy. Instead I focus on the conversation and dodge the questioning looks from my mother. She didn't say anything when Radcliff explained I fell asleep on Niall's couch, but, if I know her—and I do—she's just waiting to have a private word with me.

After dinner, Niall and I are sent to bed like we are a pair of misbehaving teenagers. Different beds of course. Radcliff uses the doctor's orders excuse for Niall and I'm just nagged until I relent. My mom follows me into my room for—you guessed it—a girl talk. We sit on the bed and I set the record straight about how everyone has jumped to the wrong conclusion— because they have even if they didn't say so aloud. But I endure the lecture and pay attention to my birth control options. What else can I do? My mom has my best interests at heart and this talk is more for her than me. Huh. I must be maturing.

When she finishes, I say, "Can I ask you a question?"

"Of course. Anything. You know that."

I do, but this is personal. "When was your first time?"

She hesitates. Perhaps anything doesn't really mean

anything. But then she straightens. "I was twenty and it was with your father. I'd like to tell you that we made an informed decision and used protection, but we were drunk." She laughs. It's almost a giggle.

My mother giggling? Wonders never cease!

"We lucked out or your brother would have been born five years before we were ready."

I can't imagine Mom not being anything other than a confident parental authority. Being drunk? Irresponsible? No. Not going there.

"Your father and I waited until we got to know each other and were in love. I think that's important. Do you love Niall?"

Do I? We've only been dating fifty-four days, but I think of him a lot, I'd rather be with him than anyone else, and he's in all my future plans. Not that I have a set course of action except to survive Jarren and the shadow-blobs. I'm hopeful that I'll have a happily ever after and Niall will still be by my side. Is that love?

"You don't have to answer that," Mom says after a lengthy silence. She gives me a gentle hug, being careful not to inflame my injuries. She pulls the blanket up to my chin and kisses my forehead. "Don't give me that look. You're never too old to be tucked in."

True. Plus I secretly enjoy being tucked in all safe and secure, but I'll never tell Mom that—well, maybe when I'm older. She leaves and turns off the lights and I lie there remembering the afternoon with Niall. Too bad we fell asleep as I would have loved to make him shiver again. And more. I unleash my creativity, imagining many ways to accomplish that.

I drift to sleep, dreaming of kissing Niall. We're on his couch. After a while he stops and stands, holding out his hands. *Come on*, Dream Niall says, grasping my wrists and tugging me to my feet. *Let's fly.*

And then we soar through the Q-net, dipping and twirling and racing across the Galaxy. I'm surrounded by softness—safe and secure, all tucked in.

Thank you for protecting me, I say, but Niall is no longer with me. I'm addressing the Q-net and it...understands. So while I'm in this crazy dream state, I ask it to let Officer Radcliff know if anyone tries to worm into our protections. It agrees. Or I think the warm pulse inside my chest is agreement.

Through the Q-net, I zip back to Planet Yulin. The security measures we've woven surround the planet like a bubble. But there should be connections to DES branching off it like tentacles. Beyond our measures is a black balloon that encases the planet—it's Jarren's web of programs. It's blocking us from reaching DES. The answer to our problem is to pierce Jarren's balloon without popping it and connect to DES. Difficult to do from the surface of the planet. Could DES create a connection to us? Perhaps if they were aware of the problem.

In my dreams, I fly to DES and navigate through their security like a river through the mountains. It's fun and exhilarating, zooming around curves and plummeting over the cliffs. Seeking out any navigators not in a time jump, I reach Chief Vasily who is entangled with the Q-net. In order to avoid scaring him by just popping into his head, I compose a message:

2522:205: Chief Vasily, the scientists and security personnel on Planet Yulin are NOT dead. We're alive, but being blocked from communicating with DES by looters who have a wormer working with them. Please find a way to reach us without letting the looters know.

Then I debate about who to list as the sender. According to DES, Lyra Daniels is on Yulin—status unknown. My records show my internship with Chief Hoshi so that will give Vasily more evidence that I have the skills to send the message. But I'm still a minor and he has no idea of just how accomplished I am. I make the message from Chief of Security, Officer Tace Radcliff. Of course, this is all a dream so it's moot.

My duty done, I play. Zipping and spinning, I cross the Galaxy in seconds and hover at its edge. The void between galaxies yawns wide and dark. Our closest neighbor is the Canis Major Dwarf Galaxy at forty-two thousand light years away from the Milky Way's core. But it's being slowly pulled apart by the Milky Way's gravity and its long filament of stars, gas, and dust wraps around the Milky Way three times. And while I'm being an astronomy geek in my dreams, that filament is called the Monoceros Ring.

Yet even that short (when you consider the size of the universe) distance to Canis Major is impossible to cross. The Q-net's star roads end at the edges of the Milky Way. Did the developers believe that exploring the Galaxy would take so long that we'd outgrow the Q-net and invent a new technology that would take us beyond our Galaxy? Amusement from the Q-net over that thought fills me. I'm aware of how ridiculous it sounds, but I sense it all the same.

A strident sound emanates. It yanks me from the edge and I fall toward it. I resist—flying in the Q-net is too much fun. But it's stronger and more persistent and I can't remain. I'm ejected into my own body with a blaze of pain that jolts me awake.

Clutching my head, I curl into a ball, only dimly aware I'm on the floor. My "you overslept" alarm is screeching. Its high-pitched tones stab into my skull like a sharp dagger. All I can do is press my hands over my ears to keep my brain from being squeezed out like a pimple. I'd laugh at the image but I'm afraid I'll expel the contents of my stomach. A horrible pressure builds on my skin. My bones creak under its weight.

Blurry black boots appear in front of me. The alarm stops. Thank the universe! Radcliff talks but nothing makes sense. He crouches down, peering at me. I see solar systems swirl in his brown eyes.

"Doctor," I gasp. "Please."

Then the world crushes me.

The pain dissolves, leaving behind blissful darkness. On the edges, I sense the Q-net. It wishes for me to fly. I resist. Flying has consequences. Instead I float in the void for…I've no idea, but it's nice here so stop bothering me.

Small noises intrude on my peace. My name rouses me. A

cold prick in my arm accelerates awareness of my surroundings. For indeed I am lying in my bed. Someone pries open my eyelid. I flinch at the sudden light and bat at the offending hand. It moves away and I squeeze my eyes shut.

"She's awake," Dr. Edwards says.

Is that relief in his voice?

"What happened?" Mom asks gently. Her fingers entwine with mine.

"I…dreamt. I…flew."

"That doesn't make any sense," Dad says.

Just how many people are in here?

"She's been referring to worming as flying," Beau says. "Maybe that incident yesterday caused some sort of delayed backlash."

I peek out. My room isn't that big, yet five people stand inside. Radcliff hovers in the doorway.

"Li-Li, is that it? Is this because you fell asleep while worming?" Dad asks.

"I…don't know." Or do I?

"The sensors in her brain could be damaged," Dr. Edwards says. "She could be accessing the Q-net through Tace's terminal."

"Without entanglers? And this far away?" Mom asks. "That's hard to believe."

The queasiness in my stomach turns sour. "I dreamt I was flying through the Q-net."

"Like when you…died?" Mom's voice catches on the D-word.

"Yes." I confess and wait for the inevitable questions.

They don't disappoint. Yes, I should have told them sooner. No, I didn't fall asleep with my tangs in last night. No, I didn't do it on purpose. Yes, it was a very vivid dream. No, I don't think I actually accessed the Q-net. 'Cause that would be impossible!

Unless I'm catatonic and still slumbering in Beau's office? No, then I would have never "woken" from my adventures. I'd still be flying and there wouldn't have been pain.

There's much discussion that doesn't involve me and I'm happy to lie there. I don't protest when Dr. Edwards schedules a late-night brain scan, because I'd rather never wake up with that excruciating pain again.

Eventually the adults leave and I'm instructed to rest. Except that's what got me in this mess in the first place.

I grab my mom's arm in a panic. "Don't let me fall asleep!"

She sits on the edge of my bed, taking my hand in both of hers. "You're going to have to sleep eventually."

And my body feels as if I'd spent the night sparring Elese. "What if it happens again? And I can't…wake up?" While being trapped in the Q-net isn't the worst thing, I'm not ready to leave the physical world. Niall's kisses are worth remaining for.

Mom squeezes my hand. "I'll stay with you. If it looks like you're having another nightmare, I'll wake you."

"You have work—"

"Hush, nothing's more important."

Her truthful, heartfelt statement slams into me like a tidal wave. "Love you, too, Mom."

Nightmare. I like that word. That explanation. And after my brain scan, Dr. Edwards is inclined to agree. My guardian lions (Mom, Dad, and Elese) stand watch for the next four nights and I've no more nightmares. All goes back to normal.

Sort of. I hesitate outside Beau's office. I'm standing in the narrow room, staring at the monitors without really seeing them. Rubbing my temples to dispel a phantom headache, I create a number of excuses for why I shouldn't be worming this afternoon. Fatigue, hunger, thirst, itchy limbs due to the healing cuts, no motivation, fear. That last one catches me off guard.

What exactly am I afraid of? Losing my mind? Not really. The pain? Maybe a little. That it wasn't a nightmare? Bingo. Because if I did fly in the Q-net how did I get past Jarren's blockade? I didn't. Then why am I scared to find out otherwise? Actually, I'd be an idiot not to be terrified. All right then. With that settled, I channel my inner lion and join Beau.

He grunts. "About time. Thought I'd have to drag you in here."

Did all the officers have super hearing? I plop down next to him. "What are we doing today?"

"First we need to fix the holes around the base's camera feeds and ensure Jarren can't access the ones in security again. Then I thought we'd try to worm through that cluster where the fake DES messages are coming from. We might be able to get through the blockade at that point."

"That's a good idea."

"Don't sound so surprised. I do this for a living, ya know." Beau flashes me a bright smile.

We access the Q-net. And the tight band around my chest eases with relief. All is normal. Not the normal from before I died, but before the nightmare normal. And I can't believe I'm defining what's normal based on those two criteria.

Strengthening our protections, we rig an alarm on the camera feeds in security to alert Radcliff if Jarren tries to view the live feed again.

Beau follows the path of the bogus messages from DES. I keep close to him. Staying out of the main pathway, we worm just below it, paralleling the route. Then we reach the blockade and angle up to get a glimpse of the incoming missives. They come in quick bursts through a gap that slams shut as soon as they pass through. There's no way to sneak out unless we know exactly when the next batch is going to come through.

Beau's disappointment is tangible.

I search for something to cheer him up. *Isn't tomorrow payday? We can send a message to DES when our pay comes in tomorrow. Did you find out when the credits are deposited?* The timing had to be precise.

I worked on that while you were recovering. Our pay dropped at the same time every thirty days except for the last one. It was delayed over two hours.

It's being intercepted. I hoped Jarren allowed routine messages to automatically come through.

Yup, and no way to know when tomorrow's will come in.

We needed another place that might provide an escape. *Jarren's been poking around in our camera feeds. Maybe we can find where he's coming in from,* I say.

Won't work. He doesn't leave a trail.

But the Q-net picked up on it. Let's at least look in the clusters for the feeds.

Waste of time. But he trails me to those clusters.

The feeds appear to be undisturbed. However, I catch a glimpse of a smudge on the alarms. It reminds me of fingerprints smeared on glass.

See that? I ask Beau. I scan for more.

What?

I explain.

Nope.

Concentrating on the smudges, I try to make them visible to Beau. No luck. We leave the feeds and work for the next couple of hours to find another way through without success. A part of me suspects we're not approaching this the right way. However, the rest of me has no clue what *is* the correct way.

Perhaps if I think of it from Jarren's point of view. How would I block an entire planet? The Q-net is such a vast network. Lots of pathways, which is why we thought Jarren had to miss at least one, leaving it open. Jarren has to be able to access DES. If we could find him, then use his link, that might work. Except we're trying to avoid him. This would be like knocking on his door and asking to use his terminal. Plus how do we find him?

The answer pops into my head. By following his fingerprints!

Too dangerous, Beau says after I tell him my idea.

There's nothing left to try.

There's always another option. Think harder, Lawrence.

Can we at least locate him? The nightmare image of his bubble around Yulin flashes in my mind.

Silence. *You can try.*

Progress! I angle so the smears are "visible." Direction is dodgy in the Q-net, but, to me, going deeper into our camera feeds is "down," so the opposite way is toward Jarren. Yeah, not the most scientific. Concentrating on the fingerprints, I worm through the upper layers. After an hour, I'm better at spotting them. I increase my speed. One quirk of worming is it's never a direct path. Finding gaps and cutting through clusters is always a roundabout route.

Another quirk is not always knowing right away when you get to the end. Which is why I barreled straight into Jarren's blockade, setting off the alarms.

Stars!

2522:209

The alarms don't wail like in the real world, but they alert Jarren in seconds. We don't have enough time to retreat. A message appears from an unknown source, but I'll bet it's the murdering looter.

2522:209: Looks like I caught a worm. Who do I have the pleasure of addressing?

I panic, remembering my last encounter with Jarren. *I got this*, Beau says.

2522:209: This is Officer Beau Dorey from Planet Yulin. I order you to identify yourself and remove this illegal blockade at once.

→You security officers sure like to order people around. I'm curious, does it give you a hard-on? I must admit you discovered my blockade sooner than I like. The little worm must have taught you something useful before her unfortunate demise.

My unfortunate demise? I was murdered by him and he doesn't have the balls to acknowledge that. I get the mental equivalent of a "calm down" from Beau.

←You are to cease and desist with the blockade immediately.

→It's cute how you keep yapping at me like a little puppy dog. I'm not going to do anything of the sort, *Officer* Dorey.

←You will be arrested and charged with endangering the population of an entire planet once we reestablish contact with DES.

→Good luck with trying to reach DES. Even if you had your little worm, you'd still be stuck. Don't worry about getting bored. You'll soon have more important things to worry about.

←Are you threatening a security officer?

→No, I'm warning you, you dolt. Not that it will matter in the end. Good-bye, *Officer* Dorey.

Jarren retreats and, without thought, I follow, trailing him along the complex path he takes to avoid getting caught in his own traps. I'm moving on pure instinct, hoping he doesn't spot me. Jarren navigates a series of clusters and then threads his way through an intricate, and fascinating, maze of alarms and programs. I hate to say this, but it's a thing of beauty.

And then, he's gone. He slips out so fast, I can't pinpoint the exact location. But I scan the programming and spot his fingerprints. After a careful inspection, I track him, moving so slow that a glacier melts quicker. I discover a tiny breach in the blockade.

Yes! *You'd still be stuck,* eh? This little worm just showed you, Jarren. But I don't hang around and gloat. I'm smart enough to retreat as fast as possible. He could be waiting to see if anyone follows him through the hole. Plus I don't know what's on the other side.

As I backtrack, I pay attention to the route, memorizing it. Careful not to cause ripples, I take my time, which gives Beau plenty of time to go from annoyed, to worried, to just about to bring in the cavalry.

Where the hell have you been, Lawrence? he demands.

I tell him, thinking he'll be happy.

That was stupid. He could have found out you're still alive.

He didn't. And now we have a way to escape.

At least you resisted the temptation to follow him.

Gee, don't go getting all mushy on me, Dorey.

He grunts. We disentangle. Fatigue beats behind my eyes in the form of a dull ache. A minor nuisance compared to the nightmare migraine. I sweep my hair behind my ears to pull out my tangs and freeze. No tangs. Did they fall out? Nothing's on the floor. I think back. Did I put them in when we started? I can't remember—usually it's automatic. Checking my pockets, I find them.

Does that mean... The room spins around me. I cross my arms on the desk and rest my head before I faint.

Beau touches my shoulder. "You okay?"

"Yeah," I lie 'cause how can I explain I just entangled with the Q-net without entanglers. Besides, it's not going to happen again. Not at all. "Just need a minute."

"Here." Something hard bumps my arm.

I raise my head. Beau hands me a painkiller and a glass of water. That was suspiciously fast. I raise an eyebrow in question.

"Thought you might need it."

"Thanks."

He shrugs, but there's a hint of a smirk. "That's what partners do."

My stomach twists, sending bile up my throat. Partners don't lie to each other. I'm a terrible person.

"When you feel better, we need to update Radcliff."

"Uh...I think I need to lie down for...ever."

"Nice try, Lawrence. Don't worry, I'll do all the talking."

I can only delay so much. Soon we're standing before Radcliff's desk. I check his eyes—no solar systems swirling inside. Whew.

Beau says, "We hit the barricade and set off the alarm."

"I hit it," I say when Radcliff tenses.

"*We* did." Beau frowns at me. "Jarren showed up so I engaged, playing the role of a sanctimonious security officer." He shows Radcliff the exchange of messages.

"What do you think he means by 'more important things to worry about?'" Radcliff asks.

"It could be he's planning another attack," Beau says.

"Or he's referring to the shadow…er…HoLFs." I can't decide which one is worse.

"We'll just have to be extra vigilant. Are you sure he didn't spot you, Lawrence?"

"Yes," I say with confidence.

"Good." Radcliff drums his fingers on his desk. "This isn't that bad."

Beau and I exchange a look.

"Jarren expected us to figure it out. And now we can test his blockade with more force. We only need to get one message out."

Remembering the nightmare, I swallow. Hard. "What about that hole I found?"

Radcliff smiles, but it's cold and calculating. "For the next few days, I want you to probe his defenses and set off his alarms. He'll get used to it and it'll be a great distraction for when we send in a second team to slip through that breach."

Very devious. I approve.

Standing outside the conference room, I wait for the signal to enter. Beau and I have been setting off all kinds of alarms as we've tested Jarren's blockade these last four days. It's fun and I hope it's driving Jarren crazy. But this afternoon we have a meeting to discuss the final logistics of the expedition to Pit 21. My parents, Radcliff, Morgan, the security officers who are accompanying the mission, the dozen archeology techs, and one medic on loan from Dr. Edwards are all already seated around the table along with my father's assistant, Gavin. All but Gavin, the medic, and the techs know about me. The reason I'm waiting is so my parents can explain to them that I'm not dead versus me just showing up like a ghost or a zombie.

I liked the idea of surprising them—even offered to wear makeup and stumble in like the walking dead—the look on their faces would be priceless!— but I was outvoted.

A disjointed burst of gasps and a few cheers erupt on the other side of the door. Aww, they care. Then all grows silent as my mom explains about the very real danger of not letting anyone else in the base know about me and how they should refer to me as Ara Lawrence in all communications and reports.

"Junior Officer Lawrence, please join us," Radcliff says loud enough for me to hear through the doors.

That's my signal. When I enter, everyone stares at me. Everyone. Amusement shines in Beau and Elese's eyes. Niall gives me a warm smile. My parents beam—no idea why. Radcliff frowns while Morgan is Morgan—neutral. And the techs…some are wide eyed with shock, others give me huge happy grins, and a few don't seem to care.

Gavin jumps up and pulls me into a rough hug. "So glad you're alive," he whispers in my ear. Gavin releases me just as fast and returns to his seat.

Wow. So much for my suspicions that I annoy him. I sit down in the empty chair between Beau and Elese.

"Now that everyone is here, we can review the plan," Mom says. A map showing the research base and the surrounding desert appears on the large screen behind Radcliff. "Pit 21 is twenty kilometers from the base."

An X materializes in the sand. There be treasure here, maties. I suppress a giggle. My mom explains how the team will drive out, open the pit, and do a survey of the Warriors inside. Radcliff describes the general role of security during the mission. I'm once again the center of attention. This time the expressions are tighter as they learn there's a chance of encountering invisible and dangerous shadow-blobs. The tension in the room increases as many of them are probably remembering the attack in the pits. One man rubs a long thin scar on his forearm.

"How do we know that looter won't worm into the satellite and see what we're doing?" one of the female techs asks.

"We have alarms in place and *I'll* be monitoring the feeds," Radcliff says.

That's a nice surprise. The man's not half bad with the Q-net.

"We need four of you to stay behind and fill in for the officers who are accompanying us," Dad says. "Who wants to volunteer?"

Eight raise their hands, including the lady who asked about

the satellite. Beau and Elese exchange an amused look. No doubt over the fact that these same techs complained about training and having to help with security.

Dad inclines his head to Radcliff. "I'll let the Chief pick."

"Malia, Tao, Rez, and Sander," Radcliff says, choosing the two women and two men without seeming to consider his options.

Radcliff also selected the woman who questioned the security of the satellite. Malia sinks back in her chair with obvious relief. I wonder if that's why he picked her.

"We'll leave the base at oh-seven-hundred tomorrow," Dad says. "Be in the port and ready at that time. Bring your field kits, including tents and sunscreen." Dad goes on to check the status on the various prep tasks the techs were assigned, gathering equipment, supplies, floodlights, a generator, a portable washroom, water, and food for the expedition.

Wow, who knew you needed so much stuff to go camping in the desert.

Before the meeting is over, Radcliff obtains everyone's attention. He waits until quiet descends and we're all focused on him. "Officer Dorey is in charge of security while you're in the field. This means your safety is his number one priority and not the dig site." Radcliff scans faces. His don't-mess-with-me scowl is firmly in place. "If he believes you are in danger, then you will abandon the site and return to base *without* hesitation." This last bit is said to my parents. "Understand?" he asks. Everyone does, but Radcliff fails to look happy.

My mom dismisses the techs, but remains seated with my

dad as they file out. Once they're gone, she asks Radcliff, "How exactly is the security going to work?"

"Officer Dorey will explain," Radcliff says.

From Beau's irritated glare, I guess this is the first time he's been asked his opinion about it. After a long moment, he says, "We will ensure the site is secure before you're allowed to set up camp. When you open the pit, three of us will go down to check for hostiles, including Junior Officer Lawrence. If the pit is safe, you will be allowed to enter. During work hours, Lawrence will stay in the pits with you and three officers will remain on the surface—one stationed near the hatch, one to keep an eye on the surrounding area, and one will sleep—the three will rotate shifts. At night, two officers will patrol the camp while two sleep—all four will rotate shifts."

Which means not a lot of sleep for me. Ugh.

Radcliff, though, nods in approval. "What's the protocol for an evac?"

Another pause. "During the day, if Lawrence spots HoLFs, she will sound the alarm…we'll take a couple blow-horns. In that case, the pit will be evacuated immediately and the hatch sealed before everyone returns to the base. At night, everyone will leave the pits and the hatch will be secured. If an unfriendly is spotted near the camp, the officers on duty will sound the alarm. I'll issue orders regarding a response if needed, or if evasive actions are required. The goal will be to get everyone safely back to the base as quick as possible."

"That sounds reasonable," Mom says. "Spencer and I will also be armed and a few of the techs as well."

"And we'll all have flashlights," Dad adds. "With extra bulbs and batteries."

It sounds as if they're planning for any contingency. Yet Radcliff's grumpy demeanor remains. Guess he's not going to let my parents forget he disapproved of this mission. My parents leave to finish the last of their packing.

Radcliff waits until the door is closed before saying, "This is a dangerous mission." He meets each of our gazes. "It's not too late to un-volunteer."

Silence.

He sighs. "All right. Dorey, you don't let anyone's opinions influence you. If you don't think it's safe, get the hell out of there. I don't care if there's no sign of HoLFs or looters. If it doesn't feel right then you skedaddle."

"Yes, sir!" Beau just barely keeps a straight face.

Heck, we all struggle to keep from grinning over Radcliff's use of skedaddle.

"If the HoLFs attack in the pit, Lawrence is in charge until you exit and seal the hatch. Got it?"

"Yes, sir!" Beau and I say together.

It's daunting to think that I'll be making the decisions, but understandable. And if I recall the two times I've encountered the shadow-blobs, I did...okay. No one died, and we all escaped with just a few cuts. I glance at Niall's forehead. The wound is healed. Only a thin dark purple line remains.

"Good. Radcliff and Keir, you're dismissed."

Niall and Elese stand and head out.

"Guess we're just the grunts for this mission," Elese jokes as she holds the door open for Niall.

Now it's just me, Beau, Radcliff, and Morgan. The woman hasn't said a word the entire meeting.

"While you two are out gallivanting, Morgan is going to be testing the blockade and annoying Jarren." Radcliff indicates the screen behind him. "Show her the areas you've investigated so she doesn't repeat your efforts and cause suspicion. We'll implement the distraction protocol when you return."

The distraction protocol—that's a cool name.

He stands to leave.

"Now?" I ask.

"Yes, now."

Morgan swivels. There's a terminal in the conference room. Beau and I insert our tangs and scooch our chairs closer. We spend the next couple of hours working with Morgan.

"We decided to test his blockade in a grid pattern," Beau says. "It's boring, but it's a standard security move, and it'll give him the confidence that he can predict where we'll be each day."

Also so he won't be worried about his escape route. He'll believe it's safe until the testing grid gets closer. Hopefully, well before then, we'll have accessed his exit with Jarren none the wiser.

Beau demonstrates what we've been doing to set off the alarms and test the measures Jarren has woven to prevent us from reaching DES. I'm struck again by Jarren's skills and the complexity of the barrier. A niggle of worry digs into my guts as I study his intricate programming.

It would be bad if Jarren learned about our mission to Pit

21. The excavation might bring him back from wherever he's hiding. Those satellite feeds are vital. Radcliff will be monitoring them, but is the security chief up to the task? I think so, but my instincts are nagging me.

Morgan copies Beau's actions and triggers another alarm. I can't help smiling. Those things are annoying when you're in the Q-net. Maybe Jarren would be confident enough to turn them off. A girl can hope.

We finish up and Beau and I return to our units to pack. Except when I'm back in my room, I realize I don't have much to pack. My security jumpsuit has been torn into rags. All I have are my security uniforms, pulse gun and kit, flashlight, and pajamas. I don't even have a bag since I haven't replaced the one Jarren took. Why didn't I think of this sooner? Too distracted by the Q-net. Guess I'll have to ask my parents for supplies.

Except my parents are too busy to join us for dinner. However, when Niall arrives, he's carrying a large black backpack.

Radcliff takes it from him and sets it on the table. He unzips it. "This is your field ruck, Lawrence." Taking out various objects he shows them to me. "Your tent, sunscreen, cap, sunglasses, communicator, binoculars, uniforms, and a jumpsuit." He hands that last one to me.

The stretchy material slides through my fingers with a familiar smoothness. Yet the color is a dark gray and there's a bit of a silver shine to it.

"It's a special material," Niall says when he notices me squinting at the fabric. "The threads are more resistant to sharp edges."

"Wear it under your uniform at all times," Radcliff orders.

Which means going to the washroom will require some gymnastics. I scrunch my nose.

Niall laughs. "It'll keep you warm at night."

"And during the day?"

"Hot as hell, but you'll be in the pit. Much cooler down there." And then his good humor drops and he peers at me in concern.

No doubt thinking about how I'll be down there without backup. His opinion of the usefulness of the techs during a crisis is rather low. I'm a bit more optimistic. They've been in training—not as intense as mine—but like Elese said, it gives you a boost of confidence.

The uniforms are the same as the ones I already have, except the shirt is a light tan color and the tactical pants are a few shades darker—almost brown.

"It's to blend in with the sand," Radcliff says. "You'll need to wear your khaki boots as well."

Oh, so that's what they're for. Radcliff gave me a bunch of stuff that I'd just shoved under my bed. Should have known he has a reason for everything.

"And the communicators are for emergencies only," Radcliff adds. "Even though they don't connect to the Q-net, I don't want Jarren discovering the frequency and listening in, but if HoLFs or the looters attack, use them."

Niall takes off after dinner to get his ruck ready. And Radcliff appears to take a particular pleasure in informing me that in order not to be seen in the base, I'll have to leave for the port much earlier than everyone else.

"When?" I ask.

"Oh-five-thirty."

I don't groan, which I think is a sign I'm maturing. Carrying the backpack to my room, I stuff all my extra uniforms into the ruck along with my pulse kit. No need for pajamas, but I do add in soap, shampoo, and a few personal items. I wonder if Niall's bringing his shampoo, but realize if one of us isn't sleeping, we'll be on duty. Boo.

With nothing left to do, I go to bed early. My dreams start with Niall and his shampoo in a hot steamy shower. The fog obscures his lower half, but I've a nice view of his bare chest. Then the ceiling retracts—like the one in the port—and there's Jarren staring down at us. He fills the sky.

Trying to have a normal life, Little Worm? Dream Jarren asks in my mind. *Don't you know I'm always watching?*

But the satellite—

Is mine along with the camera feeds. Do you really think your security measures are better than mine? I've been doing this for years. And you've been...dead. He holds his hands out to me. *Come see what I've done, Little Worm.*

A part of my mind knows I'm having another nightmare and should slap myself awake. Yet my dream self is too curious for her own damn good. I take Dream Jarren's hands and we soar up to the satellite, flying through the Q-net on invisible wings.

With my new...sight, I spot his fingerprints all over the

programming. Just like he boasted, he's in deep. My measures are not enough to keep him out since I missed most of his tricky little convoluted worm tracks. Pah!

I shoo him away. Dream Jarren smirks, takes a bow, and disappears. I study the complex programming. It's like a map. If I can find a way to reroute it so he'd go in circles, seeing only the empty desert that I recorded before, that would be super cool. I'll also need to include a shortcut just for me to see the real feed. I trace Jarren's intricate codes and the solution forms in my mind.

It'll be a tedious process and I'd rather be dreaming of Niall in the shower. But I see this as a trial run. If it works, I'll use my extra time in the port to implement this bypass. I chug through it. After…I've no idea how long, the Q-net kicks in and helps despite the fact I'm not in my cluster. Must be because this is a dream and strange things happen in dreams all the time—I accept the aid and it finishes in seconds. Show-off.

I'm considering my next move when the screech of my alarm pierces my dream. I fall to Yulin. But I know I'll get a nightmare migraine if I slam back to my body. With effort, I slow and go through the steps to disentangle with my dream. Yes, I know it sounds crazy. Dream, remember? Humor me.

When I wake, I open my eyes slowly. No pain throbs in my head. But my ears are being assaulted. "Alarm off," I say. The instant quiet is blissful. However, I'm now running late.

I dash to the washroom. Radcliff is already dressed and drinking a cup of coffee. He makes a show of glancing at the time. Rushing around, I dress, apply sunscreen, and shrug on the backpack. Its weight almost knocks me off my feet. Good thing we're not hiking.

When I'm ready to go, Radcliff's already waiting for me by the door. Since I'm on time, he keeps the snarky comment that I'm sure he was mentally composing to himself. We head to the port through the deserted hallways.

Glad that he seems content to walk in silence, I review my...er...nightmare. My subconscious must have noticed something wrong when I was worming the satellite feeds. And my worry about this mission brought it to the surface.

Despite the early hour, my parents and the techs are in the port. They're loading equipment into three sand vehicles. The trucks have big oversized tires with lots of nubs that help them gain traction in the sand. Six people can fit in the two rows of seats. No roof, but there's a thick metal roll bar arching over the passenger compartment. Two big spotlights sit on the bar like a pair of mouse ears—it's kind of cute. Behind the seats is a long flatbed that will be filled with the boxes.

Radcliff goes over to talk to my parents, but I find the terminal in the port. I'm not going to be happy until I check the satellite feeds. Not bothering to sit down, I insert my tangs and worm into the satellite. Sure enough, Jarren's little paws are all over. I curse. But then—

The modifications I did in my dream have been implemented. There's a shortcut to the feeds and Jarren is watching the uninhabited sand dunes I recorded earlier. The strength in my body drains and I sink to the floor. Pulling my knees up to my chest, I rest my forehead on them as the room spins.

I entangled with the Q-net while dreaming, without tangs or a terminal nearby. Oh my stars.

2522:214

Not good, not good, not good. The port continues to spin around me. I gulp in air, trying hard not to pass out. This is bad, really bad. Terrifying. I'm a freak. Dying has fried my brains and I'm—

"Ara, why are you on the floor?" Mom asks. "What's wrong?"

I curse under my breath and raise my head. The port tilts under me. Concern flares in Mom's eyes and she crouches next to me. "You're white as a ghost. Lean forward, head between your knees, deep breaths."

I do as instructed.

She rubs my back. "In and out, nice and easy."

Concentrating on the basic task of breathing, I ignore my chaotic thoughts. Eventually the black and white spots in my vision fade and color returns to the world.

"Better?" Mom asks.

"Yes. Thanks."

She helps me straighten. I brace for another wave of dizziness, but the floor remains steady.

"What were you doing?"

Freaking out, having a panic attack, take your pick. "I was checking something in the Q-net. And I...think I moved too fast."

"What was so important it couldn't wait?"

"The safety of the mission."

"Oh."

I explain about the satellite feeds and my solution.

"That's my girl. It's a good thing you checked, then." Mom relaxes and returns to ordering techs to load the trucks faster.

If you must know, no, I didn't share with my mother that I fixed it while dreaming. That still sounds crazy. And now that I'm thinking about it, I could have been...sleep walking last night and accessed a terminal. That's probably it. Since I'm not showing up in the camera feeds, it'd be impossible to verify. Yes, I know all about denial, why do you ask?

After I disentangle, I join Beau and the others. He explains our roles while driving to the camp. I'll be in vehicle three, which Elese is driving. She gives me a wide, slightly manic grin. This ought to be fun.

We insert our communicators in our ears just in case there's an emergency.

Stowing my ruck in the bed, I hop into the back seat. Elese takes her position. Besides us there are three techs and the medic—two in the front and two with me. The large doors of the port roll up. The metal rattles and the wheels squeal as they run up the track. Beau gets into the first truck, which my father is driving. Mom is behind the wheel of the second one with Niall. He also sits in the back.

The engines start up with a roar and we drive out into the cool darkness. Once we clear the port, the door clanks, shutting behind us. The strong peppery scent of Yulin's air fills my lungs. This is the first time I've been outside the base since we arrived. I marvel at the gorgeous night sky before I remember my duty. Standing up, I hold onto the roll bar and use my binoculars to scan the area for any signs of intruders—basically lights. Just ahead, both Niall and Beau are doing the same thing.

The vehicles trundle over the dunes. They're not moving very fast, but they still kick up clouds of sand, which coats the binoculars' lenses, gets into my eyes, nose, and mouth. Ugh. Now I know why Beau picked the first vehicle. We arrive just as the sun is rising.

Securing the camp actually means walking around a large empty area and confirming that yes, it is indeed empty. We also scan for footprints. None, although Niall finds small tracks from what looks like a lizard. Dad takes a picture of them for the biologists.

Then we stand guard as the techs unpack the supplies. I notice Niall has his cap and sunglasses on. Good idea. I dig for mine. Enjoying the fresh air and sunlight, I'm content to just soak it all in. A slight early morning breeze fans my face. Underneath the peppery scent is the dry aroma of anise. While I'm supposed to be focused on the surrounding desert, I sneak glances at the activity in the camp. Techs assemble tents, unload the equipment, and sweat. Between shouting orders and directing the techs, my mom preps the Ground Penetrating Radar. My dad arranges everything, breaking the camp into three specific areas—sleeping, working, and eating. The portable washroom is constructed near the tents.

As the sun creeps toward its zenith, the breeze dies and the air thickens with heat. I scan the horizon with my binoculars and confirm the nothingness out there. Not even another team from the base is nearby.

What I don't do, is think about the Q-net. I can rest easy out here well away from the base and all its terminals. The scientists carry portables that just run the standard plug and chug programming. You can't entangle with a portable because the device is not connected to the Q-net the same way as a terminal. Information can still be exchanged between the Q-net and a portable so all the data collected in Pit 21 will be uploaded to the Q-net when we return to the base. And messages can still be sent from one portable to another.

When Jarren had attacked, I created a worm hole between a portable and the Q-net so I could keep track of the looters through the base's camera feeds. I can't do that out here, which is beneficial. My brain can take a break and I'll be good as new when I return.

When the camp is complete, the techs carry the GPR over to where the pit is supposed to be. The initial scans of the desert marked the long narrow strip of the sixty-four underground pits—think of the planet as a ball and the pits are like a rubber band around its middle—but the accuracy is not always...er...accurate.

Mom uses the GPR to find the edges of the pit. It's square and each side is exactly sixty-four meters wide. Our camp is located to the left of the pit. A smart move. Otherwise, if the roof of the pit collapses, then the entire camp will fall in. Dad marks the edges with flags, and then my parents gather with the techs. Probably discussing the location of the hatch.

Normally, after the research base is built, the robotic diggers go from the underground archeology lab straight into the pits so no sunlight or weather can impact the Warriors. Accessing a pit from above is new. And tricky. They can't make the hole too big or that would risk collapsing the roof and they won't open one right above the Warriors' heads. My guess is they'll dig in a corner.

I do another sweep of the desert's unending expanse and confirm there's still nothing out there. It's a really good thing. Trust me, I don't want Jarren and his looters emerging from the sands. But it's still really boring.

The shovels are unpacked and handed to the eight techs. Dad places more flags in a circle and then shovels the first scoop of sand out before the techs take over. I was right, they picked a corner to dig the hole.

Standing guard is not physically challenging by any means, yet sweat collects under my arms, between my breasts, and dampens my collar. But the tech's shirts are soaked and plastered to their bodies as they work in the hot sun.

When they hit sandstone about a meter down, Dad orders

them out of the hole, which is about two meters wide and roughly circular. Now comes the tricky part. My dad and two techs carry a robotic digger over to the cavity. The thing resembles a round hedgehog about a meter in diameter. I glance at Beau. Does he feel a kinship? His spikes are tucked under his cap. But it's nice to see he's also switching between watching the action and the boring desert.

They insert the digger, turn it on, and step back. The robot puffs up to twice its size. Its spikes grow and dig into the surrounding sand, anchoring it in place. Then it hums and crunches. After a few noisy minutes crushed sandstone is ejected out its…er…rear end. Can't risk having the pieces fall on the Warriors below.

Everyone retreats past the flags to stand on "solid" ground. If something goes wrong with the digger, they won't plummet to their deaths. Mom paces as we wait and wait and wait some more before the digger breaks through. It makes a strange hiccup sound, then climbs from the hole, and sits nearby, retracting its spikes. The desire to pet it and say "good boy" pushes up my throat.

My father gestures me over. Time for my special powers of observation. I don't have the blow-horn but everyone is close enough that they'll hear my shout if I spot shadow-blobs. I stare at the gap. No shadow-blobs appear. No surprise with the sun blazing down on all our heads.

"Do you see anything, Officer Lawrence?" Dad asks.

"No," I manage to choke out because I'm just about to lose it over *my dad* calling *me* Officer Lawrence. Surreal.

We wait some more. When the pit fails to collapse, my dad nods to a young man wearing a safety harness. The tech "swims" out to the hole. Okay, he's doing a low crawl which spreads his weight out. It still looks like swimming to me. Once he reaches the edge he lowers an air testing instrument into the pit. Checking the gauge for any signs of toxins, he releases more and more rope until it hits the bottom.

"It's stale. We'll need to pump some fresh air in there," he declares and swims back.

Another tech lowers a black hose then switches on an air pump. It hums. A breeze flows from the hole. Its cool musty smell reminds me of damp clay. When the air matches the surface conditions the pump is turned off.

Now it's my turn to swim. I don a safety harness—yet another layer. The sand is super hot. The searing heat on my face is like standing in front of an oven with the door open. I'm glad I'm wearing my jumpsuit because I suspect the sand would burn my skin through the fabric of my uniform. I'm not graceful and I suspect everyone is watching my butt wiggle as I swim to the hole.

Reaching the edge, I peer down into the pit. Sand particles float in the beam of sunlight arrowing to the floor. A row of Warriors is visible. It makes my heart happy to see them whole. It's as if the doctor just declared them healthy. Strange. I check the shadows—they circle the pool of light. I wait. No movement.

"Status?" Beau calls.

"Clear for now." I swim back.

"Time to install the hatch," Dad says.

The hatch is basically a hollow pipe about two meters wide and three meters long. One end is open while the other has a cap with a wheel. Turn the wheel, pull, and the cap swings open. Spin it the other way and it locks it. Dad measures the depth of the hole and they trim the pipe to fit. Once that's done, they insert it into the hole and secure it. It's a super tight fit, which I suspect is the point.

After that, they lower two floodlights and I take another peek inside. Still no movement, but lots more Warriors are revealed. Again, I get that extra pump in my heart.

Beau and Niall pull a ladder apart until it's about six meters long. Elese helps them insert it into the hole and hold on as they slide it down. Once it's secure, Beau signals us to pull our flashlights. I tuck the blow-horn in my weapon belt.

"Officer Keir, keep an eye out for unfriendlies." Beau moves to climb down.

"I should go first," I say. "In case I…feel anything. Then we can quickly retreat."

"Feel?"

"Pressure, coldness. Warning signs."

"Oh. Okay."

I grab the ladder with my left hand while holding my flashlight in the other. Taking my time, I climb down. The air cools as I descend. The strong dry desert scent is replaced by a damp mustiness. The ladder vibrates when Beau and then Niall step on. Sand from the bottom of their boots rains on me. Now I'm really glad for my cap. However, I keep my focus and my flashlight on the shadows.

Pausing at the bottom, I try to sense if shadow-blobs are lurking. The air lacks that heaviness and bitter cold.

"Clear." I move so Beau and Niall can join me. Their boots crunch on the layer of sand on the floor.

Behind us is one of the corners of the pit carved out of an unremarkable sandstone. It is smooth and undisturbed, but in front of us is a diagonal row of thirteen Warriors—one of the eight sides of the octagon. The aliens arranged the Warriors into forty-two precise rows in the shape of an octagon. The shortest rows are eighteen Warriors long, and the longest ones contain forty-two Warriors. For a total of one thousand, four hundred, and fifty-two Warriors in one pit. Don't be too impressed with my math skills; these numbers are well known because every pit on every exoplanet discovered so far has the exact same number of Warriors standing in the same configuration.

"Look out below," Dad calls.

Another floodlight is on the way down. Beau and Niall move the two already here. Part of our job will be to set the lights all around the pit, illuminating as much as possible. They're on tripods and can be raised so they're above the Warriors' heads. The statues range in height from one-hundred and eighty-three centimeters to one-hundred and ninety-five centimeters tall. The ceiling of the pit is another two meters higher.

"All right, we'll spread out and check every centimeter of the pit," Beau orders. "Lawrence, signal if you see or feel anything."

"Yes, sir."

Beau's on my left and Niall's on the right, so I head straight into the rows of Terracotta Warriors. They're all Chinese and I've always viewed them as part of my extended family. Plus I practically grew up in Warrior pits so there's a comfort in seeing over a thousand familiar faces.

Their hair is pulled up into knots or hidden under caps. They all wear long coats that reach their knees and have high collars—or they might be scarves as some of them have the ends tied and hanging down like a ribbon. Some wear armor over the coats. The General and the officers all have ribbons on their armor—two in the front and three on the back. The archeologists have identified eight—there's that number again—basic head shapes, but their facial features were sculpted by hand, making millions of individuals. No two are alike.

Most have some type of facial hair—mustaches, beards, and little tear-drop shaped clumps of hair right under their bottom lip. They have wide noses, thin eyebrows, and slanted almond-shaped eyes. Each one stands on his own pedestal—yes, they're all male. And their expressions are all mostly neutral. Except the guys who have peaked eyebrows; they look surprised.

I weave through them, checking shadows and setting floodlights. The pit grows brighter and brighter. It seems warmer as well—a good sign. Sand has drifted around the Warriors' feet. I crunch through the piles, excited to be the first person to see these Warriors in over two thousand years. It almost makes me want to be an archeologist. Almost!

When I go to pick up another floodlight, Beau is waiting at the base of the ladder. Dangling high above us is the next tripod.

"Anything?" he asks me.

"No. It's...nice."

"Nice?"

How to explain? "I haven't felt this comfortable in a Warrior pit since Jarren attacked. And to see them all...whole. It reminds me of when I was younger and..." Safer.

"And what, Mouse?" Niall steps from one of the rows and joins us.

"And when I used to hide behind them, avoiding my mother and the long list of tasks she wanted me to do." I put my hands on my hips. "Sound familiar, Toad? Hiding in the Warriors?" He'd done the same thing to avoid me when we first arrived on Yulin.

"Ah... Look, here's the next light. Love to chat, but I gotta work." He grabs it and heads deeper into the pit.

"Chicken," I call.

Beau laughs, but then sobers as he studies the statues. "The way they stare straight ahead is kind of creepy. I can't imagine growing up surrounded by Warriors."

"Strange, I can't imagine my life without them. My brother and I used to play around them—hide and seek, tag..." A sudden pang of grief hits me.

"Brother?"

"Yeah, Phoenix, he's in a time jump to Earth." And here's another quirk of living with the time dilation. No one asks you about your family for fear of upsetting you. Instead they wait until you mention someone and then ask, figuring since you brought the subject up, it should be safe.

"That's rough. Why did he leave?"

"He wants to be an archeologist like my parents."

"Why couldn't he stay and learn from them? Aren't they the best?"

"They think so." My smile fades. "But anyone who wishes to be more than a tech has to study at the site on Earth." My parents were thrilled and devastated at the same time. Sad days, indeed.

"You can always catch up to him."

True, but that means leaving lots of other people far in the past.

The next light arrives and Beau snags it before me. I stick my tongue out at him.

"Brat," he says.

While I'm waiting, I scan the shadows. Still just normal shadows.

"How's it going?" Mom calls.

I glance up into the brightness. A dark silhouette peers down at me.

"Good so far."

"Wonderful. This next light needs to be installed in the center of the pit. It's multidirectional and should work well there."

"Okay."

She disappears and the light makes its slow descent. Nothing moves fast in archeology. Unlike navigating the stars, but that's unlike anything else I've done. And, if I survive Jarren and whatever he has planned, I can become a navigator. But is it worth never seeing my family again? The next Interstellar Class space ship doesn't arrive for another three and a half E-years, so I've plenty of time to decide on my future.

Once the light settles on the sand, I unhook it and pick it up. Ugh. It's heavier than the others. I head toward the center of the pit. There's a gap there. It's another mystery. At the very core of the rows and columns of Warriors is an open space. It's octagonal and about two meters wide. No one has figured out why it's there. Just like no one knows why the Warriors are standing in an octagonal-shaped formation, or why there are about a dozen other differences between the alien sites and the one on Earth.

I pause. Or why they have hearts. Unless Lan's theory is correct, then we do know why, but not how it works. It seems the more we learn about the Warriors, the more questions pop up. It's frustrating, which is why archeology isn't high on my future career list. At least we can check to see if these Warriors have hearts. Actually...I glance around, I know they do have hearts. I've no idea why I'm so certain, but these Warriors are...not *alive*, 'cause that would be beyond crazy, but...ready.

When I reach the edge of the gap, I slow. The statues around the gap might have special symbols on them and I don't want to disturb anything. Not that I can knock a Warrior off its feet—they weigh about 295 kilograms. But after a lifetime of being careful, it's a hard habit to break.

I'm looking at the ground so I don't trip over a drift of sand when I spot them. I freeze. Astounded is too mild a word, but I'm at a loss to find a better descriptor. Coherent thought is difficult.

Wait. There has to be a reasonable, scientific explanation. I scan the surrounding area. Nothing but undisturbed sand. I'm staring at an impossibility.

Setting the light down, I swallow to dislodge the knot in my throat, and take a deep breath. "Beau, Niall, come here!" I shout. According to Radcliff's specifications, this isn't an emergency—it just feels like one.

"Where are you?" Beau asks from my left.

"Center of the pit," I say. "But don't go past the Warriors."

"Why not? Are there HoLFs?" Niall asks from behind me.

"No."

Niall reaches me first. He halts at the edge. His pulse gun is in one hand, a flashlight in the other. "What's wrong?"

Beau joins him a second later. He, too, is armed. "Talk to us, Lawrence."

Instead, I point to the exact center of the gap. Surrounded by the smooth and undisturbed sand is a single set of boot prints.

2522:214

"That's it? You got us all worried over footprints?" Beau holsters his gun, relaxing. "Radcliff and I have been walking all over the pit."

But Niall remains alert. "I haven't been in the center, have you?" he asks Beau.

"Well, no, but—"

"Look closer," I say. "There's no other prints."

"So? There's sand everywhere. Must have covered them up."

For some reason Beau is being particularly dense. "No one's been in here in over two thousand years. And the ridges of the prints are well defined."

"So you're saying someone has entered this pit recently and didn't make any tracks except for smack dab in the middle?" Beau's tone suggests I've lost my mind.

Considering what happened last night with the Q-net he's probably not wrong.

"Think about it, Dorey," Niall says.

"What's there to think about? Lawrence is playing a trick on us. Nice one, you did a great job erasing your tracks. Can we get back to work now?" Beau heads off muttering under his breath.

I turn to Niall. "I didn't—"

"I know. They're much bigger than your feet. Stay here, let me check something." Niall points his flashlight at the ground as he weaves through the Warriors, doing a loop around the gap. "There's no other prints like that one. Did you see any others when you were setting lights?"

"No, but I wasn't really looking for them."

"I was, and I didn't see any. And if someone did erase them, then why leave one behind?" Niall asks.

"Maybe he missed it? Could it be from one of Jarren's looters?" I ask, still a bit flabbergasted.

"Then there would be lots of destruction."

Good point. A scary thought pops into my head. "What if it's a scout checking out the pit and he's planning on returning with reinforcements!"

"If that's the case, how did he get in here?"

"Through one of the walls. Have we checked them all?"

"I looped around the back, but let's look again."

I leave the light and follow Niall. We inspect the walls of the pit. They're all the same sandstone with no evidence that anyone tampered with them. Unless Jarren's thugs can walk through walls, no one entered through them. We return to the center. The set of prints is still there.

"What do we do next?" I ask.

"Report this to your parents."

Beau isn't happy about interrupting the plan. "We haven't confirmed it's safe yet."

"There's no HoLFs. And no one else is down here," I say.

"Are you sure? The person who made that footprint could be hiding in here."

I refrain from asking him how this person entered the pit. Beau orders us to do another two sweeps of the pit before he allows Niall to call up to my parents.

"Dr. and Mr. Daniels, can you please join us?" Niall asks.

"What's the matter?" Mom immediately asks.

"There's no need for concern. We'd like to get your opinion on something."

Something. Talk about vague.

Fortunately, my parents get the hint and stop asking questions. My mom mounts the ladder, followed by my dad. They join us at the base.

"What's going on?" Mom asks.

"We found something," Niall says. "Come on, we'll show you."

As soon as my mom sees the first Warrior, she exclaims and stops to inspect it.

"We'll have plenty of time later, Ming." Dad pulls her away.

"But—"

If I wasn't so freaked, I'd be amused watching my father tow my mother through the Warriors like she's a misbehaving child.

When we arrive at the center, I let Niall explain. My parents' confusion doesn't last long and they ask all the same questions we did. We show them the walls and they circle the gap, searching for more prints.

My mom swipes a strand of long black hair that escaped from her braid. "The only explanation is that a person appeared in the center of this pit, stood there, and then disappeared. Of course, it's impossible, but that's what fits." Her tone is practical as if this type of thing happens every day.

No one argues.

Dad looks at Beau. "Do you think we're in danger?"

Beau takes off his cap and runs a hand over the limp strands of his hair. "Let's say you're right and the person just popped in and popped out. The biggest danger is if the person returns and has a weapon. Or more than one person arrives and surprises us." He gestures to the center with his cap. "Since teleportation is impossible, the odds of that scenario happening are very small. However, I think it would be prudent to have Officer Lawrence stationed in this location during the day. She can watch for HoLFs and for the magician."

"Magician?" Mom asks, giving Beau a sharp look.

"Yeah, you know. Now, I'm going to disappear before your very eyes." He waves his hand in a grand sweeping gesture. "Presto!"

Dad laughs. Mom's still not amused. Niall and I cover our grins. What else can we do? It's crazy and yet another mystery added to the long list of unknowns. Might as well have some fun.

Mom leads the way back to the ladder. Once there she calls

up, "Fred, tell Regan to grab a 3D digitizer and come down here."

Two more floodlights have arrived and Niall and Beau take them. We're almost done setting them. Regan soon climbs down. She's clutching the digitizer to her chest as if it's a shield. The tech looks at me.

"It's safe," I say.

She loosens her grip and the tense line of her shoulders relaxes. Mom leads her to the center. Curious, I follow.

"I want you to scan that print in the sand. Once you finish, return to the surface so you can send the image file to Officer Tace Radcliff. Have him check it against the boots of his prisoners."

Regan gives my mom a wide-eyed stare, but recovers and starts fiddling with the switches on the digitizer—it resembles an oversized camera.

I lean close to Mom. "That's a good idea. Do you think Jarren's looters might have been in here?"

"I don't know, but it's worth looking into. Even if they don't match, we'll still know more than we do now."

True.

The rest of the floodlights arrive and the three of us set them. I move the multidirectional one closer to the prints, but not in the very center. The pit is ablaze with white light from all directions. The Warriors' shadows are either short or diffuse. The shadow-blobs would have to work really hard to hide in here.

I walk through the Warriors until I find the General in the

first row. His official position is R1, C21 (there are also forty-two columns). Standing in front of him, I study him. The generals are always the tallest of the Warriors. He's clasping his hands in front of him with his coat's sleeves pushed up. Like all the generals in the army, he's wearing a pheasant-tailed cap, which resembles one of those fancy folded napkins that are placed on the table during special dinners. This general's mustache looks like a flattened letter M with the ends curled up. He has mutton chops and a square-ish shaped head.

The General gazes forward, as if watching for the enemy. I sense all is well with the Warriors. It's...calming. Strange, I know.

"Thirty minutes to sunset," Elese calls down.

That is the agreed-upon time for everyone to start exiting the pit. Regan finished her scan and has already gone to the surface. My mom straightens from her inspection of one of the Warriors. She wipes sand from her knees. Frowning, she marches up to Beau. This ought to be good.

"There's plenty of light down here. Ara said it's safe, I want to—"

"No." Beau uses his I'm-in-command voice. "We won't be deviating from protocol, Dr. Daniels."

She stiffens. "I'm in charge of the expedition."

"And I'm responsible for everyone's lives."

"We're safer down here." Mom gestures to the lights. "It's

dark at night. Plenty of shadows in camp."

I wonder if Mom planned this all along.

"None of the research field teams has reported an attack in the desert," Beau counters with ease. "All our experience with the HoLFs has been in the Warrior pits."

Did Radcliff anticipate my mom would try something like this?

Mom crosses her arms. "In the *destroyed* Warrior pits."

"Irrelevant. Please evacuate or I'll have you escorted out."

I freeze in place. Would I have to draw my weapon on my mother? More importantly, could I? I am a security officer and it's my job to ensure everyone stays safe. But she's my mom! Except, this time, she's not considering what's best for everyone. So…yes, I could. Mom glances at me and then Niall, who has joined us. She must see something in our expressions because she relents.

"Come on, Spencer. We need to brief the teams for the morning." She grabs the ladder and climbs up.

Dad gives us a little salute and then follows her.

When they disappear above, Beau lets out a long breath. "You two go up, I'll be last."

Niall gestures for me to go first. I put my foot on the bottom rung of the ladder. The lights will stay on even though the pit will be empty. Seems a waste of batteries. But preventing shadow-blobs from invading while we're sleeping is worth a few batteries. What about invading boots? I stop as an idea occurs to me.

"What now?" Beau asks.

"I think we should erase those boot prints," I say.

"Why?"

"If the person returns tonight then we'll know."

"You don't think he will leave another set?" Niall asks.

"He could, but this way it'll be clearer."

"All right, I'll go." Beau hurries off.

Niall and I wait for him.

"Did you notice the symbols on the Warriors around the gap?" Niall asks, tilting his head toward the center of the pit.

"No. I was busy being freaked out by the magical boot prints."

He smiles. "At least they weren't alien footprints."

Good point. Except… "We can't assume that. Aliens might wear boots." I gesture to the Warriors. "The aliens chose them to act as protectors. Why? Perhaps because they are similar in appearance."

"Or the Warriors could be the aliens' equivalent to guardian lions."

"Oooh. Nice!" We share a grin. And then I remember. "What about the symbols?"

"I recognized a bunch of the ones that correspond to the different Warrior planets that Lan discovered. If I give you some paper and chalk, could you make some etchings of them while you're waiting for the boot-wearing magician to reappear?"

"Yes, I can."

Beau joins us. He's wiping his hands off on his pants. "I've a feeling I'm going to hate sand by the end of this assignment."

"No doubt about that. Those little grains manage to get into everything and then they find their friends and soon you'll have handfuls in your boots, pockets, underwear."

"Speaking from experience?" Niall asks.

"Unfortunately."

"Fifteen minutes," Elese calls down.

We climb up the ladder and my dad seals the hatch. The air is dry compared to inside the pit and it's cooling. Bright orange, yellow, and gold paint the western horizon. Next to the dig site the techs are prepping for tomorrow, assembling equipment and planning work shifts. The heavenly aroma of cooking food drifts from the mess tent like invisible tentacles reaching out to grab the unwary. Caught, saliva fills my mouth as my stomach growls loud enough for the others to hear. I haven't eaten all day.

"Didn't you pack some energy bars?" Niall asks me.

"I…didn't know I should."

"Rookies," Elese says, with a smile.

"Good thing I have plenty." Beau hands me a bunch.

"Thanks." I tuck them into the various pockets in my tactical pants. Handy.

He grunts. "Okay, time for a team meeting. We have sixteen hours of darkness to cover between the four of us. We'll each cover eight hours. Lawrence and I will team up and Radcliff and Keir will be the second team."

I glance at the mess tent with longing then at the portable washroom.

"Relax, Lawrence. It's not a consecutive eight hours. After spending all day in the pits, you'll get two hours to eat and clean up," Beau says. "Then you'll have six hours on duty."

Whew.

Beau glances at me and then Radcliff. "Tell you what. You and Niall get dinner now. Kier and I will keep an eye on the camp. Then Radcliff can fill in for me the next two hours while Kier and I take a break. Sound good?"

"Yes, sir," we say in unison, and hurry off before he changes his mind.

"At least we can eat together," Niall says.

I wouldn't mind showering together either, but my parents would mind very much. "Yeah, nice of him to switch it up for those two hours. It'll be our only time together. Do you think your dad told Beau to keep us apart?"

"No. You're teamed up with Beau because he has the most experience and you have the least. It's a standard strategy. You shouldn't put two inexperienced people together."

"That makes sense."

"There's a reason for everything, Mouse."

I huff. "Including magical boot prints?"

"Yes. We just don't know what it is yet."

"I wish I had your optimism, Toad." I take his hand. It's dark and I don't care who sees us. This is the only physical contact we'll have for the next ten days.

Niall must agree since he doesn't pull away.

The food is standard base food, but it always tastes better when you're starving. Otherwise, it doesn't compare to

Radcliff's cooking. I grab a clean uniform before showering. The lukewarm water is on a timer so I don't dawdle. I'm reluctant to squirm into my jumpsuit after sweating in it all day. Ugh. Pulling it off the hook in the changing room, I sniff the material. It's not rank. Odd.

After my shower, I have enough time to visit my parents before I'm on duty again. I enter the command center. Don't be too impressed. It's an oversized tent that has a couple tables for meetings on the right side and a double sized sleeping mat for my parents on the left. They're alone—probably not for long.

"There's my girl," Dad says, sweeping me into a hug. "Did you come to check on your mother? Make sure she's not plotting to sneak back into the pit?" There's a gleam in his brown eyes.

"Spencer," Mom says.

He ignores her. "She was just testing the limits, like a toddler, seeing what she can get away with."

"Spencer." There's more force behind it this time.

"Sorry, Ming." He winks at me—not sorry at all.

My father's been in high spirits since my parents learned Lan translated the alien symbols.

I change the subject before Mom kicks him out of the tent. "Did you figure out a plan for tomorrow?" I ask.

Now Mom's face lights up. She looks ten years younger. "Cataloging of course, and digitizing the statues. And we're going to pay particular attention to the symbols on the Warriors. I just wish..." Her excitement dims a bit.

"You had all of Lan's research notes," I say.

"Yes. It's such a phenomenal step in the right direction. Finally! And, at the same time, it's so very frustrating. You've no idea."

Oh, yes I do. Probably just as frustrating as being interrupted every time Niall and I are alone together.

"At least we're actually here," she says. "And can get some work done. Real work. I only wish…" Mom hugs her arms to her chest.

"That Phoenix was here?" I finish for her.

"Yes. He would have loved all of this."

"I know, the three of you would have geeked out together," I mock grumble.

"You can't pretend that you're not excited, too," Dad says to me.

"Well, I'm excited for Lan. And I plan, when I have time, to find all her notes for you." And for her. She deserves full credit and I'm going to do everything I can to make sure she gets it.

"We have no doubt you will," Dad says. "What we're not sure of is…"

Uh oh. I hold my breath.

"If you would have pulled your weapon on your *mother.*"

"Spencer!"

I assume a serious demeanor. "I have my orders. If Dr. Daniels is not following proper security protocols, then I will *ensure* that she does."

"Ara!" Mom jabs her finger at the tent's flap. "That's enough from both of you. Out!"

We bolt. Stopping far from the tent, Dad and I share a fit of giggles. After we recover, Dad goes to check on the techs and I find Niall so we can relieve Beau and Elese.

When they head to the mess tent, I ask Niall about the weirdly smell-proof jumpsuit.

"It's that special fabric. As long as you air it out every day it stays pretty clean. If you wear it non-stop for a couple days, it'll stink," he says.

"Speaking from experience?"

"Unfortunately."

We share a smile before parting ways and patrolling the edges of the camp. I don't turn on my flashlight. Instead, I let my eyes adjust to the semi-darkness. There's a glow from the camp so it's not pitch dark. Eventually, Beau relieves Niall. For a while it's not too bad since there's activity in the camp. But once everyone goes to sleep, silence descends. And boredom sets in. To keep alert, I alternate between staring out at the empty desert and gazing at the awesome display of stars. With no clouds, no light pollution, and no haze, there's more white in the sky than black. Also helping to keep me awake is the quickly dropping temperature as the day's heat radiates out to space. I'm glad to have the extra layer. Niall's right—the jumpsuit is warm.

My shift extends into an eternity. By the time Elese relieves me, I'm an old lady. Okay, that's an exaggeration, but six hours of nothing but my thoughts is torture.

"Any problems?" she asks while yawning and stretching her long arms.

"No. Nothing. Zero problems. Am I a bad person if I spent some of my time tonight wishing for some excitement?"

"Not a bad person. But you know the old adage, be careful what you wish for."

"Yeah, yeah. Enjoy the boredom." I wave and trudge to my tent, 'cause it's been a very long day.

It's warm inside my tent. The material resists wind, sand, and is waterproof. I debate if I should take off my jumpsuit and let it air out. But if there's an incident, then I'd need to rush to the rescue. Best to leave it on. I slide under the blankets and squirm into a comfortable position.

Sand is a pain in the ass except in one situation—when you're sleeping on it. Then it's soft and molds to your body. Ahhh…

I'm the first to go into the pits in the morning. Pausing at the bottom of the ladder, I test the air for signs of shadow-blobs—nothing—then I head straight to the center. The fake eggs and toast I ate for breakfast churns in my stomach. I've drawn my pulse gun without any conscious decision to do so. Sand crunches loudly under my boots. Too loud. I slow, easing to the edge of the gap. No new footprints. My relief is so strong, I almost stagger.

Looping around the pit to ensure there's no shadow-blobs hiding, I return to the ladder to call the all clear. My parents and the techs descend. Mom shouts orders and the techs begin scanning the Warriors with the 3D digitizers. They've been told to avoid the middle.

I stay out of the way and keep watch. But I don't remain in the gap or I'd go insane with boredom. Instead, I patrol between stretches in the center. Well, I don't stand right in the middle, just in case the magician pops up. I hover at the edges.

There are twelve Warriors around the gap. Alien symbols and Chinese calligraphy decorate their armor. At first glance, the two kinds of marks appear to be similar, but once you know the differences they no longer look alike. The alien symbols were etched on an octagonal terracotta box that I reconstructed before I left Xinji and, in time, Lan was able to use that box to translate them.

Niall was right. The Warriors around the gap have the special alien glyphs. If the looters broke into this pit, would they save these and destroy the rest? My inner guardian lion growls at the thought of these Warriors being harmed.

Beau brings me lunch and offers to stand watch while I eat— nice of him. When I finish, I ask him to stay a few more minutes so I can make the etchings for Niall. I only need to do eight Warriors, since the four in the corners don't have any of the alien symbols, which makes sense since it's a combination of eight glyphs that represent another Warrior planet. The order isn't important because only those ones together equal that planet.

It's easy to do an etching, just hold the paper over the symbol and rub lightly with the side of the chalk. Niall gave me the black chalk so there's a nice contrast against the white rice paper. I'm careful not to touch the Warriors as my mother has ingrained in me that the oils on my hands could damage the terracotta. The techs wear gloves. However, when I'm on the fifth one, the paper rips and my knuckles brush the surface.

Three things happen at once.

A zap of extreme cold shoots up my right arm.

I scrape my knuckles bloody.

And the alien symbol fills with a bright green light.

2522:215

I stare at the glowing glyph in shock. Green light fills the grooves. Impossible except…there it is. Hugging my right arm to my chest, I rub it, trying to ease the bone-deep ache from the cold.

"Is that supposed to happen?" Beau asks.

I startle at the sound of his voice. My brain registers that, no, the world as I know it hasn't ended, it just flipped upside down, and, yes, there are other people here. I turn to him. "Get my parents, please." My voice is weak and shaky.

"Are you all right?" He steps toward me with his hand extended.

I jerk back. "Don't."

He stops and a hurt expression crosses his face. "Sorry."

"It's not that. I touched the light. I might be contaminated."

"Oh. Okay." Beau dashes away.

The muscles in my legs decide to quit working. I sit on the

ground. And by the way my heart is racing, I fear a panic attack is imminent. Why does this keep happening to me? As if answering my question, the ice in my arm disappears. I wish I'd never touched that black Warrior heart and instead listened to my mother.

"What in the world could be so—" My mom skids to a stop with her mouth open.

"Ming, what—" My father's brown eyes widen until they're as big as twin moons.

They gape before pulling their gazes from the glowing glyph. It appears to be an effort, and, while my parents peer at me, I don't think they're really seeing me. Almost immediately, the spectacle recaptures their attention. I wait, but it doesn't take them long to partially recover from the shock.

"What…how…" Mom steps closer with an arm outstretched. She halts centimeters before the glyph as her archeological instincts kick in.

Normally, I'd be amused to see my mother in such a state. This time, it just adds to my panic.

"I touched the Warrior by accident." I explain what happened.

My dad blinks then shakes his head as if waking from a daydream. "That's it?"

"HoLFs?" Beau asks me.

"No."

Mom holds out her palm in front of the light. The symbol shines on her skin. "It doesn't burn." Mom leans with her head to the side. "No hum or other mechanical noise."

"Did you hear anything when it turned on?" Dad asks me.

"No, just felt a stab of cold." I'm still clutching my wrist.

"Like when you touched the heart?"

"Yes."

Mom presses her bare hand to the Warrior. Nothing happens. Then she tries the one next to it. Still nothing.

"Spencer, gather the techs and have them search all the Warriors for more glows."

Dad takes off, shouting for the techs to assemble.

"Do you want me to try?" I ask, pointing to the second one.

She clasps her hands together. "We don't know if this is…benign, or dangerous."

Her comment sends my thoughts spiraling. What if I just turned it on and it is going to explode? No, there would be evidence of explosives in other pits, especially the ones that have broken Warriors. Seems my imagination has ventured out from where it fled.

"What if I touch that one again? See what happens."

My mom glances at Beau.

"Is there any way to tell what might happen?" he asks.

"No," Mom says.

"Then it's the only way to figure it out. Go ahead, Lawrence." Beau draws his pulse gun and flashlight.

Bracing for another zap of intense cold, I brush my fingertips on the Warrior. The glow dies. No spark or zap or anything. It's rather disappointing. And that's when the techs appear.

"What happened?" Dad asks.

Instead of answering, I touch the Warrior again. The light returns and the techs gasp in unison. I flex my fingers a couple times, but they're fine. It takes a few minutes to update the techs. A few try "turning on" the other Warriors, but nothing happens. Guess you need to have touched a Warrior heart in order to wake them. But now the big question is: can I do it again?

I stand, brush the sand from my pants, and tap the Warrior beside the glowing one. Icy pain shoots up my arm. Yelping, I step back, just as the alien glyph flares with green light. Gasps ring and I need to sit down again.

"Go check to see if any others are lit," Mom orders the techs.

They scatter in twelve different directions.

My dad crouches next to me. "You okay?"

"Just need…a minute."

He settles next to me, rubbing my upper arm. "Deep breaths."

By the time the pain dissipates, the techs have returned. No others are glowing.

"The Warriors around the gap must be important," Mom says to no one in particular. "Any conjectures?" she asks the techs.

They offer a few guesses, but I'm no longer listening. Since I'm sitting on the ground, I've a good view of the smooth spot of sand that use to be marked with a pair of boots. What if the lights have something to do with those prints? I scan the Warriors around me. What if I wake all eight of them? Would a person appear in the center? Yes, I know it's a big leap in logic and doesn't follow any known laws of physics. But deep inside me is an instinctual need to test my theory.

"Dad," I whisper.

He pulls his attention from the discussion. "Yes?"

I explain my idea. Dad pales, which is quite the feat considering his skin is the color of alabaster.

"Too dangerous…yet…" He touches the hilt of his pulse gun.

Ah, he's tempted. After a few moments, Dad waves Beau over.

"Does her arm still hurt?" Beau asks. "Should I fetch the medic?"

"She's fine." My dad fills him in on my theory, but Beau's shaking his head no before Dad can finish.

"We can evacuate all the techs, you can bring your full team down here, and the trained techs will stand guard on the surface," Dad tries. "This is the first time *anything* has happened with the Warriors; we need to investigate every possibility."

"I can be ready to turn off one of the symbols if things go sideways," I say.

Beau hesitates. "We need to consult with Dr. Daniels."

My mother doesn't need as much convincing. She's willing to try. Of course, I didn't remind them that each touch will cause me a great deal of pain. The techs are sent topside. Niall and Elese join us below and are briefed.

"This is highly dangerous," Niall says. "We need to bring in the astrophysicists to study this first, and then consult with them and my father before testing anything."

He's right. That's the smart thing to do. Sure that they'll agree, I glance at my parents. My mother's cheeks are flushed with excitement, and she's tense with determination. I wonder if that's what I look like when I'm being stubborn.

"By the time we study and consult with everyone, this phenomenon might disappear," she says. "This will just be a quick test. If nothing happens, then we'll rule out one theory."

Deep down, I suspect this isn't temporary, but I keep it to myself. Yes, I'm excited and don't want to wait either.

"Come on, Radcliff, where's your sense of adventure?" Elese asks, which is the wrong thing to say.

He stiffens. "If we do this, I want it noted that I advised against it."

Everyone glances at Beau. It's his decision.

"Noted. We'll do this," he says. "Everyone aim your weapon at the middle of the gap. If the magician appears, stun him. Lawrence, if you sense anything amiss, you turn it off. I want your hand a centimeter above the last Warrior."

My parents, Niall, Beau, and Elese all spread out, surrounding the center but standing between the Warriors. I brace for the pain as I reach for the next Warrior. It's just as bad, but I keep from wincing as another green light shines. However, the next one doesn't add any new pain. Bonus! I wake the other four in quick succession. Then stand right next to that last Warrior, ready to touch it again. I have my pulse gun in my other hand. My heart bounces in my chest. Did I just kill everyone?

We wait in a tense silence. There are no sounds. No

additional lights. No sudden appearance of the magician or his boots. Nothing.

Five minutes later, still nothing.

Ten minutes, and nothing.

"How long are we going to wait?" Beau asks.

"A few more minutes," Mom says.

I'm torn between disappointment and relief. Besides, just because I have a gut feeling doesn't mean— A small black oval hovers over the center of the gap. It expands. My lungs stop working.

"Does anyone else see a black shape?" I ask with a squeak.

"Yes. Is it a HoLF?" Beau asks.

"No."

The blackness grows until it's about as tall and wide as a Warrior. The hair on the back of my neck stands on end. Niall is opposite of me and, behind him, a wave of green light rises, washing out the white floodlights.

"The Warriors," Mom gasps. "They're all glowing!"

"Lawrence?" Beau asks in a tight growl.

"Still no sign of hostiles." But I sense a state of readiness from the Warriors. Focusing on the blackness, I strain to see inside its depths. The temperature drops and the air thickens, growing heavy. Both signals of shadow-blobs. Yet, I don't spot any.

The edges of the blackness pulse as if something inside it is straining to break through. Another wave of green light crests. It's almost as if the Warriors are pushing against the shadow-blobs. Maybe fighting them or protecting us. After a few more waves, the blackness stills. The edges sharpen into a rectangle.

The blackness dilutes and it's like peering through a window. And I spot— I slam my hand down on the Warrior. All the green lights from the Warriors in the pit go out except the seven statues around the gap. The blackness shrinks to fist-sized and winks out of existence.

"What happened, Lawrence?" Beau asks.

"I saw…"

"Don't keep us in suspense."

Unwilling to influence them, I ask, "Did anyone else see anything inside the black rectangle?"

"Just more blackness, but I thought seeing that was exciting enough," Mom says.

I scan their faces; everyone agrees with my mother. They also haven't moved since I ended the experiment.

"What did you see?" Beau asks me.

"I saw the back of a person, standing in another Warrior pit."

I can't say they didn't believe me, because the last time I claimed I saw something that they couldn't, I ended up being right. Yet there's a general sense of disbelief.

"Was the person human?" Dad asks.

"Yes."

"Then why did you turn off the lights?"

"Because he could have been one of Jarren's looters." And it was a knee-jerk reaction.

Silence.

"Let's say that the blackness is a portal to another Warrior Pit," Mom says.

"That's a super huge leap, Ming."

"I'm speculating. It would explain how the looters have been getting around without using a space ship."

"Unless there's no air in there. Or if it leads to an alternate dimension," Dad says. "At this point we've no idea."

"What was with the light show?" Elese asks.

"Could be an energy source," Mom says.

"That's ridiculous, we haven't found anything inside the Warriors that would suggest they're capable of doing...well, anything!" Dad shoves his gun back into the holder on his belt.

"There's hearts inside the Warriors," I say. Recalling the sequence of events, I try to pinpoint when the lights flared. "I think the HoLFs might have tried to get through and the Warriors stopped them, maybe even helped to create a safe passage."

"Did you see ghosts?" Niall asks.

The ghosts in the factory seemed to keep the shadow-blobs away when we were attacked. "No, it was too bright, but I sensed the struggle."

"This is all pure conjecture," Dad says. "And once again, we're no closer to any answers. We need to bring the astrophysicists here and let them figure out what the hell is going on."

"Maybe we should open another intact pit and check if there are boot prints there," Mom suggests.

"Not without Officer Radcliff's permission," Beau says. "I suspect I'm already in trouble for allowing this deviation from protocol."

And I suspect we're *all* going to be in trouble. From their queasy expressions, so do my parents. Perhaps we can blame gold fever.

"All right." Mom returns the pulse gun and her flashlight to her belt. "We'll proceed as normal in this pit and won't do any more testing of the alien glyphs. Spencer, send word of the…glowing symbols to Dr. Carson and request that she and Dr. Zhang come out here. Ara, please turn the rest of these off before the techs return."

"My team, as you were," Beau orders.

Before Niall heads to the ladder, he gives me a significant look. It promises that we have much to discuss later and he's not happy. I go around and turn off the Warriors. Now that the excitement is past, the ache in my arm comes to life and my knuckles sting.

"You okay?" Beau asks.

I roll my shoulder. "It'll go away."

"Did anything escape that portal?"

"No. The pit's still safe." More than safe. Protected. Huh. Another idea pops into my head. One of these is going to kill me if my colleagues don't do it first. "If we relocate a bunch of these Warriors to our destroyed pits, they might keep the HoLFs at bay."

Beau sighs. "There are so many things wrong with that sentence." He rubs his face. "Okay, I'll bite. If we did that,

230

would you go into the pits and risk your life?"

Would I? I glance around at the imposing figures of the Warriors. "Yes, I would."

"Good to know."

I finish my etchings without causing another mind-blowing discovery. Beau goes topside and I resume my duties while thinking about the glowing glyphs and the portal—yes, it was a portal. I know what I saw. Would the Warriors in Pit 21 glow if the magician returned? Or do the glyphs only glow when opening a portal from this side? The person's back was turned to the portal. If the lights in their pit turned on, you would think they would have spun to look to see who's coming through. Unless they didn't have time. Either way, I hope that person isn't working for Jarren.

Elese calls down the thirty-minute warning, jarring me from my thoughts. Planet Yulin turns on its axis once every twenty-nine Earth hours. It has enough of a tilt that right now the sun is up for thirteen hours and down for sixteen. Inside the base, the difference between Yulin and Earth isn't noticeable, but out here, it's...strange. Good thing we don't start right when the sun rises, or else it'd be a very long day down in that pit.

Niall is waiting for me when I exit. We stay until Dad seals the hatch before heading to the mess tent.

After a couple minutes of silence, Niall says rather gruffly, "I can't believe Beau authorized that test. What the hell was he thinking?"

"I suspect he wasn't," I say.

"What do you mean?"

"Excitement is contagious. We all got a case of gold fever."

"Gold fever?" Niall lifts an eyebrow.

"It happened on Earth a long time ago. They discovered gold and everyone went crazy trying to mine it. The moral of the story is they made bad decisions."

"Over gold?"

"Yes. And that's what happened today. We were blinded by the light. Except you—the sensible one."

Niall grunts.

"You gotta admit it was super exciting." I do a little skip.

"It was super dangerous. My father is going to explode."

My good mood sours. We reach the mess tent, fill our plates with…what appears to be the exact same menu as last night—lovely—and find an empty spot to sit. We eat in silence. Halfway through the meal I remember the etchings and pull them from my pocket.

Spreading them out on the table, I say, "At least we can figure out what planet these symbols represent."

Niall studies them. "I wish I'd brought my sketchbook. Guess we'll have to wait until we get back to determine which one."

"My mom should have the files on her portable."

"But there's no terminal for the Q-net."

"We don't need it. Remember the colored-octagon project?"

"The one we never finished."

"Details, details." I wave a hand. "My point is we kept the data from that project on Mom's portable and didn't send it to DES because we suspected Jarren was monitoring our files." Little did we know he was also blocking them.

"Your mom has to report to my father about today. What are the chances of your mother letting us borrow her portable?"

"Are you going to counter everything I say?"

"I am the sensible one."

"No, you're being Mr. Negative. We'll get nothing if we don't ask. Besides, we only need the portable for a minute or two."

We finish dinner and head to the command center. As soon as I enter, I get the parental once-over. Yes, I'm fine. No, the arm doesn't hurt.

When they're satisfied, my mother says, "I'm glad you're here. I need you to clarify a few things for me about the…incident this afternoon."

Niall gives me a smug look.

"I'm happy to help, Mom. In fact, if you let me borrow your portable for a couple minutes, I can tell you what planet those symbols represent." Now it's my turn to give Niall a smug smile.

"You can do that?" Not waiting for an answer, she hands me her portable.

"Yes." I bypass her files and access the ones Niall and I made for each pit on Planets Xi'an and Anqing. We didn't have time to finish the others. Once I reach the colored octagon files, I realize it's going to take me longer than I thought. I need to look at every single pit until I find the one that matches.

I bring up the first pit and glance at the etchings, comparing the two. Nope. On to pit two. Nope. Pit three. No. Four. Nada. Five. I wish I could access my Q-cluster. It would have this done in— The portable's screen blurs and is replaced by the Q-net's vast landscape as if I'd just inserted my entanglers. I didn't. In fact, they're in my pack, in my tent. And the closest terminal is over twenty kilometers away. My Q-cluster pulls in the file I'd just been looking at. I swallow as it takes over comparing the symbols.

How I reached the Q-net from the middle of the desert is…I've no words. I swallow again. The cluster matches the symbols in seconds. It's Planet Dongguan—one of the closed Warrior planets, which means no one is living in the research base, therefore, no one should be in the pits.

A strange spinning sensation causes my stomach to flutter as I'm disconnected from the Q-cluster. My vision once again focuses on the portable's screen. Its edges dig into my palm.

"Ara? Something wrong?" Mom asks.

Oh yes, lots of things. Like the fact your daughter has massive brain damage. I draw in a deep breath. "It's Planet Dongguan."

My parents and Niall are quick to come to the same conclusions. Someone is living on Dongguan without permission, or the pit I saw isn't on Dongguan but another planet, or I really didn't see a person in a pit—I'm okay with that one, especially after accessing my Q-cluster from a portable.

A portable kilometers away from a terminal!

Another thought occurs to me. What if I tapped into a part of my brain that can do these things really fast *like* a Q-cluster? I've heard you only access ten percent of your brain's power—not sure from where. What if I can use all of my brain? That would be cool. So I could figure out what one hundred and ninety-seven times forty-three is in seconds. Uh. It's... If I round it up to two hundred and times it by forty that's...er...eight thousand, then I need—a new theory. 'Cause that one's wrong.

"...Ara?" Mom asks.

"Huh?"

"Are you finished with the portable?"

"Oh. Yeah." I give it back to her. Everyone's staring at me in concern. Time to get the focus off me. "You said you have questions about today?"

"Yes." Mom asks Niall and I to clarify what we each saw, felt, and how long it took for the blackness to go from a fist to a two-meter tall rectangle.

After we finish, I take a quick shower, and fill in for Elese while Niall relieves Beau. My thoughts are a chaotic tumble of all that happened today so Niall surprises me when he grabs my arm before we part.

"You saw something in the files. What was it?" he asks.

"I..." Damn, he's too observant and I can't come up with a good answer fast enough.

"Mouse." His tone is growly.

"It's not what I saw, but…" He's not going to believe me.

"But what?"

"It's…I…" I sigh then blurt it out. "I can access the Q-net without a terminal or tangs."

He rocks back on his heels as if I just slapped him.

"Go ahead, tell me it's crazy. It's impossible. That I have significant brain damage." I've joked about this in the past. However, I'm no longer being flippant. No, now I'm terrified.

"Sounds like you already covered the basics." He pauses. "Do you think it has to do with touching that heart?"

I consider. "No, or it would have happened sooner."

"When did it start?"

"After I fell asleep while worming."

"But that shouldn't—"

"I know! I've been telling myself that for the last ten days."

"The migraine."

I nod. "At least I don't get headaches anymore." Small mercies, but still…what else can go wrong? The answer pops into my head like the magician. "Are you going to break up with me?"

"What? No. Why would you think that?"

"'Cause I'm a freak of nature. 'Cause of all the problems I cause like turning on the Warriors. Although that was an accident, but I'm the only reason the symbols glowed. 'Cause I can't follow simple instructions. Don't you want a *normal* girlfriend?"

"I hate to break this to you, Mouse, but you were never ever, not in a million years *normal*." He moves his hand down my arm and entwines his fingers in mine. "If I wanted normal, I wouldn't be with you."

In a strange way, that's really sweet. "But…the Warriors and the Q-net. It's all…too much for one person to deal with."

"It is." Niall releases my hand.

A crack races through my heart. I knew it was too much for him.

Instead of stepping away, he pulls me in for a hug. "But you don't have to deal with it alone. I'm not going anywhere."

I melt against him. Best boyfriend ever.

"You know what you need to do," Niall says.

I tilt my head back. "Kiss you?"

A smile. "We're in uniform."

"We're hugging."

"I'm providing emotional support. Which also includes the advice to inform your parents of what's been going on." When I grumble, he adds, "Face it, Mouse, if I can figure out something is wrong, they probably already suspect."

"Yeah, but they're distracted. Plus this'll just add to their worries."

He gives me the you're-making-excuses look. Mr. Sensible in all his glory.

"How about I tell them when we get back to the base?" I ask. "I'll stay away from the portables and won't connect with the Q-net until I talk to them."

"You're just delaying the inevitable."

"Other than requiring me to stay disconnected, what else

can they do? Send me to the base for more brain scans? What happens to the dig then?"

Niall presses his lips together. "I guess you have a point."

I wisely keep from gloating. Instead, I promise to fess up once we're home.

As I'm making my rounds in the pit the next day, I encounter my parents at the base of the ladder. They're both huddled over a portable. Because of my vow not to tangle with any tech, I veer away.

"He can't do that." Mom's tone is harsh.

Uh oh. I slow and glance over my shoulder.

"Technically he can," Dad says.

"There's no danger, Spencer."

"You can't be sure of that. What's to stop someone from Dongguan from just...popping in here?"

"The laws of physics."

"Tell that to those boot prints. Come on, Ming, you know he's right."

"He's—" Mom spots Beau, who is climbing down the ladder.

Beau is pale and his brow is creased with worry. "Dr. Daniels, I've orders from Officer Radcliff to cease all activities in Pit 21 and return to base as soon as possible."

2522:216

My mom faces Beau with her hands on her hips. Uh oh, I brace for her to blast the poor guy—because Radcliff is the one who ordered us all back to the base, not Beau.

"No," Mom says to Beau. "We're not leaving. We've only been here two days and—"

"It's not up for discussion, Dr. Daniels. Tell your team to pack up."

I give Beau major credit for standing up to my mother. She glares at him and he stares right on back.

"The security team is welcome to leave. We're staying," Mom says in her don't-argue-with-me tone.

"We can come back." Dad appeals to Mom. "We'll bring the astrophysicists and more security."

Mom rounds on him. "Do you really think Tace is going to allow that?"

My father looks downright grim. "He's going to have to.

This is our only way to get answers."

Or more questions. Remembering the swell of lights and the strange black rectangle, I rub my arm.

"Fine," Mom spits out. "But we're coming back. If Tace won't agree to sending security with us, we'll bring all the techs instead. Most of them have been training with pulse guns."

Which might be effective against the magician, but not shadow-blobs. However, I don't remind her of them or she might change her mind and stay. And I don't want to be caught in the middle if she orders me to remain with her.

The rest of the day is spent packing up the camp and enduring lots of grumbling from the techs. My dad rigs the floodlights so he can turn all of them on from the surface when we return. Smart.

Beau, Niall, and I switch off the lights, starting with the furthest set and moving toward the ladder. When I reach the center, I pause. If the magician returns, he'll see our footprints and the big floodlight. Hmmm. It might be a bad thing if he's working for Jarren. So I smooth out the sand in and around the center, trying to make it appear...natural. It's not perfect—far from it, but it's...better. Then I move the light deeper into the Warriors.

We finish and stand at the bottom of the ladder. There's enough sunlight so it's not completely dark.

"Anything?" Beau asks me.

"No HoLFs."

He peers at me, then nods at Niall. "You go first."

Niall mounts the ladder, then Beau, and I'm last. I take a

moment to wonder if we'll be back. I hope so.

After I arrive at the surface, the ladder is pulled out and retracted to its smaller size—basically Niall pushes one end and Beau the other until the ladder's only a couple rungs long. The action reminds me of crinkling space, which brings two distant points close together. And then I wonder if the black rectangle that appeared in the center of the pit is a form of crinkled space.

The BP Crinkler engine works in silence as it compresses large sections of space. The rectangle is on a much smaller scale, but there wasn't any noise. Except the distance between Yulin and Dongguan is…uh, I'll have to look it up. Would the time dilation also be a factor? One of Jarren's goons said the time dilation sucks for us, implying it didn't for them. So say Jarren is using the Warriors to travel around the Galaxy like my mom speculated, then there isn't a time jump. That would be amazing! And it would explain so much.

"Oh no," Niall says next to me.

I jerk in surprise, reaching for my gun. "What?"

"Your brow is furrowed and you have that look."

"What look?"

"That you're thinking big dangerous thoughts."

"I'm not—"

"Lawrence, are you ready to go?" Beau asks.

"No, sir."

"Then get your ass in gear. We're leaving in ten minutes."

Niall mouths "later" as I hurry off to pack my ruck. I shove everything in and am back in time to climb into vehicle three.

Kier drives while I scan the horizon and my thoughts mull over impossible things.

We arrive an hour before sunset. Radcliff is waiting for us in the empty port. I'm confused about the lack of workers until I remember that I'm supposed to be dead. It was nice not to worry about that at the camp. Really nice. Add in the fresh air and night sky to the things I'm going to miss. Sigh.

Radcliff approaches us. His movements are stiff with anger and a white-hot rage burns from his gaze. I brace for the reprimand.

"Report back to my office, now," Radcliff says in an even unemotional tone, which is worse than any of his growls. "Lawrence, keep your hat and sunglasses on and follow close behind Dorey and Radcliff."

"Yes, sir," we all say in unison and hurry off.

I glance back. Radcliff is aiming for my parents. I suspect this might be an end to family dinners.

No one says a word as we travel through the mostly empty hallways—good thing it's dinner time. The few people we encounter don't bother to do more than glance at us. Both Niall and Beau are taller than me so I doubt the couple of scientists even noticed me.

When we enter the office, Morgan is sitting behind Radcliff's desk. "That must be some kind of a record—shortest field trip or maybe shortest time to trouble," she says.

Ha ha, not funny. I resist the temptation to explain. I'm sure Radcliff is going to want a complete report—no sense telling it twice. We pile our rucks in the corner.

I spot the guest terminal and that reminds me. "Did anything unusual happen in the Q-net yesterday afternoon?" I ask Morgan.

"Unusual as in…?"

"While you were testing the blockade and setting off Jarren's alarms. Was there any…indication he might have noticed what happened in Pit 21?"

"No, but you and Dorey probably have a better handle on that. Maybe you'll see something when you go in again." She pauses. "*If* you go in again."

Beau and I share a horrified look. Radcliff wouldn't ban us from the Q-net? Would he? No. It's too important that we find a way to reach DES. Then I remember my promise to Niall to tell my parents about my terrifying new abilities. Yeah, I'll be a hundred A-years old before anyone lets me near a terminal again.

The wait for Radcliff is torture. I'm ready to confess all my transgressions. And it's scary just how many I've had over my very short life. When Radcliff does arrive, his presence slams into us like a supernova. It's an effort for me to remain on my feet. We all straighten to attention, standing almost shoulder-to-shoulder in front of his desk. Morgan relinquishes the seat and stands behind Radcliff. Her expression remains neutral.

Radcliff accesses his terminal and pulls up a report on the screen before he turns his attention to us.

"Tell me everything," he orders in that chilling monotone.

I start with the discovery of the boot prints. And we all take turns describing what happened. Elese doesn't say much because she was on the surface most of the time. When we reach the decision to turn on all eight glyphs, Niall fails to mention that he advised against the test. It's a nice gesture of solidarity, but I'm not going to let him get into trouble when he was being sensible so I speak up on his behalf.

Radcliff grunts but doesn't say anything. We continue with the story and end with our arrival at the base. Silence fills the room. It thickens and presses on us. And I swear all four of our heartbeats are audible. The air in the room is pulsing along with the quartet of thumping sounds.

"Keir and Radcliff, you're dismissed," Radcliff finally says.

They hesitate for a fraction of a second before bolting. Not that I blame them.

"Lawrence—"

"It's my fault, sir," I blurt out. "It was my idea to turn on all eight symbols."

"Why would you suggest it if you had no *clue* what would happen?" Radcliff asks. His words are ice cold. "Do you have any *sense* of how *dangerous* that was?"

"But that's the thing, sir. I *sensed* it was safe. That the Warriors would protect us."

Radcliff stares at me as if I've gone insane. Morgan struggles to keep her neutral expression. One day, I'm going to make that woman laugh out loud, but obviously not today.

It takes him a few minutes to form a response. "That type of thinking is going to get you killed, Lawrence."

I dig my nails into the palms of my hands to keep my snarky response inside. It's an effort.

"You don't…" He rubs a hand over his face. "You're new to this, and you weren't in charge. Except for a complete disregard for everyone's safety, you are not at fault." Radcliff glances at Beau.

I sense it isn't going to go well for my partner. And I decide to risk what's left of my credibility. "Permission to speak freely, sir?"

His shoulders droop and he leans back in his chair. "This should be good. Go ahead, Lawrence."

"One of the reasons my parents pushed to test my idea was because they were afraid you wouldn't allow them to experiment later."

"And they were right," he says.

"Not even with a full security team nearby?"

His gaze is hard. "No."

"No offense, sir, but that's the wrong thing to do." I hold up a hand to stop the tirade that's twitching his lips. "Look, Jarren killed me so I wouldn't figure out what he's doing. If we're afraid to investigate every possible clue to determine what he's up to, then he wins. He's coming for us before that Protector ship arrives regardless. We need to take risks so we're ready. Officer Dorey recognizes this need, which is why he allowed the test."

"Are you done?"

"I'd like to add that I have a special connection to the Warriors, which cannot be refuted as I…er…woke them. They *are* protecting us. And I think we should find another intact pit that has the symbols for an active Warrior planet and try to contact the scientists working there and have them alert DES about the blockade. Now I'm finished, sir."

Radcliff once again studies me as if I'm stark raving mad. I suppress a sigh. Without any scientific proof, no one is going to take my advice. And without experimentation, we won't gather any evidence. It's one of those paradoxical situations—a catch something or other. Basically, it'll all come down to trusting a teenager with brain damage. So not happening.

"Your comments have been noted. You're dismissed, Lawrence."

I meet Beau's gaze. He nods and I give him an encouraging smile. Poor guy is about to have his ass handed to him. I grab my ruck and leave. When the door closes behind me, Radcliff's muffled voice sounds and I rush to increase the distance. No way I want to overhear that lecture.

Niall's door is open and I pause outside. He's sitting on his couch, but jumps to his feet when he spots me. Niall grabs my arm and tugs me inside his unit. "How was it? Bad?"

"No. Other than being told I have a complete disregard for everyone's safety, I did more talking than your father."

"You did? Should I be worried?"

I recount my comments. "He gave me permission to speak freely," I add before Niall can tell me I've just dug my own grave.

Niall laughs. "And I bet he's regretting that."

"Hey!" I punch him on the bicep.

He rubs it even though I didn't hit him hard. "I wonder if

he's going to take your advice."

Now it's my turn to laugh. "Doubtful."

Turning serious, Niall steps closer. "You have a point. We should test another pit."

Mr. Sensible agrees with me? That's scary and sweet. I wrap my arms around his neck and pull him in for a kiss. It starts out chaste but soon turns deep and passionate.

Sometime...later, Niall breaks away. "Wow, I should...agree with you...more often."

"You...should." I'm having trouble catching my breath.

"Now that I have the proper incentive..." He dips his head for another kiss.

This one is just as fiery. And my two layers of clothing are suddenly hot and restrictive. I'm about to suggest we continue this in the shower, when he stops. I groan.

"We need to be on our best behavior, Mouse. My dad's bound to be upset for a few days."

"Fine, but in ninety-eight days, *you're* mine." I poke him in the chest. "*You* and not Mr. Sensible."

He smiles. "It's a date."

"Good." I step to leave.

Niall touches my shoulder. "Thanks."

"For what?"

"For standing up for me."

"Why didn't you?"

Niall fidgets with his sleeve, yanking on the stretchy material. "Beau and I don't have the best relationship so I didn't know if he included my objections in his report. And I didn't want to come off all, 'I told you so.' Plus we're a team."

"*Were* a team. I doubt your dad will let us be one again."

Niall meets my gaze. "Then my dad's an idiot."

"Is that so? I wonder what he would say to that?"

"Mouse." He mock growls.

"Oh, look at the time. I better get to my unit since I'm being on my best behavior and all." I smirk.

He raises his hands, bending his fingers into claws. "Don't make me resort to tickling you into submission."

"An empty threat. Remember what happened last time you tried?" I did. His touch had been far from ticklish.

Dropping his hands, he says, "Ah, hell."

"Later, Toad."

After a long shower, I help myself to leftovers. When Radcliff arrives, I brace for...I've no idea. However, he doesn't say a word as he heats up a dish. I'm almost done with my meal and I gauge the distance to my room.

He grabs his meal and pauses. "You're to report to training with Keir tomorrow morning and then a meeting with the astrophysicists at thirteen hundred hours in the conference room."

"Yes, sir." The words pop out of my mouth automatically.

Nodding, he heads into his bedroom, leaving me wondering what the meeting is going to be about. Did he consider my idea?

Will my parents be there? Have the astrophysicists discovered anything about the shadow-blobs? I hope we'll actually get some answers this time and not a lecture.

I can't believe I'm admitting this, but after two days of doing nothing but guarding the workers at Pit 21, I miss the physical activity. Who knew? Don't worry, I'm not going to turn into one of those exercise nuts. It's just nice to stretch my muscles. Also, so far, my experience as a security officer is not what I expected. At all.

"Pay attention, Recruit," Elese says as she sweeps my feet out from under me.

I land on my back with an oomph. Obviously, I still have much to learn.

Elese grabs my hand and pulls me to my feet. "Again."

Then it hits me. Not Elese, but the realization that being a security officer is all about *again*. Training is life-long. There's never going to be a point when I can say, yup, I'm done. But I guess that's true of any career—learning never stops.

Elese counters my jab with ease. She sidesteps my kick, grabs my leg, and slams me to the mat again. "What's going on, Rookie? Two days away and you forgot everything I taught you."

"Sorry, just thinking about my future."

"You keep fighting like that, and you won't have a future," she teases.

Except she's right. Like I told Radcliff, Jarren's coming and I need to be ready. I focus on my training.

By the end of our session Elese gives me a grudging, "Better."

I hurry back to my unit for a quick shower and an even quicker lunch. Shoving the last bite of the sandwich into my mouth, I wipe crumbs off my hands and shirt, swallow, square my shoulders, and enter the conference room.

My parents are sitting at the table with Drs. Carson and Zhang. Way over on the opposite side are Radcliff and Morgan. The tension is palpable. My mom is describing the light show the Warriors put on to the astrophysicists. I debate where I should sit—near my parents, near Radcliff, or in the middle. Sheesh, you'd think this wouldn't be so difficult. In the end, I pick a chair closer to Radcliff. I am a security officer.

When Mom explains about the black rectangle, she defers to me. I tell them about the person inside.

"Probably an optical illusion. Or a reflection of one of the others in the pit," Yenay says.

"No," I respond. "The blackness had depth."

"There are no alternate dimensions," Bertie says rather gruffly.

"What about a portal to another planet? A shortcut," I suggest. Like some of my worming tunnels. Where did that come from?

"The laws of physics—"

"Don't apply to crinkling space."

"Of course they do," Yenay says. "Or we wouldn't be able

to do it."

Strangely that makes sense.

"Wait," Dad says. "Are you saying that the black rectangle is crinkled space?"

"No, but maybe it *acts* like it," I say. "If it's a portal, then that might explain how it works."

"There's no engine, Ara," Mom says.

"How do you know?" I ask. "You found alien equipment in the factory. Maybe one is a crinkle space…er…crinkler."

"Except when you crinkle space to bring two points together, you warp the space around it. Which is why the ships do it far away from other planets and suns." Mom flares her hands out in a V to demonstrate.

I appeal to my parents. "You saw the wave of lights. Maybe the Warriors can smooth things out. Or maybe the aliens are better at it than we are." I pause, then ask Yenay, "How does the Bucherer-Plank Crinkler engine work?" The ship's engine room is one of the places that are off limits to passengers and even I'm not brave enough to risk a peek.

Bertie and Yenay glance at each other. Then Bertie sighs. "We don't exactly know. It's a highly complex theorem that takes years of study. Aerospace engineers are the ones who designed the engine and who understand how it works."

"I don't suppose there's one in the base?" I ask.

"No."

That's unfortunate. "We could test my theory in another pit and try to send something through."

Everyone looks at Radcliff. He'd been quiet during the discussion. Too quiet.

"If we're to figure out what is happening, we will need to see the rectangle," Yenay says.

"It's highly dangerous," Radcliff says in an even voice. "We need to focus on the more immediate threat of the HoLFs. However, I don't have the authority to stop you."

"But you have the authority to prevent your officers from accompanying us," Dad says.

Radcliff tenses so much I worry his lower jaw is going to crack. "If you decide to proceed with this line of inquiry, you can request volunteers." He shoots me a weighty glance. "I cannot guarantee anyone will do so, but I will support their decision."

By my parents' surprised reactions, I guess this is quite a change of heart for Officer Radcliff.

"When can you be ready to go?" Mom asks Yenay.

Once again she turns to her colleague and they do that silent communication thing.

"Officer Radcliff made an excellent point about the HoLFs. I think we should finish collecting and analyzing the data from Pit 1 before we make plans to go to Pit 21," Yenay says.

"Good idea," Dad says before my mom can voice her objections. "In the meantime, I'll ask for volunteers." Dad meets my gaze. "Officer Lawrence?"

Nice of him to ask me instead of assuming I'm going. There's no test without me after all. And even though it's my idea, I'm still smart enough to know there's risk involved. "I'll go as long as there are four other security officers with us."

The silence is complete.

My mother is the first to recover. "That's a tall order. We do have a number of techs who can use pulse guns."

"They don't have the experience. We need trained and seasoned officers, not rookie techs." I'm probably imagining the warm glow of approval from Radcliff.

"All right," Dad says. "Officer Morgan, will you volunteer?"

Asking the second in command—bold move.

"I wouldn't miss it," she says.

Crack—there goes Radcliff's jaw. Not really, but the man is not happy.

"Thanks," Dad says. "Three more to go."

Mom breaks the tension by asking the astrophysicists if they have an update about the nature of the HoLFs.

"Not yet. We're hopeful the data from the sensor will point us in the right direction," Bertie says.

Yenay and Bertie then leave the conference room with promises to contact everyone once the data has been examined. I've no idea what they really thought of my theories. Time will tell. Speaking of tell, I've a promise to keep.

Before my parents can leave I draw in a deep breath and say, "Mom and Dad, can you stay? I've something I need to discuss with you."

They settle back in their seats. Radcliff gives me a probing look. I sigh. "Officers Radcliff and Morgan, can you remain as well?"

Now I have all four adults' undivided attention. Go me. I search for the right words—the ones that will make the most sense without causing undue alarm.

"What's wrong?" Mom asks when the quiet stretches past awkwardness.

Unable to find the perfect combination, I blurt, "I can access the Q-net without using entanglers."

Confusion dominates and I do my best to explain. "...another dream, except it turned real, but I disentangled before I woke up so I didn't get a killer migraine. Actually, I didn't have any pain."

Stunned silence.

"Can you prove it?" Morgan asks.

I don't feel particularly sleepy. But then she swivels to the terminal. Oh.

Handing my mother my tangs, I say, "Yes, I can."

They all stare at me.

"I can do it from here." It's not a boast, just part of the demonstration. They might as well learn the full extent of my freakish powers. Yes, that's sarcasm, people.

Morgan accesses the Q-net. And I concentrate on the screen like I would if I was sitting next to her with my tangs in my ears. Soon enough my vision blurs and then I'm trailing her to Jarren's blockade.

These are the areas I tested while you were gone. She shows me the grid we created to keep track. Two new sections are checked off.

Any gaps? I ask.

No. It's tight.

Are we going to implement the distraction protocol soon?

Probably not for a while. Not until this business of crinkling Warriors is settled.

Crinkling Warriors? You're quite the comedian, Officer Morgan.

And you're quite the anomaly, Junior Officer Lawrence. Before I can counter, she adds, *Time to disentangle.*

Only when I disengage with the Q-net do I learn that Morgan turned off the screen and I closed my eyes sometime during our short session. No one else knew what was going on.

Morgan spins to face the others. "She was in the Q-net with me."

Her proclamation sets off a bombardment of questions. Yes, I should have told them sooner. No, I don't have any pain. No, I don't get random visions from the Q-net. Yes, I can tangle and disentangle at will, well, except when I'm dreaming when I inadvertently entangle. No, distance from the terminal doesn't seem to matter. I elaborate on that point.

"You accessed the Q-net through the portable! In the middle of the desert!" Mom presses her hands to her chest as if to keep from saying more.

Since it was more of an outburst than a question, I don't reply.

"Did it cause you any problems?" Dad asks.

"Other than freaking out?"

"Uh, yes."

"No. I was fine. And now that I know what I can do, I have more control."

"Any Q-net dreams the last couple of nights?" Radcliff asks.

"No." I recall the two others. "I think it happens when I'm worried about something. The one with Jarren seemed to be triggered by my subconscious. I think I picked up on Jarren's fingerprints in the satellite feeds. The other was just after we discovered the Q-net made changes to our security measures to protect me."

There's a pause. One of the chairs creaks.

"Could you have made those changes to the security cameras while sleeping?" Radcliff asks.

Ah, he still wants to blame me for that. "No, that was before."

"Before what?" Mom asks.

"Before I dozed off while entangled."

Another pause and then another round of questions. No, I don't hear voices, I don't see things that aren't there, unless you count the person in the black rectangle (which I don't), I don't have suicidal thoughts or thoughts that are not my own, and I don't have access to the star roads. At least I don't think I do, I haven't tried. Basically I don't have any symptoms that I'm going crazy or turning catatonic. Unless all this is just a dream or delusions and I never woke from my concussion. Might as well say it—this could be my imagination while I'm lying unresponsive in the infirmary drooling on my pillow. You have to admit I do have an overactive imagination.

"What caused this?" Mom asks.

I shrug. "The concussion. Touching the heart. Dying. Falling asleep while worming. All of the above. None of the above. Take your pick."

"No need to be snarky," Mom says.

The sad thing is, I wasn't being snarky. Just honest.

"What do you suggest we do?" Radcliff asks me.

I stare at him. Did he really just ask *me*? Oh boy. Not one to waste this opportunity, I say, "Nothing. I keep doing what I do and I promise to let you know right away if I'm having any problems."

"Problems as in…?"

"Headaches, delusions, voices, more dreams." No one says a word. "Look, I've had multiple brain scans and they've all shown no damage. Let's just view this as a…quirk of my brain's wiring due to various unavoidable events." I tap my forehead. "And I promise to use my powers only for good." That earns me a smile from Morgan. I'm getting closer.

My parents glance at Radcliff and Morgan, who meet their gazes. And I suddenly feel like an intruder.

"Ara, please return to our unit," Radcliff says. "I'll see you later."

Ah, they wish to discuss me without me. That's fine. Doubting that I'll see my parents at dinner, I give them a quick goodbye and bolt. I pause outside Niall's door. He's probably on duty or sleeping. Besides, we're supposed to be on our best behavior. Ugh. I do as ordered.

A knock wakes me up from a nap. Radcliff didn't say what I should do after I returned to our unit. Loophole! "Come in."

The door opens and Niall pokes his head in. "Where is everyone?"

"Discussing my fate in the conference room." I glance at the time—it's been two hours. That doesn't bode well for my future.

"So you fessed up. How did it go?"

"I'm not confined to a padded room for my protection. Yet." I stretch.

"That's good. And for the record, I think you would look adorable in a confinement jumpsuit."

"Watch it, Toad." I throw my pillow at him.

He catches it and tosses it back. I duck.

"Your reflexes are getting better, Mouse."

I grunt—very unladylike.

He laughs. "Come on, I'm starving."

We dig through the refrigerator. Radcliff has plenty of leftovers. Enough so I wonder if he cooked the extra food while we were gone out of habit. As we eat, I fill Niall in on the meeting with the astrophysicists and my theories.

"What about a wormhole to the pit on Planet Dongguan?" Niall asks.

"I thought the same thing. It could be like a shortcut through the Q-net."

"No, like a real wormhole. The ones that form in space and

CHASING THE SHADOWS

are supposed to connect two distant points without crinkling space."

It could be possible. "There's the power issue. What's generating the wormhole?" But then again, what's powering a Crinkler engine?

Radcliff arrives, heats up a meal, and joins us at the table. I stop shoveling food into my mouth as my stomach sours. What did they decide? Should I pack?

"Your father's been busy," Radcliff says into the silence. "He's already recruited Officers Dorey and Keir."

Niall glances at me. "Recruited for what?"

I explain about the plan to open another pit and my conditions.

"I'm guessing he'll ask you next," Radcliff says to Niall. "And that you'll say yes." His tone implies that agreeing would be idiotic.

Used to his father's ill humor, Niall ignores him. "Of course I'll go."

A grunt is Radcliff's only response. I hide my smile.

"As for you..." Radcliff stabs his fork in my direction. A poor meatball is impaled on the tines.

I suck in a breath.

"You're to proceed..." He bites off half the meatball and chews.

My imagination has no trouble filling in the blanks. Proceed to the infirmary. Proceed to detention. Proceed to a small dark room for the rest of my life.

259

"...as normal. But if you have any problems or even a niggling sense that something's not right, you are to report it to me or your parents A-sap. Understand?"

Whew. "Yes, sir."

Another grunt. But I'm relieved they took my advice and I can be...er...normal. Well as normal as I'm going to get after everything that's happened. And, thinking about it, I'm okay with that.

The astrophysicists collect twenty days' worth of data and then analyze it. They request another meeting to report on their findings. So eleven days after the last one, the seven of us are once again sitting around the table in the conference room at thirteen hundred. Seems my morning training sessions are not to be disturbed, but my afternoon worming sessions with Beau aren't as important—although we're having fun setting off Jarren's alarms. At least the tension between my parents and Radcliff has diminished. They're coming to dinners again.

Both women look tired and I wonder if they've been getting enough sleep, or if the results are keeping them up at night. Scary thought.

"We analyzed the data," Yenay says. "The HoLFs are emitting radio waves."

Radio waves? That seems so...ordinary.

"We don't know if they are using these waves to communicate or if it's a natural byproduct," Bertie says.

"Byproduct?" Morgan asks.

"For example, humans emit thermal energy, or rather body heat. You can see it if you view a person using infrared goggles. Our bodies also generate an electrical signal. So perhaps the HoLFs produce radio waves."

"How does this help us?" Radcliff asks.

"We could build a weapon that counters the radio waves. Perhaps it will kill them or cause enough harm that they'll leave." Bertie raises her hands in an I-don't-know gesture. "If they're using the waves for communication, then it would stop their ability to transmit. That also might scare them away or make them unable to attack in force."

"What counters radio waves?" Radcliff asks.

"More radio waves. A weapon could emit the same wavelength and frequency as the HoLFs', but out of phase so the two waves will cancel each other out. It's called destructive interference."

Her comments reminded me of my physics classes. "If you don't get it just right, the two waves could converge and amplify the signal."

"There's always going to be risks, however, if we design the emitter right, it will sample the frequency's phase from the HoLFs and then produce a countersignal," Bertie says.

"How long would it take to sample them?" Morgan asks.

"A fraction of a second."

"Wait, back up," Mom says. "It's been too long since my university days. Can you explain the difference between wavelength and frequency?"

Bertie explains. "Wavelength is how long the wave is—think of it as a piece of string curved up and down like a snake. The wave is measured from the middle of one crest to the next crest. For the HoLFs, the wavelength is zero point nine two meters. Radio and infrared waves are longer than X-rays and Gamma rays. Frequency is how fast the wave is moving—like a wave in an ocean racing to shore."

"If we create a signal that has the same frequency and wavelength, but the crests of our waves are at the same time as the troughs of the HoLFs' waves, they will both disappear," Yenay adds.

"Okay, that makes sense. How long will it take to build the emitter?" my mom asks Yenay.

"Building it should only take a few days. That's not the problem. The difficulty will be designing it with the supplies we have on hand. It's been a long time since humans used radio waves. We're also going to need an engineer to help."

"Do we have an engineer on base?" Mom asks Dad.

"I'll have to look at the personnel list." Dad accesses his portable. "Maybe Jim McGinnis has an engineering background. He's in charge of the base's maintenance crew."

While my dad checks, I'm struck by Yenay's comment about humans using radio waves. "Could we also build a radio receiver? If the HoLFs are using radio waves to communicate, we could hear what they say."

"The likelihood of the aliens speaking English is infinitesimal," Yenay snaps.

Is it me or is she just all gloom and doom? "Do we have any

linguists on base? They could try to translate it. Even if we don't, we should record it so when we reestablish contact with DES, we can send it to their language experts."

"That's actually a good idea," Bertie says, sounding surprised.

Sheesh. Tough room.

My dad glances up from the portable. "Jim has a mechanical engineering degree. Will that work?"

"Yes, that's perfect," Yenay says without a snap. It must be me.

Finally something going right for a change. Don't worry I won't relax, there's still plenty of things that can go horribly amiss. Curious about the HoLFs' radio wave, I ask Yenay what the frequency is.

The scientist scrunches up her nose as if in pain. Bertie swallows. Her face pales—quite the feat considering she's already rather pale. What did I do now? I didn't think it was a hard question.

"It's three hundred and thirty megahertz," Yenay finally says.

Three thirty. Why does that sound familiar?

"Is that significant?" Radcliff asks.

Trust the man's internal something's-wrong-detector to pick up on their discomfort.

"It's the same frequency of Sagittarius A-star. That's the name of the supermassive black hole at the Milky Way's galactic center."

2522:228

Wait, what? We all stare at Dr. Zhang. Did she just say that the shadow-blobs are emitting the same radio waves as the black hole at the center of our Galaxy? That would be cool except…

"I thought nothing escapes a black hole," I say.

"Once past the black hole's event horizon, nothing does. Not even light," Yenay says. "But the signal is from the region around the black hole."

"Are you implying that the HoLFs might be from the galactic center?" Mom asks.

"No, that would be impossible."

"Why not?" I ask before my internal filter can stop me from questioning an astrophysicist with a doctorate. "The HoLFs had to get here from somewhere? And if there's a portal in the pits, then why can't they use them, too?" And then the logic catches up. "Oh, right. Those pits were destroyed. The shadow-blobs aren't using the Warrior portals, but something else." Now everyone is looking at me. "What?"

"We haven't confirmed the existence of your portals, Ara." Yenay's words are clipped.

"Is having the same radio frequency significant?" Radcliff asks again.

"It's just a strange coincidence."

Radcliff and I exchange a glance. One of the things I learned by reading the security handbook is that true coincidences are rare.

"What's inside a black hole?" Mom asks. Apparently it's been too long since her last astronomy class.

"Gravity," Yenay says. "Matter is crushed down to a mass of zero, and gravity is all there is."

Definitely not going to be vacationing there. And no chance shadow-blobs could live there either.

"There is a theory that a black hole exits into another spacetime, acting like a wormhole," she adds.

I perk up at the mention of wormholes—perhaps Niall's theory has merit and the shadow-blobs are traveling through black holes.

"Of course nothing but gravity can survive the journey," Bertie says.

Boo. But I wonder… "Is there the same frequency radio waves coming from all the black holes in the universe?"

"No. They're all different. And only the radio-loud active galaxies produce radio wave emissions. They range in frequency from 10 megahertz to 100 gigahertz."

So no way our black hole is connected to another black hole in a different galaxy, creating a shortcut between them. The astrophysicists leave to consult with the engineer.

"We really could use DES's help with all this," Dad says. "Any progress on getting through the blockade?"

I glance at Radcliff. Beau and I been testing Jarren's defenses while waiting for orders to try and use Jarren's exit.

"I've been reluctant to make an attempt to reach DES until we learned more about the HoLFs," Radcliff says. "But it appears it's going to be a while before the astrophysicists are ready." He looks at me. "Can you find that breach again?"

I don't hesitate. "Yes."

"All right. Tomorrow afternoon, we'll implement the distraction protocol."

"We, sir?"

"Officer Morgan and I will provide the distraction while you and Dorey slip through the crack."

Fun. I just hope Jarren's not waiting on the other side.

The four of us gather in Radcliff's office. The countdown has started for Operation Distraction! Sorry, I couldn't resist. Plus nervous energy courses through me like electricity. If I screw this up, Jarren will know I'm alive and probably start planning to correct his oversight right away. No pressure there. Right?

"How much time do you need to worm to the breach?" Radcliff asks me.

I consider. On my own, it'd take me about an hour. With Beau trailing... "Ninety minutes."

"All right. Morgan and I will wait thirty minutes then go in and test grids one-forty-three and one-forty-four," Radcliff says.

He and Morgan will use the two terminals in his office while Beau and I will use the dual ones in Beau's. When we enter, I spot a glass of water and a bottle of painkillers on his desk. That's super nice and a pang of guilt hits me. Beau doesn't know about my new ability. Radcliff thought it was best to keep the information to those that needed to know and I'd argued—unsuccessfully—that my partner definitely needed to know. However, I'm pretty certain that there's going to be a slip-up in my future.

I sit down in front of the terminal and insert my tangs. This is too important and I don't want to drop out of the Q-net during a critical time.

"Ready?" Beau asks me.

I square my shoulders and draw in a breath. "Yes."

"Let's go."

We access the Q-net. I take point and lead Beau to Jarren's maze of hidden clusters, alarms, and programs. To say it's complex is not doing it justice. It's a work of freaking art.

Damn, Beau says. *How did you find this?*

I followed Jarren, now shush.

As I enter the maze, I have a brief thought about being the proverbial mouse in the maze searching for a piece of cheese. Queen Mouse will show Jarren, the murdering looter, just what she can do. I clamp down on a laugh. Niall's nickname for me is very appropriate right now.

What's so funny? Beau asks.

Too much to explain. And I need to concentrate. Slowing, I worm through the intricate layers with care. Beau slides in behind me with nary a ripple. After all this time working together, we've developed a synergy.

We near the breach. Jarren's Q-net fingerprints are all over like a green slime on wet walls. I channel my inner snail and squeeze through his gaps at a...well, snail's pace. It's tight and I wonder if he increased his security measures. Did he suspect someone found his exit? Fear sweeps through me, tingling down to my fingertips. I pause. I check the programming again, seeking traps. Being thorough, it takes me a while and—oh, you tricky bastard. There's a near invisible web around the breach.

Stars. The strands of the alarm are woven tight, but there are a few tiny fissures. I aim for one of the bigger ones, which isn't saying much as they're all really small. I sense Beau backing away. No surprise, getting one of us through is going to be a miracle. With two of us there's no chance in hell.

An ache throbs in my head as I navigate through the tight threads. Halfway through, I'm stuck with nowhere to go. I'm just too...heavy. It's hard to describe, but I'm like a shadow-blob with too many tentacles. Too much mass. If I move in any direction, I'll trigger an alarm. Argh!

Too bad I can't turn less dense like the shadow-blobs. Frustration pulses. I managed to get through the blockade when I was dreaming, for stars' sake. And when I flew to the satellite feeds it was ea—

Oh my stars. A terrible idea occurs to me. I mean really really bad. But it's the only play I have left. Before I can change my mind—I can't believe I'm going to do it—I remove my tangs.

My presence—for lack of a better word—lightens. The web of alarms around me no longer constricts. Fun and frightening. I fly between the strands, heading straight for Jarren's breach. When I reach it, I slow back to snail mode and slip through the crack in the blockade. Peeking out, I brace for an ambush.

Nothing except the vastness that is the rest of the Q-net. Yes! I don't waste time celebrating, though. My first task is to create an escape route through the blockade. A near-invisible one so we can contact DES without alerting Jarren. I move far away from his exit. It's easier on this side because all his programs are set to keep information in. My tunnel is like a sewing needle sliding through the tiny holes in a fabric's weave. In this case, the needle is hollow to allow messages to get through. It's a delicate and exacting process.

Once I finish, I seek a way to contact DES, even though a headache slams on my skull. I'm thinking about searching for an interstellar navigator when a life-saving device pops up from nowhere. Yeah, I know it sounds crazy. But it reminds me of those red floating survival rings we had when I was a kid on Planet Ulanqab. The research base was right next to a shallow lake. I've lots of good memories of playing in that lake with Phoenix—splash fights, dunking him, being dunked, sculpting Warriors out of sand—go on, say it, we were archeology geeks.

It's pretty obvious the life ring is a trap set by Jarren. I inspect it carefully for his fingerprints, search for hidden alarms, and near-invisible traps. It's clean. Huh. I mull over the implications for a while. It only materialized when I considered finding a navigator. Who would leave something like this so close to the blockade? And who had the skills to hide it so well?

The answer appears as suddenly as the device. I grab the ring. A message from Chief Vasily pops up. Confirmation that I wasn't dreaming when I reached out to the navigation chief. Good news, right?

> 2522:215: Officer Radcliff, DES security personnel were unable to find, let alone break through, your so-called looters' blockade. In fact, considering the planet has gone silent, most of them think your message is a morbid prank from a bored wormer. I'm not as certain since the skills needed to reach me are beyond a typical wormer. I'm leaving this hidden connection to me with the hope that you can once again "escape" the blockade and contact me.

I guess I couldn't blame the Chief for thinking my message was a hoax, but you have to give him credit for following up and for the skill needed to keep the so-called looters from finding it. He sent it fourteen days ago. I hope he's not in a time jump by now.

> 2522:229: Chief Vasily, thank you for being willing to believe me. We've created an escape tunnel through the blockade. Although I now have access

to DES, I'm still concerned about the looters discovering our new ability to communicate. Can you aid us in contacting someone in security who can guarantee us a secure and safe connection?

In other words, someone who knows how to keep the wormers out. Knowing Beau is waiting for me, I'm about to use my escape tunnel and return, when a message arrives. That was fast.

2522:229: Officer Radcliff! So glad to hear from you. I'm about to win a ton of credits from the rest of the crew. I'm patching in our Chief of Security, Officer Odette Bouchet. She'll make sure you reach the right people at DES without tipping the looters off. Here she is!

→Hello Tace! Thank the universe you're alive. Is your son, Keith, also well?

Oh no. She knows Radcliff and is purposely trying to test him. Better fess up before she asks me something I don't know.

←Officer Bouchet, this is Junior Officer Ara Lawrence. I'm sorry for the deception, but I used Officer Radcliff's name because no one would know me as I'm new to security. Both Radcliff and his son Niall are fine along with the rest of the security team and the scientists on the base. We only had one casualty, Officer Ivan Menz. Please allow me to connect you to Radcliff.

→So I'm to believe a *junior officer* is capable of reaching a navigation chief?

←I interned with Chief Hoshi and she taught me a great deal about the Q-net. Please let me connect you. It won't take me long.

→Why does the name Lawrence sound familiar?

Ha. Another test!

←It's Officer Radcliff's wife's maiden name.

→I'll wait.

Whew. I quickly retreat from the cluster and use my new escape route to return to Yulin's security. Radcliff and Morgan are still entangled, but Beau is not. Odd.

What took you so long? Radcliff demands.

His growl tells me two things, I've been worming much longer than he expected and he was worried. I briefly explain about Vasily and Officer Bouchet.

How did you—

No time, she's waiting. You need to do your security chief thing right now.

Update Dorey, Radcliff says to Morgan. *Lead on, Lawrence.*

Even though I created the escape tunnel, I'm still super careful not to make too many ripples. Radcliff follows me with ease. After we're past the blockade, I show him Vasily's message.

He notices the life ring. *Now what?*

Grab it, I say.

Cute.

I can't take any credit.

He gives me the Q-net equivalent of a grunt. *Go back to the base, Lawrence. I can take it from here.*

Can you find the tunnel through the blockade without alerting Jarren?

I've been worming in the Q-net since it was invented, I think I can handle retracing our route.

A simple yes would have sufficed, I grumble at him.

You're not the only who can snark. Then he connects to Officer Bouchet before I can snark back.

The messages between them fly fast and furious. I leave them to it. Besides, my brain has turned to jelly. And by the painful contractions in my head, I suspect brain matter might ooze from my ears. Even though I'm tired and don't have tangs in, I still ensure I disentangle properly to avoid another killer migraine.

Fire burns across my forehead. I rub it as I glance around. Beau is leaning against his desk staring at me with a hard gaze. He's holding his hand out. For a moment my exhausted brain thinks there's a couple of pain pills on his palm. Except they're—

"Care to explain these?" Beau asks.

My tangs.

I sigh. Dredging up a bit of energy, I enlighten him. He asks all the same questions as Radcliff and my parents.

"Why didn't you tell me?" Beau asks. He tries to maintain a neutral tone, but we've spent so much time together that I know he's hurt.

"Denial. If I didn't acknowledge it, then this scary new thing didn't exist. But even *I* couldn't maintain it and I'm the Queen of Denial." Then I rat Radcliff out. "I planned to tell you after this op."

"If you were going against Radcliff's order, why not tell me before the op?"

"Because of…" I wave a hand at him.

"What?"

"That expression on your face. That's what. You're not sure if you believe me or not. You think I'm a freak. And I needed you super focused today and not worried I might turn catatonic."

"Why? I couldn't get through. I didn't help."

My brain might be turning into mush, but I notice he didn't protest and say I'm not a freak. "You helped. A lot. I was more cautious—otherwise I would have run right into that web. Also if we triggered an alarm that close to the breach, Jarren was sure to investigate. You would have talked to him again. That gave me more confidence to navigate that sticky little surprise." I rub my temples as strange sparks flash and swirl in my vision. Closing my eyes just makes everything brighter so I open them.

"Here." Beau hands me my tangs, two pills, and the glass of water.

"Thanks." I down the pills in one gulp.

"That's my job, taking care of the super wormer."

It's not a compliment. I surge out of the chair and get right in his face. "Get over yourself, Beau. You're a talented wormer, and a smart guy. Yes, I'm now some prodigy in the Q-net, but it's because something or somethings fried my brain." I tap my pounding head with my index finger. "I don't recommend it as it's frankly terrifying when it happens. But you know what?" I poke him in the shoulder.

Beau's amber eyes are huge, but he manages a weak, "What?" as if he's afraid to ask.

"You're a jerk. I really need my partner to understand, to be supportive, to be someone I can tell all this crazy crap to without worrying he'll think I'm a freak. This isn't some competition, Beau. If you were the one to reach DES, I'd be jumping for joy, excited for you and the rest of the base. This is a big freaking deal. We might just survive this. But all I want to do is…" My skin flushes with a clammy sweat as the floor undulates under me.

"Do what?" Beau asks.

"Puke." I rush for the trash can. Kneeling over it, I heave out the two pain pills and the dregs of my lunch from so very long ago. A sour smelling bile gushes out next. Ugh.

Beau crouches next to me. He sweeps my hair back, holding it out of the way. His other hand is on my forehead. His palm is cool and comforting, helping to dampen the spike of pain that is hammering on my skull in time with my dry heaves. When I'm done, he pulls me from the rancid stench. Scooting back, he holds me to his chest, supporting me as I regain my breath.

"You forgot one thing," Beau says when my heart rate returns to normal.

"Oh?"

"When you said I was talented and smart."

Figures he'd remember that. "Did I say that? I must have been hallucinating."

He ignores the jab. "You did. You forgot to add how incredibly handsome I am as well."

I groan. "How could I forget your giant ego?" But inside I'm smiling because my Beau is back.

The door opens. Niall takes one step inside the office and stops. He's staring at us. At that moment, his resemblance to his father is almost uncanny. Seems a supernova glower can be inherited. Who knew? Not that I blame him. I'm still wrapped in Beau's arms, pressed against his very muscular chest. And why did I only notice his muscles now? Oh boy. Niall's nose crinkles and he glances at the noxious trash can.

I try to move away, but Beau's arms are like iron.

"You good?" Beau asks me.

"Yeah."

"Help her stand," Beau orders Niall, releasing me.

Niall grabs my wrists and pulls me to my feet. Except my legs have turned into two overcooked carrots that refuse to hold my weight. I sag, but Niall scoops me up as if I weigh nothing. Opening my mouth to protest, I meet his gaze and wisely keep quiet. I suspect this is more for him than me. Men.

"Should I call Dr. Edwards?" Beau asks.

"No. All I need is food and rest," I say before Niall can say yes. "I'm sorry about your trash can."

"No, you're not," Beau says with a smile.

True.

"Go get that rest." He shoos us.

Niall carries me out. Radcliff is still at his terminal. Although his gaze is aimed at his screen, his stare is distant. Morgan has disentangled.

She spots us. "You know most people would have escaped the blockade, made contact with DES, and called it a day."

"You mean the lazy underachievers?" I ask.

Morgan laughs. The sound erupts from her gut in short bursts. Finally! Is it strange that I'm more proud of making her laugh than breaking through Jarren's blockade? Probably.

"They also know their limits and wouldn't need to be carried because they exhausted themselves," Niall says.

"I'm feeling better, you can put me down."

His hold tightens. Guess that's a no. So I endure the indignity of being carried like a baby back to my unit and into my bedroom.

Niall lays me on the bed. "No one showed up for dinner so I came looking for you. Are you hungry?"

"Starving."

"Stay here." He jabs a finger at the bed before turning on his heel and leaving.

As much as I'd love to remain, the vile taste in my mouth just won't be ignored. I sneak into the washroom while Niall is busy in the kitchen. Brushing my teeth is pure heaven. Of course, he's standing on the other side of the door after I finish freshening up—that's code for using the toilet, washing my hands and face, and combing my hair. His arms are crossed.

"It's been a really long day, and I needed to use the washroom," I say in my defense. No softening in his posture. Fine. Let's see if he can maintain his overprotective stubbornness. "Okay, you're right. I'm still not steady." Ah there's a bit of give. "I need a shower. You can join me and make sure I don't fall."

He drops his arms in surprise and steps back.

Score!

Then he squints at me in suspicion. Guess I shouldn't have smirked. A beep sounds from the kitchen.

"Your ass better be in bed in one minute," Niall growls then heads to the kitchen.

Despite the pain gnawing on my skull, I'm in bed within thirty seconds. Niall arrives soon after with a tray. On it are two bowls of delicious smelling beef stew, two glasses of water, and two cups of chocolate pudding. He sets it down and then joins me on the bed.

"Thanks," I say.

A grunt, which is better than a growl. We eat in silence and each bite revives me. I scrape the sides of the cup with my spoon, trying to get every last bit of pudding.

"There's more," Niall says. He takes the tray and returns with another pudding cup.

My hero.

He sits on the edge of the bed while I suck it down. It doesn't take me long. Gotta love a sugar rush. But he's still uncharacteristically quiet.

"Are you mad about Beau and I?" I finally ask. "That wasn't anything. I was sick and he—"

"I know. No. I'm just worried."

Not what I expected. "About me and Beau?"

"No. Although at first…" He shakes his head. "No. About you." Niall stares off into the distance. "Remember when I said you reminded me of a comet?"

"Yes." Now I'm worried. Where is he going with this?

"I'm afraid you're too much like a comet. Burning so bright, doing impossible things, going full speed. I'm worried you'll burn out or crash. You've no sense of self-preservation. You'll give your all until you collapse."

Considering what happened today, it's hard to argue with that last comment. But… "I'm not suicidal. I have a good sense of self-preservation."

"Okay, tell me one example where you didn't risk your life for someone else or risk your health to accomplish something."

I search through my memories. There has to be a time. "Ah ha! There was a rodeemian spider in my room on Planet Wu'an. Those suckers are deadly and I called my dad to take care of it." Knowing my dad, he captured it and tossed it outside the base.

"That doesn't count."

"I think it should." Rodeemians are hairy, hand-sized, horrible little monsters. I shudder.

"How about just in the last two-hundred and thirty-three

days?" he asks.

Basically since I've known him. Okay fine. I sort through all that has happened, and can't find an example. "That's not fair. Lots has happened in those two-hundred and thirty-three days."

He waits.

"Okay you made your point. What else am I supposed to do? I'm a security officer. Isn't that part of the job? Menz died saving *my life*."

"You did it *before* you were an officer."

"Then that means I'm doing what I'm supposed to." Huh. Never thought of it in that way before. "What's really bothering you?"

Niall runs his fingers through his hair, leaving behind little spikes. "The plan to open another pit and portal. You're going to charge right on in and go through that portal. I just know it and I'm going to lose you forever. Like…" His fingers curl into fists. "My mom."

The last two words were almost a whisper. His grief is so raw, it's like sandpaper scraping across my heart. Oh, Niall. I scooch in close behind him and wrap my arms around his shoulders. Pressing my cheek against his, I say, "I'm sorry. You're right, I'm doing too much, going too fast. I'm…scared and I just want all this with Jarren and the shadow-blobs to be gone so we can just…be. I will be more careful and more considerate in the future."

He twists and pulls me forward. I end up in his lap, facing him. Niall hugs me, pressing me against his chest. "Thank you."

His embrace is warm and comforting. I close my eyes,

breathing in his scent.

"My mom…died nine hundred and eighty-three Actual days ago. Before we headed to Xinji, the ship stopped at Planet Omikron to deliver supplies and drop off passengers. She went planetside with my dad to, as she liked to say, 'refresh her creative batteries.'" He clears his throat. "There was an…incident at the port." Every muscle in Niall's body tenses. "A guy with colony fever demanded the shuttle pilot take him to the ship. Of course the pilot refused so he grabbed a little boy. Threatened to kill him. Mom was behind them and, according to Dad, she didn't hesitate. She tackled the guy, knocking the boy away. But the guy had a knife and he stabbed her in the leg. Son of a bitch hit her femoral artery. Nothing my dad could do but watch."

"That's terrible." But it did explain why Niall was so upset by my behavior.

"Captain Harrison broke the news to me. I'd volunteered to stay on the ship that first day." Niall huffs. "Elese was climbing the walls days before we obtained orbit. I could wait another day." He pauses. "I went down for the funeral, though. She wanted to be cremated and…"

The silence stretches. I glance up at him.

Niall's gaze is on one of the paintings. "This is going to sound strange, but to me it makes perfect sense. She wished for us to mix her ashes with paint. Mom gave me a canvas with a landscape drawn on it in pencil. It's a picture of her favorite place in the Galaxy. I'm supposed to paint that landscape with *her* paint."

Wow. No wonder Radcliff had been so against Niall using his talent—not only reminding him of his wife, but of her request. "It sounds rather morbid," I say.

"I know. But she always said she put her heart and soul into her paintings so why not *be* a painting and brighten a room, maybe make someone's day a bit happier. Mom would say, "Better than being shoved in some ugly urn or buried in the ground and forgotten.'"

When he put it that way… "You're right, that does make sense."

"You would have loved her, Mouse."

"No doubt." This earns me a brief smile.

Then his smile fades. "I haven't painted her landscape. It's just too hard. And frankly, creepy."

"I understand." Not that I've any experience with cremated remains, I imagine if it's mixed with paint it would be thick and gritty and crumbly when dried. Like a Warrior heart! Did the aliens who built the Warriors literally put their hearts and souls in the statues? An interesting thought. Too bad there's no way to test that theory. Just like all my ideas.

"Do you think you'll ever paint it?" I ask.

"Eventually. There's a museum on Earth that has a bunch of her paintings on display. I promised them a dozen or so more for their collection. One of those is going to be her painting. I figured she'd love it there, being with the people who appreciate her art the most."

"That's lovely, Niall."

He meets my gaze. "I haven't told anyone about the

museum, not even my dad. Thanks for listening to everything."

"Anytime." I'm rewarded with a kiss. It's tender and sweet and if he keeps it up, I'm gonna melt right in his arms. My birthday can't come soon enough. And if you're the type that believes I should wait until marriage, honey, I might not live that long!

A harsh clearing of the throat interrupts us. Radcliff is standing in the threshold.

Niall and I break apart.

"We're having a team meeting at oh-seven-hundred tomorrow. You're both expected to be there."

"Yes, sir," we say in unison.

Radcliff hesitates, but then shoots Niall his heavy stare before leaving.

Unaffected, Niall chuckles, but he stands. "You need your sleep, Mouse."

Grrr. Radcliff has rotten timing. And I don't want Niall to leave, so I do what I used to do as a kid when I wanted my mom to stay longer. "Can I ask you a question?"

He stills as if wary. "Sure."

"What is colony fever?"

"Oh." He blows out a breath. "It's very rare, but occasionally a colonist realizes that he is millions of kilometers from home. And he can't go back. Even if he manages to return, all of his friends and family that he left behind are long dead. So he snaps. Some with colony fever kill themselves, others go on a rampage. It's a mental state and not a virus. It happens on space ships as well."

"Ship fever?"

"Yeah, not very original. There's milder cases of it. Like Elese. She was new and our trip to Omikron was the longest time she was on a ship. I doubt she would have snapped, but she was driving us all crazy with her inability to stay still."

"And standing guard for hours…"

"Pure torture."

That I believe. I lean forward and take Niall's hands. "I've one more question. It's really important."

His grip tightens. "What is it?"

"Are there any more pudding cups left?"

He laughs. "Good night, Mouse."

"I'm serious!"

He turns off the light.

Not everyone on the security team is in the conference room the next morning. Bendix and Ho are guarding the pits. Morgan and Tora are watching detention. My parents are in the meeting along with Drs. Gage and Jeffries. Wondering if Beau purposely took the seat next to Niall, I sit in the empty one between him and Elese.

"Yesterday at approximately seventeen hundred hours, our security officers created a breach in the blockade without tipping off Jarren." He glances at Jeffries and Gage. "We're now able to communicate with DES," Radcliff says.

A cheer rises. My parents beam at me and Beau. And my mom can't resist smirking at Jeffries and Gage.

When the noise settles, Radcliff continues. "I was able to talk at length with Chief Security Officer Odette Bouchet. She updated me on our status and was able to arrange a secure path to DES HQ." Radcliff consults his portable.

Then his serious gaze scans each of us as if he's taking our measure and gauging our abilities to handle the news. Uh oh. I brace.

"According to DES, our planet was reported having gone silent on 2522:139. We're to assume all information received from DES since then is inaccurate."

Like the names of potential rich patrons of Jarren's operation. Jarren probably got a laugh by sending Radcliff the names of innocent people to investigate.

"Now we're getting accurate information. Unfortunately, not all the news is good. Planets Wu'an, Ulanqab, and Taishan have gone silent."

Shock rolls through the conference room. The air presses down on my shoulders and I hunch forward as I absorb the horrible news. Three more Warrior planets have gone silent. Does that mean they're all dead like on Planet Xinji, or cut off like us?

"Did they report a looter attack before their communications ceased?" Dr. Jefferies asks in a rough voice.

"No. If they were attacked, they were prevented from reporting it to DES."

Just like with us, Jarren was probably monitoring their

messages. But unlike us, I'd bet no one on those planets could see the shadow-blobs. Which means…

I rest my forehead near the edge of the table as black and white spots swirl in front of me. Over a thousand people dead. Eviscerated! Beau squeezes my shoulder in support.

Elese leans close to my ear. "Breathe."

But the air has turned from a gas into a solid, jamming my windpipe. The black spots converge. A loud hum sounds. Whack. A hand slams on my back. Pain radiates along my ribs. I cough, expelling the blockage before gasping.

"Breathe," Elese orders.

And I do. Eventually my lungs work on their own, my vision clears, and I straighten. Only to wish I could slide under the table. Everyone is staring at me.

"We're trying to stay optimistic," Radcliff finally says.

Unlike me. I skipped right to the worst-case scenario.

"Did any of those planets report finding anything unusual?" Mom asks.

"No. All the reports were normal. If they did discover anything, Jarren must have blocked it."

"So we're assuming Jarren and his looters are responsible?" Dr. Jefferies asks.

"For the time being. Until we receive more information."

"How did Jarren get to these planets when he was here only sixty plus days ago?" Dr. Gage demands.

He's somehow using the Warriors to travel. But I'm smart enough not to say it out loud. Not because Radcliff shoots me a warning look. Sheesh.

"He's obviously working with other groups," Radcliff says. "He probably organized a coordinated attack. The good news is that the Protector Class ships are still enroute to all the active Warrior planets and DES has launched a few more to check on the closed Warrior planets as well."

"What about Jarren? Are they searching for him?" Mom asks.

"Now that they know about him, they're forming a team to locate him."

I huff. Good luck with that. Beau and I exchange a significant glance. If DES couldn't get through to us, they're not going to find him.

"We're sending DES all the information we have on Jarren and also on the HoLFs." Radcliff frowns. "Seems they're skeptical about the HoLFs' existence. But they promised to have their engineers work on a design for that null wave emitter. Dr. Zhang gave me access to her notes."

"That's wonderful," Dad says. "Did they say when it'll be done?"

"No, but they're aware it's an urgent matter."

"What should we do while we're waiting for the Protector Class ship to arrive?" Mom asks.

"Nothing. At this point we are to wait for orders from DES. They made it clear that we are not to do anything." He glances at my mother, but she raises her chin at him in defiance. "I know it's frustrating, but at least DES knows we're alive."

Small comfort. How long before Jarren figures out we

contacted DES? They'd have to assign their top people who are most skilled with navigating the Q-net in order not to alert him. But I can't even be that optimistic. I'd say we have a couple days at most before they tip him off. Scary. Could we find him? It would be difficult, but we have a better chance.

"No," Mom says. "I'm not sitting here waiting for orders. They're skeptical about the HoLFs, which means they'll debate it to death—*our* death most likely. No. We're boots on the ground, in the thick of things, and have the most at stake. Drs. Carson and Zhang will continue to construct the null weapon and we're still going to the other pits."

Go Mom! Radcliff opens his mouth to, no doubt, protest, except the rest of the room agrees with my mother. Especially the officers.

The meeting breaks up soon after that and most everyone files out.

"Get your ass to training, Recruit," Elese says before leaving.

But Beau and I remain behind with Niall, hovering halfway between the door and the table.

"Are you thinking what I'm thinking?" Beau asks.

"That DES will botch the job, alert Jarren that we breached his blockade, and we'll be neck deep in looters within seven days?"

"Yup."

Niall returns to the table. "You're not thinking of doing something rash?" He's really asking me, although he addresses us both.

"Don't worry, Junior. We'll clear it with the boss first," Beau says.

"What's *it*?"

"Your girl here is leagues above what any DES expert can do. Now that we can get past the blockade, we can find Jarren's physical location for them and send them the info."

"Can you really?" Niall asks me.

"We can. And this is going to sound like I'm bragging, but we can also reconnect those other Warrior planets to DES." If anyone is still alive.

Beau bangs his fist on the table. "Damn straight." Then he hops to his feet. "I'll talk to Radcliff, see if we can start this afternoon." He bolts.

But Niall is still frowning.

"I remember my promise," I say to him. "Actually, it's safer for us if we search for Jarren. I really don't think DES fully understands just how skilled he is. He's managed to fool them for so long. And his alarms are almost impossible to spot." And because worry lines crease his forehead, I add, "I won't do too much in one session. There won't be a need to carry me back to my room."

This earns me a half-smile. "I don't know about that. You're already late for training. Else is going to run you into the ground."

I groan.

"Get moving, Recruit. Chop chop." Niall hits his palm with the edge of his other hand, making a chopping sound.

"You'll pay for this later, Toad." I sprint past him.

"Looking forward to it, Mouse."

Every muscle in my body is sore by the time I report to Beau's office. Niall wasn't kidding—Elese made me pay for being late. Neither Radcliff nor Morgan are around, which is unusual, but not oh-my-stars alarming. As soon as I enter the back room, Beau shakes his head.

"Radcliff said no. We can't search for Jarren."

I plop into my chair. The room smells of lemon and pine— a major improvement over yesterday. There's a shiny new trash can in the corner.

"What about helping the other silent planets?" I ask.

"That's a no as well." Beau rubs his face. "He said, and I quote, 'That we are *all* employed by DES. They own the base and we will abide by *their* decision.'"

Steepling my fingers, I lean back. "Did he also add something uncomplimentary about my mother?"

Beau waves away my question. "There might have been some other comments. It's not relevant."

"Uh huh. So what are we supposed to do?"

"You'll like this. We're supposed to keep testing Jarren's blockade so he thinks we didn't find a way through."

"Oh joy."

Beau presses a hand to his chest. "My stars, girl, contain your enthusiasm." Then he peers at me. "What are you thinking?"

"I'm thinking Radcliff is going to need to be convinced."

"I know one way you can do that."

"Really, how?"

"Take him with you into the Q-net. Show him the maze of Jarren's programs you navigated to reach DES. If that doesn't change his mind, nothing will."

It's worth a shot.

Except Radcliff is too busy sending information to DES to "waste his time" worming with me. My frustration builds with each day. And my fear. Any little noise sends me to the ceiling, convinced Jarren is attacking the base.

But there is some good news. Four days after we reestablish communication with DES, they message us diagrams for the null wave emitter. The design is easy to read and uses supplies we have on hand—double bonus. Drs. Carson and Zhang along with Jim McGinnis excitedly promise a prototype to test in a couple days.

The problem is, I'm worried we don't have a couple days. DES hasn't found any signs of Jarren. Not in the Q-net or his physical location. It's not a surprise his hideout is…well, hidden. DES only has access to satellites and messages from people living on the colony planets—all of which can be wormed. But I'd hoped they'd spot the clusters he's been using.

I use my extra time—'cause let's face it, it doesn't take Beau and me long to test the barricade—to train extra hard. When Jarren attacks, I'm not going to worry about my aim. Oh no. Mr. Orange Light is mine.

You'd think with all the physical activity, I'd sleep well at night. But I toss and turn. Each night gets worse. It's all my fault. I'm the one who said to Beau that we'd be neck deep in looters in seven days. So here it is, the night before day seven. Exhausted, I stare at the ceiling, willing myself to sleep.

Except my heart is acting like I just ate four pudding cups. It's thumping out: *Gotta be ready. Gotta be ready. Gotta be ready.* In double time.

The desire to crawl into bed with my parents pulses through me. When I was little and something scared me at night, I'd sneak in under their covers. I doubt Radcliff would appreciate a midnight visitor. Imagining his reaction, I huff in amusement. Then I give up and go into the kitchen. Maybe a warm drink will help. I brew a cup of one of those flowery weedy type teas that are supposed to make you sleepy. I take a sip. Ugh. Needs sugar. Lots of sugar.

Sitting on the couch, I spot Radcliff's portable on the table. I access the chapters on how to deal with a combative prisoner— yet another fact-filled assignment from my training officer. I wonder just how much of these lessons will stick with me. Once a situation goes sideways and the adrenaline kicks in, I find it hard to believe I'll be able to maintain a clinical detachment. Sipping my tea, I spend the next couple hours reading. And the dry protocols do what the tea could not: I fall asleep on the couch.

Jarren invades my dreams. No surprise as he's been a frequent visitor of late. This time he's standing in the hallway on the other side of the door to our unit.

Come out and play, Little Worm. It's been so boring without you, Dream Jarren calls.

Go away.

It's too late for that. I'm coming for you. The door opens and he strides in. He holds out a hand to me. Let's fly!

No. I'm not supposed to. DES—

Is handling the situation? You do realize I've been building my network for years and they've no clue what I'm doing? They're not a threat to me. His tone implies they're more a threat to me. *Actually, they're quite useful as I've learned a few things.* Jarren gives me a significant look. What started as a dream just veered into reality.

His sly cat-ate-the-mouse smile turns my blood into ice. We're in the Q-net. And I'm communicating with the real Jarren as if we're worming together like we used to do back on Xinji. Did my dream self inadvertently reach out to him in the Q-net or did he come looking for me? And, more importantly, does he know it's me or think I'm some other wormer? All scary questions.

I panic. *Go away.*

He sighs. *You're no fun, Lyra…or should I call you Ara?*

His last words render me speechless and confirm he's well aware of who I am despite not seeing me in the camera feeds.

You can change your name, but you can't hide from me. See you soon. Jarren leaves.

Without thinking, I follow him. Well, I track him. I zip through his breach, cut through a number of clusters, and dip toward the star roads—they call to me. Ignoring them, I focus on Jarren. But his trail is gone. *Where is he?*

And then the Q-net says, **HERE**.

And I about faint from the shock. But I'm too busy falling

toward a planet. It's bright yellow and a desert covers sixty-eight percent of its surface. The other thirty-two percent is carpeted by forests. Tall green trees with big canopies of leaves spread out over the rolling landscape and effectively hide Jarren and his thugs from the satellite's cameras.

The planet is Yulin.

2522:236

Oh my stars! Jarren has been hiding on Planet Yulin this entire time. Even though the desire to get far away fast pushes on me, I need to move through the Q-net without causing ripples. I don't want Jarren to know I've located him. Before I wake up...er...disentangle, I check the satellite feeds, searching for a shuttle flying toward the base or an army of looters crossing the desert.

The early morning sun washes the sand with its golden light. Other than a few field teams, nothing else stirs. I create a program to alert us if there is any movement from Jarren's camp. Tucking it into Jarren's own protections to hide it is somewhat fun—I'm still freaked over the fact he's so close. And that he knows I'm alive. And that we had a conversation through the Q-net.

Although I shouldn't be surprised Jarren knows. Beau and I predicted DES would bungle it. Then I disentangle, ensuring I don't take any shortcuts to avoid a killer migraine, and ignoring the tight ball of panic in my chest that's squeezing out distress signals: *Hurry! Hurry! Hurry!*

When I open my eyes, Radcliff is standing in the living room. He's frowning down at the portable in his hands.

"Why are you on the couch?" he asks.

"I couldn't sleep." The truth.

He taps the portable. "So you were worming instead?"

Talk about a trick question. Smoothing my hair away from my face, I sit up. "No. I was reading. Then I fell asleep and then I was worming." Which didn't sound as good as it did in my head. "But not on purpose."

"Ara—"

"Jarren knows I'm alive. And he's here. On Yulin."

Radcliff's grumpy annoyance transforms to steel. "Where?"

"Other side of the planet. In the forest."

His fingers dance on the portable for a minute. Then he hands it to me. "Show me."

There's a map of Yulin. I scroll, searching for an area that looks familiar until the rest of my brain wakes up. Connecting with the Q-net, I request a marker. A big red dot pulses over a large swathe of trees. I return the portable to him and disconnect.

"Sonovabitch," Radcliff says, striding to the door.

Before he can take off, I say, "I've set up an alarm. If he leaves that area, you'll be alerted."

He pauses with one hand on the door. "I don't know whether to discipline you for disobeying orders or give you a commendation."

I know which one I'd pick. "Let's get through this first and then you can decide."

"Nice dodge, Lawrence." He leaves.

And I hurry to report to training on time. I know not to say anything to Elese, but I have to admit it's killing me not to confide in her. The need to hear her say, "It'll be okay" is almost a physical ache. A hug of support would be nice, too. I'm even willing to overlook the evidence to the contrary. Yup, I'm that easy.

My sessions with Mr. Orange Light have progressed. Now he swings back and forth, ducking my shots. And I know it's a cliché to say that it's hard to hit a moving target, but it is *really* difficult to get the timing just right. While my misses outnumber my hits ten to one, I wonder how Jarren managed to shoot me from a hovering shuttle, while I was running. He must have practiced during those extra twenty years.

Other than plotting to take over the Galaxy, what else was he doing? Probably figuring out the Warrior mystery and other nefarious deeds. I have to admit when he said he'd explain everything to me and that we'd be heroes, I was tempted to hear him out. But... If he can figure it all out, then so can we.

Determination pumps through my veins. I aim, wait a few seconds, and fire. Direct hit! Yes! Mr. Orange Light winks out.

And so do the rest of the lights in the shooting range. I count heartbeats. One. Two. Three. Four. Then they turn back on along with my panic. Expecting to see looters streaming into the training room, I race out with my pulse gun in hand and stop.

Zaim and Rance are using the weight machines and Elese is pummeling a punching bag with her bare knuckles. No one appears alarmed. But then again no one knows about our unfriendly neighbor.

"Something wrong?" Elese asks. Sweat streams down her face, but she's not out of breath. The bag creaks as it spins and swings on the end of the chain.

"Did the lights flicker out here?"

"Yeah. Must have been a glitch. Why?"

"Ah, I thought it might be a sandstorm." Hiding an army of looters!

"More like sand in the machinery."

True. Those little grains of annoyance get into everything.

"How's target practice?" Elese asks.

"I decided to take pity on Mr. Orange Light. Let him feel like he's doing well for a change."

"That good, eh? Just wait until he starts shooting back. I doubt you'll take pity on him then."

"He can shoot back?" Yikes.

"Only way to learn how to aim and fire during a battle situation. You think it's hard now, wait until you're jacked on adrenaline, in a dark room unable to see the enemy."

Like the shadow-blobs. "I get it."

"No you don't. But you will."

Those ominous words echo in my head as I return to the shooting range. Mr. Orange Light no longer appears friendly. And I no longer allow distracting thoughts to wreck my concentration.

No surprise, I'm ordered to report to the conference room that afternoon. As I take a seat, I consider asking Niall for some of his mom's paintings to brighten up the place. I spend more time in here than my bedroom. Granted, I don't have many other options.

The usual suspects are here: Mom, Dad, Radcliff, and Morgan. All in the same seats, which is kind of funny. However, no one is smiling. Nope. It's easy to guess that Radcliff told them Jarren's location.

"Please explain to everyone what you were doing last night," Radcliff says.

It doesn't take me long.

"I thought you said you had control," Mom says to me. Her tone is harsh.

"I do. Except when I'm worried about something."

Dad touches her arm as if to say ease off the girl. Her posture softens.

"How does Jarren know about you?" Radcliff asks me.

"I'm assuming DES tipped him off about our escape from his blockade, then, when he examined the breach, he figured out who created it."

"Are you sure it wasn't due to worming in your sleep?"

It's a valid question, yet the desire to shout, *Why do you always blame me?* burns in my throat. "Yes. At first I thought he was just a bad dream because I've been fretting about him. But

I think he was searching for me."

"We'll assume Jarren has been monitoring our communications with DES since yesterday. Please limit your messages to unimportant communications and say nothing of our security measures," Radcliff says.

In other words, don't tell DES we know where Jarren is hiding.

"We also need to train and arm as many people as we can before he arrives," Radcliff continues. "Morgan, I want you to organize this A-sap and coordinate with Spencer regarding personnel. The archeology techs can help."

"Yes, sir," Morgan says.

"What I want to know is why didn't the satellite pick up on their thermal signatures?" Dad asks.

"They're smarter than the average criminal," Morgan says. "They located their base of operations on a hot spot. Deep underneath that area are thermal vents from volcanic magma. There's hot springs all over. Jarren and his goons are probably enjoying nice hot baths every night."

"And can't he worm into the satellite and alter the feeds?" Mom asks.

"He can and did," Radcliff says, then he meets my gaze.

And he can again. "I better check all our security measures to ensure he hasn't overridden them."

"Good idea, Lawrence. I also need you to find out how many people are at Jarren's base, what weapons they might have, equipment, and if they have security patrolling the forest."

"You're not thinking of attacking them, are you?" Mom

asks.

"It's an option. Depends on their numbers and readiness. If they're not expecting it, an attack could be quite effective."

"And dangerous." Mom is looking at me.

"It's just as dangerous if they attack us. We need more information A-sap."

About that. "I'm going to require Officer Dorey's help."

"Update him about Jarren's status," Radcliff says. "The rest of the team will be informed later this afternoon. Dismissed."

I hop up and head for the door, but my mom cuts me off.

"We need to talk," she says.

"Now?"

"No. Tonight after dinner, just thought I'd warn you."

I clutch at my chest in mock surprise. "That's a first. Who's dying?"

She swats me on my bicep. "Brat."

"Takes one to know one," I tease.

"That's mature."

"True, though."

"Go, before I show you just how bratty I can be."

I resist the urge to stick out my tongue at her before leaving. Beau's waiting for me in his office.

"Another meeting? What's the big secret this time?" Beau asks.

Ah, he's still sore over the whole worming-without-tangs thing. "You're going to regret asking that question."

"I am?"

"Yup." I fill him in.

He slouches down in his chair. "Stars, girl."

"I warned you."

"You did." He stares at the screen for a few moments. "Looks like we have a ton of work. What do you want to do first?"

Outwardly, I don't react to the fact he asked me my opinion. Yes, we're partners, but he's always been in charge of picking what we're going to do in the Q-net. "Check our security measures."

"All right. Let's get to it."

I insert my tangs. It doesn't take us long to see Jarren's been snooping around. The scary part is he didn't set off a single one of our alarms.

Has he altered any of our programs? Beau asks.

Not for the cameras in the base, nor the ones in the satellite. I check the feeds for security. *He's hit these pretty hard. Oh no.*

He's watching live feed in security now?

Yes. He's bypassed it.

But you don't show up in those feeds. Or has he found that special Q-net trick, too?

Trick or no, the Q-net ensures I'm not visible in the security camera feeds. *No. That's still intact.*

That's good. If he doesn't see you, then he'll question whether or not you're alive. Might slow him down.

Nice of you to try to make me feel better, but it's too late for that, Beau. He called me Lyra and Ara. My worming style is too obvious. I focus on our next task. *Are you ready to infiltrate enemy territory?* I ask.

How do you want to do this?

Obviously without tipping Jarren off. *On tiptoes, silent as the night, unseen, and—*

No more clichés please. I get it. So how's your head? You know he's going to be hiding behind some serious protection.

Ah. Going snail speed is extra hard and I made a promise. *We should probably take a break. Do you want to work on this after dinner?*

Is that enough time off?

Should be.

Ara, if we tip Jarren off that we know where he is, he's coming straight for us. And we're not ready for him yet.

It's enough time.

Dinner is a strange affair. Everyone is sneaking glances at me. Well, they're trying to be sneaky, but I notice. I don't say anything, though. 'Cause that would just give them all permission to ask me how I'm feeling about Jarren. And truthfully, I'd rather not have that discussion. One of the ways to be good at denial is to not examine your emotions too deeply, but to rather focus on other things. Like Niall's T-shirt and how it clings to his shoulders and chest.

He catches me looking at him and I'm rewarded with one of his I-know-what-you're-thinking smiles. I raise my eyebrows in a you've-no-idea-just-what-I'd-like-to-do manner. His eyes narrow in a I'd-like-to-see-you-try squint.

Too bad Radcliff interrupts our silent communication by asking for an update on the security measures. I fill them in on what Beau and I found.

"Any info on Jarren's hideout?" Radcliff asks.

"We're going back in tonight. We needed a break," I say, meeting Niall's gaze.

Universal approval. Wow, never thought that would happen.

"Don't stay up too late," Mom says.

I wonder if it's an automatic Mom response. Do the words just pop out of her mouth?

The rest of the dinner limps along with awkward small talk. Again, no one is brave enough to speculate what will happen if Jarren attacks. Although I suspect it's one of the reasons my mother wished to have a talk with me.

After dinner is cleaned up, my dad leaves to recruit volunteers to help with the base's defenses. Niall washes dishes while Mom and I go to my room to have our chat.

We sit on the edge of the bed, facing each other. If we wore the same clothes, I could almost imagine I'm staring into a mirror that reflects my future. Her silky black hair never stays confined in a braid, just like mine.

"I'm being careful," I say.

"You don't even know what I'm about to say."

"I figured that would cover all the bases."

She tucks a loose strand of hair behind her ear. "I want you to stop."

"Stop what?"

"Everything."

Oh no. She's in panic mode. I know it doesn't seem like she is, since she waited until now to freak out, but, think about it, I learned the fine art of denial from someone. "Mom—"

"Don't *Mom* me. Jarren *killed* you and the first thing he's going to do is come after you. No. I won't let it happen. You're staying here." She points a finger at the floor.

"Are you grounding me?"

"Yes. You're not eighteen A-years. I'm still your legal guardian and what I say goes. You can only leave this room for meals and to use the washroom."

A snarky response—why don't you just have Radcliff throw me in detention—wells up my throat. But I swallow it down. Logic is my only play. "Hiding won't keep me safe, Mom. And while you can order me to stay here, you can't enforce it."

"Tace will."

"No, he won't. He needs me. Mom, everyone on this base needs me." Huh. That's a ton of pressure. Maybe staying in my room isn't such a bad idea.

"Then you're coming home, Lyra. Back to your room in our unit. That door can be locked."

She used my real name. She's really upset. This must have been building all day. "I can't be seen."

"Yes, you can," she snaps. "The cat is out of the bag, Lyra. Jarren knows. Besides…" Mom glances at her hands. They're clutched tight together in her lap.

"Besides, what?"

"I'm tired of pretending you're dead. Of ignoring the pitying looks. The awkward conversations. And there's a few people who I thought were my friends that have been…avoiding me."

I'm a selfish idiot. I had no idea what she's been going through and it didn't even occur to me to ask. I'm also a self-absorbed idiot. Scooching closer, I wrap an arm around her shoulder. "I'm sorry. Is Dad having problems, too?"

"I'm sure he's getting the same response, but you know your father."

"Yeah, not the most sensitive when it comes to others' emotions."

"Just like your brother. I swear I could give him my fiercest scowl and he had no clue I was upset with him."

"Yeah, I had to tell him to go apologize to you and he was always clueless as to why." But he would do it. A pang echos in my chest. I miss my brother, but I'm glad he's safe. And I understand why my mom's being such a…well, a mom. "I'm sorry you had to pretend I was dead."

"Not your fault. We needed to keep you safe. But now—"

"Locking me in my room isn't the answer. You know that, right?"

"I know." She sounds just like a pouting two-year-old.

I hide my smile.

"It's just I don't trust Tace to keep you safe. He has the entire base to protect."

"Then you're just going to have to trust me to keep *me* safe."

"It'd be easier if, when I look at you, I don't see my little girl with her pigtails and chubby cheeks." She strokes my cheek.

That isn't chubby. At all. "Would it make you feel better if I roll my eyes and act like a hormonal teenager?"

"Actually yes. I think this trouble with Jarren has robbed you of your youth. You should still be attending soch-time and complaining about it."

"I don't miss soch-time. At all. Do you want me to tell you why?"

"I know why."

"Then you know why I need to go help Beau discover what Jarren's hiding out there in the woods."

"Smart ass."

I tsk. "Name-calling? Now who's acting like a teenager?" Ah, there's a smile.

Mom stands and smooths her shirt. "I'm not going to apologize for being a mother."

"Don't worry, I know it can't be helped."

"Be careful tonight, Little Miss Know-it-all." She gives me a kiss on my forehead.

As she leaves my room, I silently disagree with her. I'm not a know-it-all. Otherwise I would have realized that her and Dad's lives have been altered by Jarren's attack as well as mine. I vow to be less self-absorbed in the future.

I join Niall in the living area. He's sitting on the couch. "Was it bad?"

"She wanted to ground me."

"Really?"

"Don't give me that look. It's *not* a good idea."

"You can't blame me."

I just shake my head. "I'm sorry we won't have any time together tonight."

"That's okay." Niall stands. "I need to get some sleep. My duty schedule's been changed and I have the night shift."

"Is it because Jarren's on Yulin?"

"No. We all have to take a night shift rotation. It's just my turn."

"How long are the rotations?"

"Fourteen days."

I step in close, wrap my arms around his neck, and pull him in for a kiss.

"Not that I'm complaining, but what was that for?" Niall asks.

"Because I can."

He dips his head and gives me a kiss. "Same reason."

"Nice to know we're in agreement."

"Don't worry, I won't expect it all the time," he teases.

"Well that would just be boring."

"Nothing wrong with boring, Mouse."

"Sorry, but I draw the line at sensible."

"Whew. I better quit while I'm ahead."

Beau's already in his office and ready to go. This time I don't insert my tangs. Beau raises a thin eyebrow in question.

"They make me too heavy," I say.

His other eyebrow joins the first, but he doesn't ask me to clarify. Without another word, we connect and use my escape tunnel to worm deep into the Q-net. As expected, Jarren is hidden behind a mountain of protections, alarms, and hidden traps. It reminds me of the game world of *Mutant Zombies from Planet Nine*. Every blind corner could lead to certain death. Well, not that dramatic, but still...

Worming through his defenses is like climbing up a slope filled with loose rocks and dirt. One wrong move and the entire thing will avalanche. Snail speed is too fast. After four hours, we're no closer to Jarren. We've no idea how many people are with him. Nothing.

We disentangle.

Beau swigs a couple of painkillers and hands me the bottle. "I felt like I was walking a tightrope the entire time. One slip and... Pow!"

I stretch my back. "I think we need another approach. Instead of hitting him straight on, maybe we can loop in behind his defenses."

"What are the odds that he's going to leave a gap for us to exploit?"

"Not very good." I gesture to the terminal. "I need to be—" No. Not going to say it.

Of course Beau asks, "Need to be what?"

Sigh. "Asleep." I rush to explain. "When I'm sleeping, it's not worming. It's flying. I have no difficulty going anywhere."

"Even the star roads?"

"I haven't tried. Nor will I. Even my subconscious knows not to mess around with them."

"But you don't have control."

"Not at first. Not to connect to the Q-net, but once I'm there and I realize what's going on, I have full control of where I go and what I do."

"It's still dangerous."

"I'm not planning on doing it on purpose, but if it happens, I'm going to take full advantage."

Beau walks me back to my unit. Radcliff's still awake even though it's oh-one-hundred hours. He waited up only to hear we were unsuccessful.

"Report to Dorey's office at oh-nine-hundred hours," Radcliff says to me. "I'll inform Officer Keir you won't be training for the next few days. Gathering information about Jarren is your and Officer Dorey's priority right now."

"Yes, sir," I say. Nodding good night to Beau, I go to my bedroom.

Resting my pounding head on my pillow is a small slice of heaven. I'm asleep in seconds. No dreams or invitations to fly through the Q-net interrupt my sleep. The next day, Beau and I spend eight hours getting absolutely nowhere. We break for dinner and try again. Then it's bedtime. I wake up and repeat.

I lie in bed and stare at the painting of the Chinese guardian lion. It's been three days of utter failure. Three days of frustration. Three days of discovering I'm not as good at worming as I thought. Eventually, I fall asleep.

Radcliff wakes me at oh-three-hundred hours. He's wearing a jumpsuit. Never a good sign.

Fully awake, I sit up. "What's wrong?"

"Get changed. We've a situation."

"Jarren attacked." It's not a question.

"No. The HoLFs."

2522:239

By the time I wiggle into my security jumpsuit and clip on my weapon belt, Radcliff is gone. I slow to a stop. The emergency lights are on, which means the base has lost its main power. Weak orange-ish-yellow light illuminates the room. Not near bright enough. Lots of shadows everywhere.

We're so dead.

A mind-numbing fear freezes me in place. The shadow-blobs are going to slice everyone on this base into little pieces. When the Protector Class ship arrives, they'll find bits of us scattered all over the floor.

"…Ara!" Elese shouts from the open doorway. "Let's go. You can have your freak out later."

I snap from my paralysis and join her. We run through the hallways, encountering no one.

"See? All those laps you complained about. They came in handy," Elese says, breathing easy despite our speed.

"Groaning is not complaining." But I gotta admit it's nice

not to be gasping for breath. However, I am sucking in more air by the time we reach the stairwell that goes down to the archeology lab. It's the only lab that is below ground level so it's easier to access the Warrior pits.

Other members of the security team are already at the entrance to the stairwell along with a big battery-operated floodlight. Everyone has their flashlights in hand. I pull mine and check the beam.

Radcliff spots me and says, "Any HoLFs in the vicinity?"

I search the shadows as I test the air. "No. What happened?"

"They attacked the officers in the lab. Tora escaped, but…"

There's always two on duty and guess who has the night rotation. I scan faces. Tora presses a cloth to her cheek. Splotches of bright red stain the white fabric. All my blood suddenly rushes into my heart. It expands, pressing painfully on my chest as if ready to explode.

"Niall's still there," I say, my voice barely a whisper.

Radcliff nods.

I turn to go down the stairs, but a hand clamps on my shoulder and yanks me back.

"Where do you think you're going?" Radcliff demands.

"To save Niall."

"Tora said the HoLFs were everywhere. We need to wait for more lights."

"He could be dead by then!" I shout.

"And so could you." Radcliff grabs my other shoulder and leans in so we're almost nose to nose. "Once the lights get here, we'll go in, until then sit tight."

Sit tight? Sit tight? My heart's about to erupt. And— Deep within Radcliff's gaze is raw pain. That's his son in danger. I nod and he releases me.

"Where's Beau?" I ask.

"In the Control Center, trying to get the lights back on."

"What caused them to go out?"

"We don't know."

It's suspicious and the urge to worm into the Q-net wars with my panic over Niall. One way to help him is to get the lights back on. But my full attention is needed here just in case shadow-blobs escape. Grrr.

Dr. Carson races toward us. She's wearing her lab coat over pajamas. A step behind her is a tall lanky man with black hair. He's carrying a long cylindrical object.

"Officer Radcliff," she calls.

Not waiting for an invitation, I join the three of them.

"...still testing it. We don't know how effective it will be," she says.

"What *do* you know?" Radcliff asks.

"It will emit a counter radio wave, but you have to aim it directly at the HoLF."

"Not a problem," I say. "Show me how it works."

Bertie looks at the man. "Jim?"

He's staring at me with his mouth open.

I suppress a sigh. "Yes, I'm not dead, get over it and show me how this damn thing works."

Jim recovers. "Um...here." He hands it to me. "Hold it like

this."

There's a short post underneath the front. I grab it with my left hand, making a fist around it. The cylinder rests on the top of my hand. It's about ten centimeters in diameter and approximately a meter long. Jim places the back end over the crook of my right arm. The sucker is heavy.

"The controls are where your right hand is. Do you feel it?" he asks.

"There's two...teeth?"

"Close enough. All you need to do is aim the weapon, and squeeze those two teeth together, which will trigger the counter wave. And don't forget this." He puts a leather strap over my neck. "In case you lose your grip."

I move my left arm so the strap sits across my body. It helps hold the weight. I swing the weapon around, getting a feel for it. "How long do I need to keep this aimed at the HoLF?"

"Sorry, all we know is it emits a counter wave. The rest is up to you to figure out. It's not like we have a HoLF in the lab to test it on."

True. Well there's no time like the present. "All right, here's the plan," I say. "I'll take point. I need two people who will grab Niall and carry him out. The rest can follow with flashlights and—"

"*Junior* Officer Lawrence, you are *not* in charge. You will not be making plans," Radcliff says. "We're waiting for more floodlights."

"But we have the emitter."

"Which may do nothing at all, like the lasers."

"We should take the chance. Time is not on our side." Niall could be bleeding out as we argue.

Just then my parents arrive with a bunch of techs in tow. They're carrying more portable, battery-powered floodlights. Thank the universe!

Radcliff shouts orders and details a plan that is almost exactly the same as mine. But I'm not going to quibble over whose idea it is, because I don't care. There's a primal wild impulse in my core that's pushing on me to *go, go. GO! Run, run. RUN!* Right into the archeology lab and get Niall.

When Dr. Edwards appears with a couple nurses, I bite back a scream. Or I think I do. My mom gives me a wide-eyed look as if I've turned feral. And that's fine with me. I'll go all feral on those shadow-blobs—just let me at them!

Bendix, Ho, Elese, and Rance heft the floodlights. They enter the stairwell first, illuminating the steps. But I'm right between them, sensing the air. No cold sensations. I think. It's hard to tell since I'm sweating.

"Clear," I say and start down with Ho on my right and Rance on the left.

Right behind us are Bendix and Elese, then Radcliff, Morgan, Zaim, and last is Dr. Edwards, who insisted on coming along. Good for him.

Drops of blood on the steps gleam in the bright white light. My heart rate ratchets up from super-sonic to the speed of light. But I keep an even pace. We reach the bottom of the stairs. Beyond our position are the doors to the lab. They're wide open. One is marked with a bloody handprint. Not good. I swallow.

Breathe. Breathe. Breathe.

The temperature drops, turning my sweat into ice. Pressure builds on my skin.

"Lawrence?" Radcliff asks.

"There are HoLFs in the lab." Also there are no emergency lights on. It's pitch dark inside.

"Where are they?"

"I'll know better once we're inside. Ready?"

A chorus of yes. Flanked by the floodlights, I enter the lab and gasp. Just to the right of the doors is Niall. He's lying on the floor next to the wall. And he's curled into a ball with his hands laced behind his neck—it's a protective posture. Except he's not moving and there's a large pool of blood underneath him.

No. No. No. NO!

"Lawrence, focus on the HoLFs, we've got him," Radcliff says as he and Dr. Edwards rush over to him.

My priority shifts. I need to protect them so they can save Niall. "Fan out around Niall," I bark.

Rance, Ho, Elese, and Bendix spread out in a semi-circle around the group on the floor. I scan the shadows. They're alive.

"Aim your flashlights at the shadows."

"Which ones?" Elese asks.

"All of them."

They do. It doesn't take long for curses and grunts of surprise to echo in the lab as the shadow-blobs sneak weaponized tentacles through the gaps in the light. I target the shadows with my weapon, but I can't see the individual HoLFs. I step out of the ring of light.

"Where are you going?" Bendix snaps. "Damn things are everywhere."

"It's too bright." I aim at the middle of the first shadow-blob that dives for me. Squeezing the trigger, I brace for…well, I've no idea.

The shadow-blob slows, then there's a sizzle-zap sound and the HoLF explodes into a million little black dots that wink out of sight. I whoop. The rest of the shadow-blobs pause as if in shock. Then they dive for me. I backpedal until my back hits a wall. Then I aim at the closest HoLF. Sizzle-zap! And the next. Sizzle-zap! Sizzle-zap! Sizzle-fun!

Tentacles lash at me with sharp blades. I duck the strikes as my training kicks in. And I keep aiming. Sizzle-zap! A handful of slashes run along my shoulders and arms, but the jumpsuit's material protects my skin from getting cut. Sizzle-zap! Sizzle-zap! Sizzle-zap!

A jagged knife of agony pierces my side as a shadow-blob gets past my defenses. I zap it, but I realize that the jumpsuit won't protect me from a straight thrust. And they've figured it out, too. Plus I'm outnumbered. Sizzle-zap! Sizzle-zap! Sizzle-zap! And I'm quite a few meters from the protective semi-circle of light. When did that happen? Sizzle-zap! Sizzle-zap!

"Lawrence, retreat," Radcliff orders.

Not until Niall—but he's gone. One less thing to worry about. I step toward the lab's doors when another burning puncture erupts on my upper right thigh. Remembering Niall's mother, I freeze. A tentacle stabs into my left shoulder. I fumble to squeeze the trigger of my weapon, but my fingers are numb. And I've no feeling from the knees down. Am I bleeding out?

Bright white light shines on me and the shadow-blobs flee. A hand grabs my arm and yanks me to my feet. When did I sit down?

"Ara, move!" Radcliff pulls me along.

I stumble up the stairs. The light holders are just two steps behind as they protect us. We burst out into the hallway. Radcliff shouts orders about stationing the floodlights in the stairwell. The air is warm and light. Too bad the base is spinning.

"...HoLFs?"

"Huh?" I blink, trying to focus on Radcliff.

"Did any of the HoLFs escape?" he asks.

I scan the area. Other than the walls undulating, everything appears normal. "No." Then I remember. Fear clears my unsteady thoughts. The base stills under my feet. "Niall?"

"Alive," Radcliff says, but he doesn't look relieved. "He lost a great deal of blood."

Oh no. "Where..."

"Dr. Edwards and his team rushed him to surgery."

"Why aren't you there?"

"Nothing I can do for him at this point. Besides, I have to ensure my team is all right." His gaze slides to my shoulder. "How bad is it?"

It was fine until he asked. Multiple injuries flare to life. The emitter in my arms all of a sudden gains a hundred kilos. I try to take the strap off, but my shoulder is having none of it.

Radcliff lifts the weapon with ease. "Did it work?"

"Yes. It did great. Just too…many of them. And they…" The floor buckles under me and I stagger to the side.

Radcliff puts his hand on my waist to steady me. I hiss in pain.

"You need to go to the infirmary." He calls for my parents to escort me.

They admonish me for not saying something sooner. Dad puts my good arm around his neck, supporting me as we navigate the hallways. My mom clucks at me, but I've no idea what she's saying. It takes all my concentration to stay on my feet. The nurses in the infirmary frown at me.

They shoo my parents out of the exam room. And then they torture me by taking off my jumpsuit and cleaning my injuries. Trust me, I'm not exaggerating. Too bad I don't have the good sense to pass out.

Another doctor comes in and inspects my wounds. She introduces herself as Dr. Bharathi. After the examination, she declares that two of the four punctures are shallow enough to heal on their own, but the other two are going to require minor surgery. My parents are fetched to give permission.

Before I'm wheeled out, I ask about Niall. "Any news?"

"Still in surgery."

I grab Mom's hand. "Is he going to make it?"

She hesitates. No doubt trying to put the best spin on what she knows.

"Please don't lie to me," I say.

"I'm not. I just don't know his prognosis and was trying to come up with something encouraging."

"Sorry." I squeeze her hand. "Did you think of something?"

She gives me a wry smile. "He's young and healthy and was smart enough to curl into a protective ball. They're all points in his favor."

"Thanks, Mom." I focus on those positives as I'm prepped for surgery. He's my last thought before everything spins to black.

I wake. My old friend, the mechanical beep, is once again keeping watch over me. *Beep—you got that right.*

The lights are dim and my father is sitting in the chair, reading from his portable. The clock on the wall says it's sixteen hundred hours. I slept all day. It takes me a few moments to remember why I'm here. Fear sharpens my groggy thoughts. "How's Niall?"

"He's out of surgery," Dad says.

"That's good, right?"

"He lost a lot of blood, Li-Li."

Oh no, he used my nickname. *Beep—calm down. Beep— you're jumping to conclusions.* Dad frowns at the machine behind my head. I take a few deep breaths to steady my heart.

Once the beeping slows, I ask, "What does that mean?"

"He could have brain damage."

Beep—he said could. *Beep—doesn't mean he* will.

"When will they know?" I ask.

"When he wakes up." My father glances away.

The unspoken, *if he wakes up,* hangs heavily in the air.

Dad clears his throat. "How are you feeling?"

"Sore. Tired. Was anyone else injured?"

"Minor cuts and bruises."

At least there's some good news. "What happened down in the lab?"

"According to Officer Tora, all the lights in the lab just died without warning. Both she and Niall immediately turned on their flashlights in time to see the doors to the pits break open. She mentioned a wave of cold air hitting her before Niall pushed her toward the stairs. HoLFs attacked and she ran, thinking he was right behind her."

And Niall was worried about *me* risking myself. "What happened to the lights?"

"Officer Dorey is still working on figuring it out, but he did restore power to the rest of the base."

For how long? "Dad, what if the lights go out again?"

"We've opened all the shades in the labs to let the sunlight in. And we have the portable floodlights for night. Also we're working on an evacuation protocol just in case we need to leave the base."

All good measures. "What about—"

"That's enough questions. If you get plenty of rest, the doctor said you might be able to leave tomorrow."

No way I'm leaving. Not without Niall.

After reassuring my parents a half-dozen times that I'm fine, they go to catch up on some much needed sleep. Since it's pretty late, I try to doze, but my thoughts keep circling back to Niall. What if he doesn't wake? Or if he has brain damage? Or he dies! Each scenario is scarier than the last. And after cycling through them all for the hundredth time, I can no longer stand it.

I sit up. My stitches pull on my tender healing skin, reminding me that I probably shouldn't be doing this. I ignore them. Except for the IV in the back of my hand, the rest of the sensors on my body are wireless. The bag of IV fluid is hanging from a pole that has wheels. Bonus.

Easing down from the bed, I wheel over to the closet, find the robe and slippers that are waiting for me inside, and put them on. Some would think multiple trips to the infirmary to be a bad thing, but there are perks—like insider knowledge. I peek out the door. All is quiet and empty. The wheels squeak as I roll the IV down the hallway. I head toward intensive care. There's a nurse behind a station, but I don't pause. Instead, I turn down another corridor, aiming for the glass rooms. Well, they're not constructed of glass, but instead of a solid wall and door, there's a half wall with a large glass window and no door to allow the nurses easy access.

Sure enough, there's a dim light shining from one of the rooms. I brace for the worst and keep going. Radcliff is sitting beside Niall's bed. From this vantage point all I see is black hair on a pillow. There's a single lamp on and Radcliff's reading something aloud, although he stops when he spots me. He opens his mouth, closes it, and rubs his temple. Poor guy doesn't even have the energy to scold me for being out of bed.

"He hasn't woken," Radcliff says.

All I can manage is a nod. Words would no doubt be accompanied by lots of tears. I move closer to the bed. To say Niall is white as a ghost is an insult to ghosts. He's beyond pale and his lips are slightly blue. Cuts mar his cheeks and forehead. But his machine beeps and the screen behind his bed lists that his vitals are all at normal levels. His brain is showing activity, although there's no way to determine if it's abnormal or not.

I wrestle with my emotions until I can speak without crying. "What are his injuries?"

Radcliff peers at me as if debating what he should tell me.

"I can either hear it from you or find out by worming into his medical files."

He sighs, but then says, "He's been stabbed multiple times. The good news is nothing vital was damaged beyond repair. The bad is the loss of blood. During the surgery, he flatlined, but Edwards was able to revive him. Now it's just a matter of time."

Flatlined! That means he died! I tighten my fingers around the IV pole until they ache, but it is the only thing keeping me upright.

"Go back to bed, Ara," Radcliff says. His tone is gentle.

It's a struggle, but I regain control of my emotions. "Unlike you, I slept most of the day. Give me the portable, I'll keep Niall company while you get some sleep."

Radcliff hesitates so I hold out my hand for the device.

"You do realize, *I'm* the one who gives the orders," he says, but he stands and hands me the portable. "If he wakes—"

"I'll let you know A-sap." I wheel my IV pole next to the chair and settle into it without wincing. Go me. Reading aloud from some story involving small troll-like people, I ignore Radcliff.

Eventually he leaves. After waiting a few more minutes, I stop. Sitting next to Niall just won't do. His bed is bigger than mine. I move some tubes aside. With my stitches protesting my every movement, I lie down next to him. I reach under the covers and find his hand. It's warm and also has an IV needle stuck into the back of it. Careful not to jostle it, I entwine my fingers in his. Much better.

"Hey, Toad, it's Mouse," I say. "You need to wake up. We still have lots of things to do together and I need you. Your dad needs you. The team needs you. The people on the base need you. We're short one guardian lion. That just won't do. And…" A wave of sadness builds behind my eyes, filling my nose. I sniff. "I love you, Niall." Why didn't I tell him I love him before? I'm a short-sighted idiot.

"Don't leave me." I kiss his cheek. Then I keep talking to him, telling him all kinds of goofy stuff until I fall asleep.

The nurses wake me in the morning, but I refuse to leave Niall. They argue that they'll keep an eye on him. Sorry, but not good enough.

Elese shows up soon after. "Causing problems already?" She tsks. "Maybe you're well enough to run some laps."

I fake a cough. "I'm having a relapse—cough—must get back to bed."

"How convenient." Humor sparks in her brown eyes. Then she sits down next to Niall. I hand her the portable. "What am I supposed to do with this?"

"Read to him."

"And that helps how?"

"So he hears a familiar voice. Let him know he's not alone. Or you can just tell him stories. That's what I did."

"All right." She squints at me. "How's that cough?"

"Going!" I wheel my IV pole back to my room, endure my nurse's half-hearted admonishments about being out of bed, and eat my breakfast.

The morning briefing is held in my room in the infirmary. Officers Radcliff, Morgan, Beau, and my parents are all in attendance. No, the place isn't that big, which is why Morgan and my mom are on the bed with me. I'm sitting up with my legs crossed to give them space. No one mentions my night-time excursion.

I recount what happened when I encountered the HoLFs, including how the weapon worked.

"Jim said they can build more," Mom says.

"How many and how soon?" Radcliff asks.

"Enough for the security team, but it's going to take a few

days."

"What about if we increase the number of people working on them?"

"We already did," Dad says. "They're tripping over each other. Plus there's only so much they can do."

"How long will the batteries on those floodlights last?"

"A couple nights, but we have extras. Plus we installed a bunch of ones that are plugged in behind the others just in case. The lights should work until the weapons are ready," Dad says.

And they're all failing to see a bigger problem. "Even with the weapons, the officers can't see the HoLFs," I say.

"Does it matter?" Morgan asks. "Can't they just aim at the shadows?"

"It's more complicated than that. The HoLFs I shot were close to me and I aimed at their core."

"We'll just have to do the best we can." Radcliff glances at his notes.

"It's not going to work. We need the team to see the enemy. We need to get to the Warrior hearts."

Everyone looks at me.

"No, too dangerous," Radcliff says.

"Please hear me out." When no one protests, I continue. "I know we don't have any evidence that touching the heart is the reason I can see them. But, think about it, it's the only play we have left." I explain how we can reach the hearts.

Once again, I'm the center of attention. I'd feel special except the expressions are not ones of awe and amazement over my grand plan. My idea is quickly vetoed. Too bad.

Radcliff moves on to another topic, asking Beau about the base's power.

"The lab is cut off from the rest of the base," Beau says. "I can't get it back into the grid. All the other labs and housing units are fine for now. I still don't know why the power went out. The last time the HoLFs attacked, they cut the electrical wires going into the pits. And they chewed through the floodlights in the lab because they were plugged in. But it's not so easy to do that for the rest of the archeology lab. Those wires are behind walls." He glances at me. "I'm hoping Junior Officer Lawrence will be able to assist me today."

"The doctor said she'll be discharged this afternoon," Mom says.

"I can help you, Beau, but I'm not leaving the infirmary until Niall wakes up," I say. And just in case they forgot, I add, "I can access the Q-net anywhere."

Everyone looks at Radcliff as if he alone has the power to persuade me. I'd be more amused that my parents believe this as well, but I'm preparing to dig in my heels for some major resistance.

"As long as you're not in the nurses' and doctors' way," Radcliff says, surprising me.

The meeting breaks up. Beau and I plan to connect in the Q-net at thirteen hundred hours. My mother fetches me a couple clean uniforms and personal supplies. When I'm discharged, I settle in Niall's room.

Elise vacates the chair, handing me the portable. "That's one crazy story. I hope I didn't give him nightmares."

I open my mouth to reply, but my thoughts have snagged on her comment about nightmares. I wonder...

I've no memory of Elese leaving. Taking Niall's hand, I tell him I'm here. Then I stare at the screen behind him. It's twelve thirty so I have half an hour. His name is at the top: Niall S. Radcliff. I don't know what the S stands for. Huh. Does that mean I'm a bad girlfriend? I shake my head and concentrate, accessing the Q-net.

And am surrounded by medical programs. No surprise given my location. Although tempted to read through Niall's medical file, I worm into my perceptive cluster. I focus on Niall. He died during surgery. Did he fly in the Q-net during that time like I did? Perhaps he's lost and can't get back to his body. But the Q-net's as vast as the Milky Way Galaxy...well that's how it feels to me. How can I—

NOT HERE, the Q-net says.

My relief wars with shock over the Q-net communicating with me again. I'd been hoping that other time was just a fluke, or my overactive imagination kicking in. My first impulse is to disentangle, but I pause. Within the Q-net is a massive amount of information. There are surface programs that will search through it, but I suspect asking the Q-net directly might yield better results. Although I have to admit, it's either the craziest thing I've contemplated—on par with asking the bureau which drawer my socks are in—or the scariest.

What are the Hostile Life Forms? I ask.

HERE. The Q-net deposits a file in the cluster.

I don't waste time thinking about why or how that worked.

Instead, I check the file. It's one of Lan's. And not just any one, but the one reporting on her translations of the alien symbols. It was one of the missing files from Planet Xinji that Jarren deleted. Yet here it is and it's complete. Amusement flows over me. It's official, I'm going crazy. Not only is the Q-net interacting with me, I'm imagining it has emotions. Beau enters the cluster. *I'm here.*

Giggles threaten to unhinge me over him echoing the Q-net.

He notices the file. *What's this?*

I wait a beat.

Stars! Where did you find this?

In the Q-net.

Not funny, Ara. Getting this file is huge.

I know. The Q-net gave it to me.

Silence. How?

I asked.

Beau sighs. *We'll worry about it later. Right now, we need to figure out the power situation so it doesn't happen again.*

I agree. We worm through the base's maintenance programs. Beau shows me the wiring schematic and how the power is distributed throughout the base. At first, they appear normal, but I look closer. Jarren's fingerprints are all over. And it appears—

Stars!

What did you find? Beau asks.

Jarren wormed the base's power programs. He's the one who

turned off all the lights in the archeology lab. And…

There's an and?

Unfortunately. He's programmed the entire base's power to turn off in stages.

Stages?

Yes. Starting at the stairwell, more labs will lose power each night until the entire base goes completely dark.

When?

In four days.

2522:240

Four days until we lose all power? Beau asks, his thoughts shrill with panic.

That's what Jarren's worm shows.

Why do it in stages?

My guess is so it appears to be a glitch and not outright sabotage.

Can you stop it?

Can I? I scan the threads of his worm. It's super complex and woven in deep. *I'm not sure. And if I do, it will alert Jarren that we found it.*

Don't touch it. We need to report to Radcliff.

All right. Where's he at?

On the way to the infirmary. I'll meet you both there.

We disentangle. Niall's hand is now in both of mine and I'm pressing it to my heart, which is thumping hard enough for the vibrations to reach my fingertips. I relax my death grip on Niall, but don't let go, then I sit on the edge of his bed.

"You're not going to believe this," I say to Niall. Talking aloud helps organize my frightened and chaotic thoughts. "Jarren, the murdering looter, is planning on killing us all. He's going to use the shadow-blobs to do his murdering for him. Why now? Good question. He knows we escaped his blockade and that DES is searching for him. Jarren wants this planet without us on it. Probably to use the Warriors. And time's running out."

"Time's running out for what?" Radcliff asks as he enters the room.

I explain what Beau and I learned. Radcliff's expression darkens. It promises pain to anyone stupid enough to cross him. I'm glad it's not aimed at me.

"Why wait?" he asks.

"He's either sadistic or he's hoping we're too busy fighting HoLFs to notice he wormed the power."

"How hard was it to find his worm?"

"Hard. I don't think anyone else could have spotted it."

"But you think Jarren is hoping that by spreading the power outages over five nights, we won't think to look for a worm."

"Yes."

"Can you stop it?"

"Maybe, but if I do, it might alert Jarren."

"And he'll try another tactic to kill us." Radcliff scrubs a hand over his face. "What's the perimeter of tonight's blackout?"

I grab the portable and pull up a map of the base. Then I connect with the Q-net—it's getting easier to do—and have it show the areas for each night in different colors. I hand the device to Radcliff.

He studies it. "I don't think we can contain the HoLFs past the stairwell. We're going to have to risk you warning Jarren."

"I said I *might* be able to disable his worm."

"I've complete confidence in you."

No pressure.

"All right." Then I get an idea. "We could send a bunch of panicked messages to DES to distract him during that time. Have you contacted them since Jarren found our escape tunnel?"

"No."

"You might not be able to."

"You think Jarren closed the tunnel."

"Yes, and that's probably why he's trying to get the HoLFs to kill us, so we don't find another way to contact DES. The timing makes sense."

Beau shows up. "Did you tell him?" he asks me.

"Yes. He knows about the four days."

"What about the file?"

"I forgot." And when they both look at me, I say, "I'm sorry but only having four days to live has me quite distracted." I fill Radcliff in on the Q-net file. "I'll send it to my parents through their portables, they're the best ones to read through it and see if there's anything useful." Of course I plan to examine a copy as well, but no need to mention that.

"Good. I'll go update your parents and discuss options," Radcliff says, but makes no signs of leaving. Instead, he's gazing at his son.

Oh. I release Niall's hand and slide off the edge of the bed. Then I hook my arm in Beau's and tow him to the hallway.

"What are you doing?" Beau asks.

I point my chin through the glass window. Radcliff is standing next to Niall's bed, resting his hand on his son's head.

"Oh." Beau stops resisting. "Any improvement in his condition?"

"No."

We go further down the hall and stop. I fill him in on the part of the conversation he missed.

"I hate that guy," Beau just about growls. "Jarren has balls to threaten us. I can't wait to see Radcliff cut them off and feed them to him."

"Actually, after learning Jarren's responsible for Niall's injuries, I'd like to be the one to feed him his balls."

Beau claps me on the back. "That's my partner."

"Are you two conspiring?" Radcliff asks, joining us.

"Always, sir," Beau says.

"Should I be worried, Officer Dorey?"

"Not *you*, sir." Beau and I share an evil little grin.

"I'm not going to ask. Dorey, you're with me. Lawrence, check if we still have our connection to DES and take a closer look at Jarren's worm. I want to know how much time it will take for you to disable it."

"Yes, sir. Should I try to reach DES again if we don't have contact?"

"No. Hold off on doing anything for now. Message me as soon as you find out."

"Yes, sir."

They continue down the hall and I return to Niall's room. He hasn't moved and he still looks like he's one step away from death. Feeding Jarren his own balls is going too easy on him. I check the screen, but Niall's vitals are the same. I kick off my boots and lie next to Niall.

"How about a bribe?" I ask him. "You can help me castrate Jarren, but only if you wake up." Nothing. Not even a twitch. "Think about it, but not too long or you'll miss all the action." I reclaim his hand. "All right, I'm going into the Q-net." Keeping up a running commentary, I explain everything I'm doing as I first send Lan's file to my parents' portables and erase all evidence of it in the Q-net. Then I take a closer look at Jarren's worm.

Complex just doesn't do it justice. And it doesn't feel…right. There's layers here that are like one of those optical illusions. They appear to do one thing, but then it switches to another. Confusing. It's going to take me hours to figure out how it works before I can even start unraveling it.

Unless I embrace the crazy and ask the Q-net for help. Why not? I might get a "not here" but I might get a "here." So I do.

HERE.

A red line snakes through the worm, then a green one. I study them. Assuming red means danger or stop and green is go, I see the solution. It will still be very difficult and time consuming, but it's now doable. The tightness around my chest eases a fraction and I move on to my next task, checking on the escape tunnel to DES.

It's still there. Except there's a misdirect worm on it, which means all our messages are being sent to Jarren. I'm beginning to hate when I'm right. Because it usually means we're screwed.

My parents, Radcliff, and I are all sitting around Niall's room eating Niall's favorite dinner—roast beef and mashed potatoes covered in gravy. The hope is that he'll smell the delicious food his father cooked and wake up. I steal glances at him. Come on, Niall, yummy food. Better than that IV solution you've been on for the last thirty-eight hours. Dr. Edwards said he needed to wake within the first seventy-two hours after the attack.

I fill them in on what I discovered that afternoon. Because of Yulin's spin, we have another six hours of sunlight, which should be enough time for me.

"At this point, we'd rather you keep the lights on even if that means alerting Jarren," Radcliff says to me.

"Even if I don't tip him off, eventually he's going to find out we survived."

"We know and we're making plans for Jarren." Radcliff's grin could be described as almost criminal. "And we're going to need your help."

I glance at Niall.

"Don't worry," Mom says. "I'll stay with him when you can't be here."

"Thanks. What are your plans?"

"They're based on a number of assumptions and things I

learned from your file, Li-Li," Dad says.

"It's not mine. That's twenty-eight years of *Lan's* research."

"Yes, of course."

"What did you learn?" I ask.

Dad reads from his portable. "She confirmed that the Warriors are protectors against a dangerous predator. I'm assuming they're the HoLFs even though Lan refers to them as demons. The Warrior planets were chosen carefully. Besides being habitable by humans, the planets are also located at an entanglement point in the Galaxy."

"Entangled like when you connect to the Q-net?"

"Not quite. It's called quantum entanglement. Basically you have two particles that are entangled—if one particle jumps, then the other jumps at the same time—they're in the same quantum state. These entangled particles can then be moved far apart and if you manipulate one, say make it turn blue, then the other will turn blue as well. Einstein called it 'spooky action at a distance.' It's one of the reasons we can communicate to other planets without our messages being affected by the time dilation."

Wow.

"Lan also says it could be translated as a crossing point as well," Dad adds.

"Crossing as in a portal to another planet or into another dimension?" I ask. Lan also speculated the demons came from an alternate universe.

"It's not clear."

"Maybe the aliens figured out how to entangle the Warrior planets with each other."

"Unfortunately, the translations don't go into that much detail."

I recall Pit 21 and feeling the presence of shadow-blobs, but then the green lights from the Warriors pulsed as if pushing back the HoLFs. "Maybe in order to cross to another Warrior planet you have to go through some alternate dimension. But that dimension has HoLFs so they built the Warriors to protect against the HoLFs when crossing."

"We've no idea if there *are* portals, Ara," Mom says.

"Then where did the HoLFs come from?" No answer. So I forge ahead. "If you assume that there *are* portals, everything else makes sense."

"She has a point," Radcliff says.

An unexpected ally. Nice.

"The file also mentioned the factory for the Warrior hearts," Dad says. "According to the symbols, only a few planets have these factories and that a person 'must claim the heart of a Warrior' in order to cross over."

"That's more proof of my theory," I say.

Mom scowls at me, but asks Dad, "Did she say which planets?"

"Yulin, of course, Xi'an, Dongguan, Kaiping, Suzhou, and three planets we haven't reached yet. Eight total." Dad gives us a wry smile. The alien builders have a thing for the number eight.

"Jarren was on Planet Suzhou for ten years," Radcliff says

thoughtfully. "He had access to Lan's notes prior to when she cracked the code; he may have discovered the hidden factory before she did."

I gasp as a memory hits me. It was something Jarren said when he caught me.

"Don't keep us in suspense, Ara," Radcliff prompts.

"Jarren said that shadow-blobs was 'a rather accurate name.' How would he know that if he can't see them?"

"Then we need to assume he and his people can see them," Radcliff says.

"Does that change any of our plans?" Dad asks.

"No. Actually, if it's true, it'll work in our favor."

"Great," Dad says, then he turns to me. "Li-Li, except for the Warrior hearts and the factories, most of Lan's translations have not been proven and we don't have the luxury to test her theories. Like I said before, we're taking a few things on faith and will need your help."

In other words, it's dangerous and might not work. "I'm in."

As soon as everyone leaves, I entangle with the Q-net and worm to the programs for the base's power. The red and green guidelines are still there. I carefully untangle Jarren's worm, fiber by fiber. I thought escaping Jarren's blockade was difficult. That was easy in comparison. It takes me over five hours, but I separate the instructions to knock out the power from the grid's main programming. Then I sever it without removing it. If

Jarren checks on his worm, it will appear as if it's working as intended. Unless he picks it apart, then he'll see where I disconnected it. But he might be too busy.

Beau's been tasked with transmitting panicked messages to DES about losing power and the HoLFs attacking and killing people. They'll get more desperate before we go "silent." This will hopefully convince Jarren his plan worked and give us a few more days.

I send messages to Radcliff, Beau, and my parents that I was successful. They're all waiting with the security team near the stairwell just in case I failed. Glad I don't have to race to join them to sizzle-zap shadow-blobs, I change into my bunny pajamas and collapse next to Niall. Sleep is instant.

By the end of the next day, my head aches from the delicate work of worming around Jarren's...er...worms. Now that the threat of losing power has been mitigated Radcliff gave me a list of tasks to do for his grand plan. Most of it is with the satellite. No, I don't know all the details and I suspect there's a reason for it.

After dinner, I crawl into bed with Niall. It's been sixty-seven hours and he's still unconscious. Worry and fear for him are my constant companions. Come on, Niall. You can't do this to me. Or to your father. Not after what happened to your mother. That's cruel.

Of course I don't voice those thoughts out loud. Instead, I settle next to him, dig his hand out from underneath his blankets, and lace my fingers in his.

"I spent the entire day worming," I say. "Don't worry, my

brain didn't turn to mush. I took breaks." I did. "I can't believe an Actual year ago, I never would have thought I'd be worming legally and be part of a security team. I thought I'd be still on Xinji, hanging with my best friend, Lan, and waiting to go to university on Planet Rho. That girl was so young and innocent." I laugh. "Okay not so innocent, but she was definitely a brat. And her worming skills were rudimentary. Now I'm worming to save everyone's lives. No pressure there." Another memory bubbles to the surface. "Maybe you should have arrested me for worming. Remember when you were still acting like a jerk and threatened to throw me into detention? My antics drew Jarren's attention so maybe if I stopped sooner... No, Jarren planned to attack the Warrior planets before I meddled. He only came back for me after he destroyed the Warriors." Small comfort. But still...

My thoughts turn to Jarren's plans and I mull it over, voicing it out loud for Niall. "So if I'm right, and the Warriors can open portals to other planets without causing the time dilation, then those that control the...technology—for lack of a better word—will not only be obscenely rich, but extremely powerful. DES will have no way to stop them because of the time dilation. They'd have no choice but to relinquish space travel to Jarren and his partners. And then what?

"Let's assume we live through the takeover—I know, a big assumption since we're trying to stop Jarren—then all our lives will change. I could take the...Warrior Express to zip over to Earth and visit my brother. Except he's still in a time jump so I have to wait twenty-five years for him to show up. Imagine his surprise, though. It'd be worth waiting to see the shock on his face." I pause. "That is *if* I can afford the fee. Right now DES doesn't charge colonists or scientists to travel from planet to planet because we're all basically working for them. No tourists in space. Unless you count the people who keep volunteering to colonize the newest planet. And what about the people who like time jumping? Like Captain Harrison and the Interstellar Class space ship crews. I suppose that will always be an option unless Jarren completely takes over DES. No, that would be too hard— he'd have to control the Q-net as well. Better to just steal the Warrior technology from DES and then offer it to everyone to use at an exorbitant price.

"Which wouldn't be that bad, except removing and destroying Warriors has a high cost—the shadow-blobs. Of course he could just abandon the Warrior planets and let the shadow-blobs have them. But why do I think it's not that simple? Probably because of the aliens who went to a considerable amount of trouble to build and place those six million plus Warriors at entanglement points on sixty-four planets throughout the Milky Way Galaxy. Too bad we don't know exactly what an entanglement point means. I'd bet Jarren does, though." And I wasn't going to figure it all out right now.

I tell Niall what Beau and I have been doing. "And we could really use you right now, Toad." No response. Swallowing a sigh, I switch topics, telling him about my brother, Phoenix. "...constantly driving me crazy, picking on me, but if someone else tried to give me a hard time, he'd be right in that kid's face. You would get along with him. Although he'd have yelled at you about being a jerk way before I did."

Sadness swells, closing my throat. I miss him and I miss Niall. And I just want…all this to stop. For Jarren to just…poof and be gone. Or to sizzle-zap out of existence. For my greatest worries to be making it to training on time and shooting Mr. Orange Light before he shoots me.

My tight control over my emotions slips. Sobs bully past my defenses. Burying my face against Niall's shoulder to muffle the noise, I let loose, crying and gasping until my back muscles and throat are sore. Then I fall into an exhausted sleep.

But my worries follow me, disturbing my rest. Soon, I'm flying in the Q-net, desperate and alone, searching for Niall. His mind is shattered and I need to find the fragments and bits of him. Once I have them all, I can reconstruct him. As I seek the shards of Niall's consciousness, Jarren intercepts me and I'm no longer dreaming. Cold fear sweeps through me for two reasons. One, he knows I'm alive, and two, his skills with the Q-net are also freakishly good as I've only ever been able to "converse" in the Q-net with those who I entangle with, like Beau. Unless it's my own super power that's allowed me to reach Jarren.

Do you know you're dangling on a hook, Little Worm? Jarren asks. *Every time you're worming in the Q-net I know you're there, squirming helplessly. You can't bypass my measures. It's only a matter of time before a big fish comes along and snatches you up for a nice little snack.*

Real cute, I say, suppressing the terrible thought that Jarren figured out what we're doing. *Did it take you all day to come up with that metaphor?*

Ah, that teenage snark. I missed it. How about this? Since we have a history, if you stop worming, I'll let you, your parents, and a couple friends live. I'll send all of you back to Earth. Promise.

It's tempting for about a nanosecond. I'm not going to abandon my team or the scientists on the base. *No. You want me to stop, because you're scared of what I can do. And, no offense…actually with* lots *of offense, you're nothing but a murdering looter. You're the scum of the universe and I'm not stupid enough to trust your word.*

Laughter. *Gotta love your spunk, Little Worm. I wonder if you'll still be so fiery when your boyfriend dies. I read his medical file, he's in a vegetative state. There's no chance he'll wake. No one wants to tell you because they need you, Little Worm. Need you to dangle on your hook and bait me to swim closer.*

You're lying. And how does he know Niall's my boyfriend? If he's guessing, then my reaction just confirmed his guess. Argh.

That's right, tell yourself that. You've always been good at denial. Good night, Little Worm. Enjoy your last days.

He's gone before I can counter. Anger over his comments surges through me. Niall is *not* in a vegetative state. Or is he? That held a ring of truth. No. Jarren's just trying to goad me. I'm scaring him, which means he doesn't know what I'm doing. But now I have to worm into Dr. Edward's files. Or do I? Ignorance is bliss. Not in this case. Nothing is bliss. Argh!

Now a helpless fury heaves through my core, creating a primal scream that rips from me. *How do I fix Niall?*

The Q-net answers: **HERE.**

A schematic glows before me. It's a jumble of pathways with tangles, loops, swirls, branches, dips, and spirals. Star roads? No. This is a map of the Q-net. *How is this supposed to help?*

HERE.

Light pulses along various routes. Am I supposed to follow them? Then the schematic shrinks until it's—oh my stars! It's a map of a human brain. The lights tracing neural pathways. And some appear to be damaged. *Is this Niall's brain? Send this to Dr. Edwards! Maybe he can repair them.*

NOT.

After an impressive light show, the diagram disappears. *What does that mean? Is Niall beyond repair?* No answer. Nothing else happens. I disentangle from the Q-net and glance around the darkened room. One of the nurses must have come in and dimmed the lights. It's oh-three-hundred. I glance at Niall's vitals on the screen. They're the same. He hasn't moved and it's been seventy-two hours.

Despair washes over me and I stumble to the washroom to indulge in another crying jag. Then I blow my nose, wash my face with cold water, and gather what's left of my optimism. He's young. He's healthy. Brains can heal. I'm not giving up on him. With that settled, I return to his side.

Beau wakes me at oh-nine-hundred. We spend another long day in the Q-net, ensuring our efforts these last few days are hidden from Jarren. And we repeat for the next day. I haven't done anything physically taxing in days, but each night, I'm exhausted.

The Q-net wakes me up at oh-two-hundred.

HERE.

At first, I've no idea what's going on. But it soon becomes clear and terror stabs me in the guts with its icy blades.

A missile was launched from Jarren's base a minute ago.

It's heading straight for us.

2522:244

I trigger the alarm in Radcliff's bedroom.

Radcliff contacts me almost instantly. We connect as if we've been worming together—just like with Jarren.

What's going on? he demands.

Incoming! I yell, showing him the missile's trajectory.

Sonovabitch. How soon?

Fifteen minutes. Should I sound the evacuation alarm?

No. I've got this. Sit tight.

Again with the sit tight! *What can you possibly do?*

Trust me and hang on. It's going to get loud. He disconnects from me.

Loud? Is he nuts? Helpless, I track the missile as it arcs around Yulin's pole. The Q-net displays its flight with a graphic. It'll hit right in the middle of the base.

Eight minutes.

We never would have evacuated in time, but still... In a

bizarre twist of the universe, time slows. Each second an infinity of torture. The missile inches closer.

Six minutes.

At least almost everyone is asleep. They won't know what hit them. Anger that Jarren's going to win pulses red hot. I stare at the missile's course as if my hatred alone would turn it around. It doesn't.

Four minutes.

If Radcliff's planning something, he better do it quick. What did he mean by hang on? I glance around the room. There's nothing solid to hang on to. Plus there are windows on one side and the wall on the other side is almost all glass. Oh my stars!

Two minutes.

I race out to the nurses' station. Plenty of glass around them as well. "Get down," I yell. "A missile's coming!"

They stare at me. Probably wondering what medication they should administer to calm me.

"Get down! Get down! I'm not kidding."

Then a whistle slices through the air. An unmistakable sound that raises every single hair on my body. The two nurses hit the floor. I run back to Niall and dive onto the bed, covering him with my body.

A deafening explosion roars like a sun going supernova. Blinding white light shoots through the windows a split second before a force slams into the base. I cover both our heads as glass shatters and the bed moves. Something—probably parts of the ceiling—rains down on my back. I hang on until the world stills.

The silence is just as loud with a ringing in my ears. I sit up.

Emergency lights turn on. The room is a mess. But then the significance of the emergency lights hits me. I jump off the bed, search for my boots, cutting my feet in the process. Don't care. I find them under a fallen curtain. Jamming my bleeding feet into them, I sprint for the door.

"Mouse?"

Skidding to a stop, I whip around. Did I really hear that? It was muffled and faint. Niall's eyes are open and he's staring at me! He looks confused. That would make two of us. I hurry back.

"You're…bleeding. What's…going on?" he asks.

Joy floods through me. Yes! "I'll explain later. I love you, Toad!" I kiss him and dash out.

"Mouse!"

The nurses are brushing dust and glass off their uniforms.

"He's awake!" I shout. "Go check on him, please." Then I race through the hallways, my boots pounding over glass and debris.

When I arrive at the stairwell to the archeology lab, Zaim and Bendix are both shaken, but the floodlights are intact.

"Did the floodlights go out?" I ask Bendix.

"I don't think so, but I'm not sure. The whole place shook and the lights in the hallway cut out for a minute." He's holding the emitter even though he really can't use it effectively.

I take the weapon from him and search the halls and nearby labs for any shadow-blobs that might have escaped. None. I sag against the wall in relief.

"What the hell was that?" Bendix asks when I return.

"Missile, compliments of Jarren."

He curses.

"We should all be dead," Zaim says.

I agree. So why weren't we? I remember Radcliff said, *I've got this.* "It must have detonated before it hit us."

Even though I want nothing more than to race back to Niall, the emergency lights are still on. They're much dimmer and I need to remain here just in case the shadow-blobs try to bypass the floodlights.

As I wait, the adrenaline wears off. The burning starts in my feet and climbs up my legs. I glance down. Pieces of glass have pierced my skin. Blood stains my pajama pants. Soon my arms, ribs, and the sides of my face throb. I try to ignore the pain. Except the harder I try, the more it hurts.

"Nice P-jays," Zaim teases me.

"I'd let you borrow them, Zee, but they're not your size."

Bendix snorts at Zaim's expression.

Radcliff arrives about five minutes later. "HoLFs?"

"None escaped," I say.

"Good."

"What happened?" Bendix asks.

"You'll be briefed in the morning. The base's lights should be on soon." Then Radcliff peers closer at me. "You're bleeding. What—"

"Niall," I blurt out. I can't believe I waited this long. "He's awake!"

His entire demeanor changes. Transforming into Niall's dad, his elation and relief flare in his eyes. We beam at each other. Then he resumes being Officer Radcliff. He tugs a piece of glass from my arm. "The windows?"

"Yes."

"Is Niall—"

"He's fine."

When the regular lights turn on, Radcliff and I head back to the infirmary. I'm limping by the time we reach Niall's room. The nurses descend on us, talking excitedly.

"…called the doctor…"

"His memory is…"

Except I'm not listening. All my attention is focused on Niall. He's sitting up and, while he's still pale, it's a vast improvement. The broken glass has been swept into a pile and someone fetched him a bowl of soup. The spoon clatters onto the tray when he spots us. We hurry to his bedside and he gives us a wan smile.

"How are you feeling?" Radcliff asks.

"Weak. Why are you bleeding? What's going on? The nurses won't tell—"

"Dr. Edwards is on the way," a nurse says. She gives Radcliff a stern don't-upset-my-patient glare.

I hide a smile as her significant look bounces right off his broad chest. Giving up, she focuses on me. Oh no.

"My stars, child, you're a mess. Let's get you cleaned up." She reaches for my arm.

"But—"

"Go with the nurse," Radcliff orders.

"But Niall—"

"Go, Mouse. We can talk later."

Later never sounded so good. A promise that he'll still be here, awake and able to communicate. I allow the nurse to tow me to an exam room. And do you want to know the sad part? The fact that I know the routine. This is my fourth time being covered with cuts. I carefully strip off my clothing. My pajamas are ruined. And the bottom of my feet are scored with deep gashes. I lie on the table. The nurse plucks shards from my skin with tweezers, cleans my wounds, and bandages the shallower ones.

After Dr. Edward checks Niall, he stops to examine me and stitch up the lacerations on my soles. When he finishes, he says, "Stay off your feet for a couple days." He pauses. "If you can. I understand this is a…difficult time for everyone. Here's a few extra strength pain meds. Only take them in an emergency. Understand?"

"Yes. Thanks, Doc. How's Niall?"

"I can't divulge his condition, but I'm pleased. And I'm sure his father will fill you in."

"Did anyone else get injured in the blast?"

"A few minor bruises and a couple broken bones—mostly due to falling out of bed. I hear we have you to thank for that."

Not really. More like the Q-net, but I did ask it to alert me so I guess I can take partial credit. I nod.

Dr. Edwards puts a hand on my shoulder and gives me a

squeeze. "Thank you." Then he leaves.

Not waiting for any more orders, I dress in the scrubs left for me, including soft booties, grab the bottle of pills, and limp over to Niall's room. Radcliff is sitting on the chair next to his bed, but he stands when he sees me.

"Get some rest, I'll be by again in the morning." Radcliff rests his hand on Niall's forehead for a moment. Then he turns to me. "Follow me," he orders.

But this is my *later*. Huffing with frustration, I shuffle after him. He heads down the hall until we're well out of hearing range then he stops.

"I told Niall about what Jarren planned with the HoLFs and the missile. Please don't tell him about our counter strategies. I don't want him to insist on being a part of them. Dr. Edwards says it's vital he rests as much as possible and doesn't get upset."

"I won't. What happened with the missile?"

"The satellite has defensive weapons that I can access. Since your and Beau's worming allowed us to keep command of the satellite, I was able to destroy the missile before it hit the base."

Nice to know. And now Jarren knows as well. "Jarren's going to try to regain the satellite. I should strengthen our protections."

"It's imperative that we maintain control. Can you do it now, or are you too tired?"

As if I could sleep knowing that Jarren might be messing with our only defense. "I'll do it now."

"Good. Keep me updated." He strides away.

I find an empty room and worm into the satellite's programming and into my protective measures. They haven't been tampered with, but I layer in another shield just in case. Then I ask the Q-net to alert me if anyone tries to bypass my worms. Once I finish, I hobble back to Niall's room.

His eyes are closed and I've a moment of panic. But he opens them and gives me a sleepy smile.

"Hey, Mouse."

"Toad." I climb into bed with him.

He raises an eyebrow. "Aren't you worried the nurses will kick you out?"

"Nope. They haven't been able to for the last five nights."

"Five..." He clutches the blankets. "No wonder Dad avoided the question."

So much for not upsetting him. "You didn't miss anything."

"Really? I think a missile strike counts as *a big thing*."

"Look at that, you can still be sarcastic. You're well on the way to a full recovery."

"Now who's being sarcastic?"

"I've many talents," I tease.

He scoffs. But then says, "Dad said you alerted him about the missile. Do you think Jarren will launch another one?"

"What I think is that you should let your father worry about that. But you won't. Neither will I. I've no idea what Jarren will do next. What I do know is there was one good thing about that strike."

"There is?" His tone is incredulous.

"Yup. It was loud enough to wake you up." I lie down next

to him. "I missed you."

He puts his arm around my shoulders and pulls me close. Or tries; he's still pretty weak. I scoot until my head is resting on his shoulder.

"Thanks for staying with me," he says.

"You're welcome. But don't do it again. That was the worst five days of my life."

"Not including when you were shot by the looters," he adds.

"Nope. Including that. I'll take getting shot over you almost dying every time."

"Love you, too, Mouse."

It's one thing to propose a plan. At the time you're safe and warm and it's all just speculation. It's quite another experience to be implementing that plan. Doubts and worries about the success of the mission gather like sand grains in your shoes or in this case, my boots. And reality is cold and windy and dark and—what the heck is that smell? Who ate garlic for dinner before a mission?

Unfortunately, my night vision goggles do not show noxious odors. But otherwise they're super cool. To my sight, the desert is bathed in a green-tinted twilight despite it being about twenty-two hundred hours. Eight members of the security team, including yours truly, are walking in a single line toward a spot in the desert that my father marked earlier. Elese is close behind me and Beau is right in front. Morgan leads our little parade and

Bendix is in the sweeper position—that's last.

After the missile attack, Radcliff changed his mind about my plan and agreed it was worth the risk. Much to Niall's frustration, but to my relief, he remained behind with Radcliff, Tora, and Vedann. He'd said he loved me! I'm still giddy over that.

Unable to use the dune buggies due to the heat they generate, which might give away our activities to Jarren via the satellite, we all take turns pulling the cart of supplies. It's not too heavy, not at first, but it's awkward, especially when trudging up a dune, then it weighs a million kilos. Okay that's an exaggeration, but when we started out, I was freezing in my security jumpsuit and now I'm soaked with sweat. I silently thank Dr. Edwards for the extra strength pain meds that I downed before the mission.

Good thing our destination is only a few klicks from base. We reach it without trouble. It's been less than a day since Jarren's missile attack so we're betting that his people aren't nearby, watching us or ready to ambush us. Of course, we could be wrong. Not a pleasant thought.

We unload the cart in silence. No need to talk when we've all been briefed on exactly what we need to do. Morgan positions the robotic digger and turns it on. Its spikes shoot out and then it grinds and scrapes into the sand. The noise shatters the quiet night. We flinch and grab the hilts of our weapons, certain the sounds will trigger an attack. It's loud enough to reach the other side of the planet, for stars' sake. Nothing happens.

Morgan hands four of us shovels. While the others stand

guard, we clear the sand ejected from the digger. It piles around the hole. When the digger is too deep to spew the material high enough, we deploy a second digger to relay the crushed sandstone. The addition of another noisy machine is going to cause me to go deaf. The combined cacophony dances along my nerves, setting my teeth on edge. Or it could be due to half expecting Jarren's shuttle to come swooping out of the sky to kill us all.

Diggers weren't designed to dig straight down that far. They're made to work in collapsed Warrior pits, clearing dirt and sand away from the buried statues. Which is why we add one more digger.

It seems like forever before the diggers reach an open space underground. They they pop out of the hole like ping pong balls, retract their spikes, and roll to a stop. Like at Pit 21, the urge to praise them on a job well done pushes up my throat.

Morgan and two others set up a rope and pulley system. The tunnel is too narrow to use a ladder. First to go down is a camera and light. Rance is crouched over a portable, watching the feed.

After another eon, he says, "We hit our targeted location."

Then it's my turn to peer into the darkness on the portable's screen. It's one of the equipment rooms of the factory under the Warriors. There's no movement or shadow-blobs although it's hard to be sure without being able to sense the air pressure or temperature. "It appears clear."

Morgan's scowl is clearer. I don't know why since I'm going to be first. It's my life on the line. I step into the harness and secure it around my waist before clipping onto the rope. Then from the cart I grab one of the six emitters that Jim and his crew were able to build in the five days since the HoLFs attacked. Settling the strap across my body, I heft the weapon in one hand. Its weight steadies me. I can do this.

"Ready," I say and turn on the communicator in my ear. We're risking discovery by using them, but they're vital to the mission.

"Just say *up* and we'll pull you out. Got it?" Morgan asks.

"Yes, sir."

I grab the rope and step into nothing. Dangling, I hold onto the rope with my left hand while clutching the emitter. They lower me down. The sandstone walls of the shaft surround me. As I go deeper they squeeze in tighter. The certainty that I'm going to get stuck gnaws on me. And there's not...enough air... I...can't...breathe...I'm...

"Status, Lawrence," Morgan barks in my ear, startling me out of my panic attack.

"Good," I reply and even manage to sound convincing.

Breathe. *You're not claustrophobic. You're not claustrophobic,* I repeat over and over. When I drop out of the shaft and into the open, I relax. The cool air is light and refreshing. Soon my boots hit the floor.

"Touchdown," I say. But I don't unhook my harness. Instead, I pry my fingers off the rope and draw my flashlight. I shine it around the room. There is a row of tall boxy alien machinery along one smooth wall. However, the shadows are normal. "Clear."

Now I detach from the rope. And I attach my flashlight to

the top of the emitter's barrel. Velcro is a wonderful thing and in the five hundred plus years since its invention, no one has designed anything better. I check the adjoining rooms and then follow Dad's directions on how to find the large cavern with the Warrior hearts.

Sand crunches under my boots as I traverse the corridors. Otherwise it's silent. After a short walk, I enter the main factory. Warriors lie prone on hundreds of tables throughout the space as if they're waiting for surgery. Even though I've been here a couple times before, it's still creepy. Along the back wall are more tables, but this time they are filled with Warrior hearts. I shine the beam over them. The silver alien symbols engraved on them gleam, but the black porous material drinks in the light.

They're the same shape and size as a human heart. And now to test if what I witnessed the last time I was here actually happened or was due to panic because all the lights went out, I switch off the flashlight. The blackness is instant. Then I blink and a row of ghost Warriors appear. They're identical to the Terracotta Warriors, standing tall and staring straight ahead. Except they're white and a bit translucent. Nice to know I didn't imagine them.

"It's a go," I say. Toggling on my flashlight, I wait for the others to join me.

It doesn't take long for Morgan, Elese, Beau, Zaim, Ho, and Rance to arrive. Bendix stayed on the surface in case that's our only way out. The team peers into the shadows with anxious expressions.

"No HoLFs down here," I say, but don't add it's peaceful

because they already suspect I'm crazy. No need to confirm.

"What do we do?" Morgan asks.

She and the others are lined up by the table.

"It's easy. Just pick one up. It's going to crumble in your hands, but there's no way to avoid it."

"Anything else we should expect?" Beau asks.

"Yes, it's gonna feel like your hand's been stabbed by an icicle, but it doesn't last long."

"Wonderful," he mutters.

Everyone hesitates as if no one wants to be first. Then Morgan huffs and grabs a heart. As expected, it disintegrates, raining fragments. She wrinkles her nose, but doesn't remark on the pain.

Beau shrugs and picks one up. Or he tries; it's dust by the time he lifts his hand. "Ow, that sucker stings." He wipes his palm on his leg.

The rest follow. Four more hearts are destroyed—sorry, Mom. No one else comments on the pain. Rance and Elese rub their arms as if their muscles ache.

"How do we know it worked?" Morgan asks me.

"Everyone turn off your flashlights," I say.

They do. Elese curses in surprise. Zaim and Beau reach for their emitters.

"Can you all see the ghosts?" I ask.

"Hell, yeah," Rance says. "And to think we made fun of you about them."

Nice.

"And we really didn't believe you, either," Zaim says. "Sorry, Ara."

"Yeah, sorry," Rance and Ho echo.

I glance at Elese and Beau.

"Don't look at us, *we* believed you," Elese says, giving the others her hard stare.

"The real test will be if we can see the HoLFs," Morgan says. "Flashlights back on for now. Rance, get the floodlights ready."

"Yes, sir."

Since we only have six emitters, Rance is in charge of the floodlights. With Morgan in the lead, we creep over to the hatch. I'm surprised the ladder is still there, although I don't know why. Icy air pours from the hatch.

Morgan pauses at the base. "Lights off. Time to set up the perimeter."

By the creaking sounds, I guess Rance is climbing the ladder. I'm right behind him. Once he reaches the top, he triggers the floodlight before stepping out. The bright white beam slices the darkness. He sets the tripod down.

My turn. I scramble into Pit 4. The heavy air presses against my skin as I slide onto the floor, keeping below the brightness. Lying on my stomach and elbows, I hold the emitter so it's pointed straight out. Shadow-blobs fly toward us.

"Incoming!" I sizzle-zap the closest ones.

Elese is next. She hands Rance another floodlight on a tripod and dives for the ground. "They're ugly little blobs," she says and then sizzle-zaps a bunch.

The rest of the team bubbles from the hatch, bringing more lights and more emitters. They waste no time taking up similar positions. A few curses and a gasp echo around me as they get their first look at the enemy. We're in a circle around the hatch fanned like flower petals around the middle. A strategy that will hopefully keep us safe.

Morgan settles next to me. "You weren't kidding about the tentacles."

Shadow-blobs rush us with their weapons already formed. We aim and fire repeatedly. Sizzle-zaps crackle in the air. So many it sounds like an electrical fire.

After a few minutes, Zaim asks, "How much juice do we have in these things?"

"Like I said at the briefing," Morgan says, zapping a couple HoLFs. "We have a few hours before the emitters need to be recharged."

"There's a million of them," Rance says.

I check over my shoulder. Does he need help? He's adjusting the beams to protect us from an attack from above. His other job is to keep the HoLFs from breaking the bulbs. He appears to be okay.

Focusing forward, I concentrate on the shadow-blobs. A million is an exaggeration. It's more like hundreds. But we're holding our own. Mostly. A few sharp tentacle tips stab forward faster than I'm able to aim and fire. The damage is minimal. Being on our stomachs, we present a smaller target. Plus they're having a harder time puncturing the jumpsuit's material. The chemists brewed up a chemical agent—don't ask me what it is;

all I know is it strengthened the fibers to counter against a stabbing motion. It's not impenetrable, but it's much better than before.

After an hour…or two, my arms ache with fatigue and my fingers are stiff. A loud pop then the crackle of a bulb shattering sounds amid the sizzle-zaps. I glance back. Rance is wielding his flashlight like a sword as shadow-blobs try to stab him. Another couple of bulbs blow.

"Lawrence, help Rance," Morgan orders.

I scramble to my feet and sizzle-zap the HoLFs harrying Rance. Sharp appendages snake between the gaps in the lights, stabbing us. His uniform is damp with blood, but he keeps moving as he rearranges the remaining lights, but then more pop behind us. I spin in a slow circle, shooting as I turn.

The HoLFs are smart enough to wait for my back to be turned. I stumble forward as the force of their blows increases. Great, they figured out our uniforms are more resistant. We lose a few more lights.

"On your feet," Morgan orders the others.

Smart. Now the rest can duck and dodge.

"Status?" she barks.

"Keir, check."

"Dorey, check."

"Zaim, check."

"Ho, check."

"Lawrence, check." I jump back from a vicious looking saw-toothed blade just in time to be stabbed in the arm. Ow.

"Rance?" Morgan asks.

Nothing. I turn and Rance is lying on the ground. Blood is pouring from a cut on the side of his face.

"Man down," I say and rush over to him. Crouching next to his prone form, I feel for a pulse. It's there. I've no time for relief as two more shadow-blobs advance on us. Sizzle-zap. Sizzle-zap.

"Status on Rance?"

"Alive. Don't know for how long."

Morgan curses. "Are you sure the HoLFs are being killed and not just re-forming in the darkness?" she asks me, shouting over the sizzle-zaps.

"Yes."

Zaim cries out in pain and crumples to the ground.

"Retreat," Morgan orders.

More bulbs pop, spraying glass over us.

"We can't," Keir says. "As soon as we turn our backs they'll be on us."

"At this rate of attack only a few of us will be able to get down the ladder," Beau says. "Those left behind will be quickly overwhelmed."

"Stay the course," Morgan orders.

We do. It's brutal and the metallic stink of blood mixes with the almost continuous sizzle-zaps. I catch sight of Ho. He's firing his and Zaim's emitter. Those long lean arms must be stronger than they look.

After a while, I reach a state of numbness. Sounds are muffled and my breathing steadies. Actions slow down. I think of Niall. He's going to be mad if I don't survive this. I wonder if he needs more rice paper to draw on. Strange and unconnected thoughts pop up in my mind.

And then Bendix is there. He grabs Zaim's emitter from Ho and aims. Sizzle-zap.

"You disobeyed orders, Officer Bendix," Morgan says. But it's half-hearted.

"You can yell at me about it later. You guys needed my help." He shoots a few more. "Ugly suckers."

"That's what I said!" Elese grins at him. "Welcome to the party!"

Bendix's arrival turns the tide and, after another hour, what's left of the shadow-blobs retreat. We glance at each other in surprise. Is this a trick?

"Check on Zaim and Rance," Morgan orders.

Elese examines Rance, while Beau inspects Zaim's injuries. Both men are bleeding from multiple cuts. Beau and Elese apply pressure bandages to the worst ones.

"They're stable for now," Elese says. "But we shouldn't linger."

"Fan out," Morgan orders. "Clear Pit 4."

We find a few shadow-blobs hiding in the corners and behind mounds of debris. The temperature warms.

"Do you feel that?" Beau asks.

"What?" Elese swings her weapon around, shooting a fleeing HoLF.

"The air is...lighter."

"You sure the strain hasn't gotten to you, Dorey?" Morgan

asks.

"Ha, ha."

"Four is clear," Morgan says. "Check Pit 3."

Not many shadow-blobs remain in Pit 3. In Pit 2 we find a black slit in the air above the place that is the middle of the octagon of Warriors had they still been standing there. Instead pieces of broken Warriors lie in scattered heaps courtesy of Jarren and his looters.

Slit is the best word to describe the slash of black—it's thicker/wider in the middle at about fifteen centimeters and tapers at both ends. The bottom point is about thirty centimeters above the ground and the slit is about two meters long.

"This is nuts," Bendix says.

"Heads up," Morgan says.

A handful of HoLFs rush past us. We shoot half of them and the others disappear into the slit.

"That's it, run home crying to your mamas," Elese shouts after them.

"Now we know how they're getting here," Beau says.

"Aim your emitter at that…tear," Morgan orders.

We do.

"Fire!"

Nothing happens. Too bad.

"Stop. Shine your flashlights on it."

We do. The blackness thickens and darkens—yes, I know it's strange—but it's as if the slit is feeding on the light. It doesn't grow or shrink or do anything else.

"That's enough. Let's clear Pit 1." Morgan takes point.

Within the next hour, the pits and lab are cleared of shadow-blobs.

Dr. Edwards brings in a crew of nurses and they rush to attend to Rance and Zaim. Bendix and Ho accompany them just in case we missed a HoLF. We're all bloody and exhausted. But it's a good kind—a triumphant exhaustion. The team's mood is jubilant. Operation Warrior Hearts was a success. Radcliff and my parents meet us in the archeology lab with their techs. Jim arrives with a bunch of maintenance people and they work on restoring power to the pits. Quite a number of people who are all probably annoyed at being awake at oh-five-hundred hours. The rest of us are ordered to allow the nurses to inspect and clean our injuries. We all look like we lost a fight with a thorny bush. But it appears none of us has anything too concerning.

"I feel like a pincushion," Beau complains without much energy.

Soon the power is reconnected to the pits. Lights shine in all four of them and the astrophysicists plan to install emitters on the walls to constantly flood the pits with null waves. Despite the brightness, the slit remains.

"We'll keep the pits off limits and post guards here with emitters until we figure out how to close it," Radcliff says. "We'll have six more of the weapons by tomorrow afternoon."

"We might need to bring in intact Warriors from the other pits," I say. And when Radcliff and my parents glance at me, I add, "There were no HoLFs in Pit 21."

"Yes, but they might need all fourteen hundred and forty-eight of them to keep the HoLFs out. If we skim a few off, it might not," Mom says.

Good point. The mood sobers as Dr. Edwards and his team carry out Rance and Zaim.

"How are they?" Radcliff asks Edwards.

"They'll live. Officer Rance has a concussion. I'll know more about Officer Zaim when I get back to the infirmary."

In other words, stop bothering the good doctor so he can do his work.

Radcliff, my parents, and the techs go to touch the hearts just in case the HoLFs invade again. I follow them down to the factory along with Morgan. We turn on our flashlights as we enter the big cavern.

"I hate to ruin these, but I'd rather see the enemy," Mom says as she picks one up. She winces. "Stabbed by an icicle is an apt description."

My dad and the techs follow.

"Yikes, that's cold." Dad rubs his hands together.

Morgan reaches for one and I say, "Don't—"

"Don't what?" Morgan is holding a heart in her bare hand and it hasn't disintegrated.

"I was going to say not to touch it because you already destroyed one."

Morgan stills. "Maybe it's a dud?"

"Give it to me," Radcliff says. It turns to dust as soon as he grasps it. "I felt the pain, does that mean it worked?"

Only one way to find out. "Turn off the flashlights."

The gasps are like music to my ears as I'm sure all the techs believed I was lying about the ghosts. Vindication is mine! I'd chuckle evilly, but that would probably put a few techs over the edge. It wouldn't do to have them running away screaming. Or would it?

We experiment and it appears that since we've already touched a heart, we can now pick one up. Which means we can move the hearts to a safer location and we can distribute them to other key personnel, like the rest of the security team.

"I guess once you have a ghost, you can't get another," I say.

My mother rounds on me. "Don't say that."

"Why not?"

"Because it's…"

I wait, but my mother is at a loss for words. Wow.

"It's scary," Dad says. "To think we're hosts for an alien spirit."

"Spencer," Mom admonishes.

"It's true, though," I say.

"We don't know that for sure." She's wiping her hands over her chest and arms as if brushing away crumbs.

Talk about denial. "Think of it as a super power, Mom. Now you have X-ray vision…well, you have radio wave vision, but that doesn't sound as cool. And you might be better at accessing the Q-net."

"Did you get better after touching a heart?" Radcliff asks.

Figures he would ask that. "No, but it could have been a contributing factor."

"Guess time will tell," Dad says, looking thoughtful.

We all carry a heart up from the factory. I plan to give mine to Niall. A giddy warmth spreads through me as I realize I've already given him my heart. Yes, it's sappy, but hey, we're in love.

As soon as I enter the archeology lab, the Q-net sounds a strident warning in my head. My happy thoughts sizzle-zap away. Another missile? I concentrate and connect to the Q-net.

Yes! And it's not coming at us.

My parents and Radcliff turn around when they realize I stopped.

Then where? The trajectory shows it heading straight to—

"Lawrence?" Radcliff barks.

"The satellite!"

"What about it?"

"A missile is on its way to the satellite."

2522:245

Cursing, Radcliff strides over to a terminal. He shoves his tangs in and accesses the satellite's defensive controls. The screen shows the hash marks of the missile's projected path. My parents stand behind Radcliff. I monitor what's going on through the Q-net.

Radcliff targets the weapon as it closes in. Suddenly he's blocked from the controls. "Sonovabitch. Jarren took over. Lawrence, can you get me back?"

I try. But Jarren has set up a convoluted program. A helpful green line glows. I follow it as fast as— Everything goes black as the satellite is destroyed.

"Sorry," I say. "I wasn't quick enough."

"Not your fault," Radcliff says. "Jarren had it timed out perfectly."

The Q-net sends me a second warning. I squeak in surprise.

Radcliff asks, "Another missile?"

"No. Four military shuttles." I do the math. Forty-eight invaders are flying toward our base.

"Four shuttles?" Dad asks. "Is that bad?"

"It's better than a missile," Radcliff says. "It means he plans to invade instead of just killing us all." He pauses as if in thought.

Things are really screwed up when an attack is considered the lesser of two evils.

"Lawrence, is Jarren aware that you can track his shuttles without the satellite?" Radcliff asks.

"He shouldn't be. I wasn't able to get past his defenses around his base," I say.

"Plus the timing of waiting until the satellite was destroyed might mean he's not aware," Dad says.

"Regardless, we have six hours until they arrive, people. Time for Operation Looter Attack." Radcliff starts barking orders.

A part of me is relieved. Strange, I know. But the threat of Jarren's return has been hanging over my head for the last seventy-four days. And now it's here. A part of me is ready for it. Bring it on. Yet another part is worried and scared and wants to run away. But that last part is just wanting it to be all over. Win or lose, let's be done.

"Lawrence," Radcliff says, startling me from my thoughts. "Get in position."

"Yes, sir."

Mom grabs my arm, pulling me in for a hug. "Please be careful."

"I will."

Then it's Dad's turn to embrace me. "Don't give yourself up for us again."

"Then don't get captured and I won't." I get a set of parental scowls. "What? It seems pretty straightforward to me."

"Go, before we ground you," Dad says.

I laugh then run into the base. My thoughts turn to the mission. It would have been nice to have a few extra days for Niall, Rance, and Zaim to recover. Instead, we'll have to rely on barely trained techs.

At least I have some time to swing by the empty cafeteria and grab a few snacks. It might be a while before my next real meal. Then I report to my "position."

It's one of the hidden areas in the base that aren't on the map. What Officer Morgan called my hidey holes. In fact, it's my favorite one that I used the most when I was a kid and hiding from my parents.

The hidden space is the size of a coffin and only accessible by an oversized duct that cuts across the chemistry lab. When I was younger, I'd access the duct from a storeroom next to the lab. But today, I use a conveniently placed table in the lab that is right underneath one of the grates into that duct. Getting in the duct is both harder and easier—harder because I'm bigger, easier because I'm stronger.

Once I reach the space, I wiggle into a comfortable position, lying on my left side. I fit better a few years ago. Shafts of artificial light cut through the grate which is about a meter away. It reflects off the shining metal walls, giving my hiding place a nice glow.

I know what you're thinking. If I'm caught here, I've no place to run. Well, if I'm caught anywhere, I'm done, so this is better than being in my bedroom, which would be the first place Jarren will check.

Waiting for the action to begin is torture. After eating half my snacks, I try to empty my mind and calm my racing emotions. A few hours of sleep would help as well. But the reality is me swatting at my thoughts as they buzz and swarm around my head.

The roar of the shuttles' engines over the base breaks the quiet. At least we don't have to worry about a sneak attack. I steady my nerves and access the Q-net. Jarren worms into the controls for the base's port. The retractable roof opens to allow a shuttle in. The port isn't big enough for all four, so one lands, deposits looters, and takes off. It doesn't take them long to unload about forty-eight people. The last shuttle remains in the port.

I pull up a map of the base and red dots fill the area representing the port. Each dot a looter. Worming into the camera feeds, I bring up the images from the port and scan the invaders. They're wearing gray form-fitting jumpsuits. Probably stolen from DES security, which means they can't be knocked out with a pulse gun unless the gun is aimed at their heads. They're checking behind all the equipment, probably looking for an ambush. Each wears a belt with a weapon holstered on one side—they didn't come to talk—and a flashlight on the other.

They're wearing jumpsuits. They have energy wave guns and flashlights, I message my team, sending it to their portables. I'm the only one who is connected to the Q-net.

I keep searching. Come on. Come on. You have to be here. No way Jarren would remain behind when there's an opportunity to gloat. There! I spot Jarren and one of the red dots turns to yellow. The perfect color for a yellow-bellied coward. I'm not sure where *yellow-bellied* comes from, but Beau said it's appropriate.

Jarren looks the same. His long brown hair is tied back into a low ponytail. He trimmed his beard and his light brown eyes shine with anticipation. The murdering looter in all his glory. His belt has two weapons and a flashlight. My stomach clenches as I recognize the kill zapper. The weapon that spits purple fire and killed Officer Menz and me.

Yellow belly has two weapons—EW and KZ, I send.

Sending the map to the rest of the team, I message that it's *go time* even though I have a communicator—that's for emergencies only. Because Jarren could worm into them just like I'm about to do to his. One. Two. Three.

"…the door," Jarren orders.

"It's locked," a man says.

"Not for long, but first…" Jarren goes over to a terminal. "Let's get all the shades on base open, letting in the sunlight." He worms into the maintenance programs.

A mechanical whirr sounds below me as the shades in the chem lab retract. The light in the duct brightens. Ah. He's worried about the shadow-blobs, which proves he can see them and also explains attacking us when the sun is high in the sky—fourteen hundred hours. It's not going to be as bright as they think, since the maintenance crew covered the shattered windows with boards until new glass could be installed.

In the port, Jarren returns to the door into the rest of the base and keys in the override code.

Oh my stars. I send another message. *Jarren has override code!*

The door unlocks. He steps back and says, "Alpha and Beta teams take security and free our people from detention. Delta team sweep the labs. Epsilon team the housing units. My team with me to the Control Center. Watch for hostiles both alien and human."

We're right, Jarren's people can see HoLFs, I send.

The red dots burst out of the port and scatter in different directions like ants searching for food. A few remain behind to guard the shuttle. I switch to the cameras in the corridors. Looters run through the empty hallways with weapons drawn. Watching them reminds me of when I came here with the security team to check for intruders before the rest of the scientists shuttled down from the Big Fat Frog.

Delta team bursts into the biology lab as Alpha and Beta reach security. I wait. After a couple of minutes it starts.

"Delta team commander to Boss."

Boss. Jarren has such an ego.

"Go ahead, Delta," Jarren says.

"There's no one in the bio lab, sir."

"Follow the plan and check all the labs, Delta."

"Yes, sir."

All is quiet for a while.

"Alpha team commander to Boss."

"Go ahead, Alpha," Jarren says. He's almost to the stairwell to the archeology lab. There are twelve looters with him.

"Security is a ghost town, sir."

"Did you check detention?"

"Yes, sir. No one there."

Jarren curses. Then he sees the floodlights and stops. "They're battery powered. Smart."

"Can you repeat that, sir?"

"They obviously evacuated, Alpha. They're probably hiding in the Warrior pits."

"What about the hostile aliens, sir?"

"Not those pits, Alpha. There are sixty others." Jarren sighs. "Boss to all team leaders, clear the base and ensure no one is here. I'm continuing on to the Control Center. Once I'm there I can find out where they're all hiding."

I grin. You can try. I wait until the red dots are spread out all over the base and Jarren's in the Control Center.

Show time, I message my team.

Worming into the maintenance programs, I close all the blinds. Then I turn off all the lights. My hidey hole is dark, but I don't need light to access the Q-net. I close the ceiling in the port.

Jarren's team leaders call in right away. All are very concerned.

"Wait for orders," Jarren says, turning on his flashlight. The others with him do the same. He sends two of his men to check on the floodlights and report back. Then he sits at my dad's terminal. Too bad for him, Dad disabled it. So fun to see Jarren punch the screen in frustration.

I check the port. There's enough light from the flashlights to see Ho and Bendix sneaking out from the hidden room near the port's exit. Elese and Beau were harnessed to the ceiling, but now they drop down on ropes. The four of them quickly disable Jarren's crew that was left behind. Boo yah!

The two men Jarren sent to check the lights reach the stairwell. The floodlights are off and they shine their flashlights at the stairwell as if that will protect them.

"Conner to Boss," one says, backing away.

"Go ahead, Conner," Jarren says.

"The floodlights are out."

"Return to the Control Center, now."

Too bad they're not fast enough. Radcliff and Morgan emerge from the stairwell and shoot them in the head with their pulse guns. They drop to the ground. Morgan has a squeeze bottle full of fake blood and she uses it to make the unconscious men appear as if they had an unfortunate encounter with the HoLFs. Radcliff and Morgan retreat.

Cuing the shadow-blobs, I send. I switch on the projectors in twenty key locations in the base. The reaction is instant as the looters in those areas get a nasty surprise.

"Hostiles in security!"

"Hostiles in the cafeteria!"

"Hostiles near the housing units!"

"We're under attack in the geology lab!"

Under attack? They must have a good imagination. All the projectors are doing is casting static images of the shadow-blobs. But it is dark and creepy in the empty base.

"It's a trap!" Jarren yells. "Everyone retreat to the port. Now." He runs for the door. "Boss to Flyboys. Come in, Flyboys."

Oh no. No calling for help. I block his communications. Sorry, not sorry. As I watch all the little red dots head toward the port, I take a moment to admire Radcliff's amazing plan.

You see, he reported to DES that the wave emitters were an utter failure and we needed a new way to counter the shadow-blobs. So Jarren's people are in panic mode, racing for escape. Except when those red dots reach the port and squeeze through the small door, there are four security officers waiting for them. And they can't retreat because the rest of the security team, the techs, my parents, and I will all emerge from our hidey holes and pick them off from this side. Radcliff's a devious genius.

I wait until all the dots are past my position, then I ease from my hiding place. Ugh, my muscles are stiff from the hours I've spent here. And my various injuries protest the motion. Guess I need to take a couple more pain meds.

I remove the grate and climb down to the table. The lab is semi-dark so I pull my flashlight and creep toward the door. The cameras show the corridors are shafts of blackness except where the looters are fleeing. The beams of their flashlights dance as they run. One of the best things about being a Q-net freak, I can access it anywhere. Like when I slip out into the hallway and know the exact location of the red dots.

Turning on my flashlight, I start toward the port. Then something grabs my braid and yanks me back.

"Ow, what the—"

A hard round coldness presses to my temple. A weapon. I freeze as all my blood drains to my feet.

"Hello, Little Worm," Jarren says right in my ear.

He removes the communicator from my other ear. It clinks as it hits the floor, then crunches as he smashes it with his boot. My pulse gun is taken next.

I swallow. Why didn't I keep track of the yellow dot? I check, but it's not on my map. That's because Jarren turned his flashlight off and the Q-net could no longer track him.

"Nice trick," he says. "Almost had me fooled. I was halfway to the port when I realized that Officer Tight Pants would never kill so many people. Good guys don't unless there's no other way. It didn't take me long to figure out that other way. Was this your plan?"

Help, I message, hoping that someone on my team is paying attention to their portable despite being very busy and preoccupied with shooting lots of looters. *Jarren caught me. We're outside the chem lab.* "No. Officer Radcliff gets all the credit." My voice squeaks.

He snorts in derision. "I wouldn't say *all*. *You* provided all the worming needed to execute the plan, and to find me on Yulin, and to alert him about the missile, and to tip him off about this attack, and to keep me from communicating with my people." His hold on my braid tightens and the barrel of the weapon digs in harder. Pain spreads along my scalp and forehead as fear's icy tendrils snake around my heart.

"How did you find me?" I ask, hoping to delay him.

"You shouldn't have picked your favorite hiding place, Little Worm."

He remembered.

"Come on." He grabs my arm and drags me back into the chemistry lab, pushing me in front of him.

I stumble, turn around, and stop. Jarren has the energy wave gun leveled at me. Pure panic sweeps through me as my heart decides to tunnel its way out of my body through my stomach.

"You know what this can do?" he asks.

"Yes." The energy from the weapon can pulverize all the bones in my body. Death would be instant. I hope.

"Don't try anything or this time I'll make sure you stay dead before I leave." He aims over my shoulder.

I duck as the windows and blinds behind me shatter. Shards pelt my back. Again with the glass. Good thing I'm wearing my jumpsuit.

"Out the window," Jarren orders. "Now!"

Going outside the base through the chem lab, I message. I crunch over the debris and climb over the sharp shards still clinging to the window frame. Then I hop down onto the sand. Jarren thumps next to me.

"This way." He grabs my wrist and tows me along the outer wall of the base.

I'm not sure where we're going until we reach the end. Three shuttles sit in the sand like giant beetles. He tugs me toward the closest one.

Oh no. If we fly away, I'll never see my parents and Niall again. I glance back. Two sets of footprints trail behind us. No one is in sight.

Heading toward a shuttle on the west side of the base, I message. *Follow tracks.* This is probably an exercise in futility, but denial is a survival instinct. Right?

We reach the shuttle. Jarren keys in a code: seven, two, five, one. The door opens, slowly settling on the sand. He pushes me up the steps. The pilot is standing in the aisle, aiming her weapon at us, but she lowers it when she recognizes Jarren.

"What happened?"

"Walked into a trap. Get this bird in the air and tell the others to take off. We're going back to our base."

The woman hesitates. "What about—"

"They're caught and we will be soon if you don't—"

"On it." She hurries into the cockpit.

Jarren pushes me down into a seat right behind the pilot's seat. "Buckle in," he orders.

In the shuttle, I message. *Code seven, two, five, one.* I pull the straps over my shoulders and hips, snapping in the five-point harness. Jarren pulls a thick plastic ring from his pocket. Then he grabs my forearm and puts it on the armrest. Before I can move, he clamps my wrist to the seat with the plastic ring—it must have a hinge. Then he does the same thing for my left arm. Between the buckles and the rings, I'm effectively secured.

When the shuttle's engine roars to life, breathing becomes difficult and tears threaten to leak.

He crouches so he's at my level. "This is so you don't run off again."

"Why take me?" I'm physically unable to say, *why not just kill me* out loud.

"I could have sent another missile after I destroyed the satellite—we have plenty of weapons—but I just couldn't." He peers at me as if I'm a strange creature he can't quite figure out. "I had to come get you. My ghost in the Q-net who has been giving me such trouble."

"Ghost?"

"Yes, layering in extra security, fixing the camera and satellite feeds, getting through my blockade all without making a ripple. Drove me crazy trying to figure out who was ghosting through my programs."

"How did you figure it out?"

His derision is clear. "Do you really have to ask?"

"DES."

"Inept DES. They clued me in and then it didn't take me long to find you in the Q-net." Jarren gives me a patronizing smile. "I'm very curious how you managed to get past my defenses. And how Officer Tight Pants took care of the hostile aliens. And lots of other questions."

"You're a murdering looter. I'm not going to tell you anything." My words are brave, but inside I'm terrified.

"Yes, you are. And do you want to know why?"

This sounds bad. Do I? Not really.

"I've lots of cool toys to play with, including this pretty pink liquid. Once it's injected into the bloodstream, the person just can't stop talking."

Not good. Not good at all. "Where did you get all this stuff?" I ask. Perhaps he'll be too busy talking to me to order the pilot to take off.

"I've partners in crime, Little Worm. Very rich and well connected partners who get me anything I need."

"Incoming," the pilot says. "Three dune buggies."

My rescue!

Jarren whips around. Standing, he goes to the front window. I crane my neck, trying to peer around Jarren. Who's here? Radcliff? Morgan? Bendix? Jarren shifts slightly as he taps on a few of the controls.

When I spot the drivers of the buggies, it's too much drama for my heart. It gives up and cowers in my chest. Niall, Zaim, and Rance are in the buggies. Somehow, they've been monitoring my messages. And instead of recruiting others to come to my rescue, they decided to save me. Three people who are recovering from severe injuries.

Of course Jarren doesn't know that. My survival might depend on their poker faces.

"They're sending us an ultimatum," Jarren says to the pilot.

"Already?" she asks. "No trading insults first?"

"I know. Rookies." He tsks. "They say if we don't release our prisoner, they'll damage our engines so we can't escape. But if we let her go, they'll allow us to leave."

"Nice of them," she says. "Do you want to tell them about our extra armaments or should I just blow them to pieces?"

Fear spikes through me. I need to do something to stop Jarren. Then it hits me and I'd slap my forehead if I could. The Q-net. But can I worm into the shuttle's programming? Shuttles and space ships have high level protections for just this very reason.

"While I'm tempted to gloat," Jarren says, "I suspect they're trying to delay us, which means more of them are on the way."

I shove the doubts aside and concentrate. The barriers around the controls for flying the shuttle are impenetrable. Maybe if I go into the program for the weapons. The defenses are thick and complex.

"All right, I'm targeting all three at once," she says.

No time to be delicate, I bulldoze right into the protocols, sizzle-zapping everything. Desperate, I call to the Q-net to help. To stop them. To do something. *Anything! Please!*

The engines and lights turn off.

"What the—" the pilot says in the sudden quiet.

I sag back in my seat. *Thank you.*

"What's going on?" Jarren demands. "Did they hit us with an EMP?"

An EMP is an electromagnetic pulse. If it's strong enough, it can knock out anything that uses electricity.

"No, we're shielded. All the shuttles are. It's just turned off."

"Can you turn it back on?"

She pushes various buttons, but nothing happens. I suppress

my smile as her actions become more frantic.

"No. There's a disconnect from here to the rest of the ship."

"That's…" Jarren turns and meets my gaze. "What did you do?"

"Nothing."

He aims the kill zapper at me. "Want to try that again?"

I lift my hands and spread my fingers. "I'm stuck here. I can't do anything. No tangs. No terminal."

"Don't kill her," the pilot says. "We need her alive to negotiate."

Jarren curses. "Safe passage in exchange for her?"

"That's our only play. We can take another shuttle," the pilot says.

He slams a fist into the seat next to me. I jerk in surprise.

"Going to another shuttle will expose us," Jarren says. "And they can cut the engines like they did to this one."

"If they're honorable, they'll keep their side of the deal," she says. "We don't have anything else."

"I can't leave her behind or she'll ruin everything. DES doesn't get to win. I'll do anything so they don't. Even die."

A buzzing sounds in my ears as all the air is sucked from the shuttle. Except no one but me notices this lack of oxygen. What little comfort I scraped together during their conversation has fled. No way I'm going to survive this.

Jarren returns to the cockpit, but the pilot is eyeing me with a piercing gaze. A dark brown braid spirals around her head like a cap. There's nothing friendly in her expression.

"I've an idea," she says and then leans close to Jarren and

whispers in his ear.

His frown deepens and he shoots me a look. It's not encouraging. He appears sick to his stomach. In the end he agrees. To what, I've no idea.

While she goes to the back of the shuttle to rummage around for whatever supplies, Jarren messages Niall and the others. There's a bit of back and forth until Jarren's satisfied.

He comes over and unbuckles my harness. This is it. My one chance to escape. Then he frees my left wrist. I brace. When my right wrist is free, I surge to my feet, striking out with the heels of my palms for his Adam's apple. Jarren steps back with a cry so the blow isn't as hard. That's okay, I aim my fist at his face and—

A sizzle sounds behind me right before I'm hit. I collapse on the ground as a million pinpricks of fire spread out from my back. My jumpsuit keeps me from being knocked unconscious. Although as the pain increases, passing out seems like a really good idea. I curl into a ball. Enduring another minute of torture, I suck in deep breaths to keep from losing the contents of my stomach. Eventually the sensation eases.

Jarren yanks me to my feet. "A wasted effort. You're still dangling on your hook, Little Worm."

"I caused you pain. To me, that's well worth the effort."

Instead of answering, he shoves me toward the door, keeping one hand on my shoulder. "Do you have it?" he asks the pilot.

"Yes," she says.

Jarren turns me so I'm facing him. He holds my upper arms, keeping me still. Before I can figure out what's going on, something is pressed between my shoulder blades. It's cold and hard and little hooks sink into my skin through the jumpsuit's fabric.

I bite down on a cry of pain. You would think I'd be used to sharp objects piercing my skin by now, but you'd be wrong.

"Done," the pilot says.

"Ready?" Jarren asks.

"Yes."

Before I can sort out what's going on, he releases one of my arms and keys in the code. The door opens. Bright light outlines the hatch as it peels away from the shuttle. Jarren steps behind me. He hooks an arm around my neck and presses his weapon to my forehead.

"Show time, Little Worm," he says, pushing me down the short steps. A group of people stand a few meters away. He keeps me between him and them as we walk sideways to another shuttle about fifteen meters away. I assume the pilot is behind us.

No one says a word. I scan faces: Niall, Rance, Zaim, Radcliff, Morgan, and my parents. They're all glaring at Jarren, which is good. If they were scared, I'd be sobbing by now. I meet Niall's gaze and he gives me an encouraging nod.

When we reach the shuttle, Jarren tells the pilot to go inside and ensure it's empty and is able to fly. While she checks it out, we wait at the base of the ladder.

The shuttle engines roar to life. After a minute the pilot pokes her head out. "We're good to go."

Jarren addresses the group. "I'm holding up my side of the

bargain and leaving Little Worm behind. Do not try to stop the shuttle," Jarren says. "If you do, I'll blow her to bits." He spins me around. "There's an explosive device on her back."

2522:245

A new level of terror slices through me. Did he just say—

"Once we are safely away, I will disarm the device."

I meet his gaze. He's holding my shoulders. Jarren's comments replay in my head: *I can't leave her behind or she'll ruin everything.* And the other one: *I'll make sure you stay dead before I leave.*

"You picked the wrong side," he says. "And it killed you. Twice." He pushes me down and sprints for the shuttle.

I land on my butt, but scramble to my feet as the door raises. My family and friends start toward me, but I hold out my hand. "Stop! Don't come any closer!"

Because Jarren is going to detonate the device as soon as he's out of danger.

And they'll all die, too.

And I can't let that happen. Jarren doesn't get to win.

So I do the only thing I can, I take a running jump and grab onto the leg of the shuttle as it lifts off. Shouts sound below me. I look down. My family is staring up at me. Their mouths are moving, but I can't understand a word. Which is probably for the best, since I'll never see them again and I don't want my last memory to be of them yelling at me for being an idiot.

Then I pull the rest of my body up onto the foot so I'm not hanging by my hands. It's a tight fit, but at least the leg doesn't retract into the shuttle. Now, if he detonates the explosives, I'll take him and the pilot with me. I wonder if Jarren will check before—

The shuttle banks hard to the left. I tighten my hold on the metal structure. And that would be a yes. He knows I'm here. Then it makes a wild dive to the right. Wrapping my legs around the leg as well, I cling with all my strength as the pilot does a series of maneuvers to fling me off. I actually regret not doing more push-ups. Who knew push-ups would be *that* important?

Eventually, the shuttle levels off. I've a second to catch my breath before the door opens. Oh boy. Shifting to put the leg between me and the door, I adjust my grip.

Harnessed to the shuttle, Jarren steps out. I've a flashback to when he shot me from a shuttle before. But then I was in the port and he was up above. Now I really am a worm dangling on a hook. Crazed laughter bubbles up my throat. He meets my gaze and just shakes his head as if he can't believe it.

He pulls the energy wave gun, then pauses. That's right, figure it out. The force from that weapon will shatter the leg and damage the shuttle. Jarren switches to his kill zapper. Except that too will harm the shuttle, knocking out the electronics. Then he touches my pulse gun, but no one can shoot that but me. Well, unless he reprogrammed it to his own electrical signal. I've a moment of panic before he drops his hand.

Grinning, he shouts over the noise, "Guess you're coming back with us. Hold on or not. Either way is fine with me."

Oh my stars! I didn't quite think this through. To be fair, it was one of those spur-of-the-moment decisions. Although not dying is preferable to dying.

He retreats into the shuttle and the door closes. Now what? The ground blurs far underneath me. It'll take six hours to get to his base. Can I hang on that long? They're flying straight and my weight is on the foot. It's windy and cold, but not enough to shake me loose.

The big question is, what happens once we get there. He'll interrogate me with his pink liquid and I'll tell him everything, including how I can access the Q-net without— The Q-net! With all the stress, I'd forgotten. I close my eyes and confirm I'm still connected. Amazing.

I could ask it to shut off the shuttle's engine. Except we'd crash and die. How about the explosive device on my back? Concentrating, I focus on it. No. It's a straight communication from the device to the trigger. No need for the Q-net. Disappointment stabs through me. At least I can send a message to my parents and Niall. But what should I say?

2522:245: Mom and Dad, I'm sorry for putting you through such grief, but Jarren was going to kill me no matter what happened and this way I'm able to save your lives, which is a huge comfort to me. Even though I only worked in security for sixty-two days, I tapped into my inner guardian lion and it feels good to help others. I know, I'm shocked too. <grin> I'm not sure what's going to happen next. I'm going to try to stay alive, which means Jarren will have me. But that's better than the alternative. And I'll try everything in my power to escape and send you messages from time to time. Jarren's going to regret this. Trust me. I love you both. Please send a message to Phoenix for me and tell him I love him. I never told him that before and it's a shame it has to come to *this* for me to tell my brother that I love him.

I send it, imagining Phoenix will not be too upset about the news. After all, he left knowing he'd never see us again so this will just be more of a regret. Something like: it's a shame, she had such potential. The next message is going to be harder to compose.

2522:245: Niall, I'm sorry we didn't have more time together, but I had to get away or risk killing everyone I care about. The security team has become my family—and not the distant cousins or annoying crazy uncle family—but actual deep level love. Surprising! Who knew I'd be worried about Bendix and Rance? And speaking of Rance, the man is supposed to be in bed recovering. And so is Zaim.

And YOU! Thank you for disobeying orders, though. I'm glad I was able to see you one more time before...whatever happens next. I'll never forget you, Toad. And do me a favor the next time you meet a cute and annoying girl your age? Don't be a jerk! Love you!

Composing those messages is emotionally exhausting. But the fact that I can when I'm hanging onto a flying shuttle is a good sign that I will be able to communicate with my parents and Niall in the future. And maybe, if I can get this damn device off my back, I can strike a blow for the good guys. Hope warms me from the inside out. I've a new sense of purpose. Plus, I've plenty of time to plan.

It's dark by the time we arrive at Jarren's forest base. The temperature is near freezing. My hands and face have long since gone numb. Lumpy blackness spreads out below. We descend closer to the forest. The moist scent of living green warms the air. I breathe in deep. It's been a long time since I've been this close to trees. Probably a little too close for comfort as we skim above the canopy.

Lights pierce the darkness and we aim toward a clearing in the forest that's getting...bigger? Ah, it appears to be a retractable forest roof. Jarren has all the upgrades. Must be nice to have rich and well connected patrons. I send a report, describing everything I see and my location. Might as well do it while I can.

Landing is a bit stressful. I make sure to keep clear of anything that pivots and flexes so my fingers and other appendages aren't caught, which is hard to do when your entire body has turned into a giant popsicle. Once the shuttle settles and the engines turn off, I assume a wilted position—super easy to do—and rest my forehead against the shuttle's leg. Time for my very own Operation Worm on a Hook.

The door opens and footsteps clatter. A beam from a flashlight shines on me.

"Little Worm? Are you alive?" Jarren asks.

I lift my head as if it weighs a thousand kilos. Blinking blearily into the light, I say, "Are we...here?" I gaze around as if confused.

"Yes, you made it."

Sighing, I try to release my hold, but can't quite get my limbs to move correctly. Jarren comes closer. He's pointing a weapon at me. Hard to tell which one in the semi-darkness.

"Help her," he orders the pilot.

She huffs, but grabs me under the arms and pulls. I hook my left foot and become a dead weight just to make it more difficult. And after a bit of grunting and bumbling, she sets me on my feet. I sway and hold on to the leg.

"Gotta admit I'm impressed you stayed on," she says.

"I was...motivated."

She laughs until I clutch my stomach and bend over slightly. "I...don't feel...very good."

The pilot jumps back. "She's all yours, Boss." Then she strides away.

"Come on, let's get you inside." Jarren holsters his weapon.

I sink to both knees and cradle my head in my hands. "I don't...I'm..."

He reaches me and holds out a hand. I wrap my arms around his legs instead.

"What? Let go!"

"Please take the explosive off me!" I cry, letting all the fear and desperation of the last six hours pour out. "Please," I sob with real tears running down my face. "I'll cooperate, tell you anything. Just. Please. Take. It. Off!" What's funny in a sad way is that he has no trouble with the idea of killing me, but my tears and groveling are making him very uncomfortable.

"Last time you—"

"I didn't have a bomb on my back!" By this point I'm hysterical.

"Promise?"

"Yes, please!"

"All right, turn around."

I do and I try to calm my hiccup breaths and runaway sobs. There's a bit of pressure and then it pulls away. Cold air kisses the sweat and pain burns where the hooks were, but I'll take it. My relief is genuine and I scramble away on all fours from Jarren and the device. He leaves it on the ground and follows me. When I'm far enough away, I collapse onto the ground.

Jarren kneels next to me. "Just breathe, you'll be fine."

"I'm sorry," I mumble and shudder—it's not an act. "It's— that was just so horrible!"

"It's over now, Lyra. Come on, let's get inside. It's warm and there's plenty of food. You must be starving." He helps me to my feet.

Huh. So he's not *entirely* evil. Who knew? And he called me Lyra. "My legs—"

"That's all right." Jarren hooks my arm around his shoulder. "I'll help you."

"Okay, thanks." I sniff.

I limp next to him agonizingly slow, but once I'm inside the base, it'll be harder to execute my plan. The hum of another shuttle cuts through the quiet. Jarren stops and turns us around as it gets louder.

A bright beam spotlights us for a second and it's just the distraction I've been hoping for. I straighten, yank my pulse gun from his belt, and shoot him in the head. He jerks, stares at me with wide eyes, and thuds to the ground.

"I don't have to keep my word to a murdering looter." I grab his kill zapper then bolt for the forest, diving behind a tree. No way I'll be able to navigate it in the dark. And who knows what creatures lurk inside. My best bet is to stay close to Jarren's base until I figure out a way to return home.

The shuttle lands, but doesn't turn off its engine. I aim both the weapons toward it. Figures hop out, they go to Jarren's prone form and one bends over him. Heads swivel as if looking for something…or someone. Did they spot me when the light hit us?

"Mouse?" Niall calls.

Such is my relief, my legs give out for real. And more tears fall. Lots more. My team came for me.

"Mouse?"

"Here!" I stagger to my feet. Then I stumble from the trees and right into Niall's embrace. It's better than flying in the Q-net.

His hands run over my back. "Is it gone?"

"Yes."

"How?"

"Hysterical tears. Another super power."

He laughs then sobers. "Can you walk? We need to move fast." Niall releases me.

"I—"

Radcliff arrives. "Let's go before they figure out we're here." He sweeps me over his shoulder and runs to the shuttle as if he isn't carrying an extra…er…fifty or so kilos.

Niall's right behind him. We enter and Radcliff orders the pilot—Morgan—to take off. I'm dropped gently into a seat while he goes into the cockpit. Beau and Elese are securing an unconscious Jarren into another seat, while Niall claims the one next to mine. Within seconds, we're airborne.

The shuttle suddenly veers to the left. I scramble to click into the harness as the craft makes another hard turn. I clutch Niall's hand. A bright white light stabs through the windows. It turns an angry red as the roar of an explosion rams into us. The metal floor shudders under our feet. We spin around and drop through the air, becoming weightless. My stomach pushes into my esophagus. Terror wars with nausea. A brief thought flashes that, despite my efforts, I'm still going to get the people I love killed. At least I'm taking Jarren with us. It's not as comforting as you'd think.

The shuttle lurches forward then accelerates. I'm pressed back into my seat as the engines howl with the strain. After an eternity, the craft levels off. The engines ease into their normal growl. Niall glances at me and I relax my death grip on his hand, but I don't release it; there might be another missile.

A few minutes later, Morgan calls, "We're clear. No pursuers."

They must have figured out that we have Jarren on board. The four of us share big goofy grins. Elese whoops.

"Thanks so—"

"None of that," Beau says to me. "This is what we do."

"And we're extra motivated when it's one of our own." Elese hands me a couple of energy bars. "Figured you'd be hungry."

The adrenaline in my blood has worn off and my stomach growls in response. But my hands are shaking and the wrapper is being…stupid. Niall takes it from me, peels it off with ease, and hands it back.

"Aren't you supposed to be on bed rest?" I mock growl between bites.

"I thought you were glad I disobeyed orders."

Ah. He received my message.

Lacing his fingers in my free hand, he says, "Besides, no way I'm lying in bed when my girl calls for help."

I squeeze his hand. "What about Rance and Zaim?"

"I didn't even have to ask. They also wanted to come along in the shuttle, but they're not as good at disobeying orders."

"And you've had lots of practice," Beau says sourly, but it's obvious from his grin that he's kidding.

"You must have taken off soon after we left. How did you avoid getting spotted by Jarren?" I ask.

Beau's grin widens. "We went the other way."

Too much has happened for me to puzzle it out.

"We flew around the *other side* of the planet," Beau says. "Jarren picked almost the exact opposite side of the world for his base. We could dig straight through it and come up right next to him."

"But still you were only a few minutes behind."

Elese laughs. "They wasted some time trying to shake off a hitch hiker. And Morgan pushed this bird well past the speed limit. Girl is a serious adrenaline junkie."

"I heard that," Morgan shouts back.

"Sorry! *Officer* Morgan is a serious adrenaline junkie. Better, sir?"

"Much."

She smirks, leans toward me, and whispers, "Girl is a bit of a diva, too."

I shake my head. Someday I'm going to threaten to tell Morgan she said that in exchange for running less laps. Then again, being in better shape certainly helped me today. My arms and legs ache, but I'm alive. A shudder rips through me at the thought of how close I came. A phantom pressure sits between my shoulder blades.

"Hey," Niall says, sensing my panic. "It's all right. You're safe. And it worked out better than expected." He tilts his head at Jarren.

True. I dangled on the hook and caught a big smelly fish.

"What about his people? Did anyone get hurt? Are my parents—"

"Other than being worried for you, your parents are fine."

Good news. "I should message them."

"Already done," Radcliff says from the cockpit.

"Other than minor injuries, no one was harmed in the attack," Niall continues. "Our team was successful. The looters who were not unconscious surrendered. They'll have to be detained with the others from the first attack, along with Jarren. He'll be put into detention once we question him. The others will be housed in Pit 1. We just don't have the room or the manpower to guard them any other place."

And the good guys don't kill people if they can avoid it. "Plus the threat of HoLFs might keep them on their best behavior."

"Yup," Elese chimes in. "Y'all be good or we'll turn off the radio waves and let you be HoLF food."

The shuttle lands with a slight bump, waking me and Niall. We curled up together and fell asleep during the last couple hours of the trip. Despite his claims of feeling better, he's still recovering from the blood loss. My parents are waiting for me in the port. I'm squished in a parent sandwich as soon as I step down. Considering I never expected to see them again, I don't mind at all.

There's excited chattering and explanations all the way to the infirmary. Niall hasn't been officially discharged and the doctor wants to observe him one more night. And the various cuts and bruises over my body need to be—you guessed it—cleaned and bandaged.

"It's a good thing for you that we've invented accelerated healing," Dr. Edwards says. "Or you'd have more scars." He taps his chin with a finger. "Probably dozens. I wonder…you might have enough lacerations for a record. I'll have to check your file."

"Not funny, Doc," I say.

"No, Miss Lawrence, it isn't." He gives me a long look before leaving.

After I've dressed in scrubs…again…I go to Niall's room. He's no longer in intensive care, but this room faced the explosion, too. The broken windows are boarded over, which is good since the sun's been up for a couple of hours. At least someone has cleaned up the glass. I shudder just thinking about those sharp little shards. Ugh.

He wakes when I crawl into bed with him.

"I can get used to this," he says sleepily. "Makes me want to stay here longer. Because as soon as I'm discharged—"

"Back to normal," I say. "Or as normal as it gets for us."

"Which is pretty crazy." Then he frowns.

Uh oh. "What's wrong? You don't like crazy?"

"How can you ask me that? I'm in love with you. Crazy is part of the package."

"Hey." I swat him gently, because it's true and he said he loves me. Can't get enough of hearing that! "Love you, too, but why did you frown?"

"Just thinking about all the stuff we still have to figure out."

"Like who Jarren's working with and what they're planning?" Knowing Jarren, he won't tell us anything. Unfortunately, that's not the only thing. "And what's going on with those portals and how do we close that rip in Pit 2 to keep the HoLFs out forever?"

"Yes. We have Jarren—a major coup—and, without him in the Q-net, we'll be able to reestablish contact with DES, but I think the bigger battle is still to come."

Ugh. "Why don't we worry about that tomorrow? Today, I've a more important question that needs an answer."

"Oh?"

"Yes. Your middle name. What does the S stand for?"

He smiles. "Sensible."

The next morning Radcliff and my parents come to Niall's room for a short debriefing. I tell them everything that happened. Mom scowls when I recount my reasoning about grabbing onto the shuttle's leg. "Staying close to Jarren was the only thing I could do to keep him from detonating the explosive device."

"The HoLFs are too good for him," she mutters under her breath.

The thought of what my mother might do to him... No. Not going there.

"I'd like to get a closer look at his base, but I don't have the manpower right now," Radcliff says. "Jarren has clammed up as well. Too bad we don't have any of that pink liquid you mentioned."

"You couldn't use it anyway," Niall says. "Jarren has rights." His tone is full of disgust.

"Yeah, the right to suffer horribly," Dad says.

Wow. No love for the murdering looter. Not that I can blame them. "Maybe since I've been there and Jarren's no longer in the Q-net, I can worm into their files and find out how many people are still there, what weapons they have, and how they're traveling," I offer.

"All right," Radcliff says.

"Once she's *fully* recovered," Mom adds.

"Of course." He turns to me. "I'm giving you a commendation for your quick thinking with the bomb. And for your role in making Operation Looter Attack a success."

Suddenly uncomfortable, I squirm. It's a wonderful gesture, but I don't really think—

"Stop frowning," Mom says. "You deserve it. Accept it with grace."

Typical Mom. "Thank you."

"You're welcome," Radcliff says. "Now the question is,

which record do I list it in? Ara Yinhexi Lawrence's or Lyra Tian Daniels'?"

Ah, good question. I don't have to hide from Jarren, and the rest of the base knows I'm alive. No reason to be Ara Lawrence anymore. Yet...I can't go back to being Lyra Daniels. She's an entirely different person than I am now. We have a few things in common—like the best boyfriend in the Galaxy, great parents (shhh...don't tell them I said that!), and a tendency to be in the middle of the trouble—but I've found my purpose and I've experienced so much since then. No, Lyra Daniels is gone.

"Ara Yinhexi Lawrence." I shoot a glance at my parents. Will they be mad?

Both are smiling. And when they leave, I get another parent sandwich. Bonus. Niall is discharged late that afternoon.

"Don't entangle with the Q-net for the next seven days," Dr. Edwards says to Niall. "I'll do another brain scan then and you can try again."

"All right," Niall says.

I'm curious, but refrain from asking Niall until we're alone. As we're walking back to security, a few scientists stop to thank us for saving everyone in the base. It's nice and weird at the same time. They were all evacuated to Pit 21 before Jarren showed up. Many of them will be helping to guard the looters in Pit 1 and will be training to fight as well. It's still another five hundred and eight-five days until the Protector Class ship arrives and Jarren's cohorts will probably come after us. The scientists no longer have the luxury of doing research, but will be helping us to fight for our survival.

Once we reach Niall's unit, I ask, "What's with Dr. Edwards and the Q-net?"

"Oh. It's a strange side effect of losing so much blood. It's nothing serious," he hurries to add. "It's just I can't entangle with the Q-net anymore."

That's not serious? Not by my definition. "How—"

"Dr. Edwards said it's probably temporary. That my brain might need to heal some more. Or maybe the HoLFs damaged the sensors." He shrugs. "I'm not too concerned. It's not like I'm a super wormer or a navigator. I can still use the surface programs and a portable, all I basically use anyway."

Niall continues to downplay it. He gives me a kiss before going in to take a shower. My thoughts, however, are racing and replaying that light show the Q-net displayed when I mentioned fixing Niall. It couldn't have healed him. Right? That's all kinds of scary. Which you'd think I'd be used to.

Except people have gone insane when they're connected to the Q-net for more than twelve hours. And I've been connected since Jarren attacked over forty-eight hours ago. I haven't disentangled. No, I just reach out when I need it and there it is. Like another part of my brain. I hurry to my room to sort it out.

Of course all I manage to do is freak out more. I access the Q-net and go to my perceptive cluster. Then I search for information on brain damage and miracle healing and entangling and the science behind the sensors we all have in our heads. Who designed them? Which leads me to the Q-net's origins and the original inventors. And...ugh. Way too much information and none of it helpful. Then I try to figure out if anyone else in the Galaxy can do what I do with the Q-net. I can't be that special. Can I?

YOU ARE, the Q-net says.

Have I gone a little bit more insane? It has extended its vocabulary past *here* and *not here*. But I've exhausted all my emotional energy, so I just go with it. *What did I do? What happened to me?*

NOTHING. I CHOSE YOU.

There's so much wrong with that sentence—the Q-net referred to itself as I—but I hold off on my freak out. Instead I ask, *Why me?*

YOU SHINE.

A video feed of me in the pits plays. I'm scrambling to hide the hatch to the factory, but, when I finish camouflaging it, it's too late for me to escape. My actions prevented the looters from finding and destroying the Warrior hearts.

YOU BELIEVE.

A series of images of me flashes. I'm lying on the ground of the port with Menz over me. Then there's one of Dr. Edwards shocking my heart. That was the first time I flew with the Q-net.

YOU HELP.

Another video plays. This time it shows me, the other security officers, and the astrophysicists in the archeology lab when we installed the sensor.

I make a sudden realization. After each series of events, I was able to better work with the Q-net until I didn't need tangs or a terminal and now I don't even need to entangle and disentangle.

And it's all because the Q-net picked me?

YES.

Wow. *Did you heal Niall?*

YES. YOU ASKED.

Another staggering statement. And again I want to know, *Why me?*

NEED YOU.

An image of the rip in Pit 2 and shadow-blobs disappearing inside it. I mull over the implications and it hits me that this...thing I have with the Q-net started around the time the shadow-blobs showed up.

YES.

You need me to help stop the HoLFs?

YES. NO LONGER PROTECTED.

We're no longer being protected because the Warriors are being destroyed?

YES.

Okay. That fits the timing. Except why does the Q-net care? Has it become self-aware and believes if we die, it will die too?

PROTECT YOU.

A picture of the entire Milky Way Galaxy spreads across my vision.

I AM HERE.

Then a strange thought forms in my mind. And there's a good chance it's not my own thought—'cause this entire exchange with the Q-net is beyond anything else I've experienced. However, the idea is that perhaps the Q-net wasn't invented by the scientists on Earth. No, it was *discovered* and tapped into. Used.

NO. PERMITTED.

Why?

YOUR TIME.

Our time? I consider. *We've advanced in technology far enough to earn the right to use the Q-net?*

YES.

Why didn't you let anyone know?

NOT READY.

Not until we destroyed the Warriors and let the shadow-blobs in. And once I think about it, we're still not ready. No one is going to believe me. I'm not sure I believe it myself. I need to clarify a few things.

Did you build and place the Warriors on planets throughout the Galaxy?

NO. OTHERS.

Okay. *And where are they now?*

GONE.

Where did they go?

BEYOND THE EDGE.

Of the Galaxy?

YES.

And you were...

LEFT TO PROTECT.

Back to this again. *Why didn't you stop Jarren from destroying the Warriors?*

CAN NOT.

I suspect there's more there, but I'm still trying to wrap my brain around all this. *Basically, you were left behind to protect us and also help us when we reached a certain technological level.*

YES.

And you're an alien consciousness. Do you have a physical body?

NO.

What are you?

I AM THE MILKY WAY.

Oh. My. Stars.

THANK YOU

Thank you for choosing *Chasing the Shadows*, book 2 in my Sentinels of the Galaxy series. The third book, *Defending the Galaxy*, will be out in November 2020!

If you like to stay updated on my books and any news, please sign up for my free email newsletter here:

http://www.mariavsnyder.com/news.php

(go all the way down to the bottom of the page). I send my newsletter out to subscribers three to four times a year. It contains info about the books, my schedule and always something fun (like deleted scenes or a new short story or exclusive excerpts). No spam—ever!

You're also welcome to come join your fellow MVS fans on my Facebook reading group called Snyder's Soulfinders. Why Soulfinders? Because according to Plato, "Books give a soul to the universe, wings to the mind, flight to the imagination, and life to everything." The Soulfinders are all about books, especially mine, but also others as well! It's a great place to find fellow readers and make friends from all over the world. There are perks, too, like exclusive give aways, getting all the news first, and an insight into my writing process. Please answer at least 2 of the 3 questions as we don't want any trolls in our group, just Soulfinders. Here's a link:

https://www.facebook.com/groups/SnydersSoulfinders/

Please feel free to spread the word about this book! Honest reviews are always welcome and word of mouth is the best way you can help an author keep writing the books you enjoy! And please don't be a stranger, stop on by and say hello. You can find me on:

- Facebook: https://www.facebook.com/mvsfans
- Goodreads: https://www.goodreads.com/maria_v_snyder
- Instagram: https://www.instagram.com/mariavsnyderwrites/

ACKNOWLEDGEMENTS

I always wonder if anyone—besides the people being thanked—ever read the acknowledgments. And, if they do, are they bored with mine, since I practically thank the same group of people book after book after book. This is my eighteenth time writing an acknowledgment, and, truthfully, I'm a little bored. Not with thanking people, because I'm eternally grateful for the love and support of my network of family, friends, and all the hardworking people at Harlequin Australia! But with the format.

In an effort to make my acknowledgments more fun, I've written this quiz. The answers are all the people who have made writing this book a blast! Thank you ALL so much!

The Acknowledgment Quiz (answers on the next page)

1. Who designed yet another perfect cover for the book?
2. Who helped to turn this rough meandering story into a smooth page-turner?
3. Who does all the grocery shopping, post office runs, and finds all the missing commas and typos?
4. Who expertly hawks my books to their customers, helping to expand my herd?

5. Who is my Chief Evil Minion and beta reader extraordinaire?

6. Who deftly deals with all the contracts, royalty payments, and business issues that are all a part of being an author?

7. Who helped me format the book so I can publish it worldwide?

8. Who taught me all the cool space stuff so it's as accurate as possible for this science *fiction* story?

9. Who is somewhat patient when her mother is distracted, reads every book, and provides feedback before publication?

10. Who provides all kinds of writerly support and commiseration during our bi-annual writing retreats?

11. Who gives me an ego boost and lifts my spirits when I'm having a bad day?

12. Who are still my good friends even after I've ignored them for months to write?

Answers:

1. Josh Durham.
2. The editorial Dream Team of Rachael, Julia, Laurie, and Annabel! With an assist from Natalie, Rodney, and Jenna.
3. My husband, Rodney.
4. Michelle, Jeff, and all the wonderful booksellers who hand-sell my books.
5. Natalie Bejin—CEM for the win!
6. My agent, Bob Mecoy.
7. Carrie Miller.
8. The Launchpad team of Dr. Michael Brotherton and Christian Ready.
9. My beautiful and super smart daughter, Jenna.
10. Author and friend, Mindy Klasky.
11. The Soulfinders!! Love you!
12. Judi, Kathy, Jackie, Jess, Quin, Brian, Christine, Maverick, Al, Dave, Mike, Melissa, Nancy, Jeri, and Kristy.

ABOUT MARIA V. SNYDER

When Maria V. Snyder was younger, she aspired to be a storm chaser so she attended Pennsylvania State University and earned a Bachelor of Science degree in Meteorology. Much to her chagrin, forecasting the weather wasn't in her skill set so she spent a number of years as an environmental meteorologist, which is not exciting ... at all. Bored at work and needing a creative outlet, she started writing fantasy and science fiction stories. Over a dozen novels and numerous short stories later, Maria's learned a thing or three about writing. She's been on the New York Times bestseller list, won a half-dozen awards, and has earned her Master of Arts degree in Writing from Seton Hill University, where she is now a faculty member for their MFA program.

When she's not writing she's either playing volleyball or traveling. Being a writer, though, is a ton of fun. Where else can you take fencing lessons, learn how to ride a horse, study martial arts, learn how to pick a lock, take glass blowing classes, and attend Astronomy Camp and call it research? Maria will be the first one to tell you it's not working as a meteorologist. Readers are welcome to check out her website for book excerpts, free short stories, maps, blog, and her schedule at MariaVSnyder.com.

CPSIA information can be obtained
at www.ICGtesting.com
Printed in the USA
LVHW012242080121
676100LV00001B/56

9 781946 381040